DIAMOND SPRING

by S. C. Dixon

PublishAmerica
Baltimore

Hardcover 978-1-4560-1921-1
Softcover 978-1-4560-1920-4
PUBLISHED BY PUBLISHAMERICA, LLLP
www.publishamerica.com
Baltimore

Printed in the United States of America

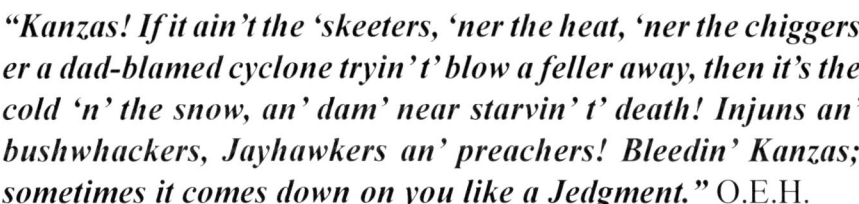

"Kanzas! If it ain't the 'skeeters, 'ner the heat, 'ner the chiggers er a dad-blamed cyclone tryin' t' blow a feller away, then it's the cold 'n' the snow, an' dam' near starvin' t' death! Injuns an' bushwhackers, Jayhawkers an' preachers! Bleedin' Kanzas; sometimes it comes down on you like a Jedgment." O.E.H.

Chapter 1

Seems t' me I was a sittin' in a lodge up north, somwhars. I know'd right off that it was a dream 'case I was the only feller in the room there that warn't daid.

It was the worstest kinda dream, too, 'case it started out plumb crazy, like most dreams does, but then it turned into somethin' else entire, an' it became awful real. Like a' lookin at a old tintype photygrap' er a'watchin' one o' them movin' shows. It scairt me some an' it was sad some, too.

But then I reckon they ain't nothin' that's much sadder than a old man's dreams.

Anywise, I was a sittin' in a lodge up north an' they was this ugly old Injun man a leanin' over me, a' singin' like they do, in a trance, like. I rekinized his face from the time I met him in the real worl' years before. It was Sittin' Bull.

(Oh, I reckon I've know'd lots o' "famous" folks in m' life, but back when I know'd him, he warn't famous none a'tall. I reckon some white folks didn't find people like ol' Bull much more famouser than a yaller dog or any other class o' Injun.

(They's been a lot writ an' a lot said 'bout him since them days, I reckon, an' I s'pose some o' it is even true. But a whole lot was jest plain made-up.)

Now Bull warn't no chief, like you prob'ly been told. He was teacher an' a preacher an' a magic man, what some calls a "shay-man," an' in this here dream I was dreamin' he was a dancin' round me, shakin' a rattle at m' haid. It was made o' a turtle shell filled up with san' an' gravel, tied up with a piece o' buffaler leather t' a willer stick.

(The rattle I mean, not m' haid!)

Now, what bothered me most is that, whilst I was a' dreamin' I was o' two minds, so t' speak. In other words, I was in the worl' o' m' dream an' at the same time I know'd perfec'ly well that I was a' dreamin', like a part o' me was awake, doncha see?

In this here dream it was Tahecapsun, which means "December," in the Sioux lingo, and the date was the 29th. Don't asked me why or how I know'd that but I did, an' I 'member thinkin' t' m'self that Bull an' his son, Crowfoot, had been gunned down jest 'bout two weeks afore by a feller named Bull Haid an' his so-called "Indian Police," an' that he was daid. Shore nuff, I looked at him close-like when he danced around me an' I see'd by the firelight that they was a big, gapin' hole in the back o' his haid an' I could see his brains a shinin' with blood. He was some kind o' a haint, I reckon.

Welp, anywise, ol' Bull was a type o' Sioux Injun the tribe o' which was know'd as Hunkpappa but he was a' speakin' t' me either in Lakota or Minnikinjou, though I grant ye that they ain't a hell o' a lot o' difference in the two.

"Mitakeye oyasin et Unci Moka yhe Tunkasila. Pta 'ya wo wicala," which is somethin' 'bout how's we's finally all t'gither in our devotion an' faith with The Great Spirit an' our Gran'mother, the Earth.

He leaned in close t' me an' his breath stunk o' wild onions. I could smell 'em. Ain't dreams something'?

Outside o' the lodge a' risin' up on the wind I could hear the sound o' flutes an' o' drums. But they warn't Sioux drums ner Cheyenne eagle-bone flutes, neither. And they warn't playin' no Indian tunes.

They was a playin', "*Gary Owen, Gary Owen*," an' it jest sent shivers down m' nervous cord 'case I know'd jest who it was. That thar was the marchin' song o' the 7th Cavalry, Custer's old band, but I know'd fer a person'l fact that Yallar Hair had been daid fer nearly 15 years er more. Hell, even in m' sleep I 'membered that.

8

Then, all sudden like, o' all people, the pappy o' mine oldest an' bestest friend in the worl' (a feller named Tall Tree) pushed aside the buffaler skin over the lodge door an' walked inside.

This feller, m' friend's pa, his name was Big Walk an' he, like ol' Bull, had already been daid fer some time.

I was glad t' see 'im! He was straight an' tall an' he did look fine, but I noticed that they was some gray in his hair, which he had cut short, jest a bit longer than a white man might wear his.

He was wearin' a Ghost shirt, which was s'posed t' be bullet proof'. But they was blood oozin' out a hole in the middle o' his chest.

He stuck his hand out t'ward me an' told me, in Kaw, how glad he was that I had come t' see him an' The People so's that we could all fight the bluecoats an' then "go home" t'gither.

Now I ain't a' lyin' when I say that that 'ere bothered me some, too, 'case when a Injun starts talkin' 'bout "goin' home" he's a talkin' 'bout dyin'. I figur'd that if I know'd I was dreamin' 'bout daid folk, then I m'self warn't daid yet and I warn't in any sort o' a hurry t' git down that road, so's t' speak, if you ketch m' drift.

Though I know'd the date, I 'member askin' Big Walk if he know'd what year it was, in the white man's count. He said it was 1890. Fer some reason that bothered me, too. That's unusu'l in itse'f, 'case as a rule I cain't 'member from one month t' another ner kin I 'member most anything in any kind o' sequence. It's jest all jumbled t'gither in m' haid an' I 'member what I kin when I need t'.

Then I hear'd the sound o' a eagle bone whistle an' a hiccupin' rattle that sounded t' me like one o' them army Hotchkiss guns a' comin from the west then another answerin' it, the shots a' comin from the south. Then I hear'd shouts an' rifle fire.

I hear'd a short scream an' a real young woman came staggerin' in like a drunkard, fallin' through the hide a' hangin' over the doorway, pullin' it down with her when she fell out on the buffaler robes that covered the floor. It was Blossom, one o' Big Walk's adopted daughters. I had met her an' know'd her an' loved her dearly nearly 30 years ago, jest afore she had been kidnapped by the Pawnee.

She had a hole in her throat the size t' put yer fist into an' great, thick globs o' black, snotty blood came a spilin' out her mouth an' out her nose. She was a' clutchin a inf'nt child. The baby was stiff and blue, eyes sqozed shet but its mouth wide open like it was a' yawnin,' but the side o' its haid had been blow'd off.

Blossom's eyes was goin' milky an' dim, but when she looked at me I see'd a flicker o' rekinition. "Why, Oscar," she said, jest purty as you please, in English, too, which I don't recall her ever speakin' when I had know'd her, "Why on earth are you here? It has been so long! It truly makes my heart glad and my spirit soar for the chance to see you here!

"But the soldiers are coming by the hundreds and they're going to kill us all, they will rub us out, Oscar, all of us. They're still angry over what happened at Greasy Grass. Why, that's been nearly fifteen years ago!"

("Greasy Grass" is what the Sioux an' the Cheyenne called the little stretch o' meadow and pra'rie near the Bighorn River that the white men know'd as the Little Bighorn battleground.)

She winced, sudden like, an' then, calmin' herself, she mouthed, "You must go now," with what little was left o' her voice, "this is no place for the living. You are in a camp with the dead. The dead and the dying, Oscar. Surely they will kill us all here today, again and forever. Fly away. Fly."

Big Walk spoke up then, callin' me by the name he'd gave me all them years ago when I was jest a child, a playin' with his youngins back in Kanzas, "Little Badger, good brother to my son and my friend, she is right. It is not good for you to die fighting our battles. Gather up your things and go. Take to the creek and get far, far away from the dead and the dying of this camp, for today the living will join us and we will all go home by an unfamiliar road. Tomorrow only ghosts will walk here in this place called Wounded Knee."

~

I waked up in m' warm bed an', fer some crazy reason, I started t' cry. Jest a old man's dreams 'bout dry bones that cain't rest 'case they ain't no jestice. Nearly four hun'ded people died that day all them years back, an' they had jest had t' die agin' in m' dreams. A goodly part o' them was women an' children. They left this here worl' through no wish an' no fault o' they own. While a rough an' ugly ol' rip like me was warm an' alive an' in the bosom o' his fam'ly here in the center o' the Earth in Di'mond Spring.

~

M' name is Oscar Eziria Harris. I am hereby a' puttin' down this here story o' m' life as told by me t' m' own sister, Doe Harris-Mead, who has writ it down purty much as I have told it t' her in something' she calls, "short-ham".

I was borned somewhar jest south o' St. Lou in July o' 1854. M' Papa, Earl Eziria Harris, was a crop farmer an' later in his life, was a cattleman. M' Mama, Pearline Hawthorn-Higgs Harris, was 20 year' old when she birthed me, the third o' what was event' ally eight childr'n, four o' which lived passed they 3rd birthday, one who died a little older, an' three o' which lived t' adulthood.

The brood was, in order o' age: Lizabeth, Barry, Junnie (dcd), Oscar (me), Ruthie (dcd)an' her twin, Pricilla (dcd), an' Doedie, "Doe", m' littlest sister. They was a baby afore Junnie which was stillborned, but m' folks had went on an' give him a name anyways, Nathan, an' they always considered him one o' the fam'ly.

Brother Barry was killed in a accident. A horse throw'd him off an' kicked his haid in when he was still a little feller, 'bout 8 year' old, I reckon, though I'll admit right out o' the chute that I ain't much pun'kin when it comes t' dates. I might tell you 'bout Barry later. Then agin', I might not as I git sidetrack'd purty easy.

M' parents had both came over t' this here country on a boat from Irelan' 'though m' Papa was really Scotch. Somehow they had know'd each other as kids an' purty much grow'd up t'gither. They was trouble in they fam'lies what with one bein' Scotch an' t'other not, so they was no church weddin'. They had got married by a magistrate, er some sech, in the town o' Limerick, jest two days afore they boarded the boat fer here. They'd lived fer a spell in New York City, which m' Pa said was a den o' rats an' thievery'. That's whar m' eldest sister, Lizabeth was borned.

They didn't want t' raise up no fam'ly in New York (who would?) so they tailed out t' some jerk-water town in Illinois fer a couple o' years whar the stillborned baby and then Junnie was borned. When he was less than two year' old they up an' moved agin', this time in the vicinity o' Westport on the boarder of Missouri an' the Kanzas territ'ry. I was borned somewhar's along the trail durin' this trip, but nobody know'd jest whar they was fer shore at the time, 'cept that Mama told me that I came into this worl' in the back o' a kinvas-covered buckboard durin' a hellacious hail storm. Mama said that the day I was borned was so hot that the corn in the field's they'd pass by was a' poppin' itse'f, but she might have been joshin' me 'case that's somethin' I ain't never see'd an' I've been around fer awhile.

She said that the storm was a brewin' in the northwest jest as her laborin' pains was startin', an' that later that night I arrived on a bolt o' lightenin' an' a clap o' thunder. I do not 'member this.

We event' ally settled on a little place jest southwest o' Westport. Some time afore this, daddy had read in the St. Louie paper 'bout the passing o' the Kanzas-Nebraska Act. He read ever'thing that he could lay his hands on 'bout Kanzas from then on out. He even took t' reading the old Government land survey o' 1825. He was one hell o' a reader, m' ol' daddy was.

By the time I was two er three year' old, he had done sold our little farm an' we moved on, 'way down t' the south an' some t' the west o' whar we had been a livin', t' a big parcel o' land' at Di'mond Spring, near the tradin' post o' Council Grove, Kanzas which is whar I then grow'd up.

Mama said that she had been real scairt t' move t' Kanzas beca'se they was so much trouble thar what with the slavery issue an' lunatics like John Brown on the Abolitionist side an' Bill Quantrill on t'other. (Her fam'ly and pa's fam'ly had seen enough fightin' in the old country, I reckon. Some o' it agin each other, I figure.)

Anywise, I remember my ma a' sayin' that they was a lot o' what she called "gorilla" fightin' all over the eastern third o' the Kanzas Territ'ry. The town o' Lawrence had been burnt down an' a lot o' the men folk had been drug out from they homes er shot down in the streets. "Bleedin' Kanzas," it was called in the papers back east.

The Southerners an' Southern sympathizers would come over from Missouri with the belief that they could kill er scare off all the Free State folks in Kanzas, then vote in slavery during a gen'ral election. When they was shore that Kanzas would come into the Union as a slave state, why then they'd jest move on back home t' Missouri, er whar' ever.

When Kanzas fin'ly became a state in 1861, an' came in on the side o' the Free Stater's, all hell broke loose. That marked the true beginnin's o' the Great War.

I was only 5 er 6 year' old when the War Between the North 'n' South started up an' I don't recollect any thing much o' it 'ceptin' a little bit t'ward the end. M' daddy said he was in neutral 'bout the whole issue. I kin 'member him sayin' that one man shore as hell should not buy up er sell another, but he also had long discussions with the neighbors 'bout how the South could not possibly continue raisin' cotton without them slaves. He said it were as plain as the nose on yer face that the North was trying t' put a stranglehold on the South's money an' business, which was superior t' what the Yankees had, an' that they was jealous. It was also a issue o' what rights each indiv'idal state was t' have in the say-so 'bout what they did within they own borders an' 'bout they own laws an' the sech.

Pa said that if the South was defeated (which mos' folks didn't believe to be possible, early on) that the states would never agin' have the rights they was entitled t' by the Constitution an' that the Fed'ral gov'ment would grow bigger an' fatter 'til folks would have t' have another revolution t' take the country back from the politicians. I reckon Pa was astraddle the fence on the whole issue o' the War, which I s'pose mos' folks was, truth be told.

News o' the battles, wins an' losses, sometimes came weeks er even months after they happened. Whar we was livin' all news was slow in arrivin' an', t' tell you the truth, the things we hear'd didn't mean much more t' us than did the news that came from over the seas. Nobody know'd if what we hear'd was the truth er somethin' som'body jest made up an' they was no way t' find out. We was what you'd call, "eye-so-lated."

Onc't in a while a rider would come through with a yaller, tore up newspaper from back east somewhar and then we at least had a idear 'bout the true happinin's.

Besides that, I was nothin' but a danged kid, anyways, an' what does a kid care 'bout sech things? Nary a whit!

Papa had told the fam'ly t' expect t' live in a "soddy", that's a little cabin made o' sod, which is jest chunks cut right out o' the livin' pra'rie, grass an' all. The sod is stacked up like bricks an' a house is made. A sod house is warm in the winter an' is cool in the summer. Ma an' Pa had lived inside one, fer a spell, back in Illinois, I think it was, an' they both told us kids stories 'bout it.

Now, the down-side o' livin' in a soddy is that they is bound t' be some trouble with varmits.

See, them varmits don't know that it's a human habytation, don't you see? It must jest look like another hill on the pra'rie t' 'em, so sometimes they jest burrow right through yer roof' er a wall an' land' smack on the dinner table er in yer bed with you, which kin be surprisin', t' say the least.

Snakes was the worst, I reckon, especially as Ma couldn't abide by no snakes on her supper table er in her mattress. She was a Christian woman an' took no truck with swearin' unless a big, ol' black snake came a' danglin' down from the rafters whilst they was a' eatin' they supper, er whatever. Pa told us that Mama would jest say, "Dam'", then knock the thing down with the handle o' her broom then loop it over the broomstick an' haul it outside whar she would toss it into the tall grass with the warnin', "Come in t' m' home agin' an' I'll not go so gently with thee, thou vile serpent!"

But we never kilt snakes, if'n it could be avoided at all an' 'specially if it was a blacksnake. A blacksnake in the out buildin's will ketch more rats an' mice an' sech than any dam' cat will! Howsoever, we did grow up a' knowin' it was prob'ly the best policy t' kill rattlesnakes an' copperhaids if they's up 'round yer house, 'case fer heaven's sake, you shore don't want 'em nestin' thar, a' raisin' up a pacel o' youngins! But

If I see's 'em in the wild, why, I jest let 'em slither on away without so much as a how-de-doo. The Indians did it that way, too, 'case they believe that 'em rattlesnake has special powers an' is a force fer good in this worl'. Besides, I figur'd that the chances o' any particular snake what crossed m' path t' ever come upon another human bein' in this wide worl' is slight t' none. Live an' let 'em live, I always said, an' I still do, too.

So, anyways, us kids, I'm told, was kind o' disapp'inted t' find that, while the property Pa had bought did a'ready have a soddy on it, we warn't going t' git t' live in it after all 'case the feller what was a' sellin' t' us had already b'ilt a big beautiful barn an' had did consid'able work on buildin' his house. The house came second t' the barn, o' course. (A fam'ly kin always live in the barn with the animals until a cabin er a house is b'ilt. Pa told me that whar he'd come from over in Irelan' that the house an' barn was usually one an' the same thing.) Anywise, this feller had started with the soddy, then b'ilt a barn, then a cabin an' was in the process o' convertin' the cabin into a full scale house when his wife an' all three o' his childun took sick an' event'ally died with the cholera. Pa said that this feller, a Mr. Martell, as I recall, Pa says his spirit had jest beat and busted so that the po'r feller sold his home, his land' an' all his mem'ries t' us. Cheap, too, Papa said.

(Cheap fer us, he meant. Ol' Martell's mem'ries had cost him dear.)

Our place was in the part o' the state that was later t' be called Morris County. The beautiful Di'mond Spring was 'bout three er four mile away from our place, an' they was also two small springs on our land'. Springs ain't all that common in Central Kanzas, (but not so rare as they is out west) so us havin' two was a deal!

The smaller spring, the one farthest from our house, would sometimes dry up in the drouth years, but the bigger spring never did dry up. It had a good flow o' water, as big as a man's laig, flowin' all year round. It twisted an' turned through our property, makin' a nice little stream, a "slew" we called it, an' it emptied into Di'mond Crik, which, I reckon, emptied into either the Cott'nwood er the Neosho River. Mos' likely the Neosho, I reckon.

The spring was jest up from the grove whar we buried the kids (I'll tell more 'bout that later). It was always cool 'round that thar spring, water-crest grow'd thar an' Mama would fry it up with aigs an' a skillet o' fresh fried bluegill an' bass er even bullhaids if'n that was all we ketched, an' make a real supper from it. They was always wild game thar, too.

In 'em early days they was deer, elk, antelope, pra'rie chickens, mournin' doves an' passenger pigeons, wild turkeys an' all kinds o' littler' critters.

Sometimes I'd spy a cougar, "wild cats," we called 'em. One o' our old neighbors called 'em "catamounts". They never did give me no trouble 'cept fer once, years later, which I will prob'ly tell ye about if'n Sister Doe will remind me.

One time in the fall, a wildcat killed Pa's hogs. Well, actually what happened was that Pa had decided t' butcher one o' 'em hogs anyways, an' had shot it in the haid with his old muzzle loader, an' was read to slit it's throat an' hang it up t' bleed out. He was a' lookin fer a bucket t' ketch the blood in t' save it back fer cheese er scouse. He'd walked 'round t' the back o' the sty whar he was bilin' water in a big, black, iron witch's pot t' dunk the pig into so's he could scrape the hair an' bristle off'n the skin. 'Parently, the old coug smelt that blood an' came slinkin' up a shaller draw t' the front o' the sty. Like mos' cats, he weren't near as in'erested in the daid hog as he were in the live one.

The cat jumped the low rail fence, cornered our old sow an' tore her throat out. Pa still had the muzzleloader rifle with him an' when he hear'd the ruckus he ran 'round an' saw what was a'goin' on. I 'member he had t' run clear back up t' the house t' fetch his powder an' lead, then he ran back down t' the sty. He said that big coug jest stood thar a' watchin' him, holdin' the twitchin' co'pse o' that hog down with both front paws, while pa fumbled 'round reloading his gun. Jest as the coug started snarlin' an' hunkered down, a' shakin' its rear end like a cat does a' fore it pounces, Papa shot the cougar smack through between the eyes, though Pa warn't what you'd call a marksman. He was shore proud o' that shot, though! He skinned the cat down an' cured out the hide, which he later sold t' a drummer fer two Amerikin an' three Confederate dollars. Then he went on ahaid an' butchered both o' 'em hogs, so they was no big loss in the end 'cept that the sow had been bred an' we was expectin' a litter o' pigs, come spring.

Pa was also purty upset with his old dog, Toby, what had slept through the whole shebang an' never once't did so much as t' lift a paw er scratch a flea in a effort t' he'p. Toby was a good old dog, I reckon, he jest didn't git too excited over nothin'.

They was still a'plenty o' buffaler in 'em times. Some folks nowadays, they don't know that they was more than one kind o' buffaler, which by-the-bye, the folks back east refe'red as "buysun."

They was one kind what preferred rough, mountainous areas, whilst another kind, which I was mos' familiar with, they liked the woods an' streams, but they disappeared early. They was smaller an' darker colored than the big, pra'rie kind an' the meat was juicer an' more tender. Them was killed off some by settlers, I reckon, but mos'ly by the Indians.

(When the time came that these "woods" buffaler started t' git scarce, why, the Indians got in a big hurry t' kill off they share 'case they was scairt that a new round o' white hunters would migrate in an' take 'em all. It didn't take long t' wipe them big, dumb buffaler all out, really. Sometimes it seems t' me, in m' mem'ry, like 'em big shaggy beasts was always 'round, grazin' on the grassy hillsides by criks an' streams, er eatin' acorns in the woods by the rivers. Then, it was like I jest waked up one mornin' an' they was all gone, all a sudden, like.)

But, as it turned out, these smaller buffaler warn't the targit fer the skinners after all, anyways. They was after the big brutes on the higher plains which, 'case o' they size o' course, pr'vided bigger hides an' it was less work t' take a hide off'n a larger beast. So the Indians wiped out all the woody buffalers fer nothin', as it turns out. No matter. If they hadn't o' did it then the whites would 'ave, sooner er later fer one reason er t'other.

It was the U.S. Gov'ment an' little feller named General Phil Sheridan what later decided that the only true way t' keep the "Injuns" on they reservations an' from follerin' the great herds, was t' jest wipe *all* the buffalers out, no matter whether they was the woods' kind er the plains' kind, the mountain kind, whatever. (Little Phil thought it was an even better idear t' simply wipe out ever' Indian man, woman an' child, but they was a few white folks, mos'ly back East, who didn't cotton much t' that idear so he settled on killin' the buysun instaid).

Then the farmers an' the ranchers started bellyachin' 'bout how they wanted the buffs gone t', so's they could graze they insipid cattle on the pra'rie, which is jest how farmers an' ranchers is by nature. I guess they was a'feared that some critter that they couldn't put a brand on, er corral an' sell off fer a profit, might git a mouthful o' that precious grass that they wanted t' save only fer they herds o' Hereford an' Angus an' Jerseys.

The gov'ment he'ped create new markets fer the buffaler meat in rest'rants an' in army rations an' the like. It cut into the cattle market some, but the ranchers stood by. They know'd that if they bided they time, the beef market would rise jest as soon as the buffs was gone an' that it wouldn't be too long. They was right, o' course.

And, if'n you want t' know, beef warn't the meat o' preference in them days anywise. The society crust would only eat pork. But pork didn't travel that good, 'less you salted the bejesus out o' it, then it would sometimes turn green anywise and afore you know'd it, it had worms, salt er no salt, so soldiers and trappers and miners and prospect'rs perfer'ed the beef. It sometimes got worms, too, but the worms in beef was harder t' see so's it didn't matter so much t' them fellers.

Buysun bones by the boxcar load was shipped off t' fact'rys an' was turned into hairbrushes, combs, mirror frames, geegaws o' all types. They was so many bones fer the pickin' that they was ground up by the ton fer fertilizer. Fer a little while there a feller could earn a middlin' livin' jest pickin' up bones from the pra'rie. An onc't in a while if'n' some daid injun bones er the bones o' some unlucky set'lers got mixed up in thar, who was the wiser?

The hides was used t' make the very warmest coats, hats, an' blankets an' the best saddles in the worl' was made with buffaler leather.

The Gov'ment he'ped support all this an' made deals t' ship these goods off 'cross the ocean, an' he'ped t' keep prices high so's the hunters would stay in'erested. As the frenzy fer killin' buffaler grow'd, they encouraged the railroads an' private landowners t' pay bounty money t' the hunters an' t' the skinners, besides. I reckon they figur'd it was cheaper payin' folks a bounty t' kill the buffs than it was t' pay soldiers t' kill Injuns, since, truth be known, the soldiers warn't all that good at either one, anyhows.

It only took 'em a little while, jest a couple o' years, really, an' most o' the buffaler was gone. I wondered even back then, could the Injuns be far behind?

~

They killed thousand's o' buffs a day an' that's a true fact! Sometimes they would skin 'em out, sometimes they'd jest cut out they big old, blue tongues an' pickle 'em in brine t' sell as, what they call, "delicacies", back East. The hump meat sold good in a local way. But most times they jest left 'em t' rot whar they fell.

(You know, they was still a few o' 'em pra'rie buffaler 'round clear up t' the turn o' the century? O' course, they was scarcer than hen's teeth, an' gittin' scarcer all the time.

(I 'member once't, years an' years later, 'bout 1905 I reckon, sev'ral o' us was a' standin' on the corner in front o' the Drover's Bank in Council Grove an' a feller came a' hurryin' over t'ward us from the Hays House up the street. "You feller's hear'd 'bout the buffaler," he asked?

(He told us that old Sy Wilkes had been over t' the Hays House braggin' 'bout a big bull buff an' a cow what was down on his place on the Neosho River. Well, we all got into our carts an' wagons an' up thar on horseback an' we rode on out t' the Wilkes' place an' shore 'nuff they was a big, old bull an' his mate up on the grassy rise above the river. We stood 'round an' watched 'em graze fer a while. Then old man Wilkes fetched down with a' old Sharp's 30/30 rifle what his gran'pappy had give him, an' he fetched down first the bull then the cow with a single shot each. We walked over t' 'em, still kickin' an' a' pissin' an' a' twitchin' in the dust, an' the old bull had pink blood runin' out o' his mouth an' nose, (pink an' frothy blood, that means a lung shot).

You know, that old bull didn't look nary ha'f so big, a' layin' thar in its own blood, the flies already a' drowndin' in the spit an' blood an' piss.

Turns out he'd shot the cow in the spine down t'ward her buttocksical area and she warn't daid but she couldn't move her hind laigs. It was gawd damned pitiful. Finally one o' the men grabbed a axe o'fin a wagon and fetched her 5 er 6 sharp raps t' the skully bone betwixt her eyes and killed her off, too, an' I was glad he did it.

I asked Wilkes why it was that he shot them pore critters an' the old man says that the sorry creachtures had the *mange*. I reckon he thought that beca'se they hair was comin' out in flaps, an' old Wilkes, he said he didn't want it spread t' his other animals so he jest left that old bull an' the cow t' rot thar on the pra'rie.

('Em buffaler didn't have no mange! It is perfec'ly nat'ral fer a buff t' shed its hair ever' year, why, it came out by the handfuls! I will admit they look a bit tattered an' raggedy when they shed, but it shore as thunder weren't no mange!)

A few days later the stink an' the flies got so bad that he poured coal oil over 'em carcass' an' set 'em a' fire. I never did see another wild buffaler. (Alive.)

~

I read some stories writ by folks who was raised in the wilderness like we was, an' they always cry an' moan an' tell o' the "hardships" what them an' they families endured. Well, at the risk o' disappointin' m' dear readers, we didn't have no real hardships t' speak o'. We lived right good; per'aps 'case it was that we jest didn't know no better.

We worked hard, but, hell, work ain't no hardship! Pa was a farmer an' a rancher (an' a danged good one fer a while, till he was took by drink) an' that's always hard work. M' Ma could do anything that a woman needed t' know how t' do back in 'em days. She could cook an' so (sic) an' was a good doc fer the livestock an' us kids.

We had food, humble as it sometimes was, tho it always tasted fine, an' we had clothin' an' shelter.

The real hardship came first with the cholera an' then with the smallpox what came 'round when I was 'bout 7 an' took m' brother,

Junnie. 'Parently he had come down with both ailments an' jest as he was a gittin' over the cholera, what had hit him first, he then caught the pox.

He was a sweet little feller an' Mama cried an' cried, lord, how she wept, seems like fer days. Papa buried him in that little grove o' trees down by the spring an' Mama planted daffydill bulbs at his haid an' tulips at his feet.

Four er five weeks later they buried Pricilla, m' little sis what died o' pox, right thar beside him. She was two year' old, a twin o' Ruthie, an' after all this time I kin still close m' eyes an' see them two little twin angels right thar in front o' me, in matchin' yallar dresses with little bee's draw'd on em, a suckin' at thar thumbs an' gigglin' an' a' diggin' thar toes into the dust o' our front yard. Both o' 'em girls, they shore loved t' chase the chickens.

So when the twin, little Ruthie, died jest shortly after, it was a complete ast'nishment, as she had not appeared t' be sickly. We never know'd exac'ly what killed pore Ruth. It warn't the pox as that had kinder died out as had the cholera. She jest waked up a' screamin' one night a' clutchin' at her little side. Mama an' Papa both sit up with her an' walked her 'round the cabin talking sooth t' her. By sunup she was daid but Mama wouldn't let go o' her. No sir! She sat with her in her lap all that mornin' an' into the afternoon till Pa tricked her into laying the little, blue body down on the bed, tellin' Mama that she jest had t' fix vittles fer the rest o' the brood afore we all starved. When she fin'ly laid her burden down, why Pap snatched Ruthie up an' wouldn't let Mama hold her no more.

First he took her off t' the barn an' then had one er two o' us kids draw up some fresh water, I cain't 'member if'n it was from the spring, er if our well had been dug yet. Anyways, we fetched him the water an' he worshed her face an' her tiny hands an' he brushed her hairs all back from her face, jest as purty as he could, not really knowin' how, an' he tied that hair back with a hank o' blue silk rib'in. We put her in the yallar dress with the bee's draw'd on it, same as they had did with 'Cilla as both them girls loved them matchin' dresses. Then he wrapped her up, tight, in a soft deerskin, I think it was, tho it might have been buff hide.

He buried her that evening in the grove by her brother an' her sis. They warn't no time t' make no coffin an' wood fer building with was a scarce commodity in 'em times, an' though we had trees, as I said they warn't the time to cut 'em down an' plane out boards an' build no proper buryin' box, though later Pa made a nice little cross fer all o' his chil'ren from cott'nwood an' burnt thar name's into 'em with the tip o' a hot iron spike. I had he'ped him t' dig them graves, which warn't much work as they was sech little things and whatever amount o' work it was pa ended up doin' as I was a little feller m'se'f.

Pore Ruthie an' pore 'Cilla. I reckon they'd been Pa's favorites an' he always seemed harder, tougher, after them two passed.

At var'ous times in my life I have see'd wonder'us things. From out of nowhar's like, things that may not mean nothin' in the tellin' but that was amazin' to me and was burned into m' mind, so to speak, like an important paintin' scalded into my mem'ry.

They was three Sac Indian warriors watched us bury little Ruthie from the pra'rie outside the ring o' trees. They was real quiet an' r'spectful. They was sittin' there on horseback with the sun behind 'em. Even them horses seemed t' know what was goin' on an' they didn't snort nor caper none.

I've always 'membered that, I have re-hashed it over 'n' over in my mind, an' I admir'd them redmen fer it, an' I know'd that Papa did too, as he told that story sev'ral times over durin' his few remainin' years.

M' Mama, though, she never was the same after losin' all them childr'n so close t'gither. She moped an' wept, doin' her chores all the while, though. Her eyes was always red an' swelled an' she sniffed a lot an' was always a' wipin' at her nose an' her eyes.

Then I guess it sud'nly occurred t' her that she might possible lose the rest o' us an' she got right per'tective an' was hesitant t' let any o' us git out o' her sight. We couldn't even play none much without her hoverin' over us like a old biddy hen.

A few months, mebe a year, had passed an' then, in April I'm thinkin' it was, it had jest poured rain, day after day. Well, me an' m' older sis was down at the crik lookin' at the high water, bilin' like a river, you know? I was a' standin' too close t' the edge an' the groun' give way er I slipped in the mud, fell on m' rump an' slid down the bank into the rushin' water! It warn't nothin', really, as I was a real good swimmer an', besides, I had grabbed a'holt the root o' a big old cott'nwood tree that was growin' thar on the bank. I warn't worried, none.

I never understood jest how it was that Mama saw this, but she did. Sis was a yellin' fer me t' be careful an' Ma must have hear'd the commotion, I reckon. Anywise, she ran out onto' the porch an' I reckon that mebe she could see Sis a jumpin' an' flailin' her arms. Mama come on the run, a screamin' "what's wrong, what's wrong?" an' Lizzy p'inted t' the stream an' yelled, "Oss fell in!"

Mama never even hes'tated.

She jumped over that ridge at full speed, I saw her archin' over me in mid air, her dress a' billowin' out like a paryshoot. She hit the water with a tremend'us splash an' that long dress o' hern, an' her petticoats, why they took in that water like a dry sponge!

Lord, lordy, pore Mama! She sunk like a rock! M' last mem'ry o' her is o' seeing the panic in her eyes jest a' fore they sank below the muddy water.

It happened jest like that, jest as fast as you kin tell it. They warn't nothin' more t' it. In a matter o' seconds her life ended an' ours changed ferever more.

Lizzy fell down on the ground in a daid faint. I swum t'ward whar Ma had gone down but Lord knows she could have been a quarter o' a mile on downstream by that time. Ordinar'ly that warn't nothin' much of a stream, but that water was deep an' high an' fast.

It come to pass that two Kaw Indian boys what found her body snagged up under the roots in a cut in the crik bank 'bout a week later. They rekinized her dress. They know'd her 'case she would always give 'em a handout if they came by our place as they often did.

They was jest boys theyse'ves an' had never tasted sugar a' fore. Ma would fry up bread dough an' sprinkle it with jest a little bit o' sugar.

It was precious in 'em days. 'Em Indian boys kept mum an' did not tell they friends 'case they know'd that they warn't much sugar t' go 'round an' so they wanted t' keep this little story fer theyse'ves.

One o' 'em kids, little feller named Tall Tree, was later on t' become m' bestest friend in 'em, m' early years, an' he was the only person outside o' m' fam'ly, who I know'd from then on out, through m' adulthood. It was fate, pure an' simple, I reckon, him bein' around an' him findin' my Ma an' sech. But I don't know.

The Good Book sez 'bout how mis'ry loves comp'ny, and over the years I often wondered how it was that one fam'ly could take so many hits, but I reckon in them days it didn't seem as awful as it would now in these modern times. They was folks what see'd it worst than us, an' folks who lost ever' single thing that they had and that they loved, sometimes in the merest twinklin' of a eye.

Not to be undue depressin' but things did not improve much. It did not seem to me like it could get no worse, but that's us' ally when it does. Git worser I mean.

It had only been a few weeks er a month at mos' after we had buried Mama down in the grove when m' brother Barry, who was he'pin' Pa with some chores, joined the others "up yonder." We had a' old plow horse what we called "Mike," gen'le as a lamb, Mike was, sired by a big old Clydesdale stud t' a Morgan mare, which, if'n you don't already know, is a mighty pecul'ar combination o' horse flesh.

Mike was a funny lookin' creachture, kinder small in body, delicate featured, an' balanced a' top o' the longest, spindliest laigs you kin imagine! At the bottom o' 'em laigs was huge, hairy hoof's what looked like bushel baskets on sody straws! Mike was a dam' good old horse but he was shore stupid lookin'.

Well sir, Barry he was a leadin' old Mike down t' the field an' I reckon he thought it would be more fun t' ride so he led that horse over t' a tree stump an' jumped up onto' his back. Now, Mike was a gen'le horse, as I have said, but he warn't no ridin' horse a'tall. He could pull a plow, er drag a sedge full o' rock er cord-wood, he could yank a stump out o' a field purty good, too, but he warn't no ridin' horse. He had been rode, years a' fore, but warn't used t' it no more an' didn't much like it none.

When Barry dug his heels into ol' Mike's side, the ol' feller grunted and started t' kinter t'ward the field. Barry was wild an' he started t' whip old Mike's flanks with a willer switch what he'd been carrying. Instaid o' making him run, Mike jest sud'nly balked!

Ol' hoss jest stepped short, which throw'd Barry off, an' the boy flew over the horse's haid an' landed face-first on the ground! Barry was stunned, I reckon, but I doubt if he was hurt much. I remember he was jest startin' to rouse hisself and to set up.

Old Mike strolled over t' Barry, ca'm as you please, turned 'round an' kicked him in the side o' the haid with his giant, iron shaw'd hoof! Barry was daid when he fell back on the ground. His haid looked like a watermelon what's been shot through with a shotgun.

How kin such a thing happen after what had happen'd t' us already?

Now they was jest Pa, Lizzie, Doe an' me left a' livin'. Barry's dyin', on top o' ever'thing else, didn't leave too much o' Papa t' go 'round. As I recollect, 'em days was hardships fer shore. I don't know how he stood it, pore pa. I reckon I cain't say how we youngins took it neither. We jest did. Case that's what you do.

~

You know, sometimes people 'member the strangest things, funny, little unimportant events that stick with us until the day we die. Mebe longer. One time, I was little, mebe four er five, an' I found a old piece o' rope that Papa had disca'ded. I was twirling it, like a lariat? I was actually doing purty good with it, too. Sister Lizzy, herself prob'ly no more'n 9 er 10 er 13, was a' watchin' me. She see'd that I could twirl the rope equally well whether I was usin' m' left hand er m' right. She said t' me, "Why, Oss! You! You are *amphibious!*"

This pleased me greatly!

I cain't not express t' you, gen'le reader, the degree o' embar'sment with which I look back over the nix thirty year' er so! Whether on the field o' battle er competition er during conversas'nal interludes, whether I was shootin' a pist'l er flippin' a coin, I kin 'member distinctly leaning over t' m' companion o' the time, whosomever, an' in a conspirat'rial tone announcin' t' all within earshot, "Either hand, old hoss, don't matter none t' me, m' friend. You see, I am *amphibious!*"

Many years later, in m' early 40's, I reckon, I took it upon m'self t' larn *proper* readin' an' writin' an' I asked the ol' lady what was teachin' me t' spell that word. She did. At the first opp'rtunity I found m'self a diction'ry so's that I could look up this marv'lously descriptive word. It read; *"AMPHIBIOUS 1. Adapted so as to be able to live on both land and in the water, sech as frogs, salamanders, beavers and some plants."*

This o' course 'splained why some folks over the years had looked at me the way they did when I proudly announced t' 'em that I was *amphibious!* On the t'other hand, some o' m' under-ed'cated friends seemed ever' bit as impressed t' hear the news as I had been, havin', o' course, no idear as t' what it implied. T' this day I have absolutely no idear what in tarnation dear Lizzy meant by sayin' sech a dam' fool thing. *Amphibious!*

Chapter 2

When the big, bloody war had ended an' word had come that Abe Lincoln had been shot in the haid by some Southern fanatic named Booth, let me tell you, folks t'day have no idear as t' what that meant t' people! The whole dam' country was shaken down t' its roots by that, I reckon. It had been wicked times fer as long as mos' folks could 'member, what with the war an' sech, an' a lot o' people faced a lot more hard times with the depres'ion which came when the fightin' stopped, an' then came the big bank panic whar folks lost ever'thing that they owned an' the like.

Fam'lies had been torn clear down by the killin' durin' the war an' they shore was a mess o' hardships both inside an' outside o' our little piece o' pra'rie, an' then that killin' o' Abraham, that jest seemed t' harken the end o' our days an' preacher's an' 'vivalists sounded the trumpet o' doom.

The 13th Amen'ment had passed which legally freed all the Negro's an' forbade sellin' 'em an' all, an' they was movin' t' Kanzas in a mass o' "Exoduster's" an' people was afeard o' 'em. They was a new Pres'dent named A. Johnson but nobody seemed t' like him so much. I've thought 'bout that, an' it don't seem t' me like the country would have liked anybody much that had t' step in an' fill old Abe's shoes. They tried t' railroad A. Johnson right out o' o'fice but some Senator So-an'-so, a feller from Kanzas as it was, cast the decidin' vote an' Johnson stayed in fer a while. They was crookedness an' sin an' a great deal o' gen'ral confusion ever'whar. They was Carpetbaggers 'n' Copper Haids, and the Reconstuct'on an' the Ku Kluxers. It was a mean time.

Years later I read that Abe mebe hadn't been as honest as mebe we'd all thought and that he played purty fast an' loose with the cons'tution an' had destroyed the whole idear o' the rights o' the states, but I don't reckon anybody who lived in them times cared much t' hear 'bout them there things. They had turned him into some class o' a god, I reckon.

~

Well, I guess losing' Ma, sweet 'Cilla an' Ruthie an' Barry was what you might call calamit'us. It mos' broke up our fam'ly. Pore old Papa, as I've said, warn't worth a peck o' corn after that. He was melancholy an' hang-dog an' a' fore long took t' drink. He had always made his own wine an' beer an' hard cider, mos' folks did, but now he'd cobbled up a still so's he could make his own likker, too. Seems like when he warn't makin' it he was drinkin' it. T' tell the truth an' sorry to say, we didn't hardly miss him much none when he passed on while still a rel'tively young man, in his late 40's er mebe his early 50's, somewhar's thar 'bouts. I never know'd fer shore.

Now, m' sister Lizzy was a good ol' girl an', like mos' girls in 'em days, she was a' grow'd up woman by the time she was 12 er 13 year' old. She took over as nat'ral as could be when Mama passed on, a' cookin', cleanin' an' takin' care o' Doe an' me. When Pa slipped into drink, why she shouldered up that 'ere burden too. She was tough as ol' Billy Hell, that girl was.

Doe was still a little thing, purty as a button, yallar hair an' big, chiney blue eyes. (I loved her then an' I still do.) Lizzy an' I fought a good deal, she tryin' t' do right by raisin' me an' me bein' purty shore that I was already raised up an' doin' jest fine, thankee much, missy. I was sorta a no good child', I reckon. I'm sorry fer that, too.

I sup'ose.

~

Down near the Neosho they was a big camp o' Indians. It was a mixed up bunch o' Kaw an' Fox an' Sac. Pa, who never did mind Injuns none, said they was all o' the same fam'ly anyhow an' shared the same "culture" as he called it. Over some times in the past they had lived t'gither an' he'ped on another, at other times they kilt each other off like flies. Purty much like white folks. Not only couldn't git along with each other, why, they couldn't even decide what t' call theyse'ves!

Some said "Kaw," some said "Kansaw" other said "Konza" er "Kanza." This here was the same tribe!

In case you don't know it, they *all* described theyse'ves as "the People o' the South Wind." (This here state is named after 'em folks, o' course you know. Som'body once't told me that they is over 20 ways t' cor'ectly spell the word "Kanzas" which I find dam'd amazin'.)

As I recall, it was 'bout this time that it seemed like settlers was jest a streamin' into the county. We was livin' only a few mile' south from whar the Santy Fe Trail cut through, an' 'em Indians jest didn't seem t' know what t' make o' all o' it, white peoples jest a' comin' an' goin' like a swarm o' bees!

On the one hand they was trade with the whites who had pos'essions what the Indians had never even dreamt the likes o' an' which they wanted. On t'other hand the whites cheated an' lied t' the Indians, brought pestilence an' sickness ever'whar they went an' thought that ever'thing that they see'd was tharn t' own. The Indians l'arned purty quick that, if'n a white asks fer somethin' why, best give it too him right off. Otherwise he might jest be inclined t' pull his gun out an' kill a body fer it!

But they was the good side, agin'. First off the whites had guns an' horses. A' fore the whites came from the east, Injuns in this here neck o' the woods had see'd horses, shore, some even owned a few, but they didn't own very dam' many o' 'em. If they was t' build up a herd o' Spanish ponies, why the Cheyenne er the Pawnee would swoop down from the north an' out o' the west an' steal 'em all, ever' one. An' a few o' they women, too, fer good measure, though t' some Injun braves, losin' a hoss was a consid'able grimmer loss than losin a woman!

On t'other hand agin', them whites brought mis'ry t' the tribes by way o' disease, greed an' whiskey. 'Course in 'em days nobody could have guessed the damage t' be done jest by the whiskey alone, an' all o' it was a dirty, dam' shame fer both sides, I reckon. "White Man's Wicked Water," the tribes called it.

'Em Indians o' our'n, they would ride along the Santy Fe an' pick up stuff that the trav'lers left behind. When people haided out o' Westport fer the West on the Santy Fe er the Or'gon Trails, why they would pack the dam' stupidest things what you might imagine! Cook stoves an' pianers, chester-drawers an' whole hogshaids o' rum! By the time they got t' our neck o' the woods they see'd that this here trip warn't no danged picnic. They started chuckin' this stuff out o' the wagons left an' right, t' lighten up the load so's t' make better time an' not t' put too much strain on 'em oxen.

Well, this here was jest a Sunday pie fer our Indians! They would ride the trails an' find this here stuff an' bring it into Council Grove an' trade it out at the Last Chance store. Er they would sell it t' som'body. Lizzy bought a good pianer-forty from that friend o' mine, that Kaw boy m' age named Tall Tree, who I have mentioned. (Tree was one o' 'em boys who found Mama's co'pse in the crik, if'n you recall).

Lizzy gave him half o' a five-dollar gold piece fer it (the pianer-forty, not ma's co'pse) which was a awful amount o' money, I thought, t' pay t' anybody, let alone an Injun, an' she told him she would bake him a choc'late cake as soon as she could git some cocoa, t' boot!

By gum, she did it, too, a few weeks later, an' Tall Tree shared it with me. We rode down t' the spring an' et it. Tree went clear crazy! Wild as a hog in a melon patch!

He'd never et no choc'late a' fore an' when he tasted it his eyes got great big an' slobbers started *runnin'* down his chin an' chest. I reached over fer a hank o' that cake an' he growl'd at me like a bear an' he dang near bit m' fingers off! When he had finished off the cake his face was smeared an' his belly stuck out. Then he got real sick an' throw'd it all back up! I read somewhar's years later that Plains Injuns couldn't take choc'late like they couldn't take whiskey. They jest warn't b'ilt fer it, I reckon, bit I don't know, a feller hears a lot o' twaddle in a lifetime.

~

Later on I used t' spend a lot o' time with Tree an' his fam'ly, 'specially after my Pa got so's he was drunk all the time an' then he was daid. Tree had a beautiful sister what I fell deep in love with. Her name was Blossom an' she was. A "blossom," I mean.

Let me see, now, I wish't I could put a time t' this. If I was guessin' I would say that this would have been 'round '66 er '67. I think that's right, beca'se it was jest a' fore the Katey Railroad branch went through an' I 'member that was 'round '68, which was also 'bout the time that Papa died, give er take a year er two. Er three…

Anywise, I was real sweet on Blossom an' she was sweet fer me. I must have been goin' on 12 er 13 er 14 (er 15) year old, near as I kin recall, an' she was prob'ly all o' 16. As I said, a branch line o' the Katy railroad was comin' through an' I got a job haulin' water t' the workers, mos'ly "hard cases", vet'rans o' the war who couldn't find no other work, the Chinks, as they was know'd, an' the Negros. I'll tell ye, these fellers worked ***hard***, hard as any slave! But now, what I did, jest a' carryin' water an' a' runnin' er'an's, that warn't all that bad, an' I ernt ha'f a dollar ever' two days! Don't seem like much now, but it was a helluva lot then, 'specially fer a boy m' age I was a savin' m' money up t' buy somethin' nice fer Blossom, mebe a bolt o' cloth er some sech. Er mebe a horse t' trade t' her pa fer her. But it was not t' be.

One night in late July a party o' Pawnee warriors came down from the Dakotas t' steal ponies. They set the village afire an' stoled Blossom an' her ma an' her little sister (whose name was Redbird), along with sev'ral other women, some horses an' two er three o' the tribe's winter caches o' food, dried meats an' berries, roots an' the like. Two Kaw men was shot daid, one o' 'em was sca'ped, an' quite a few more was wounded. (You know, all these years later, I ain't never met with anyone who's had dealings with a Pawnee that had anything good t' say 'bout 'em.)

I never laid eyes on Blossom agin'. 'Cept of course in dreams.

Tall Tree never would let on that he missed 'em womenfolk which was the Injun's way, but I know'd he did. Now that his ma was gone, it was jest another thing fer us two t' have in common me bein' a orphant, too.

Like mos' Indian youths his age Tree was considered a grow'd adult an' ask nobody's permission t' do anything. He asked me would I like t' ride west fer a few days an' t' hunt. He had been lucky not t' lose either o' his two ponies in the raid as he always kept 'em hobbled in a shaller draw what led down t' the crik, with his brother's an' his pa's, but separate from ever'one else's, which turned out t' be a piece o' good luck fer him, doncha see?

Lookin' back, I know'd I should feel mighty low fer leavin' pore Lizzy an' little Doe alone on the farm, but by this time Lizzy was keeping comp'ny with a Welchman's son with the unlikely name o' Domination Jones. I figur'd that since "Domm'" couldn't keep his eyes *off'n* Liz I should rightfully expect him t' keep an eye *on* her, as well.

~

Back in 1825, long a' fore Tree er I was born'd, they had been a big council under a spreadin' oak in a grove o' trees between representatives o' the U.S. Gov'ment an' the Greater an' the Lesser Osage Indian Tribes. The gov'ment liked t' make a show out o' stealin' land with lots o' flags and fellers dressed in showoff uniforms with brass 'n' braids an' the sech.

Now, this here council was over in the settlement what took its name from the event, that bein' Council Grove.

Basically what it was that took place was that the white men lied t' the Indians an' "bought" the rights t' survey a big parcel o' land' an' paid fer it with cheap trinkets an' mirrors, whiskey, gunpowder, rifle balls, old-timey muzzle loader guns, some rundown, flea-bit, wore out horses, wormy beef and wormier pork, buggy flour an' jarred food. Plus they paid $500 in somethin' called "reserve notes," not gold er silver but jest paper, all fer the right t' jest "survey" the land' in question. They didn't even claim that they was buyin' it. Now, this same land, though the Indians didn't know it yet, had already been claimed by the whites through papers filed in the territ'rial capitol, at that time in a little stink-hole town called Lecompton, I think, an' in Washingt'n, D.C., by writ o' some feller know'd as *Emmett Domain*.

Now, tellin' true, these Osage Indians lied t' the white men, too, telling 'em that they was willin' t' commit t' sech terms although they had no more right t' "grant title" t' the land' than did the Kaw, Tree's people, er any o' the other 10 er 15 er so tribes what crisscrossed the area.

Whar'as the Osage didn't own the land', how could they legally sell it, accordin' t' Tree? But as gifts was exchanged an' as hands was shook, then that made 'er so, ever' thing was all legal-like when the Injuns "tetched the pen," an' then later o' course ever'body got drunk. Then a fist-fight broke out an' things turned ugly, as they gen'ally did.

Nix day the white men sent word t' Washingt'n by telygraph that the survey rights, an' the land' that went with 'em, was had, lock, stock an' barrel! Meanwhiles, the Injuns went on they merry way an' more than likely never give the inc'dent another thought, having no real idear what they had did. (How does a man who has t' sign his name with an "X," er "tetch the pen," as the Injuns put it, how is that thar man s'posed t' read over the document that he's jest "signed?" It's plum' dam'd silly, if'n you ask me, which o' course, nobody did!)

Over the years the Gov'ment kept on sending "gifts" from time t' time includin' more wormy salt pork, which the Injuns wouldn't eat anywise 'case some o' 'em saw the pink meat an' thought it was butcher'd up human bein'. They was also dried beef, which the Indians would eat, an' other staples like flour, salt an' a sugar ration t' all the area Injuns which they considered t' be either Osage er Lesser Osage whether they was er whether they warn't. An' blankets.

Now, it is a disgustin' but dirty-true fact that some o' 'em blankets had been prev'ously used t' wrap the daid co'pses o' soldiers or other Injuns what had died with the small pox!

A kinda greasy feller know'd as Little Phil Sheridan, mentioned earlier, an' some o' his boys in Washingt'n had said they shore did feel bad t' larn 'bout this, 'case, o' course, they hadn't know'd nothin' 'bout whar 'em blankets had come from other than that they'd been turned in by Indian Agents up in Powder River country. You tell me if that ain't one o' the low downdest dam' tricks ever' played on anybody by anybody an' it is a hist'rical fact! Makes you proud, don't it?

Anyways, the point bein' that, with all these goin's on a'goin on, Tall Tree was travelin' as a stranger in a strange land' even when he was at home! The Osage had done give away his right t' be here fer any reason, let alone the fact that it was where he was born'd and was where he still lived!

In them times, a white rancher would as soon shoot a Indian who might be ridin' 'cross his land' as he would be t' shoot a woof. Sooner, prob'ly.

Tree's people was not partic'larly violent, as Injuns go. Still, they was not a welcome sight on the farms, ranches er towns in eastern Kanzas at that time. Whether er not they was mean, they was indeed mayhaps a little theify, if'n you ketch the drift. Yer chicken er yer dog er yer bucket er a cow er a broke-back ol' hoss er a child er two might as soon as not turn up missin'.

Well, as we had already decided to go a huntin' turns out that now I was a travelin' with that ere Indian. I figur'd that me bein' see'd with Tree might've been a good thing fer him. The whites we came upon must've assumed that I was his keeper, like he was m' Injun like a man might own a negger. Other people thought that mebe we was both scouts a'workin' fer the Army er Gov'ment surveyors, the idear o' which, speakin' frankie, I kinder liked.

Ever'body must've thought somethin' 'case they left us alone! It shore as heck warn't a nat'ral sight t' see a white an' a Injun travelin' t'gither an' the fact that we might be friends jest never did cross folk's minds. It jest didn't occur t' 'em that we, neither one o' us, would *want* t' be friends with t'other one!

Anyways, him an' me was a goin' huntin' an' that was it! We lit out an' had rode fer nine er ten days an' see'd hun'deds o' buffaler. Only trouble was they was all daid!

Bones bleachin' in the sun. Carcasses all swelled and bloated up on the pra'ries. The humps hacked off an' the tongues cut out t' be pickled an' sold t' the fancy folk.

Hell, nowadays they didn't even take the hides! Tree an' I skinned out a few o' the buffaler what warn't too putrificated an' later we sold 'em hides fer 3 dollar apiece!

It was a mighty good time fer the crows an' the tu'key buzzards, the woofs and coyotes!

It was a good ride, too, 'cept fer 'em daid buffaler. Thar was still more game in that country than a feller nowadays would er could believe.

It was drawin' in on the middle o' late September, which is m' fav'rite month in Kanzas. The days is warm t' hottish, the nights is cool t' coldish an' they is a certain crispyness t' the air an' t' the colors o' the countryside.

The sky was deep, deep blue an' the pra'rie grass, 12 foot tall in places, was the color o' ripe wheat. The land' was dry as tinder, but was crisscrossed with streams o' fresh, cold water. We rode clear on out t' within a day er so from Fort Dodge, a hell o' a ways from home, when the weather started turning agin'' us so we decided t' haid back fer Di'mond Spring.

On our way back we sat high up on a ridge an' watched a long column o' soldiers, "blue coats," Tree called 'em, file past us, proudly bearin' up the stand'rd o' the 7th Cav'ry. Even from this distance I could see the strawberry tresses o' Colonial Custer's "long hair" flowin' behind him in the wind. He was some. He was somethin'. He know'd it, too.

Shore, I know'd who he was. Mos' ever'body did. He was the talk o' the land' in 'em days durin' an' after the War. I had see'd a tintype photygrap' a' fore that a travelin' drummer had, but I would have know'd him anyways, jest havin' hear'd folks talk.

He had been a real big hero in the Great War and they was talk that someday he would be the pres'dent. But at the moment he was none too pop'lar in Washingt'n as he'd had more than a few disagreements with Useless S. Grant and the rest o' the brass. They'd more or less exiled him out t' Ft. Riley, Kanzas which was Sunday pie fer old Yallar Hair.

(I reckon that Custer's hair was more red than yallar, but that was the name what the Indian's give him and it stuck. Mebe they'd seen him in a younger day or when he'd been goin' a spell without his hat and it bleached out his hairs, I don't know…)

Jest the day a' fore we had spied a big huntin' party o' either Cheyenne er Sioux, couldn't tell at the range we was at, but they was haided in this gen'ral direction, an' we had kept a good distance between 'em an' us. After watchin' the troops fer a spell we decided we best keep a'movin' so's not t' git ketch'd in 'twinxt the two.

Now, as I said, Injuns called him Yaller Hair, but Custer's own men called him "Old Iron Ass," among other things, as he was famous fer his exhaustin', "forced" marches. Could've been that these here fellers was jest coming back from the Washita River fiasco down in Indian Territ'ry, whar they had killed over a hun'ded "hostiles". (You know, even back then I was smart enough t' wonder how an Injun on his own land' could be considered a "hostile"?) It was common knowledge that two thirds er more o' these "fierce" hostiles was women an' childr'n, shot down like dogs as they ran from they lodges, awakened at dawn by the gallant 7th, the marchin' ban' playin' the old-timey strains o' "Gary Owen, Gary Owen".

Some o' 'em Injuns had gather'd fer pertection 'neith a Amerikin flag what had been gave t' 'em by they "white fathers" at one treaty pow-wow er 'nother.

The whites had promised 'em that they was safe so long as they stood under that flag. Truth was it jest made 'em targits, all the easier fer the brave men o' the 7th Cavalry t' surround 'em an' t' cut 'em down, er, as the Injuns say, t' "rub 'em out".

(Sometime' you need t' pick up a *real* hist'ry book an' read up on the Washita River campaign. I guar'ntee it t' make yer skin crawl an' yer blood bile!)

So now it was that Old Iron Ass was back in Kanzas. Years later a feller told me that 'round that time Custer had been up in Fort Leavenworth whar he was having more trouble with the Army brass. He'd had some o' his men shot fer desertin', some whipped bloody fer "insubordination", an' he had abandoned his troops so's he could ride off, back t' Fort Riley an' galyvant with his wife, Elizabeth.

Besides that, Pres'dent Grant didn't cotton much t' Custer since he had testified agin' the Pres'dent's brother, Orville in a hearin' 'bout graft in Washingt'n.

Lot's o' people think o' Custer as a great soldier, mebe he was, mebe he warn't. But bein' a "great soldier" don't necessarily make a feller a great man.

I know'd enough 'bout him t' reckon that he had been a real hero in the War Between the States. I know'd his brother Tom had won the Medal o' Honor twice fer bravery in battle!

Ain't no doubt that them boys was plucky.

I know'd that George Custer was the youngest man in hist'ry t' be made a General, but it was what is know'd as "brevet" and now that the war was over he was a Colonel agin', though he rarely referred t' hisself as sech, preferin' t' be know'd by the higher rank.

But what some don't know is that he was Court Martialed. As rankin' an as brave as he was they was something' in him that jest rubbed the army brass the wrong way, I reckon, and so he was allays in hot water, if you ketch the drift. Now, a Court Marshal. (I don't know if this was jest a' fore we see'd him er jest after.)

Anywise, I asked Tree if he know'd who that feller down thar with that long hair was an' he said no, but that he must be a great warrior t' ride sech a fine pony an' t' lead so many men an' t' have sech long, beautiful hair and t' wear such fine, white buckskin.

We sat fer a spell an' watched that schemey old Norseman lead his troops off to the west t'ward Dodge. I must admit that I felt a little something' a stirrin' in m' breast an' a certain guilty pride a'watchin' 'em ride away into the dust an' haze. I was tempted t' foller an' t' watch what happened jest in case they was t' cross paths with that red huntin' party we'd see'd earlier.

(A year er so a' fore he died, ol' Yallar Hair writ a book called *"My Life On The Plains."* Some o' his Army buddies called it *"My Lie On The Plains,"* behind his back o' course. Event' ally I had m' own experience with old Iron Butt that convinced me that they was likely right in sayin' that. Remind me t' tell you 'bout that, sometimes.)

When I think back on it, I don't s'pose a third person listenin' in could have understood the conversation between Tree an' me. I spoke mos'ly English an' a little bit o' Kaw. Tree spoke Kaw an' Kiowa, which is quite a piece differ'nt from each other, as well as some consid'able English. He claimed he could also talk Lakota, Nakota, Comanche an' Cherokee (in his later years, some Latin, Frenchy an' some German) an' I reckon that he could, too. He was a smart feller, Tree was.

He said that a white woman had lived once with his tribe an' that she'd taught all o' the childr'n some o' her talk an' some Mex, too. He said that one o' his uncles had traded a old mare, blind in one eye, an' two ugly, yallar, Injun dogs fer that white woman from some Mexico traders. The woman had been bad abused, which happened a lot when they was kiddy-napped, I reckon, an' had died a short time later. She jest broke down, I figure.

Tree's mama had been a Kiowa. They was 'riginally from down 'round the Yallarstone an' kindly migrated into Kanzas an' the Territ'ry by theyse'ves. Tellin' the truth, they was sort o' like pore relations, I guess. Like the Pawnee, I have never hear'd too much said kindly 'bout the Kiowa from neither Indians nor white folks.

We rode on slowly, windin' our way back t'ward Di'mond Spring an' this time we did see a small herd o' buffaler, abut 20 er so, I reckon. Tree asked me if I wanted t' chase after 'em but I said no. I was starting t' feel rightly sorry fer 'em critters, I s'pose, but I didn't mind if'n he chased 'em a spell. So he did. He didn't kill none, though 'case they warn't no need t'. We had our pickin's o' small game an so why kill sech a big feller as a buff fer only one or two meals?

But I always will remember the look on his face when Tree wheeled his pony down mungst that herd and rode with 'em fer a spell, hoopin' an' hollerin' like a red injun, which o' course he was. He shore looked the part, and he shore did look happy, too.

An' he was happy. When he came back he was pantin' like an old hoss, and sweatin' and smilin' and laughin'. He was a good feller, as good as any feller that lived is m' 'pinion. He slapped me on the back and off we went. I looked back and them buffs was already standin', haids down, grazin' as if nothin' at all had happ'nd, as though they was nothin' wrong.

It was a hell o' a hunt, it was. A hell o' a ride, and I wouldn't trade them mem'ry's fer nothin'.

But as a feller gits older he sees things through differ'nt eyes, if you know what I mean. Years later, a' lookin' back, I could see sev'ral things what had happened near 'bouts this time which did not bode me well. I reckon I should have know'd that rough times was a' comin' m' way. I rar'ly know'd o' any other kind.

It had all began sometime' a' fore. The first ill omen, I reckon, had been all o' the dyin' in m' fam'ly an', finally, Pa's passing away. I know I already have talked 'bout that some, earlier, but let me 'splain jest a little more, so's t' sort it out.

Pa had been very morose an' morbid an' would not leave his bed even fer likker. Why, he was so bad off that he let the fire in his still burn out! He had laid in that bed nigh on three weeks. Sud'nly one night he sat up an' cried out, "No! Not the boy! Not the boy!"

I fear'd like hell that he meant me!

He looked crazy as hell, too, eyes as big as a hooty owl, he was sweaty all over, a tremblin' an' a shakin'! He let out with one more long "noooooooooo," an' fell back in the bed.

Lizzie dashed over t' comfort him an' t' dab some cool water on his brow, but he jest trembled and shook like a cold, wet dog and within a few hours he was daid!

Nix day Tree an' I dragged his body down t' the grove, he was a purty big feller, m' Pa, an' we couldn't carry him, though we tried, an' it was slick walkin'. It must've either early in the winter er late spring 'case the ground was still froze. Naw, I 'member, it was right at the start o' winter!

Whatever, it don' matter none. The ground was hard an' I must admit we made piss-pore job out o' diggin him a grave. When we was done they was 'bout as much o' him left sticking out o' the ground as they was buried under it.

Finally, Tree thought t' hook up a travois t' his pony, which would have been the best way t' move the co'pse if'n we'd a thought o' it right off, but we didn't, an' we hauled limestone's up from the crik an' b'ilt a mound over the co'pse t' keep the varmi'ts out.

Tree's people don't hold much with handling the daid, 'specially daid whites. I appreciated his he'p an' I know'd that it was a sacrifice that he made as a show o' respec' fer me. I asked Lizzy if'n' she couldn't bake him a choc'late cake without so much cocoa in it fer him an' she did. I made shore he et it real slow an' only let him have a piece er two.

He woofed it right down as quick as I doled it out t' him, but at least it didn't make him so sick this time. Nix day though he had developed sech a case o' the "runs," an' could not even ride his pony!

~

It snowed a skiff that night after we buried Papa. It snowed a' might more the nix day. This was good, 'case it froze his body and kept the smell down and the critters away.

By the morning o' the third day the sky was low an' menacing. I saddled up Pa's old ridin' horse, Maggie (he'd traded Mike off after the incident with Barry) an' I rode over t' the Kaw village. They camp was semi-perm'nent an' was jest a mile er two from a ford in the Neosho whar the whites claimed that the famous Spanish explorer Cor'nado had passed through in 1541! I don't think the Kaw gave a hoot nor holler 'bout that, seein's what Cor'nado unleashed on 'em! ('Course, he did bring along horses, an' fer that alone the Injuns always said they could almos' fergive the whites fer ever'thing else!)

Tree was thar an' he invited me into his lodge whar he lived with one o' his brothers, Shield, his pappy an' his old granny "Two Moon." Two Moon had fixed a big skin full o' game birds, antelope meat, wild onions an' cattail root which taste a good deal like Irish 'taters.

(Do you know how the old timey Injuns cooked a' fore they had a steel pot? Well, they took a goodly-seasoned, smoked buff hide, jest the skin, I mean, with the hairs scrapped off, an' hung it near a fire on a wooden tripod. 'Course they couldn't set the hide right over the fire without it burnin' up, but they kept it close by, filled with water an' the stuff fer the soup. Meanwhiles, they heated up smooth, river rocks in the coals o' the fire an' when they glowed they would reach down an' grab up a rock er two with a horn spoon an' dump it into the hide pot! A' fore long it would heat t' a slow, rollin' bile, then they would cover the hide with a grass mat er another piece o' skin t' hold in the heat. It was a dam' slow way t' cook but it made fer laripin' good vittles. If they had been a recent hunt, why, then, druther than usin' a smoked skin, they'd use the fresh buffaler gut which imparted its own flavor, which I will tell you without fear o' contridic't'n is a mighty fine tasty treat.)

Old Two Moon had herself a iron pot, though. She had two as a fact, but on this partic'lar morning she had decided t' cook the old way an' she had a fresh deer's belly a' hangin' on its stand an' was a' fillin' it up with good things fer a stew. I ask her why it was that she was a cookin' sech a'way an' she jerked her haid t'ward the low sky outside an' said in English, er somethin' sorta like it, "No hurry. We stay here a long, long time."

She busied herself by putting some large deer bones into the fire t' roast. Later they could be took out an' busted , an' the marrow sucked out. It was good tastin' an' gave a feller energy.

She also made some cakes out o' groun' corn that she would pat into dried cornhusks what had been soaked in water with ashes in it an' then shoved the whole pack'ge down into the coals t' bake.

They warn't no set mealtime fer Injuns. They et when the food was done. Any time o' the day er night if the food was thar, why, someone, *anyone*, a' walkin' by a skin full o' soup would jest grab up a horn spoon an' have hisse'f a mouthful er two. The Kaw could farm, some, mos'ly corn which was a big part o' they diet, an' o' course they hunted deer an' buffaler when they could git it, thanks fer which was gave at ever' meal t' the Great Spirit. Who ever grow'd er killed the food warn't given much o' any credit fer they work, all thanks was given t' they heathen god.

The Kaw camp had many kinds o' "houses." First off, they was a tipi. These was the homes o' the true nomads like the Comanche. When the Kaw an' other tribes saw them tipi's they liked so much that they stoled the idear.

Gen'ally tipi's was small, light, quick t' move an' purty comfor'ble t' live in, 'specially in the summer time when the side flaps could be raised up t' let in the breeze. The size depended on how many they was in a partic'lar fam'ly and how many skins could be scrounged t'gither. Some of 'em was really big, surprisin' big, and could sleep 8 er 10 folks.

Men carried a smaller tipi with 'em on the hunt, small enough so's that could be carried by one horse, an' set up in a matter o' minutes t' serve as cover fer one man, two at the mos'.

Another kind o' dwellin' among the Wichita, Osages, Kaw an' Pawnee, an' the same kind o' home that Tree an' his fam'ly lived in, was a lodge made o' grass. Some called them "wickiups" er "wigwams."

They would build a frame o' cedar wood covered with willer entwines an' then that was covered with long, swale grass which was used like shingles. The door would face east so's the morning sun came in like a 'larm clock t' wake ever'body up. Mos' Injuns was early risers.

Mos' o' 'em houses had holes fer windows which was covered with heavy hides hung up fer curtains. Often as not they was also a door on the west side so's the Indian could say his prayer o' thanks fer another day o' life an' ask pertection from the night. Mos' major prayers was said in the mornin' at sunrise an' agin' in the evenin' time, 'round sundown.

(Yer average Indian was a religious fool! They talked with they gods on a person'l level, ever' day, sometimes all day. They was much more religious than the whites was, at least that's how I see'd it, as they lived minute t' minute with The Great M'stery which was another name they had fer "God.")

'Course they was superst'ious fools, too, believin' as they did that all things had spirits an' some o' 'em spirits was fer the Injuns ways an' some was set agin' 'em.

(I had t' laugh at ol' Tree one time! He was worried that a feller in his camp, a kind o' medicine man, might be puttin' the evil eye on him so, o' course, I told the superst'ious knothaid how a sprig o' holly er juniper over his lodge door would he'p keep the bad luck away almos' as good as a iron horseshoe sprinkled with salt will, which any blamed fool should know.

(Well, shore enough, he went out a found hisse'f a small cedar tree but then the danged dunderhaid went an' said a prayer o' apology t' the tree's spirit a' fore he would cut limbs off'n it! It's a mighty superst'ious feller who says a prayer t' a tree a' fore he puts it t' it's intended use!)

As I say, them lodges could be huge, as was Tree's, which I guess was between 70 er 80 feet 'cross! They was always a fire burnin' in the middle o' the floor an', jest like in the tipi's, they was a round hole cut up in the roof' t' allow the smoke out, but not big enough t' let in too much in the way o' rain an' snow. Truth is it was almost always smoky in them places

The lodge was also used t' store food up near the roof' amongst the crosspieces, mos'ly tied up in twine made from dried grass er buffaler sinew.

Now this tribe, Tree's folks, they raised big gardens ever' summer. They grow'd peppers, corn, beans, all kinda o' squash an' gourds, melons, pumpkins, onions an' Indian taters. Kanzas dirt is rich an' often times they had enough o' a surplus crop so's t' trade off with other tribes er t' take into Council Grove an' trade off with gov'ment agents er the local farmers. If not, most of them crops, 'cept fer the melons, could be dried or stored fer use in the wintertime.

Now, what was I a' sayin'? Oh yes, 'bout the houses! Anyways, this here kinda lodge what Tree lived was big an' airy an' as comf'able as any white man's house.

(They another kind o' house sorta like these lodges I jest told 'bout, 'cept they would put thick layers o' dirt an' sod over the top o' the framework. Another way was t' build with the same mater'als but in a different shape, a long, low boxy-type o' lodge which, I reckon, is more like them 'er wigwams.)

When the lodge was all b'ilt up, a prayer t' the one they called the "Man Never Know'd on Earth" was said so as t' guar'ntee the safety o' the house an' fer those who lived inside it (as I said, they was superst'ious folk). This partic'lar village whar Tree lived had some lodges an' tipi's o' each style.

Tree's Pa, Big Walk, came in with a wove reed basket full o' pieces o' flint rocks. I guess he reckoned that he was going t' have time on his hands t' chip out some new points fer his arrows an' fishin' spears. Now, the Kaw was pore people. They had a few guns, but they was mos'ly flintlocks an' cap'n'ball pist'ls, old-timey things. They was no repeatin' rifles among 'em yet, in fact it was a violation o' Fed'ral law t' give er t' sell an Injun a repeater.

But even with guns, they was some Indians what still preferred arrows. A good warrior could fire up t' seven arrows into the air then fire an eighth a' fore the first one fell back down t' earth! He could easy fire five er more arrows in the time it took t' load up a muzzleloader. 'Sides, a rifle always let out a belch o' smoke which was a perfec' targit fer a man with a bow. Alls a feller had t' do was t' aim jest below that 'ere puff an' he had a right good chanst o' hittin' the rifleman in the face er the chest! An' a man could almos' always find somethin' t' make a arrow out o' even if he was lost er pinned down by the enemy.

Big Walk was a tall, han'some Injun o' 'bout 40 er 45 year' old, I'm guessin'. He had been at his daddy's side during the incident back in '59 what was still fresh on a lot o' folk's minds.

His pa, the village chief name o' Ah-Le-Goh-Wah-Ho, which the whites translated t' Big Horse, but who ever'body jest called "Ah."

Now, Ah was a fair man who tried t' control his peoples by settin' a good example. See, chiefs didn't really have much o' any real pow'r in a village like, say, a mayor er a capt'in er som'body like that.

A chief couldn't tell people what t' do er how t' act. Oh, he *could,* but they didn't have no oblege t' listen t' him. Gen'ally, though, chiefs was r'spected enough so's that they word carried weight an' they served by example.

Welp, it seems that a couple o' the young Kaw bucks had stoled a pair o' horses from a Mex trader, which was somewhat o' a sport amongst the Indians, kinda like white kids tippin' over the outhouse o' the neighborhood grouch. No real harm is meant by it. But white folks, and Mex's, too, fer that matter, takes great o'fense at having they horses snatched!

Well, old Seth Hays, owner o' the Hays House restaurant an' hotel in Council, he came out t' the camp jest a bilin' at Chief Ah, sayin' that the Mex's is the kinda trade the town o' Council Grove needs an' that the townspeople don't want 'em drove off by a pack o' thievin' redskins!

Old Chief Ah thought 'bout it an' he didn't like the tone of it none, so later that day he rode into town with 'bout a forty men in a effort to smooth the matter over. Seth came out an' they exchanged hot words.

Some cowboys who was in town lookin' fer trouble got t' feelin' tough an' so got t'gither a kind o' a posse. When the Injuns rode out o' town the posse follers 'em. By the time that the posse rode over the crest o' hills t' the south o' town they see old Chief Ah with his original forty men only now they's other Indians coming in from ever' direction an' the group is 'bout 200 strong! Not jest Kaw Injuns, neither, but a big band o' Arapaho, which happened t' be in the area on a hunt.

They was this feller present with the name o' Rev. Tom Huffaker. He was what he called a Methodist He-piss-co-pail preacher. He had started the Kaw Mission school jest north o' Council Grove but after a while he said he found the Kaw childr'n t' be "uneducable" so he had closed the school in '54.

Anyways, Reverend Tom comes up t' the Chief, all full o' bluster, an' he demand's that 'em two braves what had stoled 'em ponies fess up an' come along back t' town with him. He person'l guar'nteed they'd be treated fairly.

Well, ever' one was het up and the whole shebang was what you call a powder kaig what was ready to blow sky-high. Chief Ah thought 'bout all the bloodshed that he could avoid fer his folks. He was one o' 'em early "visionary's," I think they calls 'em, who could see whar the war between the red men an' the whites was haided. He ca'med ever'body down a notch er two an' he talked 'em two young fellers into goin' along with the Reverend who was, after all, a man o' God.

Well, don't you know that it was jest a matter o' hours a' fore 'em Injuns got theyse'ves a quick an' speedy trial? They was tried an' convicted o' stealin' horses from a man who warn't even a citizen o' the U.S.A.! *

Jestice was swift, indeedy it was. They hung 'em both in a stand o' trees within eyesight o' the old Kaw school!

(* That Mex who's horses was stoled was not a citizen o' the United States, but then neither was the Indians! I have always been slack-jaw that the first Amerikins warn't considered citizens in this here land' until a special act o' Congress was passed in the 1920's! I was there fer that, too, but that's another story.)

Old Chief Ah never trusted the whites agin' and his say with his tribe was brought down a heap by the whole incident.

But his son, Walk seemed t' believe the best o' folks in spite of it all. He was a pow'rful man, the kind with what the Injuns call "Big Medicine," an' I felt kindly shaky in the knees when he was around, 'specially when I looked into them dark, de-fiant eyes.

~

Walk sat down an' patted at the hide mat beside him. I'd hear'd tell that he could speak some English but would not out o' pride. I reckon. I went over an' sat down beside him an' he asked me in Kaw if I could make a point, meanin' a arrowhaid. I shook m' haid "no" an' he proceeded t' teach me. I set with m' haid down watching him clack t'gither two stones, one chippin' away at the other, sparkin', sometimes, until grad'ally an arrowhaid took shape. It was fun t' do, lessen you mashed a finger er busted yer thum-nail, an' real useful, too, an' Big Walk was a patient teacher.

When I looked up some consid'able time later an' glanced out through the leather flap-door, it took my breaths away! I was plumb amazed t' see the snow! It was already deep enough t' have completely covered the earth. Pore old Maggie, m' horse, was weighted down by it. It was clear that I warn't going t' go home in this mess fer at least a day er two. It was lovely.

They was no wind at all, which is rare in Kanzas, an' it didn't feel cold. The snowdrops was huge, the size o' a 5-dollar gold piece, I ain't never seen the likes before er since, an' they drifted slowly t' the earth like angels from above, an' my, warn't thar jest millions o' 'em?

The snow was like a blanket that muffled ever' sound. Injun childr'n an' they pack o' ugly dogs* ran through the camp playing an' shouting an' them dogs a'barkin'. But the snow swaller'd they shouts an' the barkin' an' it was as though I was dreamin' er lookin' through a pict're book o' somethin' from long, long ago.

(*Fer some reason which I never know'd, Injuns always had the ugliest dam' dogs alive! Even uglier than Mexikin dogs! If you was t' be walkin' along somewhar's an' see the disgustin'est dog you ever did see, prob'ly yallar with big, ig'n'rant brown spots, why, it would be safe t' figure that dog belonged t' a Injun! Mebe the fact that them dogs was so ugly made it easier when it came time t' eat 'em, I don't know. Remind me sometime an' I'll tell you the best way t' cook dog, Sioux style. M-m-m, laripin'!)

~

(Fer no reason in partic'lar I recall that I decided t' go out by m' lonesome that day an' try t' scare up some game, kindly as a way to "ern my keep," if you ketch my meanin'. They was a great fog, like we gits in Kanzas durin' some winters, an' I walked in the snow, up t' m' belly in places, a'lookin fer a rabbit er some sech. I came on t' a place whar a cott'nwood tree had fell over, mebe blow'd down by the wind in a prev'ous storm, mebe collaps'd from the weight o' the snow, an' I started stompin' 'round in the branches. Shore 'nough, a pair o' rabbits hided off from under that tree. They ran 'bout 30 feet an' stopped like a rabbit does, still like, prob'ly lookin' back at me an' thinkin' I couldn't see 'em, as rabbits is stupid as hell.

(I was a packin' a old 10-gauge shotgun, fer some reason, I don't recollect that it was mine. I might have borried it from Tree er one o' his folks. I had two brass cat'ridges, like we used t' use back in them times. The gun was a singleshot, so I had one cat'ridge in the chamber an' t'other in m' right hand which was holdin' the stock o' the gun.

(I raised the gun up an' sighted down the barrel at a spot somewhar's right in betwixt 'em two rabbits an' I pulled the trigger. Now 'em old guns made a hell o' a racket an' would kick you like a mule an' leave yer shoulder black an' blue an' yer ears a' ringin' like a churchy bell, but the only sound that day was this gen'le "poof", like the gun had been all wrapped up in thick cotton, an' both 'em rabbits jumped straight up in the air, 3, mebe 4 feet high, then they jest fell back t' the ground, daid.

I walked over, like I was in one o' 'em movin' pict'res I see'd once't years later at a Worl' Fair, run real slow, an' I kin clearly 'member the white o' the snow, an' the brown o' the rabbit's fur, the black o' they eyes an' the red halo's spreadin' out in the snow 'round 'em. It was so very quiet, like I was in a dream. Although them rabbits had give up they lives, it was still an' all a lovely sight to see. I remember it so well.

(I fetched 'em both up an' makin' m' silent way back by the same way back as I had came from, I took 'em rabbits back t' the camp, skin'ed 'em out and gave 'em to ol' Two Moon an' she was as giddy as a school girl to have 'em! Ain't it funny how 'em things stick with a feller? I don't know why, it ain't important, but I jest now recollected it all as clear as if I had been thinkin' o' it ever day since then.)

~

Inside the lodge was the smoky smell o' the stew, the hides, an' a rich smell o' people. Fer some reason I felt as though I might start cryin'. Big Walk moved beside me t' look out o' the flap at his camp. He put his big arm 'round m' shoulders an' shook me gently, "Eh Wakon Tanka ah tse waat, he' tse lek, meh Tskeke". That means somethin' like "God has made us a beautiful world to live in, my Son." I turned m' haid t' wipe away the tears. I never a' fore felt so at home anywhars. I don't believe I ever felt that way since.

~

It snowed an' it snowed an' it snowed! Four straight days an' nights o' snow! I have see'd snow like that mebe onc't er twice since. Mebe.

This was a big dam' snow! On the second day the wind came up hard an' bitter from the northwest an' the temp'ature dropped lower an' lower. Drifts was as high as the lodge poles an' from a distance you could see the smoke from the center hole like it was a' coming up out o' a drift o' snow, er so it appeared. What had been beautiful before had turned out 'n' out ugly in a hurry.

Big Walk brought his favorite pony into the lodge with us an' tied his other ponies, along with mine an' Tree's, t' the side o' the lodge out o' the wind. His horse, Rain, was as ca'm as a house cat an' his big body put off a lot o' heat. All the dogs was in the tent with us, too. It was warm enough, but didn't it git ripe?

T' make matters some worse, that horse had been eatin' chestnuts er acorns er some dam' somethin' that gave him the flat'lence somethin' awful! If yer city folk you might not know that a horse with the gas makes for one big dam' stink! I spent consider'ble time with m' haid underneath m' blanket.

48

Indian folks is tougher'n hell. Tougher'n any gen'ral white man kin know. Fortunat'ly fer 'em it had been a good summer an' they was all fat an' prosper'us an' they' was still a fair amount o' dried meats, nuts an' dry berries an' the sech laid by in different hidin' places in the woods which they know'd like the backs o' they hands.

All through the camp I could hear the chatter o' stones as the men an' boys sat, patiently making points. December is know'd as Moon o' the Clacking Rocks among some o' the Plains tribes, an' it shore did seem appropr'ate now.

This was a dangerous storm an' the Injuns know'd that the only thing t' do was t' wait it out.

~

Many whites, I l'arned later, was not so lucky. A branchline o' the Katey locomotive was stranded east o' Council Grove with snow drifted up t' it's smokestack. Fer months t' come, trav'lers would stop at shacks, soddy's an' farmhouses dotted 'round the pra'rie only t' find entire families o' skeleyt'ns huddled t'gither 'round a cold fireplace. Often the bones o' farm animals was mixed in with they's so's as they couldn't be told one from t'other. 'Em farmers had tried the Injun trick o' bringing the animals inside but it had jest been too dam' cold, I reckon, er mebe they animals weren't as tough as those o' the Injuns. I hear'd that some o' 'em folks had suffercated what with the house bein' buried in snow an' all o' 'em inside tryin' t' breath the same air, but I don't know. Some folks say that is "science," but I don't know nothin' about that.

They was also talk o' o' kinnibalism, but I don't care t' talk too much 'bout that thar thing.

An' lord, how the pore, wild animals suffered so! I hear'd tell that a man could walk from here t' Colorado on the co'pses o' the antelope what had froze! ('Em things never did recover an' I never see'd near as many agin' as I had a' fore that storm. This here storm along with big 'un in '78 purty much put an end t' the antelope in Kanzas).

Birds starved t' death, not bein' able t' dig down through the snow t' git t' the seeds an' sech that they needed t' live on. They didn't have no water that they could git t', neither. When the thaw finally came, near a month later, why, the streams was floatin' with daid fish that had been froze solid, the water not bein' deep enough fer 'em t' escape the freeze.

The buffaler fared a might better, though some grew mighty spare. It ain't no accident that so many trappers wore buff robes. They's warm enough fer a man an' fer a buffaler too, I reckon.

I was worried sick over Doe an' Lizzy an' first chance I made m' way back t' our farm. They was all right but had been worried sick over me, which is the one thing I had never figur'd on.

I hear'd later from a neighbor that ol' Custer an' his men had been caught in the storm out somewhar's between Dodge an' Ft. Hays. They suffered bitterly, he said, but the "Red Fox" (Custer had hisself a heap o' nicky-names) had pulled 'em through it by keepin' 'em up an' movin', force marchin' 'em all night long in a blinding snow an' all survived

It was a example o' "Custer Luck," as the Colonel an' the newspapers called it. Shore, they was some o' his men what lost fingers an' toes, some lost a whole foot er the tip o' an ear er two er the end o' a nose, but they all got in alive, god bless 'em. Old Iron Ass had pulled 'em through it an' reinforced his men's undyin' r'spect—an' hatred o' him.

All 'n all it was one hell o' a winter. Snowed at least once a week from then on till late in March! Then, I waked up one morning an' hear'd a redwing blackbird callin', "t'wee, t'wee," from down in the marshy area between the spring an' the crik an' I know'd that it was springtime agin'. Springtime leads t' summer, an' let me tell you that it was the dam'est summer o' m' life!

CHAPTER 3

As I told you at the start o' all this, I ain't much fer dates. I thought in m' mind that this must've have brung us up t' the summer o' '69 but sister Doe, who is he'pin' me t' put this all down, says that it had t' have been '68. No matter, if I cain't 'member *when* it was, I shore as hell 'member *whar* it was an' *what* it was that happened *'case I was thar!)*

I had grow'd restless that last winter, an' spring was welcomed. Me an' Tree fished an' hunted an' scrounged 'round doin' as little as possible. Now his tribe plan was fer all the men folk t' ride south in search o' the big herds. Tree an' his brother an' his Pappy would have been happy t' have me go along but some o' the others in his bunch didn't feel so warm t'ward me beca'se I was white an', as o' late, the white folks hadn't been doin' no great favors fer the Injuns an' so I warn't likely t' win no pop'larity contest an' I did not relish the idear o' bein' mistook for a buffaler er endin' up as a "accidental casualty" o' a mis-aimed bullet or arrow.

After Tree rode off I moped 'round our place fer a long spell. I he'ped a neighbor build some rock fence which is miserable hard work an' I was nearly bit by rattlesnakes on at least ha'f a dozen occasions! I he'ped the girls with the garden, but m' heart warn't in it.

I had been thinkin' some 'bout Yallar Hair Custer an' it occurred t' me that if I was t' ride t' the west that I might jest hook up with the 7th an' have me a ad-venture er two. 'Bout the middle o' August I said good-bye t' the girls an' away I went.

I warn't in no hurry so I took m' time. I was jest this side o' the Smoky Hill River an' I spied a farm house, late afternoon, gittin' 'long t'ward evening, an' I rode up t' it, thinkin' I might git m'self a hot meal an' a place t' bunk down fer the night. As I look back on it I shore do wish that I hadn't o' ever laid m' eyes on that place or, if I had, that I had jest hided out an' kept' on a' ridin'!

This here area, The Smoky Hills, got its name beca'se it is always hazy lookin', like smoke. Well, on this day they was real smoke comin' from that farmhouse. At first I thought they had b'ilt a big ol' fire, like you do fer scaldin' water when you's butcherin' a hog, say. But, as I got close, I could see that the house itse'f had been burnin'. By now the fire had purty near burned itse'f out, ha'f o' the house, that is the wood part, bein' destroyed. The remainders o' the house was sod an' it don't burn too easy but it do smoke like ol' Billy-Hell.

The flame had died back consid'able, but still, as I say, 'bout ha'f o' the place was a smolderin' ruin. Scattered 'round the front yard was a' guesome a sight as I'd ever see'd!

First they was a man. He had been stripped nekkid an' his, 'scuse me fer sayin' it, his "privates" had been cut off. They was two boys, one 'bout 10, an' the other one littler' an' they had been did the same way. They was a woman an' a girl, nekkid too, all hacked at an' cut up, an' all o' 'em was full up with arrows. When I first rode up it took me a little while t' figure out jest what the hell they was! They looked like big, white, pincushions. I would say that each body had 20 er 25 arrows a' stickin' out o' 'em, which is a sign the Indians leave. Gen'ally it only takes one arrow t' kill a person. They wanted folk t' see this an' take it as a sign t' keep off Injun land.

Them folks had all been sca'ped an' they haids was all red an' scabby looking, an' they was big, nasty blowflies an' big, green bottle flies a' crawlin' all over 'em.

Now, I ain't gonna say too much 'bout all this, 'case I don't like tellin' it anymore than yer gonna like hearin' it. I'm jest gonna say what needs t' be hear'd.

I climbed down from ol' Maggie's saddle an' looked as close as I could bear t' at the woman. B'sides bein' sca'ped, her eyes had been poked out, an' her tongue cut off. They had also mutilated her bosoms in a way that I don't care t' discuss.

The tips o' the men's fingers was missing as was they tongues. The youngest boy's haid had been hacked o'fin' his neck but fer some reason they hadn't gouged out his eyeballs. It might have been better fer me if they had, fer I have dreamed 'bout 'em eyes all these years since. They was as blue as blue kin be, wide open an' horrified! I tell you what, truth be know'd, it jest made me heave up ever'thing I'd et fer the past three days. It was mighty sad.

The girl looked t' be 'bout the age o' our pore, daid little twins. She was still holdin' ha'f o' a rag doll, like som'body had tried t' take it from her but she wouldn't let it go an' it had ripped in two.

Now, I ain't no way tryin' t' jestify what them Indian's did, it was as wrong as anythin' kin be, but they was a *expl'nation* fer it, whether or not a white person kin understan' it or not. The way they see'd it, by mutilatin' them bodies the Injuns was pertectin' theyse'ves an' they fam'lies 'n the afterlife. Cut off a man's fingers an' he cain't pull a trigger, gouge out his eyes an' he cain't see t' come after you. Cuttin' up the other parts an' a man er a woman ain't gonna have no offspring. I ain't sayin' it's right, but truth is, it ain't no worse than what the U. S. Army did t' red people. Some soldiers made covers fer they saddle horns from a woman's privates, others made t'baccy pouches from a man's.

One is jest as bad as bad as t'other an' neither one is right and god he'p them that did sech things fer whatever reason an' fer whichever side they was on.

After I got sick I figgerd I'd be all right. But when I turned back 'round an' took in the whole scene I got sick all over agin'. After I had finally throw'd up a third time, an' was weak in the knees an' covered in what they call a cold sweat, I walked off a ways an' cried some, I reckon 'case they was nobody alive none to see me.

I mounted up on Maggie an' haided on west ridin' hard, panicky like, t' find som'body an' t' tell 'em what had happened, I reckon, though I have no idear as t' who it was I thought I might find.

I hadn't rid more than a mile er two when I came up on a small group o' tall riders, Cav'rymen in grey an' a few ranchers ridin' like hell t'ward me. When they pulled up they asked me right off had I see'd anything. I told 'em, "yup" an' I said if I was 'em, I'd slow down, 'case they weren't in near as big a hurry t' git up t' that farm as they thought they was. The leader o' this band, a retired rebel soldier named McKlosky, looked at me kinda suspicious like an' told me t' "fall in." I don't reckon I know'd what he meant, they wasn't no pond or nothin' t' fall in t', so I pretended I know'd what he was on 'bout anywise an' I rode with 'em back t' the house, though I shore did not want t', let me say.

The sun was jest going down as we rode up t' the yard. I felt better seein' that some o' these older fellers got sick, too. As I have stated, it was guesome.

After millin' 'round an' mutterin' in low voices fer a while, the men formed details t' bury the daid an' a civilian feller said a few kindly words 'bout Jesus and his virgin ma. McKlosky had climbed down from his mount an' was a' lookin' the area over real good. He picked up a arrow shaft an' held it out t' me.

"Know the tribe, do ye lad?" He had a accent in his voice that reminded me o' m' Pa, harsh an' rollin' from deep in his throat, not sweet an' piping like Mama's was.

I shook m' haid "no…"

"Wichita's! Dam' right, lad! They's dirty, murderin' Wichita Injuns. Anyone t' do sech as this ain't a human bein' a'tall. It's an animal that does this sort o' devil's work!"

"Wichita?" I asked, like it was a statement o' disbelief, "Why they ain't nothin' but a bunch o' beggars an' hobos, sir."

"Aye! Er so they appear t' the casual eye! Until they think that they kin git away with somethin' as dastardly as this! They's wolves! These s.o.b.'s would slit they own mither's t'roat with ah razor if'n' it meant a free meal fer 'em, er a shiny bauble, er a bottle o' some dam' rot-gut. Lookit that paint on the shaft, lad! Lookit how the haft is tied, the way 'em spinfeathers is arranged? Wichita! Shore as hell, I'd stake m' reputation on it!"

Well, it was clear t' me that McKlosky know'd a sight more 'bout this thing than I did, or at least he believ'd he did, which is purty much the same thing t' some folk, so I jest shet up.

"Aye! We're gonna find 'em, lad. An' when we do we're gonna gut the gizzards out o' ever' las' man, woman an' chile. Animals, I say! Bloodthirsty savages! Eyre with us, then, laddy? Speak op, son! Eyre comin' along?"

Well, I was mighty het up by now, as you might say, an' so I up an' said, "shore."

We made a camp a mile er so from the house down by a crik that ran through the hills. We didn't have no supper, but I don't think that nobody minded 'case none o' us was too awful hongry after seein' what we'd jest see'd.

Sunup, nix mornin' a' fore we pulled out, five U.S. Cav'ry men, real cav'ry, in blue coats, come ridin' up on 'em big sorrel horses o' they's. They poked 'round an' asked ever'body lots o' questions. They ask t' see the remainders an' McKlosky, who didn't seem t' be all that thrilled at the prospect o' playin' second fiddle t' his former enemies, stood thar all stiff an' blow'd up, straighten' the lapel on his ol' grey coat, an' he told the capt'in in charge that the "dear departed" had been treated t' a good Christian burial an' that if'n the Army wanted t' see 'em, why then the Army could borry they shovels an' dig 'em up theyse'ves.

This here Capt'in, named H. H. Tucker, he jest rolled his eyes. Later, he looked at them arrows an' pronounced 'em as Arikaree, what we called "Kree" er "Ree" Indians. They's all the same bunch.

Well, shore, old McKlosky argued a bit that the markin's was all Wichita, but it was clear that fer a fact Tucker know'd what he was talkin' 'bout an' he told McKlosky that, besides, they warn't a plug's difference in a Kree an' a Wichita, but that they had been consid'able trouble o' late with a band o' Kree t' the west an' that since the Wichita had been peaceful fer the past 4 er 5 years, that it was mos' likely Kree arrows. Tucker had a air 'bout him o' a nat'ral borned leader an' it was clear that he didn't need t' browbeat er down-talk t' McKlosky, so it was that McKlosky seemed t' accept bein' corrected, onc't he see'd that Capt'in Tucker was a reasonable feller an' one that know'd what he was a'talkin' 'bout.

The Capt'in told us that Col. George A. Forsythe had formed a comp'ny o' men at Fort Harker in Ellsworth county an' that his men was goin' back t' they de-tachment then ever'body would ride t'gither t' meet the Colonel an' that, if'n we was inclined t' do so, why, we could join up right now. 'Course you know that I had nothin' else t' do.

"How old are you, young man?" the Capt'in asked when I raised m' hand t' volunteer.

I lied an' told him that I was 17. He kind o' smirked an' asked 'bout m' fam'ly. "I am an orphant child, sir, what was stoled by maraudin' Red Injuns an' then stoled agin' an' raised by a roving band o' gypsy pirates. I am a right good tracker an' a nat'ral borned killer. I kin skin a buffaler as fast as mos' men kin skin a buck. I am good with horses an' mules, I kin cook an' I kin shoot equally well with either hand as I am amphibious, sir."

Fer some reason, unknown t' me at the time but which became apparent in later years, he laughed right out loud an' clapped me hard on the shoulder in a frien'ly way . "Well," he said, still grinnin' like a 'postum eatin' poke berries, "you'll do, son, you will most definitely do. An officer can never have enough *amphibious* men in his command." We all mounted up an' with a wave o' his hand we was off t' Fort Hays.

~

The ride t' Hays is hellacious long, that is a fer-shore fact, but it was fun fer me. After all, they is safety in numbers as the sayin' goes, an' I had fun talkin' with all these fellers. Mos' o' 'em was vet'rans o' the Mexikin War er the War Between the States. As I have p'inted out, some had even been on the losin' side! But deep down, they was all soldiers, it was all that they know'd how t' do, an' so they r'spected each other fer that.

They shore warn't much in the way o' work fer a man in them times an' the Army paid twen'y er thirty dollars a month er thar'bouts. The gov'ment had been signin' men up fer long hitches in what was already bein' called "the Injun Wars" t' pr'tect good, Christian Amerikins who was willin' t' move on t' the West an' t' tame this here lan' an' wrest it from the heathens. Years later I l'arned that the law called it "Manifest Destiny."

By now, mos' o' the farmers an' ranchers what had set out with us whilst the iron was hot had dropped out along the way, comin' t' they senses, so t' speak, an' havin' crops an' animals an' wifes and chil'ren t' tend t'. Not me! I had nary a care in this worl'. I was off on what I figur'd to be a grand ad-venture!

CHAPTER 4

All the men treated me good an' sev'ral took me under wing. They show'd me how t' track. (I had lied t' the Capt'in when I said I already know'd how). They show'd me how easy it was t' tell a Injun's pony from a Cav'ry horse (That is easy as Sunday pie! A Injun pony ain't *never* shod, an' beca'se o' that, an' beca'se it ain't near as big er heavy as a army horse, all loaded down with a saddle, tack an' bags, the track left by a Injun pony ain't never so deep).

I l'arned a lot 'bout trackin' varmi'ts. (Know how t' tell a woof track from a cat track? Easy! A woof er a coyote er dog has a claw print in the track, but a cat's claws stay draw'd up inside the paw 'less he flexes 'em out! Never thought 'bout that, did you?)

I l'arned some little bit 'bout trappin', too, an' how t' care fer horses an' mules on the long marches. 'Bout ha'f o' them men rode mules, an' preferred 'em over horses! I vowed as I would git me a mule a' fore I would ever have another horse.

A mule is mean an' ornery, fer shore, only a fool would say otherwise, but they is also tough as nails an' kin travel twice as far as a horse on ha'f as much food an' water. An' lots o' folks don't know it but mules is fast! They kin run faster than mos' horses an' a dam' sight further! These fellers had lit a fire under me an' nary nothin' agin m' old hoss, Maggie, but I was set fer t' find m'se'f a mule!

From time t' time we came 'cross the Indian's trail, if it *was* the same group o' Indians. They ain't really no way t' tell, though'. They is some what will let on that they is but they ain't. Now, you kin tell a war party from a movin' camp, o' course. That's easy as Sunday pie, too! A war party leaves a narrow trail, travelin' in a purty straight line us'ally, no more'n two abreast, an' they will only be the hoof prints o' small, unshod horses.

A camp, though, will leave behind hoof prints, human footprints, an' trails dug by the travois an' lodge poles. You also will find the feet prints an' the "scat" left by them ugly dogs. At first glance it is all jest a big mumbo-jumbo o' tracks over tracks over tracks, but if a feller will git down o'fn his horse an' *look*, why, after a little studyin' you kin figure out purty much what's been goin' on.

They is also always trash an' litter whar a camp is moving, burnt out fire pits, disca'ded scraps o' food, bones, wore out cookin' skins er pots. They's horse an' dog droppin's an' a ways off the trail a good tracker will find human droppin's, too.

It was on this ride when I saw somethin' that has stuck with me ever since. If I could paint I would have made a picher o' it. We was ridin' down a slope into a great, flat bowl o' a valley, haided north by northwest. They was a big ol Kanzas thunderstorm comin' up on the horizon in front o' us an' I mean t' say it was gonna be a rip-snortin' doozy.

The shelf o' clouds was huge an' menacin', with big, snow white thunderhaids at the top, an' the bottom was a sickly, greenish-black color. It was pressin' hot an' they was not a hint o' breeze. 'Cept fer a few meadowlarks an' sparrows an' the dam' gnats that buzzed 'round our eyes an' mouths constant, they was no sign o' life on this rollin' pra'rie. It was like city people says, jest like a big, endless sea o' grass!

It was so sweaty an' still, I could hear ever' saddle squeak an' the sound of boots scuffin' in the stirrups an' the grunts o' the men and horses. I could hear the sound o' the horse's teeth on the steel bits and the chink of the metal rings in the tack!

We rode fer 'bout a hour, I reckon, I noticed that the deer flies was a tormentin' the horses somethin' tarrible, tho' not botherin' us much, an' I see'd that the black cloud was gittin' bigger by the minute, jest a' bilin' at the bottom.

We was jest 'bout 'cross the narrow end o' the valley an' was fixin' t' start up the ridge on the far side. A ways off in the distance we could *feel* the thunder, an' then, like the angel o' death, I saw a snow white cyclone drop out o' the clouds an' spin like a drunkard in the same place fer sev'ral minutes! Then it sucked back up into the cloud an' then, jest as sud'nly, it came back down agin' an' started t' zig-zag 'cross the tallgrass! As it rolled it picked up dirt an' dust and pulled up inside itse'f, turning from snow white t' a gashly brown.

It was off in the distance some, mebe 4 er 5 mile' away an' we all watched it, awestruck, wonderin' if'n' it was gonna come our way an' what we was t' do if'n' it did.

Jus' then, on the ridge between us an' the twister, *they* appeared, like ghosts from out o' nowhar. It was a party o' Comanche warriors! It sent shivers down m' spine an' ever' one o' our horses stopped as if on command. Ever' man's eyes lifted up t' look at 'em Indians on the horizon an' the wind started t' blow from the north an' it felt as cold as wintertime on our sweaty clothes. M' horse, Maggie, shuddered an' snorted an' stamped at the sod.

I had never afore see'd a Comanche up close and I was plum pole-axed! I am here t' tell ye that it was a dam'ed impressive sight!

If'n' you don't know it, the Comanche was prob'ly the mos' admir'd Injun on the plains. They was fearsome, fearless, fightin' men an' they was widely know'd as the bestest horsemen on the plains er anywhar's else.

They could ride a pony at top speed without a saddle *er* a bridle! They could shoot with a bow'n'arrow er a pist'l er a carbine an' they could shoot straighter from a movin' horse than mos' men could a' standin' still!

When they rode they hugged that horse so tight with they knees that they was hanging straight out from the beast on the opp'sit side o' whoever might be a' shootin' at 'em, an' that Injun could shoot you daid from betwixt a runnin' horse's laigs! It's a fact.

Them feller's up on that ridge looked like wonderful statues. They was all between 18 an' 40 year' old, an', in one way, they all looked jest alike, 'bout the same size an' all, though each one was dressed in his own partic'lar way.

They faces was all painted up, some with stripes o' bright yallar an' deep red an' black. Some, prob'ly members o' a tribal f'aternity, had one ha'f o' they faces painted snow white an' t'other ha'f painted pitch black, real scary, like some class o' goblin, I reckon!

Mos' all o' 'em wore high leggin's an' breech clouts, high, laced, buckskin moc'sin boots, a few had wore blood-red shirts with buckskin vests, some wore they vests bareback.

Now, these Comanche has got dark, wine-red skin! They's much darker than some Negro's have know'd. They hair is coal black. Some wore they hair parted down the middle with braids a' hangin' down either side o' they backs. Others was wearing they hair like Pawnee, with porkypine lookin' spikedy ridges down the center o' they haids, all stickin' up an' caked with painted, dried clay.

The horses was wild looking, with no two what looked alike an' some was colored more like dogs* than horses, with big spots o' colors an' almos' ever' last one had a colored hand print on they left flank.

(*Did you know that among many o' the Western an' Central Plains Injuns the word fer "dog" an' the word fer "horse" is the same? When ol' man Cor'nado brought 'em horses t' this country, 'em Injuns had never see'd 'em a' fore an' the only thing they reckoned they might be is a big old dog! It the truth, now, I'm tellin' you).

Each Indian man was holdin' a rifle an' even from a distance we could tell that some o' these was new, repeating Winchester's. Mos' wore they bullets on belts 'cross they chests, Mex style, an' sev'ral also wore pist'ls as well. (Fine, army-issue side-arms, purty new, and I reckon I know'd how they came acrost 'em.)

They was a bow an' a quiver o' arrows hanging down the left front laig o' each pony. In they own society these fellers must have been rich an' pow'rful men.

They shore 'nuff looked like roy'lty t' me!

We was no further from 'em than the distance 'cross a wide city street an' we could see the cyclone twistin' up behind 'em though they didn't seem t' even notice it. I think they was wonderin' 'bout us like we was 'bout 'em, only the chances are that they was more than likely expectin' us an' was consid'able less surprised than we was.

O' a sudden, hailstones the size o' hen aigs started peltin' us so hard that it knocked one o' our fellers clean out o' his saddle an' knocked him cold! It only hailed fer a few minutes an' then started t' rain like a cow a' pissin' on a flat rock!

When I peered up t' the ridge agin' through the river o' water runnin' off the brim o' m' hat, both the twister an' the Comanche was gone.

As I said, it was a thrilling sight. I won't never forgit it neither, I betcha.

~

We slogged on through the rain which did not let up until we made camp t'ward evenin'. I spent one cold an' mis'able night, soaked an' shiverin' in a stinkin' wool blanket layin' on top o' cold, muddy ground! Ever' time I hear'd a varmit make a sound er hear'd a twig snap I would think o' 'em Comanche an' set up with a start. Finally the old cook, a man name o' Hank, said, "Settle down, boy. You sceered o' 'em Injuns? Lord, son! ' Em Comanche come after you an' I g'arantee you won't hear a sound. They'll cut yer throat an' you'll never even know they was a comin' till you wake up daid t'morry mornin'!" This made me feel better, sort o', an' I event'ally drifted off into sleep.

Nix mornin' I warn't daid and the air was clean an' fresh an' I thought fer shore that I could smell autumn on the breeze. The sky was hard, clear, blue an' they was a heavy dew on ever'thing. The sun came up warm an' pleasin'. The pra'rie soaks up rain like a biscuit soaks up gravy so ridin' over it weren't too bad.

Event'ally we marched into Fort Hays, on t' the Smoky Hill River an' fin'ly t' Fort Wallace, all told over 200 mile'! When we got t' Fort Wallace we stayed fer one day an' one night, which was Sunday pie fer me. I always loved life in 'em forts. The buildin's was crude, I reckon, but they shore seemed mighty plush after so many days on hossback. Old Maggie had developed a split hoof so Capt. Tucker saw t' it that I got a new, army issue mount.

Now don't you know it was a big, chestnut brown, jack mule! It was named "Lucifer." It took me jest a matter o' mere minutes t' l'arn why that was his name.

Within a day I hated that son-o'-a-bitch mule worse than anything in the worl'!

If I tried t' saddle him he would blow his belly up real big with air. Then, when I put m' foot into the stirrup, he would fart the air out an' the saddle would slide clear down under his belly an' I would land face down in the dirt!

If I turned m' back fer even a minute that scoundrel would bite me hard enough t' draw blood! Bit clear through a buckskin jerkin I was a wearin'. I l'arned t' never make the mistake o' bendin' over 'round him. He would use m' butt as a targit an' either ram me with his bony, hard haid like a billygoat, er send me sprawling in the dust er the mud with a well-placed kick t' m' skinny be-hind!

An' *could* he kick? Why, no matter how many times that varmit let me have it, ever' time it seemed like a whole, new experience! The only word I kin come up with is "stunning," 'case it was!

One minute I was a standin' thar thinkin' 'bout this er that, doin' somethin' er nothin' in partic'lar an' then, WHAM! I was airborn'd, with abs'lutely no idear in this here worl' as t' what might have happened t' me! Fer all I know'd I'd been blow'd up in a powder magazine er had been hit on the backside by a cannonball! Then after five 'er ten minutes o' floatin' around up there with the birdies, I would come a'crashin' down, jest a plowin' a rut in the ground with m' elbows, m' chin an' the heels o' m' hands!

M' pore hands was so skinned up an' scabbed over I could hardly do no work. M' elbows was so sore and scabby that I walked around with m' arms held away from m' body till one o' the men asked me was I was pertendin' t' be a chicken er somethin' an' ever'body laughed at me!

An' that dam' mule know'd jest as well as a doct'r when I was almos' healed up, an' shore as I was, WHAM! Once't agin' I would find m'self eye t' eye with a grasshopper er a skunk er some other creachture b'ilt low down t' the ground.

An' then, when I could finally rouse up the strength t' pull m' broken body up from the earth, the laughter o' ever'body what had see'd it a' ringin' in m' ears, I'd look at that gall dern'd Lucifer an' he would be standin' thar with his loppy danged ears a' layin' back, showin' his big yallar teeth an' brayin' out with a big jackass laugh o' his own at me!

Oh, he know'd what he was a doin', yes indeedy, he know'd perfec'ly well. He was a vile an' nasty villin. He would torment me so!

I hated that beast t' the point whar I seriously considered murderin' him! That's right, murder! Why, I ain't never in m' days killed nothin' in cold blood 'cept fer a skeeter er a fly, but as the Lord is m' shepherd, they was more than once't that if'n' I'd been able t' lay hands upon a gun, a ax, anything at all, jest a long, thick board would have been fine, an' if I'd a' had the strength t' use it on that mule I'd a' felt nary a pang o' regret!

When it came time t' mount up I know'd that, first thing, I would spend 5 er 10 minutes dancin' around with that fool mule.

When I could fin'ly git up on him, he would haid off in any direction he pleased, an' if I tried t' rein him back in, he would walk in big circles, frothin' at the mouth, eyes rollin' in his haid an' gen'ally puttin' on a show, like as I was a' killin' him, while all the other fellers would sit an' laugh at me atop this dammed fool mule! Gawd, but I hated that fly-bit beast!

~

We left the Fort on the 9th o' September. (Purty good fer a feller with no haid fer dates, ain't it? Well, I cheated! I 'member'd it cause that was m' Mama's birthday). They was 49 men including Col. Forsythe who was in command.

'bout four days out a rider approached us from the west an' reported that a wagon train had been attact'ed the day a' fore by a small band o' Injuns. Four white men had been killed an' all o' the expedition's supplies had either been stoled er burnt up. The Indians was either Wichita er Arikaree er both an' they had either taken er drove off er killed all o' the livestock 'cept fer one old ox which was still alive even though it's haid had been split open with a ax, er somethin'.

The Col. said he couldn't spare no men fer t' chase the Injuns as we was on the trail o' a bigger band, an' so sent the rider off t'ward the Fort on a fresh mount. I was more than willing t' let him take Lucifer as I'd as soon t' walk. Instaid the feller rode off t'ward the Fort on a fast, Indian-style pony.

The Col. told him t' bring back a detail o' 10 men an' he wrote a note tellin' them t' do what they could fer the unfortunate trav'lers. After the rider took off we veered our course t' the west so's as we could stop by an' check up on those folks an' t' bring 'em water an' what few rations that we could spare. Mebe we could shoot some fresh game along the way an' the order was give t' shoot anything eatable what crossed our path.

I killed a cottontail an' a jackrabbit. Two other feller's each got deer, a white tail an' a muley. By mid afternoon we rode into the camp o' wagons. The folks thar was mighty glad t' see us an' they was still purty shook up, 'specially the women an' the kids. As luck would have it, two o' the old boys who'd been killed was both bachelors so at least two o' the families never lost they pappys. O' the t'other two, one left behind a wife an' a teenaged boy, the other, the sorriest, left his wife an' three childr'n, all under the age o' 10. (The childr'n, I mean, his wife was in her 20's, I reckon.)

I wondered what would happen t' her an' 'em youngins, so far from home an' a' haided fer lord knows what er whar? The folks on the wagon train had already buried the daid an' had covered they graves with flint an' limestone pra'rie rocks.

I he'ped t' clean one o' the deer an' a feller asked me how I'd l'arned t' do it so fast and slick. He paid me a compliment when he said, "Boy, you skin jest like a Injun! Whar'd you l'arn t' do it thata way?" I jest shrugged an' told him m' Pa had taught me. Some white folks, 'specially folks that has jest endured a Indian attack, might not like hearin' 'bout m' best friend an' his fam'ly.

It was late in the day when we finished up dressin' out the game, so's it was decided that we'd spend this night with the wagons, much t' ever' one's pleasure. The trav'lers felt safer with us along, the Col. felt better knowin' that this would buy 'em some time until he'p came from the Fort an' the soldiers was happy t' have the comp'ny o' nonmilitary folks, 'specially some o' the younger, unattached women folk.

I struck up a conversation with a Mr. Teal Cudahay who was travelin' from St. Lou, which I already sorter had 'dopted as m' home town, tho' I had never been thar. He was haided, along with his wife an' two youngins, first t' Santy Fe an' then on t' Californy. He said that the wagon train was mighty slow an' that folks was either bored out o' they minds er scairt out o' they minds, either way, they was mos'ly crazy on these s'journs. He feared fer his fam'ly mos' all the time, never knowing who er what was a' waiting fer 'em beyond the nix rise. The pra'rie o' Kanzas had been awful monot'nous sometimes, he said, an' I cautioned him in as nice a way as I know'd how that the worst was likely yet t' come.

As I may er may not have mentioned, the east an', t' a less degree, the middle o' Kanzas has plenty o' streams an' criks an' slews, an' they's tree lines along the streams, an' sometimes they is groves o' cott'nwoods er willers which crops up purty much in the middle o' nowhar's. They's plenty o' open plains, too, but occasionally a feller needs t' come up t' somethin' like a grove er even tall grass t' kind o' break things up an' they will, in this area.

But from the west third part o' the state on'ards is a whole 'nother story, I will say. The flatland's o' Western Kanzas reaches all the way out near t' Pike's Peak, (which was originally part o' the Kanzas territ'ry but had been left t' Colorado when statehood came). This is the part o' Kanzas that sticks in the traveler's minds fer years after they've crossed it, an' some says that they'd face Beelzebub hisself a' fore they'd cross it agin'.

It's whar strong men kin grow weak an' whar some souls, after days an' days o' rollin' grass an' sky an' sun an' wind, would actually lose they minds an' do wild things, hurtin' er killin' theyse'ves an' others 'case they jest went plumb hog wild, I reckon. I've hear'd tales o' husbands er wifes a livin' out in 'em parts in a soddy an' one day comes an' they jest snap an' kills they whole families an' theyse'ves.

Some Injuns said that 'twas evil spirits that lived in the tall grass what would take over the bodies o' the whites who had no pertection agin'" 'em, an' these spirits would twine up in they hair an' talk t' 'em an' tell 'em t' kill they families, so they did. But, as I have said, Injuns is a superstitious lot. Besides, a lump o' rock salt an' a piece o' iron in a feller's pocket will keep spirits like that away, as any fool could have told 'em as if they would have listen'd.

~

We talked fer some time an' his wife, Loretta, fixed up a laripin' trail stew made with fat an' tallow from the hindquarters o' the mule deer. She had found some wild onions, pra'rie sage an' some Injun taters an', along with the spit-roasted meat, it was as fine a meal as ever I et, I reckon.

Mr. Cudahay took out a old mouth harp an' play'd a couple o' sad tunes. I was right in'erested in it an', believe it er not, he jest gave me that harp! Said he had another, an' per'aps he did. That man started me up on a lifelong love o' things musical an' I later was t' become a purty fair hand at the *harmonica*, as it is really know'd. I believe they might have been a career in performin' fer me, but, if so, I ain't got around t' it yet.

Mr. Cudahay had a ceegar an' he let me light it up fer 'im. I took two er three big old puffs but had a bad coughin' spell what left me week an' dizzy an' not feelin' at all like a dyed-in-the-wool t'baccy man.

Mos' all o' the soldiers are t'baccy men. Some smokes pipes, others ceegars, when they kin git 'em, but mos'ly they all chew plug. They call it all kinds o' things, "horsetail braid", "dog's laig" an' "negger twist" but truth be told they ain't a hang's difference in any o' it. It is black leaf t'baccy either braided up er mashed into a plug so hard a feller could break off his teeth tryin' t' git a bite. I ain't storyin' when I say that I've see'd fellers who could spit a stream o' brown t'baccy juice 12 foot an' hit a targit no bigger than a $5 gold piece!

Often times they ain't a whole lot t' keep a feller occupied out on the frontier, so a little thing like bein' the champeen spitter in his outfit was somethin' o' a honor. (That ain't all fellers did fer distance, neither, but as I am tellin' this all t' m' little sister t' put down here, they is some areas which must be left t' the reader's avid imagination).

We left camp a' fore sunup the nix morning an' I never did say good-bye t' the Cudahay's. They was nice folks an' I shore do hope that they made it t' Californy an' got rich growin' grapes an' oranges an' lived a long time.

You know, it has appeared t' me that the one thing 'bout them times what nobody never talks 'bout, is that it was a time o' constant separation. Why, you'd meet a feller er a gal, talk some with 'em, mebe even face a tribulation with 'em, mebe share phys'cal love. Then, a day er two later, why you'd part an' like as not never ever see er hear o' that person ag'in. I 'member it as a time o' great excitement, that whole bizness of movin' West, an', yet, o' great sorrow. I've wondered how many young ladies finally made it t' whar'ever they was goin' an' then, nine months er so later, give birth t' a lifelong reminder o' they times on the Plains? What would 'em women tell they child 'bout they pappy?)

Excitement. An' sorrow. Constant sorrow, it seemed at times.

CHAPTER 5

We had been ridin' per'aps a hour an' a ha'f an' the sun was full up in the sky. The Col.'s person'l guide, a Crow Injun named Rustyblade who was one o' 'em skulky, shiftly types, he told the Col. that they was a good, sweet stream up ahaid whar we could fill our kinteens an' water the horses. Col. Forsythe said he had not slept well the night a' fore an' that, if'n the men didn't object, he would like t' take a nap fer an hour er so in the shade o' the cott'nwoods an' willers along the crik bank. O' course nobody minded even a little bit!

We rode down t' the water an' dismounted. It was stand'rd practice fer one feller t' hold the horses back a spell while 't'other filled up the water jugs, so as t' keep 'em horses from muddying up er foulin' the water. I dismounted from Lucifer without no major injury, which with 'em was a win'fall, an' I handed the reins t' a feller named Corp. John Harrington, a nice young feller I'd been passing trail time with.

He was only nineteen er twen'y year' old an' had lost his whole fam'ly t' the pox in less than a month's time! He had lost his pa an' his brothers a' fore that in the War. He had been the last grow'd man an' then the dam' pox came an' killed his ma, his sisters, an' all his fam'ly at the rate o' two er three *a day!* He was the very last one left! He told me that when he was done with the Cav. that he was going t' git hisself a homestead either here in Kanzas or down in the Injun Territ'ry, if the gov'ment opened it up, an' hitch up with some young woman an' repopulate his bloodline.

As I was bendin' over t' fill the kinteen, John was a goin' on an' on 'bout that homestead an' how he was gonna plant corn an' wheat an' beans an' 'taters, sech 'n' sech an' so's on. Right in the middle o' this here speech, he stopped talking, sudden like. I hear'd him make a funny, gurgly sound an' I looked up at him t' see what in tarnation he was goin' on 'bout.

He was standin' stock still with a far away distant look in his eyes. His mouth was wide open an' they was the leet'lest trickle o' blood a' runnin' down his chin. Right smack in the middle o' his forehaid thar was 'bout a foot an' a ha'f o' arrow shaft stickin' out! The flint tip o' the arrow was jest barely stickin' out o' the back o' his neck! I was so scairt, shamed as I am t' say it, that I pee'd right in m' trousers!

Fer a while I swear I could not breathe but soon as I could I stood up an' started screaming, "Indians! Indians!" The other soldiers looked up at me as if they was tryin' t' guess whether er not I was a' funnin' 'em. One by one, men started t' drop t' they knees with arrows stickin' out o' they chests, they bellies er groins! 'Em Injuns was smart enough t' attack quiet like, with them arrows instaid o' guns.

The trees here was purty thick an' the underbrush was too, in places, makin' it the perfec' place fer 'em t' ambush us, so they had killed sev'ral o' our boys a' fore the others even know'd that we was under fire.

I ran back t' pore John who was still alive, sorta, I reckon. He was on his hands an' knees, snots a simply gooshin out his nose an' he was a'twitchin' all over, like a dog a shakin' the water from its coat. I never did know fer shore but he might have already been daid at the time. (You see, later I came back t' him, he was still in the same position but was very cold an' fer shore had been daid fer a while).

I grabbed fer his pist'l, not a Army issue, but a mighty nice Colt Navy percuss'on pist'l, what he had said he had bought near-new in Dodge City. I was wearin' m' own sidearm but it was a old cap'n'ball from a' fore the war. John wore a pouch with his ammo in it an' I grabbed that, too but I couldn't git it loose. A fearin' I would die on that 'ere spot, I fin'ly had the since to pull out m' knife it cut the pouch offin' the leather strap he was a' wearin'. I figur'd he wouldn't mind and he shore as hell warn't gonna be needin' 'em bullets none.

By now I could hear the occasional pop o' gunfire an' I know'd that our boys was awares at last o' what was happenin'. We couldn't see 'em dam' Indians who must have been up high on the oppersite bank o' that narrow little crik. Arrows was comin' down like hailstones. One came down onto' m' shoulder blade but thar warn't nothin' behind it an' it jest bounced off without even hardly tearin' m' shirt.

The men was trying t' find each other an' t' form a front agin'' the attack. Ever'time one o' our rifle's would fire, a puff o' blue smoke would billow out, an' a' fore you know'd it, who ever had fired the shot would ketch two er three arrows in the face er chest. This is a ol' Indian trick what I have already spoke about. Watch fer smoke an shoot right below it!

Oh, my was them bowmen fast! Sometimes a third er fourth arrow would ketch a man a' fore he could fall from the first one! Course, it coulda been 2 er 3 fellers shootin' at the same soldier, but knowin' Injuns like I know'd em, I don't think so.

Fer some reason I 'member noticin' that some o' the arrows had old fashioned stone tips, but others was shiny blue steel.

I was running t'ward the Col. an' was no more 'n 6 feet from 'im when I hear'd a "snap," an' he went right down with a musket ball through his thigh! I got real scairt then 'case Indian gunfire started in fer real and I know'd I hear'd the unmistakable sound o' repeatin' carbine fire comin' from they side o' the stream. I could tell 'case the shots was comin' too fast from the same place to be a musket, 'sides, a musket an' a carbine don't sound the same. A more mod'rn rifle makes more of a "crackin'" sound than a "boom."

Me an' another feller he'ped the Col'nel, one o' us under each o' his arms, an' we fought our way through the brambles till we reached the water. This was whar the crik widened into a broad, shaller pool. They was a big sandy island' that we made our way fer, the water comin' up t' our chests. It was covered in little willer trees an', t' this day, I ain't shore why we wanted t' git onto' that island' but we shore as hell did! It seemed that all o' our men had that same idear. Per'aps it was 'case the island' was as far away from the firing as we could git without trying t' scale a steep embankment.

The Col. was in pain but he was lucid. He did a quick haid count, as best he could in the confusion, an' saw that prob'ly ha'f o' us was daid er wounded. As near as we could tell the sound o' shots coming from whar we had been did not diminish. Either our boys was makin' a stand er them Indians was finishing 'em off.

We later found out that they killed ever' one o' our horses an' mules, including that dam' Lucifer (provin' that they is something good in all things, no matters how tarrible they seems at the time.)

To this day I have no idear as to why they killed them animals. It was more Injun-like to steal 'em. I have seen men go into a killin' frenzy, jest shootin' an' slashin' at ever' thing what moves, and I reckon that is all I can fig're to a' count fer it.

The shootin' carried on till 'bout 10 er 11 of th' clock I reckon', then ever'thing got spooky quiet. The Col. had shor'ly lost a lot o' blood an' he was in then he was out o' consciousness. I think that ever'one but me had been wounded in one way er t'other. Our little island' had turned out t' be 'bout as good a place t' be as any we could have picked, even though lookin' back it was act'ally the only choice we had. All o' us, 'specially those who was bad wounded, was thirsty. After a while some o' the men started t' cry out fer water. Ever'time som'body stuck a haid er a hand out from the willer thicket we'd git shot at by at least 4 er 5 guns an' a couple o' arrows!

'Bout 10:30, I reckon, we was thinkin' hard 'bout tryin' t' git the hell out whatever the cost. A' fore we could move, though, the Indians started firin' agin'. Even though they had no clear targit they jest started shooting bullets an' arrows into the thicket in a random sort o' way. Occasionally I would hear a scream or a outburst o' swearin' an' know that one o' our men had been hit. This as'ault lasted 15 er 20 minutes, I fig're.

The Colonel asked if any one o' us thought that we would be able t' git through an' haid back t'ward the wagon train fer he'p. Things was shore 'nuff gittin' desperate, he said, an' I could hear one feller, who was layin' out, exposed down near the water, cryin' out fer one o' us t' shoot him, it was plumb pathetical.

I peered through some branches an' see'd the pore wretch out thar. The Injuns were using him as a targit, hittin' him with arrows an' gunfire in his laigs an' arms so's not t' kill him too quick. He was a' screaming an' blubbering an' cryin' out, "Fer the love o' Jesus, boys, shoot me in the haid! Thar a'killin' me, t'rtuous slow…!"

I thought 'bout doin' it, I could have hit him easy, too, but, God he'p me, I could not. Mercifully, one o' 'em Injuns had a bad aim an' an arrow caught the pore devil right whar his throat apple was. The blood went up like a goosher an' he bled t' death in what seemed like no time, 'tho I'll wager it seemed a mite longer t' him.

Well, that was enough fer me! I felt like I had t' git out o there er die a' tryin'. Me an' two fellers, Jackie Stillwell an' Pete Trudell, volunteered t' try an' make it t' the wagons er t' Fort Wallace. It was jedged that we best wait fer evenin' which seemed like it was a hun'ded year' off. Men was delirious now, an' cryin' fer water. Me an' Jackie dug deep holes into the san' an' they filled up with muddy water which was shore good enough if'n' we drunk it through clenched teeth, an' that he'ped some.

The Colonel drifted off into a kind o' delir'um. Sometime he was awake an' sometime he was asleep an' sometime I couldn't tell which was which fer he would mumble some, from time t' time, an' we didn't know if'n' he was givin' us orders, er jest what. The flies an' gnats was gathering round the blood smell and the stink o' loosed bowels. Skeeter's an' deer flies an' san' fleas all came out t' t'rment us. It was a nightmare in the daylight, so t' speak!

It jest got hotter an' hotter, sweat was stingin' m' eyes an' drippin' down o'fn' the end o' m' nose. I prayed fer rain, but the prayin' didn't take, which I've found is the case as often as not. Seems t' me that prayin' is a lot like doin' a rain-dance; timin' plays a big part.

Finally the shadows started growin' long an' th' least little breeze picked up from the south. I could hear chants an' whoops from the ridge. It was chillin'. I know'd that these warn't songs fer the daid, fer I doubt that at that point we'd so much as wounded a Indian. No, this here was the songs o' brav'ry an' o' battle an' o' vict'ry an' o' slaughter.

Secretly, as risky as it was going t' be t' try an' crawl out o' this hell-hole, I felt like m' chances was better t' go than t' stay. I had l'arned enough 'bout tribal markin's in the past few weeks t' know that 'em arrows shot at us was either Comanche er Kree. Mebe both. I know'd that these two tribes, with the mebe 'ception o' the Flathaids, was the meanest an' cruelest sons-o'-bitches on the Plains t' they enemies. I thought back t' that pore feller that they'd used fer targit practice. They'd done a fine job o' t'rturin' him even from a distance an' I'd hear'd hair raisin' stories 'bout the pore souls unfort'nate enough t' fall into they hands at close range. I kept thinkin', "Hurry up, sundown, hurry."

CHAPTER 6

It was a beautiful evening 'cept that they was a passel o' people a' tryin' t' kill us all o' the time. The south wind kicked up purty good which he'ped t' cool us down some an' also t' pr'tect us a little from 'em dam' gnats an' skeeters. The Injuns had been real quite an' we was wonderin' if perhaps they had fergot 'bout us, we was shore hopin' that they had. A private named Jimmy James stuck his haid out o' a willer thicket an' a rifle ball neatly removed the top ha'f o' his right ear leaving him deaf an' bleedin' bad an' provin' t' us that that, no indeedy, we hadn't been fergot at all!

I entertained m'self fer a while by looking 'round fer that shiftly Crow scout o' the Colonel's, Rustyblade. Nobody had see'd hide ner hair o' him an' I would've bet money t' all takers that the sneakin' sonsabitch had know'd what he was gittin' us into. I was a thinkin' that I would have liked t' talk t' him, but not in private, that's fer shore. He's one o' 'em types that would cut out your gizzards, eat 'em up an' then go t' a Sunday meetin' with a smile on his lips. He scairt me, consid'able.

Finally the sun went down over the ridge an' me an' the boys prepared t' haid on out. Jackie Stillwell convinced Pete an' me t' set out fer the oppersite shore, goin' *t'ward* the attackers, as they would never suspicion it. We would swim t' the shoreline an' then hope that they was enough current t' carry us downstream t' whar we would make our way t' the safe side, although we was purty turned 'round an' not all that shore which side was the safest!

After consid'able thought, ol' Pete an' me decided that we would give it a try. It was dark enough t' see the stars an' a little sliver o' moon 'bout midway 'cross the sky, but the Injuns was yet t' build any fires, which I found odd. (It's been m' experience that, whar' ever a Injun settles, one o' the first things he does is t' build hisse'f a fire).

Anyhow, we slips into the water as quiet as leatherback mud turtles an' made our way, real slow, over t' the Injun side. I would be a lyin' if I was t' tell you I warn't scairt t' the point o' bein' mortified. Good thing I was in the water er I would've had another wet spot on m' breeches, if you ketch m' drift.

It didn't take us long t' git t' the shaller water by the bank an' then we flipped over on our backs an' let the water carry us downstream. It warn't no big river but the current was surprisin' strong an' it felt like we was skimmin' along. Actually, this was a mighty great relief cause not a second went by what didn't take us further an' further away from danger. Er so we thought.

It seemed like a consid'able weight had been on m' chest an' that now it was took off an' I wanted t' shout an' t' laugh. O' course, I know'd better an' did neither one. I jest kept m' mouth shet an' rode the water with Pete an' Jack. I see'd a big ol' water snake a glidin' t'ward me an' I was afear'd he might decide that I looked like a nice log fer him t' slither up on, but jest at the least possible minute he decided t' change his course an' veered off, back t'ward the middle o' the stream. As I might've said, I ain't altogither afeard o' snakes, but I ain't likely t' be all cuddly with one neither.

After what seemed like a ha'f a hour er so, we came up on two deers, drinkin' from the stream. They is skittish creachtures so we took this as a shore sign that we was far enough from anybody t' be safe. We made ready so's t' climb out o' the water an' t' set off on our way. We scrambled up the bank an' haided off t' what we hoped was the northwest, which we believed t' be the direction o' the wagon train.

After we had walked fer 5 er 6 hours, jedging by the moon an' stars, Jackie said he believed he could see the light o' some campfires up on the horizon. This gladdened us consid'able. We hightailed up t'ward the fires an' was nearly in a daid run as we approached 'em. Pete, in the lead, stopped so sudden that he fell over his own feet an' sprawled out onto' the grass. He sit up, quick, an' put his fingers t' his lips an' motioned fer us t' lay down! The grass here was beat down an' we was surrounded by big dark mounds o' what looked like dirt. By smell alone we realized that these piles o' dirt was buffaler carcass', skinned an' gutted, only the prime cuts o' meat, like the shoulder, the hump an' a parcel of the rear flank, had been cut off. This was a sign o' white men, gen'ally, leaving the bulk o' the creachture t' rot.

But the sounds comin' t' us from 'round 'em fires warn't the sound o' white folk a-tall! Me an' the boys was not 50 feet from a Kree Camp!

Lord o'Friday, was we scairt! This made bein' scairt a' fore seem like Sunday pie! Over in the light we could see the men gittin ready t' ride out on a raid! They was paintin' they ponies an' greasin' they hair! Women folk was cookin' buffaler hump on spits over the fires an' peggin' out the hides. Here I was, all this time, thinkin' it was late at night, when by now it was early mornin'! The sky was growin' pink in the east. I reckon that these fellers was a haidin' over t' join the others an' t' wipe out our men once't an' fer all. The sounds o' the songs an' the bone-whistles and willer flutes an' the tom-toms was chillin'. Talk 'bout bein' too close fer comfort!

We crawled, ever so slow, over t' a heap o' four er five o' the buff carcass' an' was too scairt t' even whisper. Sud'nly five er six young Indian boys was comin' t'ward us. They was stumblin' sleepily an' tho I could only understan' a little o' they lingo, I know'd that they was mumblin' amongst they selves 'bout how they was a goin' t' foller the grow'd men an' do all kinds o' brave things. They kept walkin' t'ward us an' both Pete an' I had draw'd our knives when they sud'nly stopped not 8 feet from whar we was layin' amongst 'em carcass.

They all relieved theyse'ves, yawnin' an' scratchin' an' lookin' up at the brightenin' sky. It would be jest a matter o' minutes afore it was light enough that they'd see us.

One squatted down an' cleared his bowels not 4 foot from m' haid but I dasn't move an' I did not. When they was finished they haided back t'ward that camp.

Thinkin' it all over later, we decided that they had left so much o' the buffaler behind 'case they was in a hurry. (Years later I told this story an' a feller accused me o' lyin'! He says, "Why the Plains Injuns was the greatest *conversas'nalist* (sic) the worl' has ever know'd! They'd a no more have left that meat behind than nothin'. Why, they used ever' scrap they had!" t' which I had replied, "Bean's!"

(The Injuns' used ever' part o' the beast only cause they had t'! Not beca'se they was "conversas'nalist" an' was worried 'bout wastin' somethin', but beca'se they was hongry all the time an' they know'd that food could git mighty scarce! Hell, they whole lives was spent fightin' er lookin' fer food, which, if'n a feller thinks 'bout it, is how white men spent they lives, too, in 'em times!

(As far as being "conversas'nalists," I've know'd Injuns t' kill ever' scrap o' game in an area a' fore movin' on t' a new one. Hellfire, that's the reason WHY they had t' keep on the move in the first place, after they done et ever' blessed thing the land had t' o'fer, it was either move on er die!

(Why, I've see'd whole groves o' pekan an' walnut trees chopped down er burned t' the ground jest so's a nomad band could git t' 'em nuts! Either they didn't know how t' climb a tree an' pick the nuts er they was jest too dam lazy!

(Trees that would have dropped nuts in the late summer an' fall an' have made food fer gen'rations o' animals an' other folks was destroyed fer the good o' one travelin' tribe.

(An' don't you believe what feller's like Bill Cody an' Bill Mathewson said, neither 'bout Injuns bein' so frugal. {Ol' Bill Mathewson, you know, he was the ***real*** Buffaler Bill! He saved m' life one time, remind me t' tell you 'bout that!} An' don't think they was the only fellers famous fer killin' buffaler! I should think not! Lots o' Injuns took part in 'em slaughters, Crow an' Kree an' plenty o' others, as shooters an' skinners an' as scouts what brought the shooters t' the herds. 'Specially when they found out they could trade 'em hides fer whiskey! The simple truth is this; jest as many Injun's took a part in the senseless killin' o' them great herds as whites did. Period.

(Why, they was so thrifty, folks says, that they even used the end o' a buffaler's tail as a fly-swat. O' course they did! What is tarnation was they gonna do, *go somewhar and buy 'em a store bought fly-swat*? That's purty much the same reason why they made spoons out o' horn, they didn't have no whar else t' git no spoon and they didn't have the know-how t' work with metal!

(*Conversas'nalists, m' foot!* I'm sorry, but that feller shore got me het up!)

Now, whar was I? Oh, yes, whatever was the reason fer leavin' 'em carcass' t' rot, me an' Pete an' Jackie was laripin' glad they was thar! We had no more than crawled up inside 'em gut cavities an' was barely settled in a' fore we hear'd the ponies hooves a poundin' by all 'round us. Them carcass' saved our lives as shore as shootin'.

I kept on gaggin' retchin' an' I couldn't breathe an' they was maggots crawlin' inside m' shirt an' pants, in m' ears an' m' mouth. Finally I jest had t' stick m' haid out fer air an' I see'd by then it was full daylight. The women an' childr'n had jest struck down the camp an' was slowly haidin' off in the oppersite direction o' the way the men had lit out.

A few mangy Injun' dogs came over an' made a commotion, actin' all stupid an' mighty brave, like dogs does, till Jackie fetched one yallar cur in the nose with the heel of his boot. It yelped as if it was a' dyin', like dogs does, an' some o' the Indians looked back in our direction. I guess they jest thought 'em dogs was over playin' with the bones, cause they didn't pay 'em no mind. We had know'd better than to stand up yet, so they couldn't see us anyhows. Finally the dogs ran off t' ketch up with the camp.

We know'd it was safe when the ravens an' tu'key buzzards settled down t' peck at the rottin' meat. They won't land' nowhar's if they see human folk 'round. We did scare 'em some when we crawled out o' 'em stinkin' shelters what had saved our pore lives! The ravens settled 'bout a hun'ded yards away an' scolded at us somethin' fierce fer surprisin' 'em. The buzzards settled in a ha'f daid cott'nwood tree 'bout a mile further off an', bein' buzzards, didn't say nothin' a'tall.

We was a sight, I reckon! Our clothes was soaked with our sweat an' with fat, blood an' pee an' whatever else had been left behind in 'em carcass' an' the flies buzzed 'round us like bees t' hunny. Jackie was weak, as he had sick-puked mos' a hun'ded times er so he claimed.

We walked over t' the remainders o' the camp but they was nothin' left behind fer us t' eat er drink an' we was all near t' thirstin' t' death. We know'd they had t' be fresh water close by er the Injuns wouldn't have camped there in the first place but we hoped it was diff"ernt water than the creek we had come down on.

I was all fer lookin' aroun' fer it but Pete said we'd better not fool 'round none an' best git on our way, which was right thinkin an' so that is jest what we did.

I was turned 'round, consid'able, but I was purty shore that the war party had went north an' the camp had went south so we continued on t' the west.

It took us all that day, mos' o' that night, an' well into the nix mornin', betwixt reg'lar stops t' rest, t' reach the area 'round the Fort. Ever' so often we'd find a puddle er a little ol' crick and we had jest enough water to keep us alive. It had been a gruelin' long walk an' we'd only jest begun our s'journ after havin' a'ready been shot at an' pinned down back at the crik, so we had took lots o' wrong turns. We could only hope that the re-enforcement's t' reach the Colonel an' our fellers could cut our time in ha'f, er even more, an' they could, too, if'n they was mounted on fresh horses.

We had stopped along the way jest a' fore sunup an' since it had been a few mile since the last crick, Pete drunk some water from a buffaler waller.

Thirsty as we was, neither Jackie nor I drank any as it looked rancid an' was full o' droppin's, flies, little wiggly worms an' all. Shore enough, Pete was sick like a dog within a hour. He was brave an' uncomplainin', but still it slowed us down, consid'able. He had tarrible belly aches an' vomited an' had the diarrhea as well.

'Bout five mile' a' fore we spied the Fort we hear'd the thunderin' o' hooves. I looked up an' thought, "Oh Lord! Here we go agin'!" Within a couple o' minutes we was surrounded by a war party o' Cheyenne!

The Cheyenne is, fer the mos' parts, a mighty fine group o' people when they's happy. They are, gen'ally speaking, tall, clean, an' very han'some folks. They chil'ren is mannerly an' well behavior'd.

They play purty music on flutes an' they's right handy in all things crafty-wise, including paintin', soin', beadwork an' carvin'. They have only the cleanest, whitest buckskins on they lodges, with the brightest ornyments.

(I mention paintin', Cheyenne men love t' paint they lodges, shields, horses an' theyse'ves with pict'res o' eagles, an turtles an' sech. They brewed up brown an' black paint from bilin' walnut shells, green's from sumac leaves, grays from bark, red from the iron ore in rocks, purples an' blues from poke an' elder berries an' yallar from flower petals an' some kinds o' clay. Unlike most other Plains Injuns they is also tol'able handy t' work metals, silver an' copper in partic'lar. They was a gen'rous peoples, too. They always took good care o' they own, pore folks, orphants an' widders. I like the Cheyenne an' I speaks some o' they lingo).0

They gathered 'round us an', o' course, they didn't know I could understan' some o' what they was sayin'. They was laughin' at how we looked an' how we smelt. One feller made quite a fuss over the stains on the back o' old Pete's trousers. The riders, one by one, rode up an' tetched us each with a long stick with a curved end. Jackie an' Pete didn't know what the warriors was a' doin', but I did! They was "countin' coup."

Now what that means is this: In the old days, a' fore the whites came an' a' fore guns, Indians was always at war with each other! Always! Now, truth be told, they warn't all that many Injuns 'round, you know? Some bookish fellers claims now that they was less Injuns in this whole country than they is people a city like London, Englan' t'day! Really! So, they couldn't always be runnin' 'round killing each other off like flies, doncha see? Other wise they'd have killed 'emse'ves all off a' fore we even got here, comprende?

'Sides, it's awful dern'd easy t' jest walk up, er, after the whites brought in horses, t' *ride* up, an' shoot a feller full o' arrows. So, since they didn't always nec'arily want t' kill they enemy', instaid they used these here long, curvied sticks, called coup sticks, an' that way they could jest walk up an' tetch the feller with this here stick, er whack him with it if they felt that a' way.

It was a show o' ca'm bravery on the part o' the feller with the stick, doncha know. This bizness of "countin' coups" it was, indeed, a good deal braver a thing t' do that t' jest shoot a feller. After coup was taken, why the brave would put a notch in his coup stick. Then, at a ceremony er at a party he would take that stick an' finger it, like a priest fingers a ros'ry, an' he could "recount" his coups, havin' committed t' mem'ry ever' blessed detail o' each event.

Some o' the great warriors an' chiefs counted coup way up t' most a thousand. It was a way o' takin' a trophy with both the counter an' the countee livin' t' see 'nother day. Scalpin'? It was gen'ally introduced by the whites, the Frenchy's in partic'lar, an' came along much later. (At one time the Arizona territ'rial gov'ment was payin' a $300 bounty fer Apache scalps. Men, women er childr'n, it didn't matter, *but*, a feller had t' bring in proof' o' the kill. First they tried bringin' in cut-off ears but they stunk too bad. Scalps was a might cleaner an' easier way t' prove a kill. I believe it is safe t' say that far more scalps was taken from Indians by whites than visa-versa.)

When the whites came, this practice o' countin' coup puzzled 'em. An Injun might ride up an' tap this white feller with his stick, stand back an' laugh, 'Course, then the white feller might jest draw iron an' shoot that Injun daid, which you would think would a' took a heap o' the fun out o' it, from the Injun point o' view!

Well, instaid o' spil'in' the Injun's fun, the risk o' bein' shot act'ally made it an even *braver* thing t' do, considerin' the consyquinces an' all. The ultimate insult fer a warrior was t' have some feller walk er ride up t' him, bean him with this here stick, then turn an' ca'mly ride er walk away. It was both humiliatin' an' infuriating, er so I'm told!

So when this tall feller, the leader o' the band I thinks, whacks me fairly hard between the shoulder blades, I called out "Hokeh Hey! Tse leta kespe," which means somethin' like, "Praise be t' God! It's a mighty fine day t' meet m' maker!"

Well, these Injuns was puz'led t' hear this from the likes o' me an' went t' talking t' me so fast that I couldn't make haid ner tail o' what they was jabberin' 'bout. I did m' best t' 'splain things in ever' Injun talk I know'd, includin' words that was Kaw, Sioux, an' Kiowa.

I guess I must've included at least a little bit o' Cheyenne in thar, too. They gave us some water from Cav'ry kinteens an' gave pore Pete a tonic o' smashed poke berries, chalk, hot peppers an' fat which set him right with his belly purty quick. Then, without nary a word, 'em Cheyenne turned an' rode off like the devil hisself was after 'em. The feller I had guessed t' be the leader, as I gather'd from they jabberin', his name was White-Robed-Man-Who-Walks-The-Horizon-Jest-At-Dawn. White Robe.

As fer me'n'the boys, we had no choice but t' start walkin' agin. At least we had had a good drink o' water, though not near enough, an' Pete was purty shore now that he warn't going t' die, at least not right away.

We had been walkin' less than a quarter o' a hour when, from out o' nowhar's, a buffaler cow, all by her lonesome, came amblin' up out o' this slew (some folks call these here ravines "draws", up in Powder River country they calls 'em "coolies"). It was an amazin' thing when Jackie pulled out his army revolver, what had been soakin' wet sev'ral times by now, an' p'inted it at this 'ere beast, jest as though you could bring down a buffaler with a pist'l!

Then two things happened that was purty much what I'd call "miracles."

He aimed an' pulled the trigger and danged if that rusty ol' gun didn't fire a shot! POW! That 'ere was the first miracle. Ain't no way that them cat'ridges should have fired after what they'd been through. The second miracle was that he killed that dam'ed beast jest like he'd a' shot it with a kinnon!

As God is m' witness, he fired once't an' that cow fell down daid like she had been pole-axed between the eyes!

We stood, all three o' us, an' looked at that creachture quiverin' in the dust with total disbelief. Jack said he was thirsty enough an' could drink its blood, but I told him that drinkin' blood could make a feller powerful sick, partic'lar in hot weather, an' that I know'd somethin' better! I knelt down by the cow an' sliced a gash 'cross the bottom o' the carcass with m' knife an' reached inside till I took a'holt o' her belly. I pulled it out an' it was full o' fresh water! 'Em boys was amazed an' we drank our fill!

Now, shore, the water was hot, an' it smelt some, an' had bits o' grass an' the sech floatin' 'round in it, but by god, it was wet! I got t' thinkin' an' we backtracked t' whar she had come up out o' that draw, an' shore enough they was a little "freshlet" spring thar with a pool o' water no bigger 'n a man's hat. We drank as much as we could without pukin', but we had no kinteens t' fill an' event'ally we had t' be on our way. Years later it occurred t' me that we could have made a kinteen from that belly pouch, but I warn't smart enough t' think o' it at the time.

We sliced off some lean meat an' et it raw. Jest so's you know, raw buff meat is purty good, if'n yer hongry an' we was. I hated to leave that carcass out there to ruin 'case I had already see'd enough of that sorta thing, but we did what we did 'cause we had to.

We hadn't gone too far when we spied, comin' at us from out o' the late mornin' haze, a column o' U.S. Cav'rymen. Was we glad t' seem 'em, too! They, however, did not seem t' recognize us as white men er even as human's judgin' from the way they looked at us an' the mess that we was in, dirty an' bloody an' covered with filth. After questionin' us at length an' us givin' 'em the best infermation an' directions as we could, they made us foller behind ever'one else, ridin' on the pack mules.

Sometimes the other men would look back at us an' cuss an' hold they noses, makin' faces an' waivin' the air. I know they didn't like the smell, but believe me when I tell you, it weren't no dam' picnic fer me ner Jackie ner Pete neither!

Come t' find out we had been only 2 er 3 mile from the Fort. This was on er around September the 20th o' whatsoever year that I said it was at the outset o' this story.

(M' sister, Doe, who is, as you may remember, takin' this all down fer me, jest said a interestin' thing. She p'inted out that, considerin' we was in the middle o' a big, wild, open area o' land what had only began settlement a very few years before, that it shore had been a busy place during m' time passin' through it, what with a wagon train and all them soldiers and packs o' wild Injuns. I reckon she's right, too, but that's jest how it was!)

CHPATER 7

Col. Forsythe had managed t' pull through but over ha'f o' the wounded men had died off with fever an' from losin' blood. He later said that on the nix mornin' the Indians had opened up fire agin', but that they had lost heart an' was bored an' Ev'dently jest simply rode off as they was know'd t' do. Fer whatever reason, Injuns was like that.

'Course the men didn't know that the Injuns had left and was too scairt t' try an' leave theyse'ves so they jest stayed on that little island'. As tough as the ordeal had been on us three, it shore was a dam' sight worse fer them pore fellers what we had left behind.

Counting me an' Jackie an' Pete, they was only 14 men lived t' tell the tale, a little less than ha'f o' the original riders. Ever' horse an' mule had been shot er stoled.

We collected an' accounted fer each o' 'em men what was killed, an' they was worshed up as nice as we could do, an' then they was buried in a meadow jest above the crik an' each grave was marked with a wooden cross marker that some o' the fellers made up right there on the spot.

(You know, I passed through those parts agin' some eight er ten year' later, an' what with wind an' storms an' pra'rie fires, they jest warn't no sign left t' tell the worl' that men fought an' died an' was laid out t' rest here. Jest a big, open meadow full o' sunflowers an' yallar-breasted meadow larks a' trillin' they silly lives away. Come t' think o' it, that's prob'ly the way it should be. The Injun's have a sayin'; Nothin' lasts ferever. 'Cept fer Mother Earth an' Father Sky.)

~

Although I had lied an' said I was old enough t' join up in the U.S. Army, I now was forced t' tell the truth jest so's that I could git out! Life has funny twists an' turns that way. I hung 'round that Fort fer sev'ral weeks, fer as I have said, I do enjoy the life o' the frontier fort.

As soon as he was able I talked t' the Col. an' told him that I was wantin' t' go home an' all, that I was really not 17 er whatever lie I had told him, I give him m' gen-u-ine date o' birth, near as I know'd it, an' he jest laughed. He was a nice feller, I reckon, doin' a dirty hard job. He took out a strong box an' gave me some cash, sayin' it was "scout's pay," an' that I shore as hell deserved it 'case even if I was jest a boy I had did a real man's job. I must say that m' ears burned red and I felt fine, hearin' that!

He also gave me a army issue nag. He'd o'fered me a mule but, recalling m' exploits with Lucifer, I had perlitely but firmly declined. I asked him 'bout Maggie, the horse what I had rode in on in the first place, but her split hoof had got 'fected clear up on her laig an' she'd been put down. I asked him was they a chanc't o' gittin' 'nother horse an' he said, well, he did have some horses but that they was old an' tired an' I said, heck, that's fine by me so he gave me a choc'late colored mare named Maisey.

Maisey was indeedy a little bit long o' tooth but she suited me fine. I introduced m'self t' her by a'blowin' m' breath up into her nostrils, Indian style, an' she made a deep purring noise, like a cat, way down in her belly. I guess I was fine by her, too.

Winter was a' comin' on an' I was hankerin' t' see Lizzy an' Doe an' t' see how they was a doin' back on the home place. I was in no true hurry, though, an' so it was near a month a' fore I got thar an' the first snow fell on the evening o' the day that I had arrived. I felt mighty fine seeing the smoke comin' out o' the chimbly o' our place on Di'mond Spring.

~

That Welshman Domination Jones had been keepin' real steady comp'ny with Lizzy an' the place looked a danged sight better fer it.

Could be that he was a thinkin' 'bout mebe our old homestead as part o' Lizzy's dowry, should the time come fer that.

He know'd that morally, an' in them days prob'ly legally, he was bound t' ask fer m' permiss'on t' marry her, if that's what he had in his mind, an' that, regardless o' m' age, I mos' likely held the legal claim t' the title t' the land' by right o' inheritance. I was kind o' in the catbird's seat with old Domm' an' I know'd it an' I reckon so did he.

When he came a callin' that first evenin' o' m' return it was I what answered the door. He was a' standin' thar on the porch with his hair parted down the middle, all slicked back, like one o' them stage act'rs, a' holdin' his hat in the crook o' his arm an' a bokay o' dried wildflowers in his hand, right purty they was, too, considerin' they was daid.

He was wearin' a threadbare, but spotless clean, cord'roy suit that was 'bout two sizes too small an' 'specially tight 'round the belly. It was clear by his startled expression that he was not expectin' t' see me. I had grow'd up consid'able an' was a good deal more o' a man an' lesser o' a boy than when we'd last clasped eyes each upon the t'other.

"Why, Oscar! Lord in Heaven, Is that you? Well, hallo! Uh, hmmm, I don't know what to say… How are you, uh, *sir?*"

Well, that "sir" business jest made me laugh right out loud. "Come in the house, Domm'," I said, "Come in an' set a spell. I s'pose you're here t' see Miss Lizzy, she's inside a brewin' some chicory. I'm jest haidin' out, I'm a ridin' over t' the Kaw camp t' visit with a friend o' mine."

"Kaw camp?" he asked, like he was stupid.

"Yes, the Kaw camp! Don't look so surprised, Domm'! shor'ly you know'd you was neighbors t' a bunch o' red savages, didn't ye? I mean the camp up thar on the crik a couple mile over."

"Well, Oss, that there camp is gone. Town folks got tired of losing livestock and property. Oh, yes, they was mighty big trouble over there. Shots were fired and there was some killing. They set the whole camp on fire late last summer, September, I believe it was. Burnt it clear down! Of course, you were gone and wouldn't have heard about it, I reckon."

"No, Domm', I didn't know nothin' 'bout that thar thing," I said, already worried t' death fer Tree an' his fam'ly. Domm' told me that he would like t' speak t' me some 'bout Miss Lizzy but I told him that it would have t' wait. They was a feller I needed t' see.

I slipped a bridle on Maisey but I didn't bother t' saddle her. It was already growin' dark an' I wanted t' make the campsite while they was a little light left so's I could still see. I rode hard through the woods an' turned west at the crik. I zagged through 'em trees, a might slower than I wanted, as the horse was new t' the trail. Still, it didn't take us too long t' git out o' 'em woods into the clearing' whar the camp used t' be.

Yup, there is warn't!

It was jest gone, all gone. They was a lot o' coals an' burnt tree stumps an' ruined lodge frames dusted in fine snow but they warn't much else. I nudged Maisey an' we crossed over into the big meadow whar I counted eleven daid-stands.

Y' see, some Indians buried they daid, others would dress the body up as fine as they could an' would hang 'em in the crotch o' a tree. If they was time and inclination some might build a daid-stand out o' cott'nwood er aspen poles like a bed high up from the ground. The Kaw done some o' both I reckon. Anyways, they was eleven sech stands. As I rode closer I could see that thar had been a even dozen but that one had blow'd down, er somethin' had knocked it down, mebe hongry bear or some sech a varmit.

Kaw don't leave no haidstone. I looked at each o' 'em bodies wrapped up tight in buffaler er deerskin. Anyone o' 'em could have been m' friend, Tall Tree. I shore hoped that none o' 'em was! The snow had picked up an' was fallin' thick an' quiet as I turned Maisey t'ward Council Grove. I felt that I had t' ask 'round an' find out what had happened here, if'n' I could.

CHAPTER 8

They was lamps a' burnin at the Hays House an' at the Santy Fe Hotel as well as a couple o' gin-joints when I rode into town. It was a' snowin' heavy, now. I tied Maisey t' the hitchin' rail outside the café an' walked in.

The warmness o' the room hit me hard an' sud'nly I felt real tired, but more important, at least at the time, was that the warm air made me feel the urgent need t' relieve m'self. I' been t' the Hays House a' fore an' I know'd the way through the back an' out t' the privy, which is whar I haided.

After takin' care o' the neces'ary, I came back t' the main dinin' room an' took a seat. It always seemed right fancy t' me back then, but the last time I was there, a few year' back, I found that it hadn't changed much since an' that the kindest thing a feller could call the place was "rustic".

The main eatin' room was paneled with native wood, all kinds, which give each different wall a different shade o' color. One wall was walnut, which is dang near black, another wall was hedge, er Osage Orange, as some calls it, an' it is a yallar-green color. One wall was oak, which is a whitish tan, an' the fourth wall had been whiteworshed so I cain't say what kind o' wood it might've been.

The ceilin' was stained dark brown with smoke from the two huge fireplaces an' the smoke from feller's pipes an' ceegars, too. But rustic or not, all in all I'd have t' say that the Hays was still purty impressive fer this part o' the worl' in them days. It was solid, an' warm, what passed fer "clean" in them times.

I could smell food an' 'membered that I hadn't et, yet an' was as hongry as a gut-shot coyote. I flopped down into a chair by a little wooden table. A barkeep came 'round an' told me that they warn't servin' still, 'case o' the nasty weather an' the lateness o' the hour an' that all the rooms that they had t' let upstairs was empty o' guests.

He didn't know me so I lied t' him an' said I had been on the trail fer two days an' that I warn't askin' fer much 'cept mebe a plate o' taters an' some pork chops an' a glass o' beer. He looked at me fer a minute an' then said that he would see what he could do fer me.

He came back in a minute er two an' said that his wife was fixin' me some pork liver with onions an' that she had left-over fried taters an' some biled fall collard greens, biled turnips, biled dried green beans ("leather britches") an' cornpone. He sat a glass o' dark beer down in front o' me an' said, if I didn't mind, that he'd shore like t' be paid now so's he could lock up the day's receipts.

Now, I'm here t' tell you that a feller couldn't afford t' eat in a fancy-pants place like this very often! That glass o' beer alone cost me a 5-cent piece an' the food, although I admit that it was good an' that they was plenty o' it, cost me dang near 20 cents! I could not believe it! Why, that totals out t' near 30 cents as I reckon it! The barkeep's wife took the sting out o' it some though, when she slipped me a big ol' slab o' hot rhubarb pie with real sugar and fresh cream slathered on it!

I et it all an', I must say, I was as full as a tick when I finished up!

They was two other cust'mers over by the bar. They kept a lookin' at me, none too fri'ndly like. I would look over at 'em while I et an' ever'time that I did one er t'other o' 'em was lookin' back at me, givin' me the ol' snake eye.

Both these fellers was wearin' gun belts, fine, hand-tooled contraptions, too, an' the holsters was filled with purty iron with pearl handles, not no army issues, neither, these was real pricey pistils like comes from overseas. (Nowadays folks think that was the way it was back then, ever'body went 'round packin' iron, but that ain't how it was a'tall. A good sidearm an' holster an' belt costed more than some feller's made in a month, two months time. Now, I ain't sayin' folks went 'round unarmed, they'd have a rifle er a scatter-gun strapped somewhar on the horses tack, but I don't reckon' more 'n' mebe one man outta twenty wore no pers'nal shootin' iron.)

I called the barkeep back over an' ask him, "Say, ain't they a village o' Kaw Injuns 'round here, somewhar's?" "Not no more,' he said, "Town folk runned 'em off, thievin' beggars an' trouble makers, that's all 'em dam' Injuns was! Got t' actin' uppity, like they owned the goddam'' country an' it was time t' show 'm how the hawg eats the corn!"

He reared back, proud, an' hung his thumbs in his su'penders, "Killed a dozen er more o' 'em, you know. Wounded sev'ral more. Not me m'self, but the fellers did. Dam' fools took a shot at us! Well, we shot back an' we show'd 'm, 'deedy we did!"

I wanted t' know more, like if'n he know'd who was kilt, but it was apparent t' me that this warn't the place fer too many questions. After all, a feller might be 'spected o' bein' a "Injun lover", so I thought purty quick an' I said; "Well, say there, ol' hoss, I'm a scout a' workin' fer Colonel Forsythe up thar at Fort Harker. That'd be why I ask about them Injuns, I am down here t' arrest a buck name o' Tall Tree, er some other sech ridic'lous Injun name. Say, now, hat if anything a'tall kin you tell me 'bout him?"

(I had noticed 'em two fellers at the bar was a' listenin' an' that me mentioning the word "arrest" had caused both o' 'em t' stiffen some an' t' prick up they ears so t' speak…)

"Hell, I know'd that kid," the bar keep said, "He was one smart Injun, mebe the only one I ever know'd. Naw, I believe that he gots away. He was tryin' t' ca'm ever body down, I 'member. His pa though, well, he got ins'lent an' ended up ketchin' a rifle ball in his chest. Through his hear, killed him daid as a hammer, it did, then that Tree feller's brother started screamin' an' wailin' an' then the dam' fool pulls out a knife, so they shot him daid, too! It was a sight! Like shootin' fish in a barrel, as ol Pat Kaufman said. He was there an' he did some killin'.

"Too bad that a woman er two an' a couple o' chil'ren was caught up in the foray, but it t'weren't our fault, that's gonna happen with 'em people when they gits all riled up. They got t' larn which side o' the bread the butter is on, doncha think? 'Sides, they don't care nothin' much fer they fam'lies, not like white folks does, anyhow. They's savages, bare more than animals. Say now, I don't believe I caught yer name, stranger?"

A deep an' menacing voice from 'cross the room sez, "Yes! Just what is your name an' what is your business here? Stand up and state your claim, son, and be purty dam' quick about it."

I kind o' stammered some and coughed an' pertended that a bite o' pie had slithered down the wrong tube. Finally I told 'em m' name was Corp'al Willie Williams an' that I was a army scout from up Fort Harker way. One o' the feller's had his back t' me an' t'other, the one who'd spoke, stared me down fer a spell, like he was a spil'in' fer a fight. I lowered m' voice an' said t' the barkeep, "Well, I still gotta arrest that man, the Injun, I mean. Now don't ask me what fer, 'case it is a big military secret. Which a'way did that band move off too?"

"Aw, hell, they broke up an' went off in ever' direction. People says they see'd that boy you' askin' 'bout skulkin' 'round that old camp groun', wailin' an' a' chantin'. Said he made some stands in the middle o' the night and loaded the co'pses up on them all by hisself."

"Listen, son," he said, lowerin' his voice, "don't fret 'em two feller's up thar at the bar. They is hard cases, both 'em. I been a' tryin' t' git 'em out o' here fer the past two hours. They's mean as snakes t' begin with an' now that they're gittin' good an' drunk they've turned right down taciturn. Don't antagonize 'em none, all right? Me an' the wife would like t' git off t' bed if'n them fellers don' set up an' drink all night."

"Shore, shore," I said, "I ain't tryin' t' do nothin' but t' enjoy this fine meal your missus made up fer me. Who is 'em feller's, anyways?"

"Jest a couple o' drifters, I reckon, they's brothers, so they claim. One's named Virgil an' t'other is Wyatt. Wyatt is the one with the handlebar moustache. Ol' Jess Willard was in here earlier on an' he said one or t'other o' 'em is wanted fer horse thievin' over in Missouri er down in the Territ'ry, er some place.

"They story is that they's haided out t' Dodge er t' Hays, lookin' fer work. 'Em fellers is the desp'ate kind, they'll shoot a man fer lookin' sideways at 'em. You stay out o' they way, boy. That Wyatt was tryin' t' git up a faro game earlier when some cowboys stopped in fer a drink, but nobody'd play with 'em. They's jest got that mean look in they eyes, doncha see?"

" Well, as I said, Jess Willard had come in, sittin' over thar by the fire, a'mindin' his own bizness, talkin' frien'ly like t' ever'body. Then ol' handlebar he up an' pulled iron on pore ol' Jess, finally, fer talkin' so much an' askin' him too many person'l questions. Goddam', he's fast on the draw, though! One second he's standin' with his back t' us an' the nix that long pist'l o' his has cleared leather an' is pressed up ag'in Jess' throaty apple! It was frightenin' fast, like a strikin' snake!"

Ol' handlebar cleared his throat real loud and ol' barkeep he straighten up an' made t' leave me alone and t' fetch handlebar an' his brother another glass.

I thanked the barkeep kindly an' stood up very slow an' tipped m' hat t' 'em two fellers. The one named Virgil walked over t' me, staggerin' jest a little, an' said, "No harm meant, boy. I thought you was a sight older than you are. M' name is Earp, Virgil Earp, and the gent yonder there is m' brother, Wyatt. We're jest passin' through this fair city and are trying t' avoid confrontation with, uh, the locals, as it were. Headed west for work, are we. No hard feelings?" He held out his hand fer me t' shake, "Say, would you care for a game o' cards?"

"No, sir, no hard feelin's a'tall an', sorry, no, sorry t' say I cain't play no cards, I'm late enough as it is," I said as I shook his hand, which was cold as death an' had a grip like iron, "I'm jest a' passin' through, m'self.

"If'n you don't mind m' sayin', you ought t' find you a room if you kin, as the weather has turned right nasty outside. They lets rooms here and will fix you 'n' yer brother a laripin' breakfast too, I reckon. Talk t' the barkeep here, an' mebe he kin accom'date you. M'self, well, duty calls an' I am movin' on. G'night, Mr. Earp, an' g'night t' yer brother. Perhaps we shall meet agin', one o' these days."

"Perhaps we shall, young fella, perhaps," he said, suspicious like an' his eyes all squinty and his voice jest drippin' with oil.

He looked at me kinda spooky, sorta wild in the eyes. I glanced over t' his brother who was a' starin' at me from under the wide, flat brim o' his hat. Although they was heavy shadowed, 'em eyes glisten'd like a fox's eyes an' they was mayhem a burnin' in 'em. I tipped m' hat agin' an' the feller, ever so slight, nodded in m' direct'on. I couldn't he'p but notice that his thumb was hooked into his gun belt, his hand jest a hoverin' over the pearl handle o' some kind o' pist'l with a exceedin' long barrel.

Even when I got outside, lookin' back in through 'em foggy glass panes, I was shore that 'em eyes was on me, burning like a willer-the whisp.

I was t' hear o' 'em boys later, o' course. The whole country hear'd o' 'em. They went an' made a name fer theyse'ves in Wichita an' in Dodge as gamblers an' *lawmen!* That's right, *lawmen!* Now, don't that beat anythin' you has ever hear'd?

Then, some years later, 'em an' some other brothers an' some friends made quite a splash out in the Arizona territ'ry in a little horse town called Tombstone, kilt a few o' fellers in a gunfight, turned into something' o' a range war, as I hear'd it. I wish't I could say that it was m' pleasure t' never have been on they cross side, but I was, some time later out in Wichita. If'n I kin remembers, I'll tell you 'bout it. I was lucky, though, I reckon. I don't think that many who crossed the bad side o' 'em Earps' ever lived t' tell the tale.

~

The snow had stopped, mos'ly, the clouds was breakin' up an' the slip o' moon was uncommon bright. This was a good thing 'case it is mighty hard t' find yer way, even t' someplace as familiar as a feller's own home, when it's a' snowin' on the pra'rie. Folks died tryin'.

The air was sharp an' cold an' purty nice. As old Maisey plodded 'long I started wishin' I had took time t' put a saddle on her. Then I got t' thinkin' 'bout pore old Tree an' his pappy an' his brother an' the others. I got a lump in m' throat when I thought o' the kindliness that they had all show'd t' me an' I wondered, if I was ever t' find old Tree agin', how he was goin' t' feel t'ward me now? We was always mighty good friends but friendship has got its limits, blood bein' thicker than water, as is rightly said. I shore hoped that all would be right if'n our paths was ever t' cross agin'.

~

That night I had the dam'est dream that's haunted me till this very day: We was in Tree's old camp an' Big Walk was havin' a party. (The Indians loved t' have parties an' a well-t'-do warrior might have 4 er even 5 in a week's time.)

In this here dream the women had brought hot food in clay pots an' placed 'em in the coals in the fire hole. They was a roast dog on a spit, Sioux style. The childr'n was playin' with a ball made o' deerskin stuffed with deer hair. They was playin' ketch an' football an' a game kind o' like l'crosse, the game that the Indians up north play.

Old gran'ma Two Moon was a tellin' stories t' the kids an' t' the grow'd ups, too, which is what old women did at 'em Indian parties. People was comin' an' goin', in an' out, as was they cust'm. (Anyone could walk into a neighbor's lodge at any time without knockin' an' nobody thought nothin' o' it. 'Course it's mighty hard t' knock on a door made o' buffaler skin.) Anyhows, old granny was a tellin' ever'one t' beware o' the Night Ghost which would come an' suck they blood er steal 'em away. One o' the childr'n ask her what the Night Ghost looked like an' all o' a sudden she turned 'round an p'inted her bony finger at me!

"There he is, there he is," she was yellin' in English! Someone kicked the football at me an' I caught it in m' hands, but instaid o' a ball it was Tree's haid, all guesome an' gashly! Tree's pa, Big Walk stood up an' grabbed his shield an' lance an' started t' chant an' t' dance an' Tree's brother, Shield, joined in. Sud'nly I shouted, "Stop!"

When I did that, they all froze where they stood. Then, all o' a sudden, they flesh jest fell away an' they took t' dancin' agin', faster an' faster, an' as I looked on, they turned into dancin', wailin' skeleyt'ns!

Lightenin' flashed, er mebe it was kinnon fire, an' they alls o' a sudden jest crumpled up into heaps o' bones an' ashes an' a cold wind came bilin' through the tent flap an' the fire turned blue, then green then blow'd out an' ever'thing got pitchy dark.

That's when I waked up, breathin' hard an' sweatin' like I had been runnin'.

I didn't sleep no more that night. Them dam' dreams, I've had 'em all m' life, I reckon, and they's a pox t' me.

CHAPTER 9

While I'm telling this story t' m' sister, Doe, who is a'takin' it all down dang near as fast as I kin tell it, I sometimes gits t' thinkin' 'bout things that don't have nothin' t' do with the story o' m' life, as it was, but that I find interestin'. Sech as names; Indian names, in partic'lar.

Now, some white names is right down silly an' sometimes strange, like Lizzy's bo, Domination Jones. What in the hell kind o' name is that, anywise? But if a feller could go back far enough you'd find that fam'ly names, like the name "Jones," why, they all means somethin'. It is jest a word in a ferign language, Welch I reckon, in Domm's case, an' although it is now know'd more as a name, it was also, once't, a word, too. Like Englishter's names sech as "Smith" an' "Butcher," why it's plumb easy t' see whar 'em names come from, don't you see? From the jobs 'em peoples had, way back yonder, like a blacksmith er a butcher, er a archer er a baker. Er Mercer, as a mercer was a feller who dyed cloth, I'm told.

Take the Mex name o' Garcia. Somebody told me that "Garcia" means "little bird" in Mex talk. But if a Mex feller walks up t' you an' says, "Howdy, m' name is Hosay Garcia," why, you don't say, "Well howdy, Hosay Little Bird," 'case that ain't what he told you his name was, see? Now, person'l like? I prefer the name o' Little Bird t' Garcia, m' own se'f but that thar ain't the point I am a' tryin' t' make.

(Am I confusin' you?)

Well, it's the same with Injun names, too, only thing is that we don't say 'em in the Injun tongue, we have t' translate 'em t' ourn. When we do that they sometime come out funny an' they almos' always comes out wrong. It has always been a puzzle t' me that a white man will git mighty upset when a feller mispernounces his name more than onest er twice, some fellers will fight ye over it. We insists that folks git it right.

But, on t'other hand, we will go 'round mispronouncin' a Mex name er an Injun's name an' not think nothin' o' it. Might even find it sorta funny!

Well, fer a sample, they was once a Injun feller name o' "Man-Who-Walks-All-Day-Without-Tiring-As-Though-His-Laigs-Was-Made-O-Wood." Now in his own speakin' why, that was nothin', as far as Injun names goes, but in Amerikin that is a pow'rful mouthful o' name! Som'body from Washingt'n added this feller, who was a chief o' some kind, added his name t' a tribal roll. He shortened it t' "Man Who Walks With Wooden Laigs." Another white feller comes along an' shortens the name agin', t' "Wooden Laig." Don't you know that a' fore very long the Bureau o' Indian Affairs listed this feller on they tribal reg'ster as "Peg Laig"?

Now, wouldn't that bend yer spoon jest a little bit if we was doin' sech a thing with your own name, er yer pa's er your brother's?

I don't know why I think 'bout these things but I do. M' sister, Doe? Well, she says I am uncommon smart, not book-smart, which is prob'ly already oblivious t' you, but ever'day smart; what you might call a certified genie! I don't like t' brag, but mebe she's right! I always felt like I was sometimes smarter than the average feller. Hell, who knows? I might be a real genie after all.

~

The nix spring I went t' work fer the feller's buildin' the Northern Pacific Railroad. The actual railroad had done came through in the 1850's, so these was jest branches o'fn the main rail bed, but the work was jest the same.

This time they didn't hire me as no water boy, I was a' poundin' spikes an' a haulin' ties an' it was goddam' hard work fer $2 a day an' I hated dam' near ever' minute o' it, workin' with ever' type o' feringer that would a' cut out m' gizzards fer a sip o' whiskey! Man alive, it was jest awful! I tried t' stick it out an' I ain't no quitter an' I ain't no sissy, but it was too much fer me so's, finally, after a few days o' it, I left out!

I took a long ride out east t' an area jest the other side o' the Flint Hills whar thar is a long stretch o' rapids on the Neosho River, east o' a little town called Emporia. Thar was a trading post thar on the river an' I decided that I would swing by an' pick up some salt pork an' some ammunition.

They was a lot o' activity 'round the post which was run by a feller named Pearson who seemed t' be all right. The Indians thar was jest a mess, though. They came in from miles 'round with furs an' skins an' would trade fer dam' near any kind o' junk er geegaw, but mos'ly they jest wanted whiskey an' plug t'baccy.

It was becoming clear t' the whites an' t' the Indians alike that whiskey was they very worstest enemy', even worser than disease er the white man's greed. 'Em pore old fellers would trade a months hard work fer a big bottle o' the swill what passed fer whiskey. It was general'y jest pow'rful grain alcohol with ashes, molasses syrup an' peppers mixed in, although it was hard t' tell as mos' o' the post traders made they own an' might use any number o' "secret ingredients" sech as boot black, coal oil, buffaler blood an' mebe a daid snake er a squirrel throw'd in fer "kick".

Some o' 'em pore Injuns would git they bottle an' walk outside an' pull the cork. They'd tilt they haids back an' guzzle as much as they could, then stand thar, a' looking dazed with tears runnin' from they eyes an' snots from they noses! Some o' the women, (whites called 'em "squaws" which was fine with some Injuns yet a insult t' others. It was a term best not used if they was any doubt), some o' 'em turned t' whorin' jest t' earn a bottle er two either fer theyse'ves er fer they old man.

This feller, Pearson, he at least tried t' control the amount o' likker an Injun could buy er trade fer. He would try an' talk 'em into a nice knife er a bolt o' cloth er some foodstuffs fer the fam'ly, like flour er sugar, if they was any t' be had. He tried t' do right by them people an' still make a decent livin'. I reckon it was a tough row t' hoe, as the sayin' goes.

Then they was always other white trappers an' nar-do-wells who would swap Pearson this er that fer a drink, then go right outside an' barter that rot-gut off t' some Injun which Pearson had jest cut off from any more whiskey fer a profit.

They had been white fur traders in Kanzas since the Frenchy's came in, 'round 1822. By the time I'm speakin' o' now, they was still consid'able furs t' be took in Kanzas, 'specially here in the east side o' the state.

They was woof's, cats, 'coons, bear an' sech. Though elsewhar the beaver fur business itse'f was near daid from over- trappin', they still seemed t' be plenty o' beavers in east Kanzas at that time. But, o' course, even they didn't last too much longer. Beaver's was so dam'- fool easy t' git!

See, you kin lead a beaver into anything so long as he kin smell another beaver! It won't come near a man smell, though, so the trapper jest walks in the water an' sets the trap under the water an' ties it up t' a stake drove into the streambed. Some trappers would tie the trap down with rope, but a light steel chain works best. Now, on top o' the stake the trapper would pour a few drips o' the juice out o' a certain gland from a beaver he'd already trapped er shot.

So here comes ol' mister beaver, an' he gits hisse'f a sniffy o' that other beaver an' he stops t' 'vestigate. He'd tread water while he sniffed an' it was near impossible fer him *not* t' stick one o' his paddlin' back feet into that trap! Gotcha!

That old beaver would dive t' the bottom o' the stream so as t' drown'd whatever he thinks it is that's got hold o' 'em, like it would with a snapper turtle, say.

Now, they's a trappin' device, jest a circle o' steel like a ring on yer finger, an' when old man beaver dives, it pulls that ring down the shaft o' the stake, over a little notched tit, an' it's mighty rare that the ring will rise er git pulled back up over that notch. In simple terms, when old beaver gits down so low an' that ring slides down, the trap cain't be pulled back t' the surface eas'ly an' pore ol' beaver drown'ds! Has t' be done thata way er old beaver will chaw his own foot off t' escape the trap like a woof er a coyote will. It sounds mighty cruel an' I reckon it is. But it was real perduct've an' a helluva a lot o' moneys was made by fellers all over the worl' bein' mean t' them beavers.

A feller named Chouteaus once took *20 tons* o' hides by a flat boat up the Kaw River t' St. Lou! Upwards o' *50 thousand' hides!* His own records show's that he an' his boys clear'd more'n a quarter o' a million dollars! They was other fam'lies as well, sech as the Bent Brothers, who made mighty huge fortunes in the glory days o' skinnin' an' hide'n.

As I say, overall, beaver was gittin' kindly rare, although they still seemed t' be consid'able numbers o' 'em here in the east along the Neosho an' Maris de Cygne Rivers. They used that beaver hide t' make the fashion hats fer the rich folk back in Bost'n an' New York an' overseas t' London an' Paris. The market fer beaver pelts was yet t' collapse an', frankly, the price was higher than ever an' they was still consid'able whites an' Injuns makin' a good livin' at beaverin'.

(Now, whar the hell was I, Doe? I'm completely off o' m' track! Oh yes, the trading post!)

Well, I got thar mid mornin' an' hung 'round all day watchin' the traders an' the skinners an' 'em pore dam' dumb Injuns. I stocked up on a smallish slab o' salted side pig meat an' a joint o' jerked deer meat t' pack in m' saddle bags, bought ammo fer the side arm but none fer the rifle as the price was too dear fer me. I found a good deal on a hide robe an' a army blanket. I didn't have nothin' t' trade so I paid in 'scrip paper money from m' army pay.

I see'd two er three laripin' fights, one betwixt a Injun an' a trapper over the percen'age o' the split they was takin' from the sale o' they skins what ended with the Injun pullin' a knife on the trapper an' the trapper pullin' his pist'l in return an' shootin' it in the air behind the Injun which was, by this time, a' makin' tracks fer the trees down by the crik, apparently givin' up with no percen'age a'tall.

Another fight was betwixt two Injun men fer reasons unknow'd which didn't amount t' nothin' much but a lot o' yellin' an' swearin' an' threatenin' an' which ended with 'em both laid up agin' the side o' the cabin pullin' on a stone jug o' rot, tryin' t' sing the words t' some old Stephan Foster song which was purty bad fer 'em as neither one spoke no English.

But the best fight o' all was two Injun women, both drunk as skunks, a fightin' an' a' pullin on each others hairs, bitin' an' cussin' in both Injun talk mixed up with some white, fightin' over which one o' 'em was a sharin' her whiskey with this skinny old chief.

Whilst they was a fightin' over which one had the honor o' gittin' him drunk, he was over with two other women friends, drinkin' from both o' the fightin' women's jugs jest as fast as he could, till, by the time the fight was done an' both women huffin' an' puffin' an' bleedin' from scratches, one with a bad limp an' t'other with a big han'ful o' hair missin' from the front o' her haid an' both eyes all blacked out an' her front teeth knocked out, why, that old feller was passed plumb out, daid t' the worl', an' two empty whiskey jugs layin' beside him!

~

Well, it was a plumb excitin' place t' be an' amazin' busy, even late at night, what with the fur traders an' the hunters an' the scouts, soldiers an' tribes a wanderin' back an' forth 'cross the plains. Kanzas was a hub o' activity in 'em days an' a mighty important place fer commerce o' all kinds.

~

Now bein' a full-fledged state, Kanzas men was all het up t' pr'vide good schools. We was among the very first states t' insist that all citizens be ed'cated t' as high a degree as was possible. This was Sunday pie fer me, as I got work building schoolhouses from the east end o' the state t' the west. It was real steady work an' not too hard, I reckon.

By 1867 they was more'n 700 schoolhouses in Kanzas! We was proud! The money was set aside from the sale o' public land, 5% o' the total, plus the fed'ral gov'ment had granted the state three million acres o' land' fer common schools an' univers'ties. They set aside sections 16 an' 36 o' ever' township fer schools.

During them times it didn't take a whole lot o' ed'cation t' be a teacher. 'bout three months o' school would git you a certificate t' teach readin', writin' an' 'rithmatic. (I never did have no schoolhouse ed'cation. Folks ask me how I l'arned t' read an' t' write an' I tell 'em the truth, I don't know how I l'arned! Jest nat'ral borned smart, I reckon. Jest seems t' me like I always could! Now, I ain't no Billy Snakespear, but I kin git by. I read an' write, jest as good as I talk, an' kin cipher some, too.)

A man schoolteacher was makin' mebe as much $40 a month whilst a female made 'bout $20 er 425. Mos'ly teachers was women, though, as too many young fellers had been lost in the War. (Don't know if you know'd that Kanzas volenteer'd more men t' the Union Army than any other state, an' more Kanzas boys was kilt than 'em from any other state, too!) 'Sides, men didn't usually teach more 'n a few years a' fore they moved on t' somthin' else that paid real money. Truth t' tell, mos' o' 'em teachers was barely ed'cated theyse'ves an' some could not actual read er write more 'n a few words an' most had no haid at all fer spellin'. I coulda been a teacher m'self, I reckon, but I was busy.

Mos' folks then didn't go past the forth er fifth grade, if they could make it that far. Beca'se o' the demand's o' farmin' an' ranchin', a boy might only go t' school two er three months a year an' by the time he gradyeated fifth, mebe clear on up t' eighth grade he might be 20 year' old! Then he'd be done. They warn't hardly no higher schools.

Anywise, I got me a job an' worked fer the nix couple o' years with a one-armed feller named o' Roy Napp. Roy was a good a' man as I ever know'd. He'd lost his arm t' a kinnon ball at the battle o' Gitty'burg. We often camped out on the job sites an' Roy waked up screamin' an' sweatin' mos' ever' night o' his life. He would say no more 'bout the war than what was obv'ous. He lost his arm. An' a good deal o' his soul, I'm afear'd.

We made 'em schools out o' ever'thing, brick, rock, sod, wood, even cement. Mos' o' the time we worked with local folks an' would try t' build the struct're as near as we could t' match they budgit, which could range anywhar's from $50 t' $800. 'Em cheap schools required the local folks t' collect up all the limestone an' the timber an' have it ready fer us t' build with.

(Early on we made quite a number o' one room sod schoolhouses an' even some dugouts which was temp'rary with the idear that folks would do a more better job when the time, and the funds, was right.)

We would blow into town, like a pack o' wild dogs, ever'body know'd we was a'comin', an' the local men o' this district would git t'gither at whatever spot had been picked fer us t' build upon. They all brought they own tools. Like I said, If'n it was possible, they would have a big stack o' lumber already cut when we got thar, mebe a stone er a brick chimbly already up.

Ol' Roy would direct 'em so's they could raise the logs up into a wall an' t' leave openings fer doors an' winders. They was hardly never no glass in 'em winders in 'em times. What glass they was back then weren't much like what we gots now. This glass was all milky an' wavy an' 'bout all it did was t' let some light in, but as far as lookin' at somethin' through it, well it was 'bout like lookin' through one a' them funny-house mirror whilst drunk (not that I ever have did that). It was pricey an' fragile an', as m' old Uncle Emil used t' say, "It warn't much pun'kin," which I reckon was his way o' saying it warn't hardly worth the expense.

They was this stuff we called Isinglass which is actually a sort o' mineral that I reckon they heat up and roll out into flat sheets an' cut t' size, an' they was another kind o' milky-clear stuff made from the bladder o' certain fishes, but fer the life o' me I cain't 'member what that was called! Anyhow, they jest warn't much real glass t' be had so gen'ally the winder was jest a hole that could be covered with a hide er a little wood door t' block out the cold an' the rain.

Roy an' me, an' sometimes a third feller, hired local, why, we would split shingles from the logs t' make a roof', an' fer a floor we would hard pack the sod. Teacher would sprinkle that floor with water two er three times a day t' keep the dust down.

We split 6-foot logs with a broadax an' made 'em as smooth as we could with a plane. Then we drilled holes on the round side an' drove in smaller logs cut from branches so's we could make laigs, an' thar was a bench fer the students! It surprised some t' know that mos' o' 'em early schools didn't have no books at all, 'cept sometimes a Bible an' what they called a "primer."

Once't in a while, if we did a real good job on the school, an' we usually did, we would git asked t' build a simular place fer use as a church, separate like, although many districts used the same building as both a church an' a schoolhouse.

We was paid good enough an' they was lots o' what you call "benefits", sech as supper with the local folks, an' dances t' attend t' an' girls t' squire 'round with, an' they was gen'ally always a big party had inside the buildin' once't it 'twas finished, with food an' drink an' dancin' an' music, if they was any t' be had, an' recitin' o' pomes an' speeches an' sech other nonsense as that.

Old Roy worked harder than any two-armed man. It was amazin'.

(He told me once, "Oss, you hammer like lightenin'!" I was proud! I said, "You mean I'm fast?" Ol' Roy laughed an' said, "Naw! I mean 'case you s' seldom strike in the same place twice!" That was a good one on me, I reckon!)

They warn't much old Roy couldn't do, seriously though, whether it was choppin' er carrying, he shore did his share an' some extry.

We was a' workin' near a burg called Bitlertown at the edge o' the Flint Hills, jest north o' Madison. We was buildin' up a purty nice school an' they wanted a big ol' fireplace instaid o' jest a potbellied stove. They had cut the stone an' left it in a heap. Roy know'd consid'able 'bout stone masonin', but with his missin' arm he jest couldn't manage 'em big rocks, some o' which weighed four hun'ded pounds er more. He called me over an' introduced me t' some o' 'em town folks as his "right hand man," which brought some mirth t' 'em. He told me that he was gonna give me a million dollar ed'cation 'bout how t' mason rocks.

He 'splained that, first, we was a' goin' t' use the larger stones t' build a harth an' the base fer the chimbly. He selected the rock he was wantin' t' start with an' I bent down t' take a hold o' it. I hear'd a faint buzzing sound, like a grasshopper makes, an' in the nix instant m' hand, an' then up m' arm, felt like it was a'fire! I know'd that somethin' had stung me, but I didn't know what the hell it was! I pulled m' hand up an' took a look at her, it was beet red an' numb an' I could see two raggedy holes, one tricklin' thin, watery blood an' the t'other jest had a clear, wet trickle o' somethin' dribblin' out!

I jest kinda shrugged it off an' reached down agin' t' hoist up that rock.

Zing!

Stung agin'!

This time when I jerked m' hand up I could plainly see what had stung me beca'se it was a danglin' thar from m' wrist! Rattlesnake!

Oh, did I go wild? You kin bet I did! I pulled that snake loose with m' t'other hand an' I throw'd it down on a big hunk o' rock an' I stomped it into paste! I was real scairt 'case I was purty shore I was doomed t' die a mis'able an' unmemorable death.

Now, lemme backtrack 'case I gots t' fer you t' understan'. They is sev'ral kinds o' rattlesnakes that live in Kanzas an' this area. In the east they is the timber rattler, they is big an' very dangerous but they is mellow, fer a snake, an' like mos' critters, they would much druther git out o' yer way than t' bother you. The timber rattlers is shy, in a manner o' speakin', an' they keeps off t' theyse'ves. I've see'd 'em that'd go 10 foot long an' as big 'round as a big man's laig at the calf!

Then, out west, they is the pra'rie rattler. They is perhaps the nastiest tempered snake in the whole country! They got little horns on they haids an' great, ugly, hooded eyes. I think that these here snakes would pack a lunch if they thought they was a chance t' travel off somewhar's jest so's t' find som'body t' bite!

Pra'rie rattlers is easy t' identify. They git big, four er five feet er more, an' they have a uncommon thick body. The mos' easy thing t' recognize is that on they tail, a' fore you git down t' the rattles, the end o' the tail has bands o' black an' dirty-white, real clear distinc' rings.

They is many other kinds o' rattlers in different parts o' the country like cane rattlers, diamond backs (some people claim they is the same as timber rattlers but they ain't), an' all.

But the mos' common kind is the kind what bit me on this partic'lar mornin'. They is called by the Injun name, *masasauga,* which means "marsh dweller" er "swamp dweller" cause you usually find 'em 'round water an' moist areas, criks, ponds, streams, slews, marshes an' the like. They's a little snake, in gen'ral, though I've see'd 'em up t'

3 feet long, gen'ally they is less than ha'f that size, the ave'age bein' less than a foot long.

But they is jest as p'ison as the big ones. You know, a snake bite is a unperdictable thing. A big ol' rattler might bite you, but say he's bit somethin' else in the prev'ous day er two, a attacker like a woof, say, er strikin' at prey? Well, his p'ison sack, which is back behind his eyes inside his haid, it may be near t' dried up an' the mos' you'll git from him is dizzy with a bad haid an' belly-ache.

On t'other hand, a little bitsy old feller, 3 er 4 inches long fresh hatched outta his aig might strike you an' he ain't et fer a while an' his p'ison sack is full, an' look out! It kin git real bad. A little snake strikes you twice er three times but he's shot his p'ison all in first bite. Big snake? He bites you twice with a full load an' the second—er third—bite is equal bad as the one a' fore. Odd, ain't it?

An' don't always count on the rattle you've hear'd tell 'bout! It might jest sound like a little ol' insect. Er that snake might have been in the water er a crawlin' through dew soaked grass an' that dried skin that makes up 'em beads at the end o' his tail is soaked through an' it don't make hardly no sound at all. Er, when that old snake sheds his skin, which is how the rattle beads is form'd, sometimes the old skin hangs up, back thar, an' muffles the sound o' 'em rattles.

City folks seem t' think that they gonna walk up on this snake and it will be a' holdin' a big ol' baby rattle curled in its tail an' it's gonna shake it like a Mexi lay-koo-koo-ratchi dried gourd!

It ain't nes'arily gonna happen in jest that a'way. Now, don't read me wrong, they's times when I've hear'd 'em big pra'rie rattlers make a sound as clean an' as sharp, so's it could be hear'd fer a ha'f mile. I'm jest sayin' that ain't always the case an' that a feller shore shouldn't count none on it.

So, thar I stood jest a watchin' m' fingers swell up till they looked fat ring sausages! I ain't kiddin' you a'tall! The first bite had been on the back o' m' left hand an' the second bite was on the heel o' that same hand. The swellin' started t' move up m' hand, m' rist (sic) an' on past m' elbow, clean up t' m' shoulder! It was tarrible frightful, hurt like all git-out! Finally, m' fingers an' hand couldn't swell up no more an' the skin started t' split, like when you cook one a' them thar fat ring sausages on a hot fire! The whole dam' arm was a' turnin' black!

Roy took out his knife an' cut cross's into 'em wounds an' he squeezed an' sucked at the p'ison but, hell, it didn't do no good that a body could see! We found a jar o' coal oil an' poured that over them bites, like you would fer a snakebit dog, which he'ped consid'able in st'ppin' some o' the burn. Within five er six minutes I was feeling very dizzy an' m' haid was a' throbbin' like som'body was poundin' at it with a mallet.

Roy asked the town folk if'n they had a doct'r, well, hell no! The nearest doc was 20 mile' south in Madison an' so a couple o' young fellers, boys really, hided out, lickety split, t' fetch him. (They show'd up with him at 'bout six of th' clock that evening. I had been bit 'round noon, er a little a' fore, I reckon). I don't person'lly recall anything after the first hour er two, 'cept what Roy told me later.

He said that snots came a' bubblin' out o' m' nose an' mouth jest like that snakebit dog will do. He said I turned ashen all over an' was cold t' the tetch. He though I was a goner, shore. They tried t' give me some whiskey but I was unconscious an' couldn't swaller anyway an' they was a'feared that I would strangulate if'n they tried t' force feed it t' me.

An old ha'f-breed woman named Annie Buck prob'ly saved m' life. She made a wet poultice out o' mud dauber's nest an' yarbs, an' tied it down over them bites. She had 'em tote me over t' a stream an' they took off m' boots an' what passes fer m' stockin's, an' then put m' feets into the cool water. By then I couldn't not barely breathe. Roy said it sounded like a death rattle down there in m' throat! Ol' Annie Buck pulled out a knife an' a' fore anybody could stop her she had gouged a hole, dam' big, too, in the skin o' m' throat, right whar it joins up with the breastbone. Roy said that the snots blobbed out o' thar the size o' a hedge-apple! Annie took a big, dried sunflower stalk an' poked a piece o' wire through it an' reamed it out good, an' poked it into that hole, an' then she bent down an' breathed into it sev'ral times then stood back an' said, "He be fine, now, I guaranty."

Well, Roy said ever'body was jest shocked t' see this thing, but that within a few seconds m' color came back an' I was breathin' reg'lar like! She packed mud 'round the tube an' left it thar until that evening when that quacker they call "Doc." Bowman came an' jerked it out, cussin' 'bout "hoodoo" medicine!

I guess I didn't need it anymore anyways, as it was, since I didn't die none after he took it out. (I allays try's t' 'member t' point out t' folks that Doc Bowman, with his city medicine, died at the age o' 66. Last I hear'd, Annie Buck was at 103 an' countin'! Shucks, she might still be alive, fer all I know. So much fer that "hoodoo.")

The swellin' was real bad, though. Roy said that m' forearm was as big as a summer melon an' other folks said the same so's I guess it was true, but I don't know cause I was in what the doct'r called a "comma." He said that they 'spected me t' check out at any time, but that I was a' hangin' in thar, tight as a hair in a biscuit.

I slept fer three days an' nights a' fore I waked up an' when I did wake up I wished that I was daid! Oh, how m' haid ached an' m' arms an' m' guts. That little ol' masasauga shore did it t' me!

I recovered slowly but m' arm was all withered an' was never really the same after that thar deal. I still gots the scar on m' throat from whar dear Annie Buck saved m' bacon.

Roy had waited all this time on me t' git better, which cost him some work, as I convelesed fer neigh three weeks a' fore really bein' even close t' m' old se'f agin'. Now we had Roy, with no right arm, an' me without the use o' m' left! Jest two arms among two men! We was a sorryful pair!

Roy did his best by me. He told me some time later that he'd near'd t' die hisself from suckin' that p'ison 'n t' his mouth as his teeth ain't too good an' some o' it got down in thar whar they was rotted an' made him purty hinky. I tried t' he'p him out building 'em schools an' things but it was a bust. He paid me fer two weeks work that I hadn't did an' wished me well. He hired a pair o' orphant Negroes t' he'p him out an' the three o' em haided further west. I ran 'n t' him agin' some years later an' he was doin' all right by hisself. He had one o' 'em arms made o' cork wood attached t' his stump an' the cork had a big, nasty old hook as stickin' out o' it, like one o' 'em Barbarous pirates in a pict're book. He told me he had became a hell o' a fisherman, what with needin' no more than a wad o' worms t' hang on that thar hook, then he said he jes' bent down with his arm in the water an' started pullin' 'em in! That was a good one on him, I reckon!

~

As fer me I went back an' laid up at the farm. Lizzy an' Domm' was a fixin' t' marry in a few months (I had finally gave m' blessin') an' they was gonna adopt little Doe as they own child. I gave 'em m' blessin' on that, too, an' proceeded t' do nothin' fer sev'ral months as I was still feelin' porely from that dam' snakebite an' did fer a startlin' long time.

Once't in a while I rode over t' the old Kaw village an' sometimes I spied fresh prints made by a small, unshod pony. I shore did miss Tree an' I hoped that I would run into him but I did not.

I decided that me now bein' at the age o' 'bout seventeen er eighteen year', more er less, I should see a little more of the world than what I had see'd so far. I rode up north an' caught a stage coach, then a train, an' took m' self t' the big city o' Chicago. It was a big old worl' an' I decided that it was time fer me t' see some o' it. I planned t' be back t' Di'mond Spring a' fore winter, when Lizzy was a marryin' on Chris'mas day.

CHAPTER 10

M' sister Doe, who you might 'member I'm tellin' this all t' an' who is takin' it all down, gits riled with me when I go off on some story other than what I'm s'posed t' be tellin'. She says we gots t' keep this all in "chronogorical" order, t' which I say "beans," as I jest cain't do that. I say things as I 'member 'em happening an' I don't much give two hoots an' a holler if'n it is out o' order 'case I ain't shore that a body what has read this far along has got the brain power t' give a hang, neither.

Any way, she says that I should mention t' folks 'bout ridin' the stage coach an' the trains, seein' as the stages is all gone (good riddance) an', that by the time this here collection o' stories gits read, why, the trains might be gone too! (I know, she's a little crazy. Kin you imagine this country without trains t' carry people?)

Well, aw'right, here we go, fast as I kin git through it 'case it ain't what I'm wantin' t' be tellin'. First off, a stagecoach is the mos' miserable form o' t'rture yet devised by man. I believe I would druther som'body t' knock me t' the ground an' roll me t' whar I was goin'!

First thing is you crawl into a dirty little cramped-up box on wheels with anywhar's from 2 t' 8 other folks. If God is out t' git you, that will include a mama with two er three howlin' youngins, per'aps a coli'ky newborn'd, if the Good Lord is in partic'lar peeved with you.

If it's wintertime you are gonna freeze yer hams off. Truly, they is people who've lost fingers, toes, an' an ear er a nose tip er two from ridin' *inside* a stagecoach. Now, this bein' m' first trip an' it bein' late summer er early fall, I did not worry none 'bout the cold.

Shore enough, though, they was a lady with two young chil'ren on m' stage. We was haided from jest north Council Grove t' a stop up near Manhattan, Kanzas whar I would ketch a train round 'bouts t' Chicago. A stage ride o' this distance could take any whar's from 4 t' 14 days! I ain't jokin' with you.

People nowadays forgit that they warn't no roads back then. Trails, that's all they was, mos' o' which went through the lowest point in a crik er stream, but if it has been rainin' that low spot is the first t' fill up with water. A ford that was usually four er five inches deep could run twelve er thirteen feet during a flood! An' imagine what all that rain did t' a unpaved trail?

A stage was cons'antly exposed t' attack by ranc'rous Indians er by highway men who didn't want t' be identified an' so strived t' leave no witnesses an' who often as not shot ever' one on board! That's why stagecoaches always had at least one fool a ridin' "shotgun," him bein' the first targit o' the attackers. 'Course he was o' even less use when bein' attact'ed by forty er fifty Injuns on 'em fast little ponies o' thern.

This stage that I was on got upwards o' a hun'ded degrees inside. Travelin' over this rough ground would actually hurt a person. It jarred yer back an' banged yer haid an' turned yer kidneys into porridges. In jest a hour or two m' back ached like a eleyphant was a sittin' on it. It was truly alarmin'! They was hardly room t' sit an' a feller was always kickin' som'body by accident er was bein' kicked his own self.

The dust poured into 'em windows as they was no cover 'cept a kinvas shade an' with that many people crammed into that dam' little cheese box, includin' youngins, all with they kidneys an' bowels bein' shook t' pieces, believe me when I tell you that we didn't want 'em shades lowered! 'Bout ha'fway into our journey we ran into a hailstorm which danged near killed the driver an' the shotgun rider, an' shore as hell was no piece o' Sunday pie fer us t'urists, neither!

It was a stinkin', hot, smelly, dirty, cramped, uncomf'rtable, backbreakin', knee knockin', teeth rattlin', nerve wrackin' ordeal way t' travel!

It weren't as bad as I expected it, though, but I ain't a goin' t' talk 'bout it no more! At least we warn't held up by no footpads ner sca'ped an' shot full o' arrows by Injun's miffed over the fact we was rollin' through they land' agin' they wishes.

Oh! Doe says shouldn't I mention that we stopped at night time at stage stations? Fine. These was gen'ally o' 'bout the same quality as was the coach itself an' rarely much bigger, 'cept that these didn't move as much unless the wind blow'd hard. They fed us biled beans without no meat an' molded hardtack biscuits without no butter er hunny.

At one stop they biscuits was plumb full o' weevils that crawled out onto' yer hands when you went t' grab a biscuit from the platter!). I swear I saw, from the corner o' m' eye, the biscuit on m' plate move, like it was tryin' t' git away from me a' fore I et it! The coffee was like mud an' the water was best drunk through clenched teeth.

They had a two-hole outhouse what a feller could smell from 3 mile' off. I mean that, seriously. If'n' the winds were favorable, we could smell 'em stations 'bout three mile' a' fore we could see 'em! 'Sides, them buckets was always empty with nary no paper er corncobs t' be had. Gen'ally I jest hided off alone an' used the bushes.

They warn't no place t' bathe nor t' take a shower bath, which I've see'd in some stations, whar they takes a old bucket an' poke lots o' little holes in the bottom o' it an' fill it with rain water an' hang it on a hook inside a little outdoor closet made o' wood, you know? You goes in an' lathers up an' then a feller outside fills the bucket an' it's like standin' in the rain. Refreshing, an' it gits a feller right clean. Us'ally it cost as much as two bits extry, though, so I never did bother with it.

Some stations was fer overnight stayin' but them beds was nothin' but filthy straw ticks so I slept in a chair on the front porch so's that I wouldn't git et alive by bedbugs an' fleas. 'Stead, the skeeter's got me an' I had a tick bite in m' ear the size o' a hen's aig (sic). The lady a travelin' with us, Mrs. Emmie Bush, waked up in the mornin' with bloody sores whar she'd been bit by chinch bugs in the night. Her an' her youngins, too. They was a snivelin' bunch t' begin with so this jest made 'em that much more kintankerous.

Fer breakfast we had beans an' pone fried in rancid lard. Beans! Now what else would be stupider t' serve t' folks who is 'bout t' git on a stagecoach and be beat and juggled and pounded and shook 'round?

Then it was back on board. I felt like I warn't goin' t' be able t' force m'self back inside the stage but finally I did. Once't they let me ride on top, whar at least I couldn't smell the others.

One feller an' his wife had got off at the nix stop so it was a might more tol'able. The whole trip took four, mebe five days, I think. Time is hard t' reckon in a nightmare.

Finally we got t' Manhattan which is a sizable town, a tradin' center fer North Central Kanzas with a fine train station like a palace sech as I've see'd in books but had never a' fore see'd m'self. I checked into a hotel an' it was swank! Cost me a dollar an' a ha'f, an' I must say it was worth that an' consid'able more, after what I'd been through. I was reasonable shore that I had waked up daid and had gone t' heaven.

They drawed me a bath in a copper tub big enough t' scrape a hog in, an' I didn't even have t' share the water with nobody! It was clean, with lye soap an' a big puffy towel t' dry off with. A man stuck his haid into the door an' asked me if I would like me a shave, only twen'y five cents, he said, shave an' a haircut, 6 bits. (Golly, it seems so famil'ar t' me, 'em prices!)

I said, why, shore, shore. I shore did need a haircut but this was the first time I ever had shaved. That feller commented that the hair on m' upper lip could be trimmed with a scissor an' make a purty nice mustache so I said "ducks", an' he trimmed it up fer me while I held a hand mirror so's I'd know how t' do it by m'self. He also left the little tuft o' hair that grow'd in the holler o' m' bottom lip, like a little goatee. That is how I developed m' facial habits o' a lifetime.

Fer that price when he was done he slapped m' face with some witchy hazel, what I had never had. It stung some, right off, but then felt jest fine and smelt purty, too. Oh yes, and he also blacked m' boots.

Truth t' tell, I was sort o' dreadin' the train ride, after all that time I had spent cooped up in the stage like a ol' chicken. But it was fine as silk! Big old cars an' a feller could git up an' walk when he got cramped up, although walkin' on a movin' train did take a mite o' practice. Once't I even relieved m' bladder whilst a' hangin' in between two cars while that train was jest a rollin' down 'em tracks!

I've hear'd people complain that the trains then was rough an' crowded, well, they should have rode a stagecoach first an' then they would have see'd how fine 'em trains was!

Granted, sometimes cinders would come in through the winders an' might set a feller's clothes afire if he weren't alert, but if it happened, one o' 'em Negro porters would come along an' tap the flames out, gen'le as you please, er pour a pitcher o' water down yer front, which, by the by, they seemed t' partic'lar enjoy doin'.

An' fast? I reckon so! It was amazing fer me lookin' out 'em winders a' seein' the country fly by! Twen'y, twen'yfive, even *thirty* mile' in a hour's time!

From the winders I see'd ever' kind o' wild game, including a sizable buffaler herd. A feller said that they used t' block the trains, coverin' the tracks fer hours. We didn't see none o' that, though they say that further west they is still one er two o' 'em big herds left. We see'd sev'ral bunches o' Indians a ridin' they ponies as if t' race the train. They didn't shoot at us er nothin', a'though they was plenty o' armed men on board the train should it have come t' that. It seemed t' me more like the Indians was jest a' playin' a game.

(Jest a few months later this very train what I was a ridin' on was t' be held up by Frank an' Jesse James an' they gang when they decided t' branch out from the bankin' business. This was jest after I had met them boys, which I am fixin' t' tell you 'bout shortly. You know, I saved old' Frank's life? Keep yer britches up an' I'll git t' it. Hell, jest lemme finish this here part o' the story, what Doe wants t' hear, an' then I'll tell ye, promise I will!)

Anywise, that train ride was something' grand and it shore made me feel like a big shot t' jest have the pleasure o' bein' one o' the lucky stiffs on board. It jest beat the tar out o' ridin' on horseback er in a coach. Still, it was a mighty long trip and I was glad when they announced that we was jest outside o' "The Windbag City," as the conduct'r called it.

When we arrived in Chicago I was plumb flabbergasted. Why, I could have fit the whole town o' Manhattan into that train station. Trains, trains, trains! Ever'whar! An' people by the thousand's. I figur'd that it would have been worth the trip even if I was t' turn right 'round an' haid back home. (Lookin' back that might not have been sech a awful bad idear!)

I would have enjoyed m' trip t' the big city even more had someone not relieved me o' ever' last cent I had whilst I was inside that 'er beautiful train Station! I was a carryin' m' money in a buckskin bag 'round m' neck. I had near t' $75 in gold an' silver an' scrip. Sometimes I would reach up an' test the drawstring t' make shore it was strong.

Well, I was a walkin' along, gawkin' an' starin' up at the ceilin', an' I run smack into this feller, er he ran into me, I should say. Why, he apologized an' stood thar, a' brushin' me off with his hand an' his hat, a' sayin' jest how sorry he was, makin' me feel purty important, I must say. He goo-goo'd and hem-haw'd an' then tipped his little round hat t' me an' disappeared into the crowd.

I guess that is when it happened beca'se 'bout five minutes later I went into a cafe an' ordered me a pork steak an' reached up t' find that m' money purse was gone!

CHAPTER 11

Oh, how low did I feel? They has never been a sadder, more melancholy feller on this earth than me when I found that m' money was gone! I had not one, measly, red cent t' m' name! I was hongry as I could be an' had been all prepared fer that slice o' pork steak. Chicago is famous fer they pig business. They is the hog butcher t' the worl'! (That's true! I've been quoted by folks fer sayin' that very thing.)

A feller brought a big plate o' food, TWO thick slices o' pork an' taters an' a river o' gravy with some cut up carrots a floatin' 'round in it like little or'nge boats, an' two slices of the whitest bread an' wasn't it jest slathered in cream butter but like a fool I was honest an' I tol' him what happen'd an' he jest sniffed an' took the plate away without me gittin' so much as a taste. A few minutes later he came back, a' leadin' a feller in a fine suit an' vest with a big, gold chain a danglin' from it who asked me t' leave so I did.

Well. I jest stood 'round outside, snifflin'. I ain't ashamed t' admit that the incident brought me into tears o' bitterness fer the first time since m' adulthood. I went over whar they was a row o' buckets with dippers that all the trav'lers was welcome t' drink out o', an' I filled m'self up on water. They was nothin' else t' do an' a station guard in a beautiful blue uniform soot (sic) all trimmed up in red, he was eyein' me as though he suspicioned that I might be a footpad er a crook. I walked over t' him, real sheepish, an' I said, "Mr., some dastardly feller has done run off with m' pouch o' money."

He looked at me, studyin' m' face an' he smiled! Oh, it was sech a nice smile. I felt better already! That feller stood thar smilin' at me fer a minute an' then he said, "Welcome t' Chicago, Rube!" (I 'splained t' him that m' name warn't Rubin an' oh how he did laugh!)

It hurts me t' say it, but I started in t' blubberin' an' sev'ral folks gather'd 'round an' joined this feller a laughin' an' pokin' fun at me, callin' me "Rube," an' a "gully bull" an' some other things that I have tried hard t' erase from m' mem'ry.

I wandered out into the street whar I jest stood 'round till night fell an' then I found me a place in a alley whar I used m' carpet bag as a piller an' I finally got t' sleep, feelin' awful low an' mighty sorry fer m'self. I dreamed I was rolled up in a blanket on the Plains, in front o' a roarin' fire, a lookin' up at the stars while m' friend Tree sang some sad Injun song, an' he would stop singin' once't in a while an' take up the melody on a willer flute.

~

Nix mornin' I waked up with one o' 'em pigeon birds a' sittin' on a wire above me which had been strung from one building t' another so's t' hang wet clothes on? That dirty bird had relieved his se'f all over m' hat an' the new vest that Lizzy had bought me special fer this trip! I jumped up, a' cussin' an' I throw'd a chunk o' a broken brick at that pigeon! It was unfort'nate that the brick missed him, but came close enough t' make him squawk, but then it kept on goin' till it busted through a winder on the second floor o' the buildin'.

Right quick, a big, bald haid came juttin' out o' that winder, a feller in his shirtsleeves with a big, hooked nose an' a big, black mustache a' sproutin' out from under it like a bull's tail, an' him a' shoutin', "Hey, you thar! You done broke this here winder an' yer gonna pay fer it, goddam' it!"

I says back, "I cain't pay fer it 'case some dirty, dam' Chicago thief done stoleded m' money bag," an' he said, "Well then, I'm a comin' down thar an' I'm gonna take the price o' this winder out o' yer hide, I reckon," an' I sez "Oh, you is mighty tough, ain't you, baldy? You jest come on down an' meet the man what is gonna kick yer ass up betwixt' yer shoulder blades in two shakes o' a goat's tail," an', say boy, he got mighty mad then!

Well now, don't you think that he came jest a' flyin' down 'em stairs, an' a' bilin' out o' that door? I could hear him a' bellerin' like a scortch'd bear all the way. When he broke out that door into the sunlight I was plumb petrified! This feller was dam' near 7 feet tall an' was covered up with tattoos o' all sorts o' fearsome creachtures. He had that old, knotty, bald haid an' that huge, black biscuit-duster o' a mustache an' a big gold tooth right in the front o' his big, cruel mouth! Why that mouth o' his looked like it was big enough t' swaller up m' whole haid clean down t' m' shoulder blades!

A' fore I could say nary one single, word, why, he grabbed me up by the lapels o' m' store bought jacket an' he lifted me up, clear up over his haid, an' he throw'd me back agin' a brick wall so hard I see'd stars an' hear'd the ocean a roarin' in m' ears! A' fore I know'd it he had grabbed me up agin' an' throw'd me agin' that wall a second time, then he grabbed me up a third time, me jest a goo-gooin' an' mewin' like a pore infant child er one o' them dam'ed imbeciles, senseless-like, don't you know, all lanky like old Raggedly Ann, an' he heaves me out t'ward the city sidewalk, an' I landed on m' tailbone an' it made a loud snap!

Then he came over whar I was a layin' by a broken board on that sidewalk an' he kicked me right up side m' haid! I retched over an' snatched up that piece o' broken board an' was ready t' fetch him a solid blow t' the side o' his old slicky baldy haid when, oooo'! He kicked me in m' "gentile" area an' down I went!

He grabbed up that stick o' wood an' he waylaid it up agin' m' jawbone an' I spits out a mouthful o' blood an' a han'ful o' teeth! Oh, it was fearsome! Guesome! He walked up an' down on me like I was a set o' stairs! Then he sits on me fer a spell an' pummeled me with his fists an' slapped m' face an' boxed m' ears till they was a ringin' like a churchy bell on Easter mornin'.

Jest when I though I could take no more and was already a' hollerin', "Nuff" an' "Uncle," why, don't you know he stood up an' started kickin' me up an' down all over again? Why shore I was plumb convinced that this here feller was a madman and that he was a'gonna kill me or die tryin'!

I was jest preparin' t' start seriously beggin' fer what was left o' m' life when, finally, some folks gather'd round an' I hear'd a woman's voice sayin' "Stop that brute a' fore he kills that pore boy," an' they did.

She was a kindly lookin', middle-aged woman in a threadbare frock an' she sat me down an' dabbed at m' wounds with a dirty kerchief. She asked who I was an' what I was doin' an' I told her the whole, sorry story, best I could through busted out teeth an' a broke jawbone, m' rear end jest a throbbin' out pain, all's the while me a' babblin' an' a weepin' like a girl. I was shore that folks must hear it an' it shamed me, an' I ended up blubberin' some more out o' mortification an' had t' blow m' nose into t' that rag o' hers an' she patted m' battered haid an' said I was t' come on straight home with her, her name was Kathleen O'Leary an' that she was a widder woman with a big old house that she couldn't live in all o' jest herse'f, an' what not, an' so I did.

Chicago is a mighty *big* town. It was hot thar, an' they had been in a tarrible drouth, hadn't rained no real rain in near t' four months, they said. I hear'd people speakin' in ever' lingo you could think o'. I am not shore t' this day that all o' 'em was even real 'case some o' 'em sounded like somethin' a feller might make up if he was drunk er tetched in the haid.

This here woman, this Misses O'Leary, was a' he'pin' me hobble on down the street, people gawkin' at me, me a blubberin', an' a limpin', an' a'cryin' out in the agonies o' painfulness, "why me, why me," t' nobody in partic'lar, jest a limpin' an' a bleedin' an' blowin' snots ever'whar I went. Oh, it was pitiful! Pitiful!

After what seemed t' me t' be two or three hun'ded miles, we finally limped into the place whar she had her house. The entire neighborhood stunk real bad. You know, country folks has got the good sense not t' build a animal pen er shed too close t' the house 'case it is jest a nat'ral thing that animals kept locked up, they start t' stink, 'specially in the hot weather.

We also knows enough not t' build a outhouse very close t' whar we sleep and eat and live. An we knows t' build 'em t' the east or t' the west o' the house where the wind is least likely t' blow the smell inside the house.

But city folks warn't like that at all. It seemed like ever' house, no matters how fancy it was er how mean it was, kept a cow er two, a brace o' hogs, chickens, horses an' sev'ral dogs in the yards in back o' the house!

And the dogs! Now what use has a city feller fer a dog will you please tell me? He ain't a goin' t' hunt it, he ain't a goin' t' load it up an' make it carry a load like the Injuns do! An' he shore ain't goin' t' cook it up on a spit fer Sunday dinner. A dog in town is as worthless as a preacher in a 'ho'house, 'scuse m' language!

But it was like a rule er a law that if'n' you wanted t' live in Chicago, first thing you had t' do was go out an' git you three er four worthless hounds t' bark an' howl an' sniff an' scratch an' stink up ever'thing till hell won't have it! Lord, how it smelt!

The outhouses reeked powerful, powerful, sickenin' and that's enough said 'bout that. I will also mention that 'neith the gutters o' most houses in them days they was a trench dug so's if'n you's too lazy t' carry the chamber pot the whole four er five steps t' the privy, which most o' them folks apparently was, why it was jest fine t' open a winder and dump that pot out into that trench, a' splashin' it up agin' the side o' yer house and drawin' flies like a dead steer covered in dung!

When we got t' Mrs. O'Leary's house it was no diff'ernt, no diff'ernt a'tall! First off, two big ol' smelly hounds came boundin' out t' meet us. They sniffed me all over an' one jumped up on me with big muddy paws which put an end, once't an' fer all, I reckon, t' m' new jacket, an' hurt me tarrible bad, too, what with m' aches an' pains an' m' busted up tailbone. Them dogs licked at the blood which covered me an' then got real feisty an' panicky an' jest 'way too excited over the taste o' it till I thought they was gonna knock me down on the ground an' lick me t' death an' gnaw on me like a ol' soupy bone.

Mrs. O'Leary didn't seem t' notice, none. She finally jerked me free o' them bastard dogs and called them, "bad little boys," and sech so's t' make m' stomach queasy all over agin'.

As it turns out, her house was big, like she said, but it was a coarse, run down affair an', besides, she warn't havin' me inside the house, after all, 'case her neighbors would talk an' she was a good Cath'lic girl, she said! (She was mebe a Cath'lic, but you'd better believe me when I tell you it had been sev'ral long moons since she had been any sort o' a *girl!*) She warn't near as frien'ly t' me now as she had been a' fore an' told me curtly that I was t' sleep in the loft above a stall in the barn out back, which by the by was no more than 6 feet from that stinkin' outhouse.

I was so crimpledd up so's that I couldn't barely walk but she told me I warn't fixin' t' mooch off'n her an' that I had t' earn m' keep an' that I would have t' milk her old Jersey cow, Bossie, (I ain't never know'd a Jersey cow that *warn't* named "Bossie") a' fore I could eat er even git cleaned up. I was ready t' bust out, bawlin' agin', but I didn't. I was gittin' mad, t' tell the truth.

I limped passed them stinkin' dogs, ready t' haul loose and kick they faces in if'n they approached me, which they was a wantin' mighty hard t' do, and I walked past that stinkin' outhouse and inside that stinkin', hot barn. I stood thar, lookin' at Bossie, a old, decrepit bag o' bones, chewin' on a mouthful o' dry hay, a starin' at me with them big rheumy eyes an' a swishin' her tail at a endless supply of gnats 'n' flies.

Them flies was thick as snow in a blizzard an' they was t'rmentin' that old cow somethin' awful. She would swish her tail 'round constantly an' stamp her hoofs an' kick an' shake her haid an' do ever'thing that she could do fer relief but 'em flies jest wouldn't let up.

I know'd somthin' 'bout carin' fer animals havin' been raised on a farm. I looked 'round in that barn which was dark as a grave till I found me a jug o' coal oil. I found a old paint brush an' I dabbed that pore old cow down by paintin' stripes o' that oil acrost her back an' down her sides an' it he'ped consid'able t' keep them flies down.

(Now, a' fore you try this yerse'f an' so's you'll know, you cain't do this very often 'case that coal oil will burn the critter's skin if you use it more than once er twice in a month).

I was stiffenin' up somethin' frightful from m' injuries an' I figur'd if I was going t' milk this here cow that I'd better set t', er I was goin' t' be too stove up t' move! I looked 'round till I spied the lantern, so I found me a Lucifer match an' lit it up. I found two buckets an' I tied Bossie up t' the manger, put one bucket under her udder an' turned t'other one upside down an' set the lantern on it so's I could see.

Jest as I was wonderin' how I was goin' t' manage t' set down an' commence milkin', I hear'd Mrs. O'Leary's voice screetchin', "Boy! Oh, boy! Boy! Now whar are you off to? I'm a needin' some wood chopped if'n I'm gonna fix us some supper! Boy! Now, whar are you off to?"

I have been puzzlin' over what happen'd nix fer some years. As I recall, I was crip'in' 'round, jest a' tryin' t' git t' the door so's t' shout back at the ol' harridan that I was still out in the barn an' not off at some square dancin' contest 'r somethin'.

When I fin'ly got stood up, I took off m' hat so's t' wipe down m' brow an' I believe that m' hat must've knocked down a paper wasp nest. Nix thing I know'd, I'd got stung on both m' lips, over m' right eye an' on m' neck, so hard it made me 'member that time I got snake bit!

It stung like a hot ice pick jammed into m' face! Well I yelped an' bellered an' started beatin' at 'em hornets with m' hat, an' a waivin' m' hands an' cussin' like a sailor, an' I reckon that scairt old Bossie an' I figure that mebe some o' 'em wasps stung her too? Well, she hauled off an' kicked out with her right hind laig an' then with her left, you see? Well, her left hoof kicked that lantern off'n that pail whar it was a settin' an' spilled it on the hay on the floor an' then the flame took off an' away it went! They was coal oil on Bossie's tail an' it dipped down in that fire an' came up like a fuse on a stick o' dynamite!

She bawled an' pulled loose from whar I had her tied, tarin' the boards right out o' the manger, nails an' all, an' then she stood right up on her hind laigs like a dog a beggin' fer a bone, an' then she turned a right purty pir'uette, comin' clear 'round, an' punched me a fearsome hard blow in m' haid sev'ral times with her front hoof's like she was tryin' t' climb me like a tree, er that she thought her an' me was in a prize fight, I reckon! She finally got turned 'round an' she busted out that barn door t'ward Mrs. O'Leary an' her house, with her tail flickin' fire an' sparks, an' ever'thing bein' as dry as tender, the grass in the yard set t' burnin' an' Lord what a panic! First the grass ketch'd, then the weeds by the picket fence, then the fence itse'f ketch'd an' then some old, weedy flowers an' a tree!

I was still under the influence o' the wasps an' it was a tolerable spell a' fore I was able t' git away from 'em enough t' git outside an' t' look around and recognize jest what was happenin'. When I did I set up a powerful fit o' yellin' which hurt m' ribs right awful.

Fer a few minutes thar I tried m' level best t' beat out the flames with some ol' gunnysacks but they caught fire too an' I reckon mebe I jest throw'd 'em over the fence into the neighbor's weed patch. I considered it some an' decided that the smartest thing fer me t' do was t' git the hell out thar!

I hobbled along, fast as m' injuries would allow, south, away from the blaze, actin' like I never know'd what was goin' on, tryin' t' whistle through m' busted teeth and split lips an' t' act normal like, an' haidin' no place in partic'lar 'cept away from Chicago!

It shames me consid'able, but I read some whar's later, er som'body told me, that the fire started 'bout seven er eight in the evenin' on October the 8th, which sound near right t' me (as if I'd know). The fire kept on burnin' fer a couple o' days, anyhow. That it burned up 120 mile' o' sidewalks an' streets includin' over 2000 lamp posts an' upwards o' a *hun'ded thousand'* homes an' uncounted business buildin's!

I ain't never been one t' shirk m' responsibility an' I will fess straight up that I shore as heck play'd a major part in what happened that day. But if that old battleaxe hadn't been so mean and so connivin' then none o' it would have ever happened. Ever'body always blamed old Missus O'Leary an' her cow, not suspicionin' me a'tall an' I ain't sorry fer it! But I will contend till m' dyin' day that me an' Bossy was what is commonly called, "innocent victims."

CHAPTER 12

'Course right off I was shore that it was me t' blame fer that fire, but what was I going t' do er say that would change anything? Nothin', that's what! So I jest kept a goin'.

A' fore long they was a panic in the streets an' a lot o' people ran out an' opened up they barns an' jest let the animals run so's at least they'd have a chance jest in case the fire keep a' spreadin', which, o' course, it did. I kept a' thinkin' that I should mebe grab me one o' them horses that was a runnin' willy-nilly through the streets but I didn't like the idear o' stealin' very much besides which they ain't much lower on god's green earth that a hoss thief.

But it finally occurred t' me that since them horses had been set free, that no body could rightly state a claim t' 'em so I started watchin' the passin' hoss flesh kinda careful like till I found a buckskin colored mare that was smallish, Indian size, an' I jest retched out an' grabbed her halter an' she didn't make no protest a'tall.

I breathed "hello" into her nostrils like a Injun do an' slipped up on her, bare back, an' oh, how it hurt me so, made me jest cry out in pain, it did! I leaned over so's I could hold on t' the halter with both hands an' nudged her flank an' away we flew, bouncin' me 'round like a little chile, me yelpin' an' groanin' an' carryin' on like she was a killin' me, which I was fairly shore that she was.

She haided south, t'ward the gen'ral direction o' sweet Kanzas, whar they ain't no big city's t' burn an' they ain't very many Irish Cath'lic women an' they ain't no big, bald haided men with big, black mustaches a' livin' 'way up the stairs so's that a feller who accidentally heaves a brick through they winder kin git the tar kicked out o' him and then git all licked over an' nearly mauleded by some mess o' skinny, stinkin' ol' hound dogs!

I rode all that night till sunup, mos'ly unconscious, I do believe, from the pain in m' tail an' up m' back an' also m' haid an' m' mouth. I got up that mornin' an' I rode some more an' when I found a ol', 'bandoned lean-t' I slid off m' horse, who I had already named "Bess."

I didn't really have no idear as t' whar I was. It was right chilly outside but I dasn't build no fire. No, I didn't want *no* fire, jest yet. (In fact, it was sev'ral *days* a' fore I felt the need t' build me a fire!) I pulled up some o' the long dry grass an' covered up in it an' I slept some, till 'bout midday I reckon. I was hurt, pow'rful bad.

When I waked up the sky was clear an' very blue. Still muddle-haided from the sleep, I didn't know fer shore whar I was right off, but when I tried t' git up the soreness in m' bones an' the aches brought the memories jest a'floodin' back. I looked 'round an' I see'd blessed Bess grazin' an' I gave a low whistle an' here she come! She walked up an' gave me the old muzzle nuzzle, an' dam' if I didn't feel good, fer as bad as I felt!

I was sorry as I could be 'bout that fire, I really was, an' I still am, I reckon, but t' tell you the truth, I was so glad t' git out o' Chicago an' back into the countryside that I jest didn't give a hang. I ain't had no truck with Chicago since them days.

I was a'wearin' some leather suspender braces on m' trousers an' I took 'em off an' made a rein fer the horse. It must've took me a ha'f o' an hour, but finally I mounted up an' started south agin'. I had a small knife, but no gun, I had lost m' hat an' jacket when I left 'em behind in the barn. I had no money, food er water but I was as happy then as I 'I've ever been, I reckon, be' case I was free!

I stopped fer a minute when a shadow had gone over the sun an' I thought that a storm might be a comin' up from behind me, in the north. I looked back over m' shoulder t' see what it was? It was smoke. I reckon as far as I had rode that I still know'd whar that smoke was a comin' from.

~

Kept a' ridin', two er mebe three days, sleeping on the ground with misery as my blanket an' pain as my piller. After I had rode fer a few days more, I started feelin' a little bit better, by an' by. I figur'd that by now I must be somewhar's in Missouri, or real close to it, an' so I turned Bess t'ward the west-southwest an' back t'ward Kanzas. I got on a well-traveled trail whar I picked up an old piece o' kinvas an' I made m'self a poncho in case o' rain. I had been lucky, so far, in that the weather had been lovely, although it was right chilly after the sun went down. I have found that, gen'ally speakin', I am quite fond o' the month o' October regardless o' whar I am.

This was hill country an' it got t' whar it did start t' rain mos' ever' mornin' an' agin' come sundown. The mornin' rain was fine, it worshed ever'thing t' a shine an' dried off as soon as the sun het up. The evenin' rain was a bane, as it left ever'thing wet an' the leaves on the ground was slimy an' cold. Bess didn't mind nothin' but I was gittin t' whar I wished I at least owned a hat.

One morning I had been on old Bess' back, wishin' I could come up with a saddle since, as I have said, we was in hill country an' I was doin' a pow'rful lot o' slippin' an' slidin' as Bess climbed the ridges 'n' banks and then ginger-footed down the draws an' valleys, when sud'nly I hear'd a rooster crow. They ain't no mistakin' that sound, ain't nothin' sounds like a rooster, no other bird or creachture that I know, an' gen'ally speakin' whar they is a rooster they is a farm.

Shore 'nuff they was a little cabin up thar amongst some long-needle pines. I rode up thar an' two er three old hound dogs lifted they haids an' sniffed, then lay's back down an' went t' sleep. These here was civ'lized country hounds, not like them heathen monisters in Chicago!

Fer the mos' part, a country hound knows how t' behave. The only way they might git excited 'bout a stranger ridin' up on a horse was if that stranger was a 'coon er a postum. I foller'd hill manners an' did not dismount, instaid I called out, "Hallo! Who's t' home?"

"I am," a woman's voice replied.

A elderly lady came up an' swung open the top ha'f o' the dutchy style door an' looked out at me, a hoodin' her eyes with her hands.

"Who's a'goin, thar'?" she called. I replied, "M' name's Oscar Harris, ma'am, I am from over Kanzas way. I'm a' lookin' fer a drink o' water an' a bite t' eat but I gots me no money, jest a strong back, tho' it's a might stove up at this moment, but I'm a' willin' if'n you'ins needs some wood chopped er split, though I will tell you I cain't do it real fast. Even so, I'd be proud to do the work an' still be obleeged, ma'am."

"If'n yor' hongry, climb down from yer hoss an' come in an' set a spell. I'll feed ya, son. 'Been hongry m'self an' so has m' chillin', an' I knows what it's like. You git yerse'f down o'fn' that beast, Mister Kanzas Man, an' I'll feed ya. Take yer old hoss round back, they's a spring-fed trough back thar an' some cut alfalfy, an' let it fill it's belly, too. C'mon now! Say, now, you ain't one o' 'em Jayhawker abby'lish'nist, ere ye?"

"No, ma'am. I'm jest crimpled up and right hongry."

I slid off'n the horse, which was gittin' easier fer me t' do by now, an' let her go, knowin' she'd find her own way t' fresh water and cut alfalfy. I walked up an' sit down on the steps, kindly ginger, like.

"What ails you, son? Jest stiff from the ride, I reckon, though you look like you been through a tol'able scuffle. Well, what 'ere you a'doin' boy? We's eatin' *inside* the house. You's white, ain't ye? You ain't got t' sit out here like no Chineyman. Come inside. You in luck, Kanzas Man, I jest made a fresh pot o' chic'ry coffee."

I went inside. The cabin was small an' very clean. They was a young boy a sittin' on the floor playin' with a doll made out o' a corn cob.

"'Scuse the boy," she said, "He ain't right. Tetched. In the haid. Borned that 'a way. He's a good boy, he jest ain't all thar, that's all. Big Archie, his pap, God rest his soul, he said the Lord works in m'ster'ous ways an' that son o' mine is shore a m'stery t' me. But he's as goodhearted as he kin be, an' he ain't no real trouble. I love's him like a puppy. Now, son, set yerse'f down at that table an' I'll fix you somethin' good, Kanzas Man, You cotton t' hen apples?"

I told her I never tried me none, but that we had us a reg'lar apple tree, back in Di'mond Spring, an' she laughed a warm, throaty way that made me feel good.

"*Aigs*, boy! Lawsy, you mean t' say you ain't never et an *aig*?" an' she laughed agin', brushin' a wisp o' silver hair back from her face, jest like m' Mama used t' do, only Mama never lived long enough fer her hairs t' turn gray.

She fried me up four o' them "hen apples," soft yolks, but not runny, jest the way I likes 'em (though I reckon I would et 'em raw, as hongry as I was) an' she fixed up a pan o' sody biscuits an' a big slice o' sugar cure ham an' a little bit o' sage sausage. She sit down a blue 'namel pot o' the bestest coffee I had ever had, an' a big old glass o' fresh milk. I should prob'ly be 'shamed o' the way I et that food, but she didn't seem t' mind none. Lord in heaven it was as good a meal as I had ever flipped a lip over in my days afore er since!

"M' name is Zerelda Samuel. M' eldest boys is gone on business, they's from m' first man. They's good boys who do right by me an' they neighbors. I betcha you know 'em, m' boys, er you hear'd o' 'em. Say, how's them vittles, Mister Kanzas man?"

I doubt whether she could understan' m' answer, but the look on m' face an' the fact that m' mouth was stuffed so full that the food was a' leakin' down m' chin prob'ly was answer enough. I slopped some coffee into m' cake hole an' wiped m' mouth on the back o' m' sleeve. "It's mighty fine, ma'am, laripin'! Best coffee I ever had, I do believe."

"I makes real coffee but I add some chic'ry an' a smidge o' t'baccy leaf. It is tasty, though, ain't it?" She talked fer a while 'bout this an' that an' nothin' in particular. She asked me what I was doin' an' why I didn't have a saddle er a pack on m' horse an' why I was a limpin' an' grimacin' with pain when I moved.

I told her a short sketch o' the last few weeks, figurin' she warn't the type t' care much what happened t' the city o' Chicago, an' she laughed, some. She got up an' went into a side room. She came back with her arms loaded with two flannel shirts, worn but not wore out, a fringed, pigskin jacket, pair o' boots an' a real nice wide brimmed beaver hat.

"These here was Archie's. He got no use fer 'em now an' m' boys is too big fer 'em, 'sides, they buys all they clothes store-bought these days. I hope you ain't sup'stitious 'bout wearing a daid man's clothes.

They's a old saddle out back in the shed, probably cracked an' split some, but you kin take some pig rend'rins er some beef suet t' it, I got both, an' that will soften it out. It should do, an' come neigh enough t' fittin' yer pony. They's some other tack thar, too, take what y' can use."

"I'm obleeged," I said.

We hear'd the hounds stir an' bark ha'f-heartedly, an' the old woman looked puzzled. "Now who might that be? More comp'ny? Never rains, but it jest pours as m' Archie used t' say."

She walked over an' looked out that door. "Why, I swan!" she said, "It's the boys! The boy's is home!" She looked so happy I thought she might start dancin' right thar in her parlor! The little feller on the floor goo-goo'd some an' got up an' ran over an' hugged at her laig. "Boy's, boy's! Come on in this h'yer house, we gots comp'ny!"

Two men walked in, one tall with a heavy, black beard with little tinges o' red at the tips, the other shorter with a lean, han'some face, kinda foxy like, clever eyes that took me in quick, up an' down. Both was powerful bilt and walked like men what's shore of theyse'ves.

"Boys, this h'yer is Oscar Harris from over Kanzas way, but he ain't no Jayhawker! Oscar, these is m' boys. This h'yer is m' eldest, Frank, an' this is m' baby, Jesse".

I stood up an' wiped m' hand on m' shirt an' tried t' swaller a great, big mouth full o' food in one swaller, near choked, it brought tears into m' eyes. "Mr.'s Samuel," I said, noddin' m' haid, stupidly, from one face t' the t'other.

The short one held out his paw first an' said, "Name ain't Samuel, son, that was m' step-pappy, Archie's name. Me an' m' brother's name is James. He's Frank, I'm Jesse. Fine t' meet you. Did my Mama give you enough t' eat?"

CHAPTER 13

Well, may I simply say that this was "ducks" fer me? Frank an' Jesse James! Now, if'n' it seems that I am a gooshin' all over this, m' readers should consider that I had hear'd tell o' these fellers, an' had read 'bout 'em, some in the newspapers an' some in the "penny dreadfuls" fer neigh on a year er more.

The James boys, U. S. Grant, Custer, Honest Abe, Wild Bill, Jenny Linn an' a few others was the major celebrities o' they times! Why, I couldn't have been more excited if'n' I was a sittin' in the same room with the King o' France er the Pres'dent!

No special attention was paid t' me, I was accepted jest like I was the fam'ly dog, er somethin', an' had always been thar! Ma Samuel fired up her skillet agin' fer her boys, an' I'm ashamed t' say that I et agin'! I had been livin' fer some days on berries an' wild fruits an' sech truck as that an' I was *hongry!*

After breakfast we all went out t' the front porch. Jesse took a big chaw o' t'baccy an' Frank lit up a big old briar pipe an' we jest sat thar an' watched the mornin' go by. The boys didn't say much 'bout what they had been doin' er whar they had been er how long they had been gone er how long they was home fer.

'Course I know'd that they was still riding with Quantrill and his like, who, me bein' from Kanzas, I didn't much cotton t', an' although both o' 'em had already been in the war, on the losin' side, they was still conducting, what was called, "gorilla warfare", which don't pay much, so they had taken t' doin' a little armed robbery on the side. Then

132

they had made the paper's by doin' somthin' so bodaciously simple that it is a wonder, lookin' back on the thing, that nobody had thought t' do it a' fore, but nobody had.

They robbed a bank! Not burglarized it, mind you, but robbed it! With guns and ever'thing! In the broad o' daylight!

~

They did ask a right impressive number o' questions 'bout me an' they seemed like they was sincerely int'rested. They seemed particular engaged when I told 'em 'bout the train ride I had took t' Chicago, 'specially a part I mentioned 'bout how I 'splored the train, an' that I had wandered through a freight car stacked near t' the ceilin' with kinvas bags an' strong boxes marked "Wells Fargo".

I asked Frank was he int'rested in trains an' he said, "Not till now. Keep talkin', son," so I did. Jesse took out a nub o' pencil an' a piece o' paper an' was a jottin' down notes t' his self 'bout this particular train, whar it started from an' whar it ended up an' he asked me lots o' other questions, like did I 'members which days o' the week on which I had traveled (which I did not 'member, after all) an' 'bout the name o' the train, which I did, indeed, 'member, it was "The Pra'rie Zephyr."

They was quite excited 'bout it fer a while, one commentin' t' t'other 'bout how they should consider a' goin' in t' the railroadin' business. After a while though, ever'one settled down. Frank asked me whar I was haided fer an' I told him I was lookin' t' goin' back t' Kanzas, I reckoned. He said if I weren't in no hurry an' didn't mind stayin' on a few days, that they might jest be haided the same way if'n' I was t' want some comp'ny! Hoo Haw! Did I want some comp'ny? Well, I guess that I did! Expecially if it was with the likes o' two well-know'd folksy heroes. I said it then an' I'll say it agin', "ducks"!

That night we all loaded up in a wagon, a buckboard, really, all five o' us, the James boys on the seat an' me an' ma an' little Archie in the back, an' we rode down the side o' the mountain t' a holler whar they was a big, long, log buildin' whar they was a holdin' a Grange meetin' an' after 'ward, a dance, this bein' a Saturday.

What a time I had! I had never been t' a dance a' fore, 'cept fer back when I was buildin' school houses and them dances warn't much pun'kin, truth be told, jest some ol' string-bean farmers an' a ol' maid er two.

Why, here they was girls an' feller's an' home brew an' sars'parilla an' even moonshine, but I don't drink no whiskey. Jesse an' Frank danced with ever' girl in the place. They was a banjer player an' a feller playin way down deep on a contraption like a wood pole stuck through the bottom o' a wash tub an' strung up with a piece o' heavy, braided wire, an' they was *two* fiddle players! My, 'em boys could saw! They was also a feller a huffin' an' a' puffin' into a stone crock jug, but hell, any dam' fool kin do that.

Well, o' course I an' ever'body else in that hall know'd what 'em brothers did fer a livin'! As I said, they was the very first persons t' ever rob a bank durin' daylight hours an' they was famous fer it an' admir'd, too. I had hear'd that jest that past June they had been up in Corydon, Iowa. While they was a big meetin' goin' on at the Methodis' Church, the James' an' they gang had rode down t' the bank, covered up they faces with bandaners, an' had relieved the establishment o' over *$6,000.00!* When they was done they rode over t' that church meetin', bold as you please, an' informed ever'one thar: "We've jest been down t' the bank an' have taken ever' dollar in the till." Then they jest spurred they horses an' rode off! They was already gittin' famouser than anybody an' this jest added fuel t' the fire.

At the party I was right shy at first an' jest kind o' slunk 'round, some. I sat with Ma Samuel an' the 'tardy minded boy, Little Archie. Frank called me over an' intr'duced me t' some fellers, friends o' his, brother's named Younger. They was John, Jim, Bob, an' Cole. Cole was drunk an' a gittin' drunker, plus he had a look 'bout him like a hongry woof an' I stayed away from him. He had meanish eyes an' always seem t' have his jaw set fer a fight.

M' favorite o' the brothers was Bob. He was a' nice a young feller as you could meet. I also met some other folks, Charlie Pitts an' his brothers, an' some others includin' as mean a' lookin' an' actin' feller as I have ever did run 'cross what made Cole Younger look like a church deacon!

He was an Injun named Sam Starr. He was a puzzle t' me. He was dressed up like a dude cowboy but his Injun hair was very long an' thick, black as pitch, an' he wore it a flowin' down his back. He wore lots o' jewelry, bands o' sliver an' turquoise an' the like. He was at the dance with a old, leathery faced harridan, a white woman named Mara Belle Shirley, who seemed old enough t' be his mama. She had a child with her who was said t' be Cole Younger's daughter. She had run off an' married som'body else, a feller that was hanged fer horse thievin' down in Texas, an' now she was either a' livin' with er was mebe even married t' Sam Starr.

Like I said, Belle was one tough lookin' old sister an' it was odd t' see her with young Sam, who I must admit, was one o' the han'somest lookin' men I have ever see'd in m' life. He was good lookin' but then they say the devil is, too. I will admit it here fer the first an' only time; I ain't never been 'round a man who seemed so gut-evil an' who scairt me so. Not Cole Younger, not even 'em Earp boys that time back in Council.

It was in his eyes, his manners, an' his voice. Sam an' Belle Starr warn't the kind o' folks you invites t' your house fer lemonade on a Sunday afternoon.

Another odd thing 'bout this party was that ever' man was wearin' at least two side arms a'showin' an' I would have been plumb surprised if ever'one warn't packin' iron inside his vest er down his boot laig, 'er both. They all also had longish knives in sheaths on the backs o' they belts, what some calls a Bowie knife an' others know as a Arkansaw Toothpick.

There warn't no trouble, though, although things did git riotous loud. I overhear'd John Younger tellin' Jesse 'bout some feller named Al Pinkerton who was pokin' 'round, askin' lot o' questions 'bout the James' wharabouts, an' 'bout jest whar was the Samuel house located an' who it was that lived thar. Pinkerton had been showin' around a business card which had on it a pict're o' a eye an' the words, "We never sleep," engraved below it. 'Said Pinkerton called his se'f a "private eye," which sounded kind o' spooky t' me.

This party lasted until midnight! I don't think I have ever been up that late on purpose in m' entire lifetime. We all rode home in the wagon a singin' songs that the ban' had played like *"Beautiful Dreamer,"* *"She's More t' be Pitied than Censured"* an' *"Red River Valley"* which always makes me cry. Well, I don't actual cry like no girl er nothin', but I do tear up some.

When we dismounted from the wagon back at the cabin an' was walkin' t'ward the steps, I see'd somethin' a' glisten in the moonlight an', somehow, I know'd they was somethin' wrong. (M' sister, Doe, who, as you might 'member, is takin' this all down fer me, says I might have somethin' that they calls a "sick scent" 'bout things, whatever the hell that means).

Anywise, it was like I know'd somethin' was a' gonna happen? Fer no reason at all I turned back t'ward Frank as he was a'comin' up behind me an' I throw'd m'self into his laigs, an' I knocked him t' the groun' jest as we hear'd a 'splosion. Frank had been a' standin' right aside a block an' a tackle which was a hangin' from a tree whar beeves an' hogs was hung up fer butcherin'? Well at that very instant a shot hit that block an' splinter'd off a big ol' slice o' the wood an' sent the whole thing a' spinnin'! If I hadn't a'turned 'round an' knocked him down, they's a good chance that that bullet would have caught Frank James right in the side o' the haid, 'stead o' missin' him an' a' strikin' that block!

I was still achin' from my prev'ous injuries and I laid thar on the groun' kindly stunned like for a second er two.

We hear'd the hooves o' two, mebe three, horses take off into the night from behind Miss Samuel's barn! They was *assashins*, out t' fetch Frank an' Jesse, an' t' turn 'em in fer the reward that the Gov'nor o' Missouri had put on they haids, an' that is the true story o' how I saved Frank James' life!

(It did take me a long time t' admit t' m'self that when I had stood up an' offered m' hand out t' Frank t' he'p him up, I hear'd a very distinctive rachetin' sound o' the hammer bein' eased t' home on a Colt .45 han'gun. Out o' the corner o' m' eye I watched as Jesse eased the barrel o' his pist'l back into the holster. I figure he had a bead on me the minute I'd turned t' knock Frank out o' the way. He had his own *sick scent*, I reckon, an' I shore am glad he had cold nerves an' waited long enough t' rekinize that I had nothin' t' do with the assashination druther than commence t' open fire on me er I woulda been daid fer shore.)

~

I spent the nix few days at the home o' Widder Samuel, eatin' the finest grub they ever was an' a'rubbin' elbows with two o' the famousest fellers in the country who was, let me say, mighty glad t' have me! 'Em boys treated me like a king, knowin' now I had likely saved they lives!

Jess asked me how I had sided fer the War an' me a' knowin' they politics, I said I had been in total support o' the Rebels. 'Course I was too young durin' the war t' really give a hang 'bout either side, but I know'd I'd said the right thing 'case they both grinned an' old Frank offered me a ceegar from a box he kept on the parlor table. Ma Samuel said "Praise the Lord."

That ceegar turned me green as a frog, but I hanged on an' didn't git sick er nothin'. Bye 'n' bye I reckon I gots to whar I liked the taste of em.

Turns out, I smoked so many ceegars from Frank's box that by the time I left I had picked up a hackin' cough, an' was dam' proud o' it!

~

We took off fer Kanzas on a Thursday mornin' an' I must say I was sorry t' go. It was rainin' but I didn't care 'bout that, none. I had a saddle, a slicker, some spendin' money in m' pocket that Frank had give t' me, a new, ol' cap'n'ball pist'l what had belonged t' they step-pappy, Mr. Samuel, an' a fine, old Henry rifle that 'em generous folks give t' me. Better still I had a belly full o' grub, a saddlebag full o' jerky an' salted side an' har'tack an' pickled "hen apples." All this, an' I was ridin' with the James brothers!

It was a pleasant ride an' 'em fellers an' they taught me consid'able more 'bout campin' on the trail than I already know'd, an' I know'd more 'an mos' folks do. At least I thought I had know'd a lot, but they years ridin' with the likes o' Bill Quantrill an' considerin' the nature o' they business, they know'd a sight more 'bout livin' comfor'ble an' clean on the trail than I had ever dreamed of.

After sev'ral days ride we parted comp'ny in Fort Scott, Kanzas. I never did meet up with 'em folks agin' but I foller'd they career's closely in the newspapers o' the day. O' course they went on t' pull the first train robbery in the hist'ry o' anythin', an' more, until finally the fateful day o' reckonin' came up in Northfield, Minnesota.

What happened in Northfield is a long story which is found in any hist'ry book so I ain't goin' into it much 'cept t' say that the folks up thar in Minnesota did not see the gang as heroes a'tall, an' that them folks killed a couple o' feller's what was ridin' with Jesse an' Frank, one name o' Bill Chadwell an' also the feller I met at the dance named Charlie Pitt.

Fact is, they all got shot up purty bad, 'specially the Younger's, who was also along. Shot 'em bad, 'though they all lived but then they was sentenced t' life in the penitentiary which I reckon to be worst than dyin'.

Frank an' Jesse got away, as you might know, an' married an' settled down. It is a excitin' story, the Northfield raid, and you should look it up and read it.

A year er two later pore Jesse was shot in the back o' the haid by a coward named Bob Ford while at home with his fam'ly. Ford was pardoned by the Gov'nor fer the charge o' murder, but later he an' his brother, Charlie, who had been at the house with 'im the day he killed Jesse, was "took care of" by friends o' the James'.

Ol' Frank, bless him, had t' stand trial fer 'bout a million "crimes" but a jury o' his peers acquitted him o' all charges. They had t' hold the trial in a opry house in order t' 'commodate the crowd o' folks wantin' t' see the great Frank James. He lived t' be 72 year old an' was fortunate enough t' die, sleepin' in his bed, on his home place. An' I know'd that onc't I had saved his life!

~

I ain't gonna continue t' brag on the James boys much longer 'cept t' mention this: I think the saddest thing o' all happened jest a few months after I had parted comp'ny with 'em. This feller named Al Pinkerton was a kind o' a detective type an' he was hell bent on collectin' a big reward fer capturin' er killin' the boys.

Person'l, I always believed he was the one who shot at Frank that night after the party but I cain't prove it. Well, one January night, he er one o' his men throw'd a bomb through the winder o' Widder Samuel's place thar near Kearny, Missouri thinkin' Jesse an' Frank was thar, which they warn't. That little 'tardy feller, l'il Archie, was only 9 year old an' the 'splosion kilt him daid. Pore Ma Samuel herself lived through it, but it blow'd her right arm off clean up t' her shoulder, jest a hangin' by a muscle, I reckon, an' finally it had t' be ampertated by a sawbones.

I always thought that was a dirty, dam' trick an', while I know'd 'em boys warn't no angels, I don't think the law should have that kind o' pow'r an' do stuff like that t' innocent folks like Ma an' little Archie.

CHAPTER 14

I was kind o' depress'd an' lonely after we all had parted ways. I warn't really too shore jest what t' do with m'self. Fer a while I ponder'd ridin' down t' the Oklahoma Injun Territory an' seein' if I could find any news 'bout Tall Tree. But in the end, fer whatever reason, I decided not t' go. Instaid I did amble t'ward the boarder till I got t' the town o' Coffeyville.

This is nice country. They is hills like all o' eastern Kanzas has, but these is a might steeper. They is trees like they is all along this part o' the state, too, but they is thicker an' a feller don't see quite so many cott'nwoods an' see's a lot more o' 'em blackjack oaks. The soil here's more red than black an' the streams run clearer. They is fewer jackrabbits an' more deer. It's more like the Ozarks an' less like the Plains. It's the same but kinda different, you know?

While I was down thar I decided t' see if I could earn me some money. The James' boys had give me a pair o' $20 gol' pieces an' I still had both o' 'em, so it warn't like I *needed* the money, it was more like I needed somethin' t' do. I ran into a feller in town name o' McIlvain who was a' wantin' som'body t' come t' his place an' set up all night t' kill a cougar that was causin' problems with his livestock. It had killed his two best dogs, a hog, two calves an' 'bout 15 chickens an' ol' Mac couldn't seem t' be at the right place at the *wrong* time, if you ketch m' drift.

I had me the Henry rifle, which was perfec' fer the job. Some folk call a Henry a "buffaler gun". It has devastatin' fire power and will reach out a long, long way and fetch a mighty big creachture down lickety-split.

I told McIlvain that if'n he bought a box o' ammunition I would spend 5 nights, if it took that long, waitin' fer the cat an' if I killed it he owed me $10, gold, an' if I didn't all's he was out was the price o' the shells, which I would git t' keep any wise.

$10 is a powerful lot o' money but compared t' what his losses already was it was a drop in the bucket. He agreed an' told me that I could make a camp down on his stretch o' the crik an', if'n I was inclined, I was welcome t' share supper each night with his fam'ly. It sounded like a large slice o' Sunday pie t' me an' so I rode straight on out an' set up camp 'bout a mile an' a' ha'f from his house, which was a big, nice one that prompted me t' thinkin' I should have set m' price at $20 instaid o' a measly 10.

They was some young town boys a playin' Injun down by the crik an' nat'rally, bein' boys, they come up t' poke 'round an' t' ask me 'bout eleventy zillion questions.

"Whatcher name, mister?"

"Oscar Harris. Folks call me Oss."

"What happ'nd to yer teeth?"

"I gots 'em knocked in fer askin' stupid questions!"

"Is that why yer face is all scared up?"

"Ejactly! Any more dang-fool questions?"

"Did you steal that 'are rifle?"

"No! What a question t' ask! I didn't steal nothin'. It was give t' me. Whar's yor manners? Why do you ask sech of a thing?"

"'Case I done l'arned m' letters an' they's initials on the stock plate, they is 'F.J.' and yer's would be 'O.H.'. Who is 'F.J.'?"

"'Em is the initials o' Mr. Frank James, who is, if'n you don't know, along wif' his brother, Jesse, a *person'l* friend o' mine!"

Well, 'em boys was stupidfied, an' they stuck with me like glue as I told 'em 'bout the days I had spent so recently ridin' with the James brothers. I told 'em some o' m' other ad-ventures an' that m' best friend was an Injun an' that I had fought ag'in Injuns with Col. Forsythe an' the U. S. Cavalry. Finally I got plumb tired o' jawin' so I ran 'em off t'ward evening an' I made m' way up t' the house.

McIlvain was thar with his wife an' a parcel o' youngins. T' tell the truth they was nice enough folks but 'em kids an' the wife acted plumb insipid! They was gen'ally all sittin' with they mouths open, gapin' like carps, at either me er Mr. McIlvain, dependin' on who was talkin'. An' the food! Why, pish! It looked wonderful, an' they was lots o' it, what with a ham, 'taters, collards, jar'd corn, bread an' fresh, warm milk. But it all tasted the same! Why, close m' eyes an' I couldn't tell the difference between the ham an' the 'taters 'cept fer the way it felt in m' mouth.

It is a sin t' waste food, m' folks always said, an' that must shore include cookin' like this! It was a waste! They warn't no salt, no pepper, no grease no nothin'! I thanked 'em kindly, though, as I was taught manners. (I had even 'membered t' take m' hat off at the table, after a while).

The missus asked me was I a' wantin' a piece o' pie fer desert, an' fer the first time in m' life I declined a slice o' pie! I had right fond memories o' pie an' I didn't want her a spil'in' 'em by servin' me up a piece that tasted like ham er cabbage er a redish er a onion er some sech!

I went back down t' m' camp at the crik an' fetched the big gun, then I walked back up t' the barn an' found m'self a spot up in the hay loft from which I could see the chicken coop an' the other pens. It was a big, nice barn an' was near ha'f full o' fresh hay. It smelt nice an' was comfor'ble an' I decided t' take m'self a little snoozie, which I did, an' when I waked up it was night time with the biggest, fullest, buckskin-colored moon as ever I've see'd a hangin' overhaid. I laid thar a while, a'lookin' at the sky fer some time, thinkin' the kind o' thoughts I guess folks has thought 'bout ferever when they is alone, lookin' up at a moon like that one. Then I hear'd a muffled squawk an' a flutter. I sharpened up an' started lookin' down below. First I didn't see nothin' 'case I was lookin' in the bright spots but then I got t' studyin' the shadows an' thar I spied it!

This here was one o' 'em big old cats, a tom, movin' inside the shadows like he was a shadow hisself. He would take a step an' then pause, not turnin' er movin' at all, jest listenin', I reckon. I slipped the butt o' the Henry t' m' shoulder an' looked down the long octygon barrel. I moved the barrel 'round, tryin' t' relocate the cat but he was gone! I took the gun down an' searched the area with m' eyes, but they was no sign o' that dam' cat anywhar's!

I gathered up m' few things an', quiet as I could, I climbed down the hay loft ladder an' eased over t' the main barn door. I looked an' looked. Nothin'! Well, havin' l'arned the art o' the hunt from the best, the Injuns, I know'd that I had somehow disturbed the coug an' that I might as well haid on home as the chances was that he was long gone. I put the rifle butt first over m' shoulder an' haided back down t'ward m' camp at the crik.

I was within a hun'ded yards o' m' camp. I could smell the smoke o' m' fire an' could barely make out the glowin' o' the coals. I hear'd m' horse raisin' a ruckus an' I got t' thinkin' that perhaps the coug had come down here t' dine on horseflesh. It raised goosey bumps on m' skin an' I was jest startin' t' run down t' whar Bess was tied when somethin' hit me from behind so hard it knocked the breath completely out o' me!

I warn't even scairt 'case I was hurt too bad! I hit the ground so hard I smashed m' nose an' busted out one o' m' remainin' front tooths an' bit a fearsome hole clean through m' bottom lip. I ain't never been hit like that, a'fore er since, never! I hear'd a guesome scream, right in m' ear, follered by a blast o' the rankest breath I had ever smelt!

That dam' cat had stalked me all the way down here from that barn an' me, a seasoned hunter, takin' no notice o' it a'tall! Ol' Bess could smell him a'comin' an' had tried t' warn me, I reckon, but I swear I neither hear'd nor see'd that cat till it had me knocked me over an' pinned me down on m' belly while it seemed t' crawl up on me an' lay down the length o' m' back. Hell, I couldn't *see* him, even then, what with m' face slogged down into the dirt!

First he took a quick sniffle at me, I could feel the raspyness o' his whiskers agin'' the back o' m' haid, then he jest opened his mouth an' bared his fangs an' snatched a'holt o' m' neck, right below m' ears.

I could hear m' bones crunch as he bit down an' I could feel the blood runnin' down the back o' m' shirt an' down m' jaw, some o' it ran into m' mouth an' tasted like copper an' salt. The cat shook me real hard an' I could hear snappin' in m' neck an' along m' collarbone! It let go o' me fer a minute, takin' a break t' sharpin' his claws I reckon, which is what he did, shreddin' m' kinvas coat an' m' shirt an' diggin' his claws deep into m' hide.

He started snifflin' 'round m' haid an' neck agin', chewin' at m' scalp, an' a' lickin' the raw wound with his rough tongue, which was very painful. I was bracin' m'self fer another crunch when I hear'd voices! Sev'ral voices, an' the sound o' runnin' feet. I twisted m' face up out o' the dirt whar I had been scrunched down an' caught sight o' sev'ral people's feet as they ran t'ward me. Twistin' as much as I could, I looked up higher an' see'd they was carryin' torches. They kept on runnin' our way until I could hear that big cat hiss! He dug his claws deeper into m' back like he was either gonna finish me off er try an' drag me away with him. Sud'nly I could hear a dull, beating sound, like a ol' drum with a loose skin! It was them people a'whackin' that coug on his back an' sides with they torches! I could smell burnt hair an' hear shoutin' an' yellin' while they tried t' drive him off!

It seemed t' take a mighty long time, that cat must've figgerd he'd caught me fair 'n' square and I belonged t' him, but finally it lets out with two er three fearsome, snarlin' screams, lets go o' me, an' runs off t'ward the trees down by the water.

I guess I had been, what they call, "shocked" 'case I jest started t' drift away, like. I didn't know whether er not I was dyin' an' I didn't much care. It was peaceful. Ever' thing sounded far away an' echo'd like I was in a cave. When I opened m' eyes they was hard t' focus.

I felt hands on m' body an' I 'member bein' flipped over onto' m' back. By the light o' that buckskin moon an' the flickerin' shadows o' the torches, I could clearly see the face o' one o' 'em boys who had been a listenin' t' me talk earlier in the day. He was bended over, face only inches from m' own, a shoutin', "Are you all right, Mister? Are you all right? 'member me? Don't die, Mister! It's me, Grat! Gratton Dalton! I got a friend o' yourn with me, he's gonna he'p you, aw'right?"

Jest as I started t' drift away, I coulda swore I see'd a man's face come up over that boy's shoulder, an' I know'd that face! I tried t' talk but could not, 'cept fer t' say his name an' I said it like I was sayin' a prayer.

"Tree," I whispered, dragging his name out a long time, it echo'd in m' ears till I passed out o' cons'isness.

CHAPTER 15

They is no doubt in this worl' that 'em boys saved m' life! I was almos' two weeks a' fore I came 'round t' true cons'isness an' more than six weeks a' fore I was up an' 'round. So's not t' keep you in suspension, it was indeed m' old friend Tall Tree's face what I had see'd! He had met up with 'em same boys while he was huntin' by that crik earlier that summer. He said that the huntin' thar was good so he kept comin' back an' nearly ever' time 'em boys would find him, an' jabber at him an' ask him questions all day, till they became friends.

At first they had been a'scairt o' him, but by this time Tree had l'arned his English as well as any white man, (a consid'able sight better than mos', m'self included). He had also got t' dressin' somewhat like a white, wearin' a shirt an' trousers. But he still had a Injun way 'bout him in some things. He still wore lots o' beaded jewelry an' high-topped leather moc'sin-style boots.

He had said "howdy" t' 'em kids an' they weren't so scairt o' him no more, much. The boys know'd he was a Indian 'case o' his hair, which he was now wearin' "Crow" style, shaved on the sides with a high ridge, greased up in the middle, puttin' me in mind o' the backbone o' a razorback hog, an' he was a'huntin' that partic'lar day with a bow. He told me he gen'ally did these days 'case a gunshot often brought someone a runnin' down t' see who was on they prop'ty an' when they saw an Injun they usually went wild an' ran off screamin' into town fer he'p.

One time a feller had jest raised his gun an' started shootin' at pore Tree, without even findin' out who he was er what he was a' doin'! I guess he must've been a piss-pore shot though, as Tree said the man fired till the rifle was empty an' never got no closer than three feet o' 'im. Tree told me that he'd jest laughed at this here feller, p'inted his bow at him an' loosed a arrow what landed square between that fellers feet, then he turned an' slipped off into the woods.

I was powerful sick fer a while an' Tree was afeard I had got the rabies. 'Em boys had wanted t' take me up t' McIlvain's house but Tree 'splained t' 'em that if they did that then he couldn't watch over me an' that a dam' town doctor would shor'ly kill me. Instaid they went up an' told the old farmer that I had drove the cat off an' it would prob'ly die so I had left out o' thar. They said that I would be back in a month er two an' if that cat had come back that I would kill it then an' if it didn't that he could give me m' money when I show'd up. Tree said that the cat would prob'ly find a new territ'ry an' prob'ly would never return t' this farm.

I was what they call "decorous" fer a few days, out o' m' haid, you know? I had a fever an' 'course, couldn't eat none, couldn't even swaller thar, fer a while. Tree packed the bites an' scratches with slippery elm bark an' yarbs an' clean mud, that is mud he had laid out in the sunshine t' dry, an' then he put fresh, clean water on it t' make it mud agin'. He force fed me water with mashed up willer bark in it fer the pain, an' I kin 'member chokin' an' nearly drowndin' in it. Finally he got some hot broth down me which he made o' squirrel meat an' yarbs with ground up pra'rie cone flower in it, t' fight off the 'fection, an' I got better, but it was slow goin' an' real grad'al like.

When I was able t' talk I had 'bout eleventy million questions an' so did he. 'Em boys, brothers named Grat, Bob an' Emmett Dalton, would often come by an' listen t' what we was sayin' t' each other. If it was somethin' private like, me an' Tree would talk in Kaw an' 'em boys would set with they jaws hangin' slack in amaz'ment! I took pleasure from seein' they faces!

As fate would have it, 'em boys was cousins o' the Younger brothers! Don't that jest beat all? Cousins! It's a true fact, if'n you don't believe me it's in any old hist'ry book you care t' look at!

~

(Sister Doe says I'm gittin' ahaid o' m'self agin', but I got somethin' I want t' say 'bout 'em Dalton boys. I feel mighty guilty 'bout what happened t' 'em later in they lives 'case I believe that they idolized they cousins, the Younger's, an' the James boys. They read stories in 'em "penny dreadful" books an' they hear'd people like me a talkin' up as t' how grand' the life o' the outlaw was an' it was all a lie!

(Look at it! The only one's o' the bunch who turned out all right was Frank James. Later, after he was paroled, Cole Younger did good too, I reckon. But the rest o' 'em? Shot daid by the law, murdered by they "friends," er rottin' they lives away behind bars! Yes, indeedy, that shore does sound grand' now, don't it?

(Some years from when I know'd 'em, Doe sez it was in 1890, 'em Dalton boys formed up a gang o' they own an' was successful at a few feeble train robberies, like the James boys, but not on sech a grand' scale. Then one o' 'em came up with a harebrained idear, prob'ly little Grat who was m' fav'rite, but who always thought like a child, full o' ad-venture an' darin' do, but anyhow, som'body had an idear that would make 'em famous fer shore!

(See, they didn't rob nothin' fer money, 'case they didn't really need none, they was robbin' fer *glory,* b'case o' all 'em dam' stories they hear'd!

(Now this idear t' make 'em "famous" was that they would ride into they hometown o' Coffeyville, whar ever'body already know'd 'em, but they thought they was safe, wearin' some flimsy disguises o' fake beards an' mustaches that ever' body could see right through, an' t' hold up *two banks at the same time!* Now, that would make hist'ry!

(So, one October day, they rode into town with a couple o' they friends an' proceeded t' do one stupid thing after another, like little kids, although by this time they was grow'd up young men. First, like I said, ever'body rekinized 'em, right off, a few o' the townsfolk even waved as they rode by, callin' "howdy" t' 'em by name! The street in front o' 'em two banks, oppersite from each other, that street was all dug up fer repairs an' the hitchin' rails was down so the boys tied up they horses nearly a city block away!

(The feller who owned the hardware store nix door t' one o' 'em banks suspicioned what was goin' on so he starts passin' out his whole stock o' rifles, pist'ls an' ammunitions t' the citizens. Two o' the boys, Grat an' Emmett, I believe, went into the 1st National Bank an' took out almos' $20,000! On t'other side o' the street Bob an' the other two fellers went into the Condon & Comp'ny Bank whar a teller lied an' told 'em that the door t' the vault was on a timin' device an' could not be opened. Both sets o' boys walked out o' the banks at exac'ly the same time. In they wildest dreams they could never a' know'd what they was in fer!

(Well, I am sorry t' say that the streets was posit'vely lined with the local citizenry, fully armed an' ready, an' when them boys came out into the street som'body yelled, "Sorry, fellers," an' then 'em folks opened fire on 'em!

(Somehow beyond believin' them boys survived the initial fullisade an' actually managed t' shoot some o' the townsfolk, killin' four. A runnin' battle ensued, as they say, an' a' couple o' the boys even made it 'way down the street but then they ran into a blind alley whar they was trapped in an' killed like rats. Ever' blamed one o' 'em was killed 'cept fer Emmett an' he was shot up awful bad.

('Course he was captured an' so spent 15 years o' his young life in the penitentiary! Like I said, I sometimes wonder jest how much I am t' blame fer stirrin' 'em boys up with m' stories? 'Em boys was mighty good t' me when I needed it, an' it's a true fact that they was brave beyond they years, if not equally as stupid, an' they saved m' hide from that wildcat! I guess they got what they wanted, though. They became famous the day they was killed, you might say that they died tryin'.)

Thar, now. I had t' tell you that an' I reckon I do feel some better fer it now that it is out.

~

Anyways, Tree told me the story 'bout the folks in Council Grove a raidin' his village an' how they was a' bilin'' fer a 'scuse t' kill him an' his people. He said he had gone back thar many times t' talk t' the ghosts o' 'em what was killed. I asked him why he had never came t' our place an' he said 'case he feared fer his life an' that he weren't wantin' t' drag me an' mine into his troubles an' that he didn't know if I had ever came home er if I had been killed when I was with the cavalry. An', he said he warn't shore, fer a while any ways, whether er not he ever wanted t' be friends with a white man agin'.

The weeks dragged by an' anytime I said I was up t' it, Tree would move our camp further an' further south, away from the McIlvain farmstead. 'Em little Dalton boys found us ever'time an' finally we had t' tell 'em that we was leavin' these parts fer good an' event' ally we did that. We moved on down into the Territ'ry until I was able t' fend fer m'self. Tree said he had some fam'ly matters t' take care o', as his old granny Two Moon was still livin'. He was also kinda sweet on a Mesquakie girl name o' Wanbunaquatekwe, which is easier said as "White Cloud Woman," who was a livin' in the village with his granny.

We decided t' part comp'ny agin', fer now, as I had t' git back t' m' place at Di'mond Spring, but that we'd meet agin' 'round Christmas er the New Year. I warn't shore but I felt like it had t' be the first er the middle o' the month o' December by this time an' long ago I had promised Lizzy that I would be home a' fore her weddin' on Chris'mas Day. It seemed like years had passed since I had been home.

A' fore we parted Tree gave me a wonderful gift! You know, mos' all o' the tribes I ever ran into, with a few 'ceptions, was generous t' a fault! That's why they was sech suckers t' sign some o' 'em worthless treaties.

All the whites had t' do was t' give the Indians a few gifts an' then they would feel obleeged t' "tetch the pen" fer they "friend," the white man, who had been so open-handed with 'em! 'Course the whites was very aware o' this tradition early in the game, an' it was o'ficial, if unspoken, United State's Gov'ment policy t' take advantage o' they belief that a gift must be repaid with another gift.

Anyway, Tree walked over t' his pony an' reached into a beaver bag that was slung alongside his bow an' quiver. He brought it back over an' dug out a soft, worked, hidebound bundle an' handed it t' me. It was heavy! Inside was a Smith & Wesson Amerikin .44 De-luxe Pist'l, silver plated, scroll-'graved with ivory grips 'graved with a eagle killin' a rattler, which he told me is the emblem o' Mexico!

It was a mighty rare piece, an' a fine one, with a modified barrel, short, like the gunfighter's used (the short barrel was a sacrifice fer acc'racy an' distance, but the gun was easier t' handle, well balanced, an' would clear the holster smooth an' easy). A pist'l like this would have cost the average man 5 er 6 months salary! They was a deerskin holster, very fine, an' a tin box o' cat'ridges, too!

I was tetched an' I choked up some. While I was a standin' thar, snifflin', lookin' at the pist'l then at the ground, thinkin o' what I was goin' t' say, an' by the time I looked up, Tree had done mounted his horse an' had slipped away into the underbrush.

CHAPTER 16

I was in purty good shape by the time I started the long ride back, but ridin' made me sore as Hades, o' course. Somewhar's I took a wrong trail, I reckon, seein's how this was a unfamiliar part o' the country t' me, an' I had gone a bit too far north, an' actually a little ways back east a' fore I got m'self straightened out. I still had m' money an' I decided that I wouldn't mind sleepin' under a roof' fer a change as it had been a pow'rful long time.

I passed a homestead an' asked if they was a town nearby with a hotel, an' they said they was a little burg called Parsons but that it was back even further t' the east which was not agreeable t' me. I know'd these folks didn't have no extry room as they house was a tiny, little soddy an' I counted at least three youngins a clingin' t' they mama's skirts so I didn't even ask 'em.

They said they was another homestead called Bender's Mound yonder, jest 'bout a ha'f a days ride west, which served food an' worshed clothes an' sech, an' that sounded like the bet I needed. I thanked 'em kindly an' continued on. Bess throw'd a shoe, which is only surprisin' in that it hadn't happened a long before, considerin' the amazin' amount o' ground we had covered an' how wore down the iron was, so I had t' stop an' pry off the other three shoes. Then her hoof's was tender an' I had t' ride slow an' try t' avoid rocky ground so's she wouldn't go gimp on me.

It warn't long a' fore I could see'd the mound on the horizon an' a homemade sign by the trail said, "Lodging. Last Chanst' ahaid". I rode up into the barnyard o' a sorry lookin' dugout type o' soddy with a few wooden outbuilding's with chickens an' a few turkeys an' guineas peckin' 'round the bare yard. They was a flimsy, lean-to barn with a couple o' mules an' four er five very good lookin' horses. They also seemed t' be a great many carts an' small wagons lined up behind the lean-t' an' a corral with at least 15 more horses an' ponies an' mules. They was also four er five oxen in a wood pen off t' one side.

They was consid'able money tied up in horseflesh, it seemed t' me, considerin' how shabby the place was in gen'ral. Back in them days a horse er a mule was a mighty big investment fer any body, but lordy what a herd they had!

A tall, rangy lookin' feller came out o' the barn, a lookin' at me right suspicious like, a wiping' his hands on the laigs o' his kinvas bib overalls. A equally rangy lookin' woman follered him out into the sunlight an' in a minute er two here come a youngish feller, more a boy than a man, who looked dim witted t' me. I asked if they had a bed fer the night an' the feller an' his wife brightened consid'able.

The first words he spoke t' me, after eyein' me an' m' horse up an' down, was, "You gots any money?" I took o' fense at his pore manners an' considered turnin' Bess an' ridin' off, but she was already startin' t' favor her right front hoof an' I know'd she needed t' rest. "I got 'nuff money fer a room here fer a day er two, I reckon, if'n you got somethin' what meets m' stand'rds," I said in a snooty kind o' way.

I had already decided I didn't like this feller and I didn't mind if he know'd it or not. Fact o' the matter was, I didn't like the look o' the whole shebang and didn't cotton t' bein' talked down t' by the likes o' him.

"Fine, fine," this feller says, "Cost ye a dollar a day, though." I studied him fer a minute an' then I said that I had passed a night in a luxshury hotel in Manhattan fer a dollar an' a ha'f once't, so I was a figurin' on some laripin' food an' plenty o' it, seein's that these acommydations did not look what a feller would call, "de-luxe."

They was greed in his eyes an' if he took any o' fense at m' uppity manners he didn't show it none. "Ol' lady here, she's a fine cook, a fine cook. Here, let the boy take yer pony, mister, an' git down an' come in an' rest yer weary, travelin' bones a spell. M' name is John Bender an' this h'yre boy is John Jr. The old woman is m'wife, her name is Sarey. Gots a girl, too, a purty one," an' he winked. "She's off to town fer some supplies fer our supper this evenin'. Now, you git down from that 'ere horse an' let us accomydate you."

When he mentioned his daughter they was a kind of a leer in his voice an' in his eyes. That ol' woman noticed it too, I think, cause she looked up at him with pure hate in her tired blue eyes. You know, lots o' fellers in m' generation is a bit hushed up an' confident'l when it comes t' discussin' relations with women folk 'case that is how we was raised up an' we find it embarassin' an', frankly, nobody else's business. They way that old man acted disgusted me, I reckon. But I gots t' say that when that girl got back she was a *sight* t' see! She shore 'nuff took m' breath away!

Her name was Kate an' I have never see'd a more beautiful woman in m' days before or after! She was prob'ly 19 er 20 year old, had sky blue eyes an' yallar hair that came down in two big braids, Indian style, an' curled 'round her, uh, *ample* bosoms. Her hips had a way o' shiftin' as she walked away from a feller that made it hard not t' look, but jedging' by her manners, she didn't mind that none.

Her pa was ferever kissin' 'round on her an' a' ticklin' an' a' feelin' her in a way that I found t' be not quite right. She paid him no never-mind, though. She introduced herself t' me an' spoke in a low, intimate voice, a battin' an' a flutterin' her eyes so's I finally asked her if she'd had a cinder blow in 'em.

She slipped her arm through mine, laid her haid on m' shoulder and laughed an' said, no, but they was so much dust that it sometimes got into her eyelashes which was way too long, didn't I think? An' I said, why no, I didn't they that they was too long a'tall an' that I found her eyes t' be real purty an' she giggled an' put her chin down on one shoulder an' looked at me like she was a little girl o' eight, a'poutin' over somethin'. Tryin' t' keep m' eyes in a respec'ful mode, I foller'd her t' the door o' the soddy an' on into the darkness.

Well, it was somethin' in thar. Right big, fer a soddy, I must say, with one big room prob'ly 15 by 20 feet, I reckon, built back into the hill like a dugout. They was three doorways covered with blankets that I reckoned was bedrooms, since the big room had ever'thing else, cook stove, table, pianer. I noticed that they was a lot o' awful nice things in this rude little hole an' they kinda looked out o' place thar, lamps an' what-not's an' nice pitchers in frames an' doily's an' the like. They was a massive big table with the laigs carved with dragons and snakes and the like, which was pushed up agin' a big kinvas curtain at the far end o' the room. I asked what was behind the curtain an' the old man jumped in an' said why, they was a big storage room back thar, a "pantry," he called it.

It was disquietin' in a way I kinnot describe! The whole place had a bad feelin' t' it an' it made me uncomfir'ble. It was dark as a cellar and they was an underlyin' stink 'bout the place.

The fam'ly all seemed anxious an' they was somethin' woofish 'bout 'em, like they was all in a hurry fer somethin' t' happen, all excited, like. I asked whar I was sleepin' an' the girl took m' hand an' led me through one o' the curtain's into a tiny little room no bigger than 4 x 8 feet. They was a pow'rful fancy bed crammed in thar an' a big chest o' drawers which must have been dismantled, taken into the room in pieces, an' put back t'gither inside. It was up agin' the wall near the entrance. They was not 'nuff space t' swing a daid cat in that room! As soon as I took a step inside m' shins was up agin' the bedstead. A feller would have t' stand on the mattress t' git hisself dressed.

"It'll do," I said. I turned an' Kate was blockin' the door with her body, arms folded, laigs stanced apart as if she was guardin' it an' determined t' block m' way. I cleared m' throat an' made t' git 'round her when she reached up an' throw'd her arms 'round m' shoulders an' started t' kissin' me right on m' mouth! I weren't opposed t' it, mind you, jest surprised, more so when she jammed her tongue between m' lips. It scairt me some! I had been kissed a' fore, but not like that! Her body was hot an' softer than I could've imagined a person's could be and, lordy, she smelt good, like vaniller!

I tried t' push her away but she wouldn't let me go. Finally I put both hands on her shoulders an' braced m' feet against the laig o' the bedstead and shoved her, hard! Fer a minute thar they was murder in them purty blue eyes. Then she relaxed, smiled an' leaned forward an' whispered somethin' in m' ear that makes me blush t' this day an' which I ain't 'bout t' repeat t' m' sister, Doe, who, as you may 'member, is takin' this all down!

Kate turned an' left the room, lookin' back at me over her shoulder an' winkin' at me. I stuck m' haid out an' announced t' the rest o' 'em that I was gonna be a' sleepin' an' fer that boy t' make dam' shore he took good care o' m' horse an' that I was t' be waked up fer vittles.

Old man Bender cleared his throat an' asked if I intended t' pay fer the lodgin' in advance. I told him all I had was two $20 gold pieces an' that he would have t' be able t' make change. A sly look came over him an' he acted real frien'ly sayin' he was shore that I, ap'arently a man of consid'able means, could be trusted fer the paltry amount due.

A' fore I conked out I dragged that big chest o' drawers over t' block the entrance. His voice came through he curtain askin' what I was a 'doin' an' tellin' me I would be responsible fer any damages t' the furnishin's! If I hadn't been so dog tired I would have marched straight out of that hell-hole an' hit the trail.

Wish t' the devil that I had o'!

I waked up but I don't know how much later. You see, they is no sunlight inside a dugout so I couldn't say if I had slept a hour er a day! As it turned out, it was evenin' time an' I could smell good cookin' smells an' I was hongry. I slid the chest o' drawers out o' m' way an' walked into the main room in m' sock feet. No body was thar but the old harridan, Sarey, who was a' standin' at the cook stove. I asked her the time an' she told me she guessed it was 'bout 5 of th' clock in the evenin'. She said it was startin' t' snow a bit outside an' was a' gittin' dark awful early as it does this time o' year. She talked plenty, I reckon, fer country folk, but she would never, ever look me in the face. I ask' her what smelt so good an' I swear, she blushed!

"Why, thankee," she said an' she told me she was a' fryin' a brace o' fresh rabbit, biled 'taters, biled leather britches, oven corn bread an' flour gravy. She had set the table with four plates an' they was a cellar o' salt an' another o' sugar on the table along with a pitcher o' hunny an' a stone crock o' fresh churned butter! I asked her who was missin' from the table as they was only four settin's she looked over at me an' said, "Nobody."

A few minutes later she walked out an' yelled at the old man t' come an' eat an' t' fetch the boy with him. Katie yelled back that they was people comin' down on the pra'rie. I walked out m'self an' from whar 'em three was a standin' they could see the entire pra'rie in all directions jest as far as they eyes was good enough t' see. The snow was startin' t' blow 'round, an' it shore was gittin' dark, but down thar on the pra'rie, way off in the distance, shore 'nuff, I could see some folks comin' this way.

I thought 'bout this an' I realized, now that I was rested an' thinkin' a might clearer, that Katie had shore got back "from town" quick when I had first arrived. I bet you she was up thar a watchin' out fer trav'lers whilst the others was a' workin'. That was a puzzle t' me, too. What was it that these folks did?

You see, they warn't no crops ner a orchard er nothin' that I could see that would take up they time, other than arranging all 'em carts an' wagons, feedin' the livestock an' mebe shootin' some game fer vittles. It seemed doubtful t' me that they would be enough trav'lers in these parts t' earn very much o' a livin' specially if'n a feller liked t' own horses the way old man Bender seemed t'. Horses is a encumbrance in that they ain't cheap t' feed nor t' care for. Anybody what owns more'n three er four horses will tell ye that there's always something ailing at least one o' 'em at any given time.

I went back t' m' room an' fetched m' boots an' m' duster an' bundled up agin'' the cold. I went outside an' I walked over t'ward that lean-t' barn an' old man Bender jest came a bilin' out o' thar as if t' cut me off. He was all smiles showin' the last five er six yallar teeth what he had left in his haid, askin' me if I was needin' anything an' t' please stay away from the barn. I said that m' horse was inside an' that I was gonna check on her an' he said, no, no sir, yer horse is jest fine, no need t' go inside that 'ere barn a'tall.

"I tol' the boy to put on some good shoes on yer pony, don't know if he did it yet, but if'n so, it's only 2-bits a hoof. I know'd you'd want shoes 'case yer horse was a goin' lame. I know'd you could afford it, mister. We're gonna take care of you an' yer horse. No sir, yer hoss is fine. It's dark in 'ere, jest wait till mornin'. That's what I'd do if'n I was you…"

But I jest kinda pushed him aside an' said, "Mister Bender, I ain't a' askin' you fer permission, I am a' tellin' you that I *am* gonna check on m' horse".

I ain't a big feller but it is clear t' all who see's me that I am tough an' I am wiry. 'Sides, 'em big scars all over m' haid an' the side o' m'face left by that coug an' the beatin' I took in Chicago likely did make me look meaner than a rattlesnake, an' Bender, he jest stepped aside an' I passed.

Bess was inside all fidgety an' stampin' her hoof's an' snortin'. I walked over and ca'med her down a bit, a talkin' to her and blowin' my breath into her nostrils. She had four new shoes and it looked like that half-wit had did a helluva good job a' puttin' 'em on and trimmin' her hoofs an' sech. 'Cept fer bein' scary she seemed to be in good shape.

The place had a uncommon foul stench t' it, not a good, earthy animal smell, neither, but whatever the stink was I couldn't put my finger to it. An' the ol' man was right, it was dark as a grave, but other than that it seemed fine.

I did notice one odd thing, they was a shelf up agin' the wall an' a curtain *behind* the shelf an' the curtain was movin' as if they was a breeze behind it, like mebe it lead into a cellar, p'rhaps. On this shelf was a passel o' clothes an' boots, men's stuff mos'ly, some nearly new, some threadbare an' near worn out.

Bender caught me a lookin' an' he said, "Lookin' fer any clothin' er boots, young feller? We buys 'em off'n folks what has packed too much stuff fer they travels. That's whar we gots mos' o' the stuff o' ourn, from folks that's jest gots too much, doncha know? City folks! They shore don't know nothin' 'bout pioneerin', does they?" I jest looked at him, he bein' all hoppy an' agytated, an' I said nothin'.

I turned fer the soddy. "Supper time," I said.

Kate came down from her perch an' said the trav'lers would be thar within the hour, she reckoned, later if'n the snow picked up. We went inside t' eat an' the whole fam'ly was jumpy.

They kept tryin' t' insist that I set at the far end o' the table with m' back t' the kinvas curtain an' I kept tellin' 'em, fer no real reason 'cept t' see 'em squirm, that I did not never set with m' back t' no wall 'case I had traveled with both Mr. Frank an' Mr. Jesse James an' that they had both done taught me t' never ever sit that away. Well, finally old John said, kind o' huffy like, "Well, you suit yerse'f then! Don't give much o' a dam' whar ye set er if'n ye set a'tall."

They was all right nasty and mean t' the younger feller, an' now that the old man was in a' poutin' mood, why, he would reach out an' fetch the boy a slap t' the haid ever' few minutes, like, a' cussin' him somethin' fearful fer this er that little thing which he said the boy was a doin' jest t' ir'tate him.

O' course this made the pore boy as nervous as a long-tailed cat in a room full o' rockin' chairs and it warn't long afore he accidental dropped a spoon on the floor. I thought that old man Bender was gonna bust a vein in his neck, the way he carried on!

When the younger feller leaned over t' pick up the spoon, the old man kicked the laig out from under his chair and sent him a' sprawlin'. Then he stood up and made as if he was a' gonna kick this poor youngin whilst he was sprawled out there on the floor!

I half stood up and said, quiet an' low like, "Thar now, sit down, that's enough!"

Bender said, "You otter mind yer own business, stranger, this here is m' house and I'll do the decidin' when I wants t' discipline the likes o' this dirty whelp! I'll thankee t' be mindful o' yer own beeswax!"

Well, 'case o' where I was and who I was with, I was wearin' m' pist'l, which is not a thing I would normally do inside a house. I raised m' hand and placed it on the butt o' the gun an' said, "It is yer house, Mister Bender, an' I reckon he's yourn t' do with as you please. But I will tell ye this, mister; if I so much as see you lift yer hand t' him agin' whilst I'm a payin' boarder under this here roof', er if I hear him so much as whimper, I will pull out this choice, Mexikin pistola o' mine an' I will whip you with it 'bout yer haid and yer shoulders till either this fine, pearly handle er your skully bone cracks like a walnut! Do you understan' me, Mister John Bender?"

I reckon' I figur'd he would cow-tow t' me, right off, but fer the slightest instant I believed he was gonna lunge fer me! His face was jest purple with rage, but by the time he'd turned t'ward me I had draw'd the pist'l and had leveled, pinted straight at his bony haid. In the daid silence o' that hole in the ground, the sound o' the hammer a' ratchetin' back and the dry, turnin' o' the cylinder was right musical!

"Mister Bender, I have cleared leather and the angle of this here sidearm ain't no longer 'ntended to merely whup knots up on yer bald haid…"

He seemed t' shrink a size er two an', grumblin' t' hisse'f, he snarled at the boy an' then he went back t' his chair an' set his boney se'f down.

Katie giggled and Sarey clucked t' herse'f like a ol' hen. The young feller got up, lookin' like a whipped pup, an' draw'd his chair back t' the table as far away from the ol' man an' as close t' me as he could git.

In a minute er two ever'body had ca'med down a bit and started t' git down t' the business o' woofin' down they supper.

Kate was a settin' on one side o' the table an' I had figur'd I'd be a good deal safer as far away from her as I could git, an' though I would be lyin' t' say I did not desire fer her somethin' fierce, I had set m'se'f oppersite her fer my own well-bein'!

It didn't do no good, though, sittin' 'cross from her. She kicked off her shoe an' started runnin' her toes 'way too high up on m' laig an' I had t' scootch m' chair back farther an' farther from the table so's that event' ally I was havin' t' reach arms length t' git a spoonful o' food.

(Like mos' folks in 'em days we only et with spoons. If a feller had a side knife, an' I did, why you could pull it out an' he'p cut whatever meat you had. If'n nobody else had nary a knife why, you passed yer's 'round the table so's they could use it, too.)

Fer whatever reason I did not o'fer m' knife t' the others. Otherwise they had t' use a big old butcherin' knife, er eat with they hands, which was not considered good manners at the table. Anywise, manners didn't seem t' be none too important t' these here folks, Big John an' Little John both ate with they fingers anyways, mos'ly, an' smacked an' grunted like animals. Then the old man would belch, then the boy would, then the old man would raise his hand an' threaten t' slap him right smart on the back o' his haid, an' cuss him, some, all the while glancin' over at me an' smilin' a sickly, 'postum smile as if t' imply he was only funnin' with the boy.

Finally the boy choked on a rabbit bone an' I half hoped he'd die from it, but his daddy fetched him a bone rattlin' punch t' his back an' he spit that bone clear 'cross the table an' it bounced off'n the wall!

Afeard o' what I might do, the old man looked over at me, gravy dribblin' down his chin, an' said, "What? He was *chokin'*!"

Ever' time I'd try t' take a gulp o' m' coffee Kate would manage t' kick me in the tenders an cause me t' spill it on m' shirt. Finally, t' eat in peace from Kate, I had t' take m' plate off'n the table an' I hold it in m' lap an' et that a'way!

Kate never et nothin' t' speak o' an' Sarey did not ever sit down at the table. It had been her place that was a missin'. I reckon she et later, but I don't know. She jest a kept on cluckin' an' cookin' stuff as they was expectin' 'em other trav'lers t' p'rhaps stop in, which they did 'bout a hour er two later, I reckon.

It was a man an' a boy, name o' Williams. They was a big fuss made over 'em when they came an' I felt it was gittin' crowded an' I was unusual tired, so I 'scused m'self t' m' room. I was also a bit jealous as Kate was a flirtin' with this man *an'* his son, who was no more than 15 year old as though I warn't even thar a'tall. I will admit that it did make me pout some.

I was still feelin' somewhat hinky after m' injuries as I shore was not used t' bein' up an' 'round an' travelin' an' all like I had been, so I refilled m' coffee cup and went back inside m' room an' laid down t' rest and t' try to think.

Dam' it was dark, as they was only a kindle an' a small miner's lamp t' light things up with. They was water drippin' down the far wall from up above, a spring perhaps, an' I watched the light play on it till I drifted off.

I must've been dreamin', er so I thought, 'case I was roused up some when I hear'd a loud whackin' sound an' a sharp cry which was quickly muffled an' then two er three more whackin' sounds, like someone hittin' a pun'kin with a stick? I 'member thinkin' that old man Bender was prob'ly beatin' up on the boy again, but I didn't seem t' give a hang. I was feelin' fearful tired an' drowsly.

I was jest awful thirsty an', although I had drank near a pot o' coffee at supper, I found that I could barely git up, but I finally did, I staggered t' the curtain an' said, in a thick, drunk voice that didn't sound t' me like it was even m' own, "Howdy! Say, what's a' goin' on in thar?" I don't recall as they was any answer, an' I pushed that chest o' drawers acrost the entryway, then fell backwards onto' the bed an' slept some more.

When I waked up nix mornin' (I reckon'd it was mornin') I was groggy an' muddle haided. I pushed aside the furniture from the door and walked out into the big room. I ask whar the Williams' was an' Sarey, who was the only one in sight, said that had hided out early so's t' git a good day's travel in afore the snow started a blowin'. I noticed a dark stain on the kinvas curtain. I sidled over t' that part o' the room, nosin' 'round, so t' speak, an' my, did it make her jumpy!

"You go on an' git back from thar," she said. I asked her "Why?" but she jest mumbled an' an' clucked an' fidgeted. I jest went on a glancin' 'round, an' directly I see'd somethin' small an' white on the floor an' when the old woman was a lookin' into her oven, why, I bent down an' snatched it up. As I did, I see'd another item that looked like a man's coin purse, so I grabbed it up too, an' I walked back t' m' room. I turned up the wick o' m' lantern an' looked at them things. The first one was smooth an' white with a dark spot on one side, I looked close an' I see'd it was a tooth! A human tooth! The second thing, the thing that I thought had looked like a purse? Well, that there thing was a ear! A man's ear!

They was little, bristly hairs growin' inside it an' a hank o' bloody haid hair attached t' a piece o' skin hangin' off'n it! I had a wash basin in m' room, on top o' that chest o' drawers, which was a right handy place fer me t' vomit in. So I did.

CHAPTER 17

They was only one thing I could do, fer shore at that time, an' that was t' clear t' hell out o' this stink-hole!

I figure that they must've put somethin' into m' food er, most likely, the coffee at supper the night a' fore 'case I still jest could not think right! I will admit that I was scairt an' weak in the knees an' I was all trembly, like. I kept thinkin' I had t' git t' m' saddle pack whar I kept that Henry .44 rifle. I don't know why I thought I needed the rifle as I had the handgun what had been a gift from Tree, but it seemed at the time that only the Henry would do and I was on fire t' git it. I reckon I had fergot 'bout the pist'l.

The longer I stewed the more confused I got. I sat back on the bed an' when I did I finally thought o' the revolver but discovered I was no longer a' wearin' it! This panic'd me some and I convinced m'se'f fer shore that Katie er som'body had stoled it. I got up and paced, er what passed fer pacin' in that tiny room. Then I sit down on a chair and when I did I found m' a small, leather pack whar I keeps m' razor an' sech as that, an' I felt the pist'l! It was like a gift from Gawd Aw'mighty! M' belly flip-flopped an' I thought t' m'self, "Hally-loo! I am *saved!*"

Quick as I could, I checked the gun fer loads and found all 6 rounds snug in the cylinder. I emptied the cat'ridge box into m' hand an' shoved the bullets into m' front trouser pocket. I slipped the gun back into the deer skin holster an' started t' hook it onto' m' belt but instaid I jammed the whole thing into the front o' m' trousers, neith m' shirt.

I slid the chest o' drawers away from the entry an' walked out into the main room. I was real dizzy an' was weavin' like I was drunk!

Sarey came up from out o' the shadows an', fer the very first time, looked right up into m' face, her ol' hag's face all saggy an' lookin' like a skully bone covered with parchment, hair a' stickin' out like straws on a wore-out broom, but her blue eyes was a' sparkin'!

"Why sakes, you look sick boy! Here, let me fetch you some coffee, you need some, I'd say. Here, take a drink from this here cup (it ain't too hot, is it?) then you kin go back an' lay down an' we'll take care o' you. Go on, now son, Sarey will watch over you, now."

I meant t' keep m' voice level, but instaid I shouted, "No," an' knocked the cup from out o' her hand. It was a tin cup so it didn't break, but it made a hell o' a racket agin' the wood plank floor down in that hole o' a soddy!

I hear'd scufflin' and, shore enough, Old John an' Young John came a runnin' in, the boy was ha'f carryin', ha'f draggin' a sledgehammer! "What's goin' on h'yre," Old John asked, "What's ailin' you, mister?"

"Why, he's sick like a dog," Sarey whined, "An' he's ha'f out his mind, why he won't let me he'p him none! I jest tried t' give him a little sweet-cream coffee an' he knocked it plumb out o' m' hand! He's a might ingrateful, this one is, an' pore ol' Sarey doin' all she kin fer him. He knows I don't mean him no harm. Mebe you kin teach him right, John."

"Shet up, you ol' biddy," the old man hollar'd, an' then, fer *no reason at all*, 'cept mebe t' show his own se'f who was in charge, he reached over an' punched the younger feller with his closed fist, punched him so hard in the back o' his haid that he fell down t' his knees an' would have gone on down on his face, too, 'cept that the old man grabbed him by his ear an' pulled him back up, shakin' him an' callin' him ever' vile name in the book!

Then the old coot started slowly movin' t'ward me 'cross that big old room an' he said,"Now you hold on, son, we runs us a good house, here, an' Sarey works tol'able hard an' we cain't have you in h'yre like you was a livin' in a barn! Now you drink ye coffee, like a good feller, an' go lay down a spell. Do that, boy, an' I'll send Kate in t' check on you. I promise. An' she'll check you over right good, too, I betcha…"

He said that, leerin' like a jacky-lantern, an' it made me disgusted! I hear'd a sound an' looked behind me an' I see'd that big kinvas curtain shimmer.

I called out an' asked who was back thar but they warn't no answer. I jammed m' hand inside m' shirt an' I pulled out that Smith & Wesson an' I cocked the hammer back with m' thumb, an' as I have said before, what a plum beautiful sound that is! A fine, per'cision machine a' gittin' ready t' do the work what it was made t' do!

An' believe me when I tell you that the sound o' that hammer is unmistak'ble t' anyone who's ever hear'd it a' fore. They all froze in they tracks an' I said agin', "Who ever is behind that curtain has jest 'bout three seconds t' show theyse'ves er I'm goin' t' bore some holes an' see what comes a' leakin' out!"

Out steps Kate, jest as dainty as you might please, sayin' "Why, it's jest me, young feller! Ain't nothin' t' be afear'd o'. Jest little ol' Katie. Say, now, you know I been missin' you!" She started t' sashay t'ward me till I p'inted the gun at her face. "They is som'body else back thar, too! I see'd his boots. Now, come on out." The curtain parted agin' an' a great big, tall feller what I'd never seen a' fore came out, kinda ginger like.

He looked t' be a member o' the fam'ly, the same color eyes an' hair an' the same features on his face, 'cept he was good lookin', like Kate. I was real confused an' dizzy an' I thought I might git sick agin er fall down on the floor but I know'd I'd better t' hold on if'n I planned t' live very long. I leaned back again' the wall and said, "Who the hell are you?"

"Why that's m' oldest boy, young feller, that's John Jr."

"You said the youngins' name was "John Jr.," I said.

"Well, uh, he ain't! His name is Robert, sometimes, why, I gits 'em confused, see? That thar big 'un is John an' this little whelp here is Robert, our dear little 'Bobby'", (he retched out like he was gonna hug 'im but instaid he slapped the boy on the back o' his haid, agin'!)

"Young John, he jest got back from the Territ'ry. Been huntin' down thar, ain't ye, son?"

From the looks o' him he had been huntin' somethin', all right! He was wearin' a leather apron an' it was all shiny, wet an' black. So was his boots. I could smell him from whar I stood an' he smelt like a butcher! I walked over t'ward him, waivin' him out o' m' way with the pist'l. He moved over by his Pa an' the little feller, who was a rubbin' his noggin' an' lookin' dazed, 'n' I sidled up t' that big curtain. Keepin' a eye on 'em I peaked behind it. They was a chair behind the curtain an' beside it, on the floor, was two er three different sizes o' hammers an' a big, double-edge ax!

Behind all this was a entryway into what looked t' be a burrow! They was dark splotches on the floor boards an' drips'n'draps o' spots leadin' off down the tunnel.

It didn't take no genie t' know that it was blood what caused them stains, an' I figur'd I know'd what had been goin' on here. The chair was facin' the eatin' table so's that a body a sittin' in that spot whar they had tried so hard t' git me t' sit would've had his back t' the kinvas an' the chair behind it!

The smell from that tunnel was awful an' I thought fer shore I was a gonna heave agin. It was all crowdin' in on m' mind an' I didn't have nary an idear as t' what it was that I was a' gonna do.

I hear'd a skittery sound an' I turned 'round t' see that Old John had taken the sledge from the boy an' was a slitherin' 'cross the floor t'ward me like one o' them orangatangy apes, an' was jest in the act o' raisin' it high up over his haid.

Sarey screamed, "Look out, Pa, look out," an' a' fore I even thought 'bout it the pist'l in m' hand fired off like a parade cannon an' I dropped that ol' sono'abitch like a sack o' taters, with a hole through his chest so big I swear that in the second afore he fell I could see the lamp behind him burnin' through! He flopped some, like a chicken with his haid chopped off, an' he made some chokey, watery sounds in his throat. The blood squirted high enough t' spray the youngest boy's face an' t' drench the front o' Kate's blue dress. It seemed t' me that the sound o' the shot was still a' bouncin' 'round the room.

Nobody moved, 'cept the little feller who appeared t' swoon an' fell down on his knees agin'. The other three jest stood thar like they was stone statues, mouths gapin' open, eyes wide, lookin' down at Old John on the floor who was lookin' up at 'em with the very same expression o' surprise, only he was daid! I had never shot a human bein' a' fore 'cept fer mebe that time when we was fightin' Indian's, but that weren't the same, 'case that was war but this was real person'l and right up close.

It was a scary feelin', but it was not a bad feelin' and I'd be a liar if I said that it was. An' besides, it was one hell of a shot, right through that ol' monister's heart, which was a dam' small target, I will add.

I was tarrible excited an' I turned the gun on t' Sarey an' I motioned her over t' stand with the others. She couldn't seem t' move so I pushed her, hard, an' she stumbled over. She slipped in the blood an' her feet went up over her haid an' she landed on her back by Old John's body. She didn't cry none, but she whined like a whup'd dog an' it was plain t' see that she was scairt as hell! The youngest boy had wet hisself an' he started t' blubberin' 'bout "Please don't kill me, mister. Kill t' others, if ye must, but please don't harm me". It made me weary t' hear it.

Kate spoke up, ca'm as you please, like butter wouldn't melt in her mouth, an' she said, "He ain't a gonna kill anybody, 'specially little Kate, are you, han'some? Naw, you ain't a'gonna shoot Kate, 'case you need Katie t' take care o' you, Oscar. That's yer name, ain't it? See, I even remembered yer name!

"An', believe me, young feller, I knows how t' take care o' a young buck like you! It'll be jes' you an' me. We'll ride off from this here place an' we kin have a awful good time, if'n you know what I mean, an' I'm shore that you do. We could git married, you know, settle down, if'n you wants to."

I know'd exa'ctaly what she meant an' the idear o' bein' "took care o'" by Kate Bender was a soberin' thought! She was a she-woof an' if ever anybody born in this worl' was real, true evil, it was Katie Bender.

I told John Jr., the big 'un, that is, t' tie up the rest o' 'em an' not t' pull no monkey shines er I'd use that pist'l barrel t' whup knots on his haid faster than he could rub 'em, an' I meant it, too. I told 'em all that I had no intention o' killin' anybody who didn't need it an' that give 'em somthin' t' chew on while they was bein tied up.

M' haid seem t' be clearin' up some an' I thought 'bout this thing, fer a minute an' I told Big John t' untie L'il John er Robert er "Bobby" er whoever the hell he was, which he did. Then I told the boy t' tie up the big feller! They thought I was crazy but it had 'curred t' me that if I was a' goin' down into that 'ere tunnel, an' I was, then som'body was a' goin' with me. Now, was I gonna take a big, heavy, grow'd man who, at any turn, might overpow'r me an' break m' neck er bust m' haid?

Was I gonna take Sarey who had already had a big hand in tryin' t' kill me, who was set in her ways an' probably already plottin' revenge fer the death o' the old man?

Was I gonna take Kate? *Hell no*! That would be like a fly invitin' a black widder t' the Grange dance! In her own way she could overpow'r me a lot quicker than Big John. No! I needed t' take the littlest feller thar. He was smaller than me an' weaker; he was scairt o' me 'case he'd see'd me ruthlessly gun down the old man. An' he was young! His ways was not yet set in stone an' he might see the light an' still turn into a real person. I figur'd it was already 'way t' late fer 'em other three.

Believe me when I say that I made dam' shore 'em ropes was strong an' tied tight. I cain't imagin' no worser o' a fate than bein' down under the ground, beneath this place, an' a' worryin' whether er not one o' these birds o' prey was on the loose, stalkin' me through the darkness like a bunch o' ghosts. It gave me the creepin' crawlies jest imaginin' it!

I told the boy t' grab a lamp an' when he was slow t' react I stomped m' boot heel down hard on the floor an' yelled, "I mean now, dam' you!" He moved, right smartly.

I pushed him ahaid o' me an' we haided t' ward the doorway behind the kinvas curtain. Kate called out, "You ain't jest leavin' us here, are you? How long you plan t' be gone? What if I have t' use the, the uh, 'acomydations'? What then? Hey, now, you answer me, you sono'abitch! Hey! *You cain't jes' leave us tied up here! Come back! You hear me?*"

I could hear her yammerin' all the way into the mouth o' the tunnel. As we stepped inside I looked back at her, her face was red an' they was spit runnin' out the corners o' her mouth an' down her chin. The front o' her dress was turnin' black with Old John's dryin' blood an' I swear she looked like some kind o' fire an' brimstone demon, er a preacher, a sittin' thar, strainin' an' twistin' at her bonds. She had gone plum his'tar'ical. The look in her eyes made the thought o' us goin' into the blackness o' that tunnel right down invitin'!

I warn't shore whether er not the little feller, who I will now call Robert, had ever been down this hole afore. He acted jest as scairt an' nervous as I did an' he shore didn't seem t' have any idear whar he was a'goin'. It had smelt bad on the outside, an' now, as we was goin' in, ever' step got worst an' worst. The boy puked, but I jest dry-heaved a lot as I had already emptied m' belly earlier in the wash basin.

It is hard t' say fer shore, but I reckon we went down 'bout ten, mebe twen'y foot er so below the level o' the dugout's floor. The decline was a gradual thing, but it would have took one hell o' a bunch o' hard, back breakin' work t' have dug it out, I'll tell you!

They was areas o' red, sandy soil which would be loose an' easy t' dig an' t' haul away, but then they was big areas o' packed, black clay an' it is heavy as lead an' exceedin' hard t' dig into. Who ever b'ilt this thing had worked *toilsome hard!* I asked the boy did he know who b'ilt it an' he said "no." I said, well, was it his Pappy, an' he said he didn't have no Pappy. I thought he meant 'case I'd shot old John. Then I asked him was old John his Pappy an' he said "Naw." Gran'pappy? Naw!

I said, then whar was his Pappy an' he say's he didn't know! I was still mighty confused from the last few days occurrences an' so I stepped him thar in that tunnel, took 'em by the shoulders an' shook 'im some, an' ask him jest what exac'ly he meant.

"Ain't got no Pa an' no Ma. Don't know whar they is! We was a haidin' out West, m' folks an' me an' m' little sis, Loraine. We stopped here 'case Pa had read the sign. We sit down t' eat, a great big meal likes they fixes when folks stops. We et an' et an' we all got real sleepy, an' when I waked up I was in that room they give you an' all m' fam'ly was gone!" (He started t' blubber here).

"I asked whar m' fam'ly was an' 'em Bender's tol' me that they had took off an' left me behind 'case they warn't no room fer me anymore an' that my fam'ly was tired o' me, but that the Bender's was gonna keep me an' I could work fer 'em an' git raised up jest like a youngin son. They said they'd call me "John." I cried an' throw'd a fit an' they'd make me drink that coffee an' bitter milk an' I'd go t' sleep in m' haid an' I didn't have t' think 'bout nothin'.

"Mister, I miss m' fam'ly awful bad! That was near a year, mebe two year' ago an' I am so afear'd they has fergots me!"

The little feller jest broke clear down, havin' said this, an' he stood with his haid a hangin' an' his arms reachin' out as though he was tryin' t' hold on t' som'body what ain't thar. I started t' go over an' hug that boy but then I 'members who he was, er who I thought he was, er who he might yet turn out to be.

See thar? I was confused!

But after jest a minute er two I see'd clearly that this little feller was a' tellin' me the truth, not even Junius Booth hisself could play-act like that! His body was jest racked by sobs an' he cried till he would choke hisself an' then take in big, whoopin' breaths. I put m' hand on his shoulder an' he grabbed me like a grizzly bear! It was jest heart renderin', I'll tell ye.

I thought 'bout what this little feller must have been through an' 'bout the lowdown creachtures what had put him through it! I don't like t' throw m' ed'cation 'round a great deal, but I know'd a $5 word what describes folks like the Bender's an' that 'ere word is *"preverts"*. They had drugged this little feller an' made him a part o' they sick doin's, an' while I had loathed him jest minutes a' fore, I found that I felt right sorry fer him now.

I asked him if he know'd what had happen'd t' the Williams' man an' boy an' he shook his haid "no." But after jest a minute he said, "That's a lie! I do know! Same thing that happened t' all the others, same thing, mebe, happened t' m' folks, same thing they had planned fer you, but you spiled it fer 'em when you wouldn't take yer seat 'front o' that kinvas, an' then agin' when you wouldn't die from that p'ison in yer coffee an' then you fooled 'em agin' by havin' the sense t' pull that chest o' drawers in front o' yer door so's that they couldn't git at ye in yer sleep without makin' a racket so's you'd might wake up! You gots 'em, mister! You gots 'em, good!'"

I told him that was fine, but ask' him agin', did he know what had become o' the Williams'?

"Yessir. Like I sez, same as they did t' the others, I reckon! Folks come by, weary o' travelin' an' they'd see that sign between here an' town. Mos' folks cain't afford t' stay in no town, some folks missed the town 'case its south o' the bend in the main trail a little bit. Anywise, som'body is up here on the mound with a spyglass a' watchin' that pra'rie ever' hour o' the daylight, usually that big ol' boy, an' the others will spell him if'n he needs t' eat er t' tend t' other busyness.

"When he see's folks comin' he alerts the old man. They is lookin' fer small groups o' people, say a married couple with small childr'n er folks a' travelin' alone er in pairs, drummers, sometimes, an' tinkerers. If it's a bigger group o' folks the Bender's sends 'em on they way, either sayin' all the beds is full er that they got the quarantine fer the cholera. That moves folks on in a hurry, I'll say!

"But if the kind they is lookin' fer comes along, they brings 'em in jest like they did you. If they need extry enticements, they is always that Kate. I hate her mos' o' all 'case she is so purty on the outer side an' so black an' ugly inside her heart!

"Anyways, they slip Laudanum, er strychnine er some sech, into ever'thing, so's after the first bite er the first sip you cain't taste it no more. They puts it mos'ly in the coffee er sometimes they will bring out a bottle o' rotgut that has been laced with the stuff. When they gits 'em nice an' comfy, John, the young one, he comes an' slips up behind the curtain out o' this here very tunnel.

"Old John er Sarey always makes shore that the biggest one o' the trav'lers, the strongest one, they make real shore that he is the one a' sittin' with his back t' that kinvas. John comes up an' he selects his hammer, big man, big hammer, smaller man, smaller hammer, like that.

"Whack! Down they go an' the rest o' 'em jackals is on the survivors like flies on cow flop! They drags 'em down here an' robs 'em, I guess.

They always told me I was lucky t' be with 'em instaid o' whar it is the others go, but I ain't so shore. I been scairt since the night me an' m' fam'ly got here. I ain't never bin left alone, they even foller me t' the outhouse. I been scairt a awful long time, now, mister. I pray an' pray t' Jesus most a hun'ded times ever' day an' I'm still scairt. I'm scairt from the time I wakes up till the time I drops.

"Sometimes it feels like I'm scairt even after they make me drink that coffee. I'm scairt even when I am asleep an' sometimes I asks God t' fix it so's I don't wake up!" an' he sniffled some more, then busted right out, wailin' like a banshee spirit.

So now it was plain t' me whar all 'em fancy furnishin's an' do-dads in the soddy had come from, an' all 'em wagons an' carts an' horses an' oxen. Later I felt like I should have know'd, but how? Who would have guessed sech a thing was goin' on out here in the middle o' nowhar's?

I wanted t' let that little feller stay in this part o' the tunnel whar he might be shielded from what I figur'd on seein' up ahaid, but I know'd I might need a hand an' I felt that now we trusted each other some an' I was startin' t' feel pr'tective o' him an' I didn't want one o' 'em Bender's t' git loose an' t' find him a' waitin' here fer me, all def'nseless like, an' take him as a pris'ner er a hostage. I thought jes fer a minute a' fore I said, "Let's go on, now," an' we did.

We had our lamp but didn't need it much at first. The way was lit by lanterns hangin' from hooks ever' few yards an' kindles stuck into the clay walls here 'n' thar. I ain't goin' t' dwell on this 'case it was too guesome, I am goin' t' tell it fast an' I am only goin' t' tell it once't.

The tunnel widened into a larger room, say, twen'y feet by twen'yfive. Lord, what a muddle! I ain't lyin' when I say that the clay floor was squishy with blood what could not soak through an' fer whatever reason didn't 'vaporate. M' boots sunk into the muck clear up t' the ankle in some spots.

Mr. Williams an' his boy was hangin' nekkid, upside down from meat hooks through they hamstrings, where they was bled out. They haids had been totally smashed in. On a wood crate beside 'em they was a ceegar box full o' rings an' bracelets an' necklaces' an' the sech that had belonged t' the pore folks what came through here. Another box had loose coins an' some paper scrip money an' person'l items what a body might carry in they pockets, like jack knives, plugs o' t'baccy, tin photygraps an' the like. They was a heap o' old clothes that I guess was too ratty er too bloodstained t' sell. They was a pair o' pliers an' a glass jar with two gold teeth in it.

(I *don't like 'memberin' this!*)

They was the mounds o' sev'ral shaller graves an' they was bones pokin' up out o' the dirt floor. Rats scurried along the walls an' though it was well into winter outside, down here they was flies ever'whar an' big roach bugs crawlin' in 'n out the bones! The buzzin' was constant an' I thought it would drive a feller crazy if he listened t' it fer very long.

I asked the boy did he know'd if they was a way out other than how we'd came in an' he said he warn't shore but that they must be a trapdoor somewhar's 'case he'd see'd the ol' man go into the tunnel inside the soddy an' then see him comin' out o' the barn a few minuets later.

We kept walkin', me leadin' the boy. I had told him t' close his eyes but I bet you he peeked. But I bet you he only peeked once! It reminded me o' some kind o' a crazy, nightymare butcherin' shop. Fin'lly we had got through the worst o' it an' I had t' ask him t' open his peepers agin' 'case I needed he'p lookin' fer the way out. The only light we had in this end o' the tunnel was the lantern we had brought a long an' the wick needed trimmin', it was smoky an' flickery light, an' it weren't a whole lot better than holdin' a Lucifer match.

The tunnel narrow'd down consid'able till even the boy couldn't stand strait up. He p'inted, an' thar at the end o' the wall they was like a wood gate which I was able t' pry loose. Behind it I see'd a crude ladder made o' pieces o' scrap lumber. I climbed up first an' found m'self in the barn. The boy foller'd an' we came out standin' in the dim light right behind the kinvas curtain, behind the shelf o' boots an' shoes what I had see'd earlier, that first evenin' when I had arrived.

I hear'd a noise an' so I pushed the boy back t'ward the tunnel, then I slipped back the curtain real slow, an' thar, not three feet from m' face, was Katy an' Young John!

~

She was sayin', "You better hurry up, Johnny! It's cold out here! An' beside, event'ally that moron an' the ha'f-wit boy is bound t' find the trapdoor an' when they do I wants us t' be long gone! Shake a laig, now! They ain't gonna stay down in that hell-hole all day!"

He said, "What 'bout Sarey?" an' she said, cold as ice, "What 'bout her? T' hell with that old b—! Let her starve! Mebe she'll git lucky an' som'body will find her. Mebe she won't. Why should it matter t' you?"

I pulled the Smith from m' belt an' slid the curtain all the way back t' fully show m'self, all brave an' grand', like a act'r on a stage, an', I'll be dam'ed, they didn't even notice me a' standin' thar! They jest kept right on talkin' while John saddled up a big roan fer hisself an' then he started t' put the tack on m' horse, Bess, fer Kate t' ride, I reckon.

They was a lull in they conve'sation when I said, "Don't know whar youin's is from, but I'm a Kanzas Man, an' here in Kanzas we deal harsh with people fer stealin' our horses."

You should have see'd the look on them faces! First, they both jest jumped near out o' they skins an' then they turned white as clabbered cream! It was the element o' surprise I had needed.

John Bender was completely dazed an' turned from one side t' t'other tryin' t' look fer a clue as t' what he might do nix. He see'd the rifle he had leaned up ag'in a buggy wheel an' went fer it, but his heart warn't in it, I reckon, 'case he was real slow.

It was too dam' easy!

Little Robert yelled, "Git 'im, mister!" but a' fore the words finished leavin' his mouth m' first shot caught Young John Bender under his right ear. It made a tiny, blue hole whar it went in an' took most o' the left side o' his face off whar it came out!

I did not plan t' shoot twice, they was no need t' do so, but I did, a r'action, I reckon. The second shot hit him while he was a' goin' down an', although I had aimed fer his guts, it caught him in his right buttock, jest a little below his backbone, an' flipped him over in mid air. He landed hard on his back an' the only distinct feature left o' his face was one blue eye hangin down whar his chin should've been, an' a few shiny, white teeth a' stickin' out o' his bloody jaw bone.

Good old Kate! This had made twice t'day that she had been splattered with blood, an' this time it had got on her face an' in her hair!

"Well," she said, pullin' a lace hanky from out o' her sleeve an' a' dabbin' at a small hunk o' brain what had stuck near the corner o' her eye, like she was a brushin' away a morsel of cake from the corner of her mouth, "Well, now! That, as they says, is that! Might I say that you are a fine shot, sir? I must commend you for your marksmanship! And is that a surprise? No, I do not think so! Not to me, at least. I had you picked, right off, as som'body special! And ain't you now?

"Oscar? You are the kind of man that I have waited all my dreary life for! I am saved!"

She noticed little Robert at m' side an' I could sorta tell she was a cookin' up a scheme in her purty haid, "And you! You poor, poor child! You, at least, are safe, now, too, rescued by this here gallant knight just as I have been!

"Oh, how I have worried for you, little fellow, how I have *grieved* for your situation, so much like my own, held here aginst our will by these wild, horrid creatures! These mad, dangerous people! And as fer me? Well, as you know, I too have suffered, perhaps even more by being—*abused*— by these two disgusting men! These Benders! Trying to proclaim to the world the lie that I was one of them, involved somehow in their fiendish plots and these dreadful crimes against poor, weary travelers and their fellow man!"

"Katie," I said, "and this is a comin' from the moron and the half-wit; shet up yer pie hole! I know who you are, I jest ain't rightly figur'd out *what* you are! I ain't never in m' life shot a woman. I ain't even *considered* it. Till now, an' truth be told, I am studyin' on it, quite serious. Why, if'n someone had so much as suggested sech a thing t' me only a few days ago I would have laughed in they face! But, woman, if I hear one more sound from 'em wicked lips o' yourn, I'll take yer purty haid off at the neck an' I'll walk over a spit down the hole, so he'p me God. Jest you look down at the floor at yer brother er yer lover er what ever he *was*, an' you ask yerse'f if'n you think I am jokin' with you. Look! *Look!*"

She did, an' what was left o' that daid, mangled face was already showin' the signs o' the rigors an' they was even a big, slow, fly, up from the tunnel I reckon, already crawlin' 'cross it an' inside it an' I thought fer a minute that she was goin' t' faint daid away, er blow her gorge, but she did not.

'Stead she looked up at me an' fanned her face with her kerchief, "What now?" she asked, real matter o' fact. She was sweatin' although it was cold enough fer us t' see our breath!

I looked down at little Robert an' he said, "Shoot that lyin' she-b— down whar she stands, mister!"

From the mouths o' babes! Fer jest a minute thar, I truly considered it.

CHAPTER 18

Instaid, I had Robert "hawg tie" her, that is, her hands tied t' her feet with a few wraps 'round her middle jest t' be safe. I thought a minute 'bout Sarey an' found that, shame on me, I felt purty much the same 'bout her as Kate did. What she'd said earlier 'bout if'n som'body found her, fine. If they didn't, so what? Starvin' t' death is a tarrible way t' go, I'm told, but I didn't reckon she'd starve.

The way I had it figur'd, she'd freeze first.

~

I finished saddling' up Bess an' Robert he'ped me harness up a good, strong draft horse t' a small cart in which we throw'd Kate, none too gen'le. I covered her up with a couple o' wool blankets an' a buffaler robe as it was chilly durin' the day an' down right cold at night, an' we had already see'd a skiff er two o' snow.

We then rifled through the Bender collection o' stole goods an' loaded the cart up han'somely with things I thought we might need.

I had the boy tie the big roan that the late John Bender the Younger had already saddled t' the back o' the cart along with Bess. I figur'd we'd ride in the seat until we could git shed o' Kate, then mebe we could sell the cart an' still have a good pair o' horses t' ride home on.

We was ready t' haid out when I got t' thinkin' an' I told the boy t' find a length o' rope, which he did. I tied it 'round the feet o' Young John's co'pse an' drug him t' the ladder an' pushed him down into the hole. Nix me an' Robert went into that dam' house, though he shore resisted goin' in, an' we got Old John's body an' drug him back into the tunnel an' dumped him down thar.

Whilst we was in the dugout that old witch Sarey jest stared at us, wild eyed an' murderous. She never spake a word t' neither o' us, nor we t' her. We was haided out the door when little Robert turned an' ran back an' kicked that old dame as hard as he could in the shinny-bone! She did consid'able talkin' then, but nothin' that I care t' repeat.

Kate was trussed up, nice, but was cussin' a blue streak an' I don't much cotton t' that kind o' talk, 'specially from a woman, so I took m' bandaner an' tied it 'round her haid an' over her dirty mouth as a gag! She kept right on tryin' t' talk, an' I bet it weren't no Sunday school sermon, but it didn't matter none 'case it was jest mumbles t' us.

I he'ped the boy into the seat, handed him a couple o' blankets an' a buffaler robe t' lay over our knees, an' I climbed up beside him an' took the reins an' give 'em a snap.

"Whar we haided, mister?"

"Quit callin' me 'mister!' M' name is Oscar, boy, but you kin call me "Oss," ever'body else does. I know fer shore whar we're haided, t' m' home in Di'mond Spring. What I don't know is jest what we're a gonna do with Miss Prissy, here." (When I said that, it started a whole new round o' irate mumbles from the back o' the cart).

"Are you gonna be m' Pa?" the boy asked me, excited like! "Naw, I ain't gonna be yer Pa! Fergit that! Now, m' sister Lizzy might take you in! She's mighty nice an' yer gonna like her. She kin bake the meanest choc'late cake that you ever flipped a lip over. I got a real good friend who is a Kaw Injun, an' I bet some o' his fam'ly would take you in," I teased, "If'n you think you got the gumption t' be an Injun!" He didn't say a word but he looked up at me wide eyed an' seemed like he kind o' took t' the idear. I had only been jokin' with him, but I went ahaid an' let him ponder over it fer now.

CHAPTER 19

Fate deals us all different cards than we could ever have guessed fer ourselves! As it turns out they was no problem at all with me a figurin' what t' do with either the boy er with Kate, 'case Fate stepped in an' blind sided me, jest like she always does, an' settled the problem, though I don't think any o' us was partic'lar happy 'bout the solution.

We was 'bout five mile' from the Bender place, haidin' west. Me an' the boy was tarrible hongry as we had both vomited up whatever food had been in our bellies whilst we had been down in that tunnel. I didn't bother none t' ask Kate whether er not she was hongry er thirsty 'case I flat didn't care. She was jest cargo t' me an' nothin' else.

Any ways, we was hongry an' thirsty an' so was the horses. I had 'member'd t' retrieve m' Henry rifle an' I figur'd that we could go down by the crik an' park the wagon. The horses would have fresh grass an' water, the boy could play if'n he wanted t', though I doubted that he'd 'member how, an' I could hunt us up somethin' t' eat as they is gen'ally always game by any crik er stream, even if it ain't nothin' but a jack rabbit er a brace o' fox squirrels er a han'ful o' nuts, an' they still might be persimmons, papaws er even some late season berries fit t' eat.

So I went ahaid on down thar, an' me an' the boy dismounted the cart underneath o' a enormous cott'nwood tree. They was still a few leaves left on the tree, some t'ward the top was still green.

(Did you ever listen t' the sound o' the wind in a cott'nwood tree? It is lovely! It makes the same sound as rushin' water makes, an' it made me think 'bout m' place in Di'mond Spring. We have two big cott'nwoods on either side o' our back porch an' the sound o' the wind in 'em leaves out here on the lonesome pra'rie took me back thar, made me homesick, an' made it hard fer me t' swaller).

Neither o' us looked after er paid any mind t' Kate although she was mumblin' loudly an' was thrashin' 'round consid'able. The boy said he would druther go with me than t' play an' I considered it fer a minute but told him he'd better stay behind as the two o' us walkin' through the dry underbrush was shore t' spook the game. I told him t' take the horses down t' the crik an' let 'em drink. I took off down the bank t'ward the water ahaid o' him.

It weren't much o' a crik, I guess, but they was clear, standin' water that was not froze solid, although the edges was a bit crusty with thin ice. The cuts o' the banks, whar the sun didn't hit 'em, was still dusted with the white o' the last little bit o' snow.

It was peaceful an' quiet an' I listened close fer the sound o' squirrels in the treetops, I looked up an' noticed that they was quite a breeze way high up thar. The sky was a hard, blue color with little whisps o' white "mare's tail" clouds here an' thar. A blue jay was raisin' hell 'bout somethin' a few yards away an' 'cross the crik I spied a tangle o' gooseberry vines that was still green. I had started t' cross over the water when I felt a stunnin' hard blow, then a sharp, piercin' pain in m' back, up near m' shoulder blade! I craned m' neck an' turned m' haid 'round t' look an' I see'd the bloody shaft o' a Pawnee arrow protrudin' from m' dark blue cavalry shirt!

Chapter 20

I thought 'bout it some, in later times, an' it has occurred t' me that I would not have been any more surprised t' look back an' see a eleyphant flyin' over m' shoulder, er t' see Santy Klaus playin' a bagpipe whilst sittin' in a pun'kin, than I was t' see that arrow!

A' though it splintered m' shoulder blade bone, I didn't even feel no pain 'cept fer a minute or two after it had first hit me, t' speak 'bout.

Now, the nix arrow, the one that stuck in m' left side? I felt that one! It jest crumpled me up like a wad o' paper an' I fell down, ha'f in the cold water with m' blood pumpin' from the wounds, turnin' the pool red! Goddam', it hurt! Who ever shot that arrow was one, strong sono'abitch, 'case it had went clear through with jest the spinfeathers o' shaft a'showin' on the business end!

I rolled over an' looked up t'ward the direction o' the cart, which is whar 'em arrows had been shot from. I half expected t' see that dam' Kate a standin' thar with a bow in her hand, but instaid I see'd 'bout ten Pawnee warriors!

One had his hand over the boy's mouth an' was carryin' him like a sack o' sugar over t' a spotted pony whar he flung him up over a Spanish style saddle. (Which ain't much o' a saddle a'tall, but some o' the tribes liked 'em 'case they is a place t' carry a lance in between the pommel an' a sharp, curved kintle).

Quick as a cat the Injun ties the boys feet with a leather thong, slips under the belly o' the pony an' secures 'em on t'other side t' his hands. He has been trussed up in a matter o' seconds. He shouted, "Oss! He'p me," jest a' fore the Pawnee struck him a special hard blow behind the ear with the blunt side o' a war-club, renderin' him unconscious.

(I always *hoped* that blow didn't kill the boy, an' I doubt that it did, although it was years t' come a' fore I found out fer shore.)

Four er five o' the Pawnee flipped the cart over t' see what was inside it. Apparently, Miss Kate had been able t' scrunch 'round enough t' cover her self with 'em blankets I had throw'd over her. They was plumb delighted t' see her come rollin' out o' thar, skirts up 'round her waist. One o' 'em pulled the gag out o' her mouth, which was a mistake, as she let into 'em with the foulest language I have ever hear'd, *an' I had onc't worked on a goddam' railroad!*

The Injuns fell on her mighty rough, takin' turns, as it was, an' finally I hear'd no more out o' her. They didn't kill her, not thar at least, as I see'd 'em tear m' saddle off o' Bess an' truss her up jest like they had trussed up the boy. I had one glimpse o' her face, clear as a bell, a' fore the horse turned away from me.

Kate's whole life had been tied up with her beauty, which was somethin' the likes o' which I ain't never see'd agin' since. But that last glimpse o' her show'd she'd never be beautiful agin', one them Pawnee had slit her nostrils with a knife, which is what they did amongst they own people t' women what was thought to be harlots.

I noticed, ca'mly, that they was a' awful lot o' m' blood in the water whar I was a' layin'. I could taste it in m' mouth, too. I thought the Injuns was ridin' out, but jest then one o' 'em came a slidin' down the bank. He ran over t' me an' grabbed me by the hair on m' haid. I figur'd he was 'bout t' slit m' throat an' I was searchin' fer the words t' the Lord's Prayer.

Instaid he took his knife an' skinned off 'bout four inches o' m' scalp right down t' the skully bone! He screamed out at the top o' his lungs an' let m' bloody haid fall back down. With one eye I could see him do a little dance, a shakin' m' scalp piece like a wet rat over his haid an' his friends up on the bank cheered an' blow'd eagle bone whistles in honor o' his brav'ry.

'Course I have no idear how long I laid thar. I have no idear why I didn't bleed t' death, mebe 'case it was so cold an' I warn't movin' 'round, none. I do know that I was picked up by a pair o' skinners who thought I was a soldier 'case o' m' shirt an' m' cap which was layin' beside me. (The Injuns had took m' Henry rifle but had not see'd the pist'l in the front o' m' trousers. They took m' good ol' horse too).

The skinners was a goin' t' leave me fer daid but, lucky fer me, one was a good Christian an' he convinced his companion that what I needed was a good buryin'. As they was a draggin' m' pore body up the bank I guess I groaned some, an' so they bundled me up, b'ilt a fire, an' waited all the rest o' that day an' all that night fer me t' die, nat'ral like. I did not, so nix mornin' they made a travois behind a pack mule an' haided off t' Coffeyville with me. They dropped me off with the local quacker named Doc Blood, a ap'ropriate name, I reckoned, an' he said I was a goner, fer shore, an' that 'em skinners should have jest left me out on the pra'rie an' sav'd him the trouble o' havin' t' file a certificate fer m' death an' the town the 'expense of diggin' a hole fer me in Potter's Field.

They rifled through m' clothes and found a soggy letter from m' sister Lizzy. They got m' name an' whar I lived from that, I reckon.

They got some other news an' infermation from m' deliriums an' finally convinced a division o' Cav'ry haided out t' Fort Dodge, the Capt'in o' which was a friend t' the doctor as I was later told, t' take me along with 'em an' t' drop me off on the pra'rie if I died, er t' drop me off in Council Grove if I lived. I was obleeged fer the gen'rosity.

'Bout two days ride from Council Grove they came 'cross a ban' o' frien'ly Indians an' stopped t' do some tradin' with 'em an' t' git any infermation they could concerning hostiles who had been raisin' Cain out west. I had purty much decided that the best thing fer me was t' go a' haid an' kick the bucket, but agin' Fate stuck her purty nose into m' business.

Who could a' know'd that amongst 'em Injuns was m' friend Tall Tree, who had returned to his roots, so to say, and rejoined with a band of his own people and as a consyquince once't agin' found his self playin' nursery maid t' me an' he took me in!

The nix day he took me by travois t' m' home whar Lizzy an' Doe, who rekinized him, even though his face was now tarrible scarred from grief rituals, an' they ran out an' greeted him.

They saw me an' was wild with anguish, although by this time I was actually some better an' could talk some, though I reckon I weren't much t' look at. Hell, I ain't much t' look out still, now that I've been all healed up fer years, I kin only imagin' what I must've looked like all fresh an' bloody, with m' pore, white skully bone a shinin' out fer all t' see!

They took me inside the house an' bathed me an' dressed m' wounds. Doe told me that this was the mornin' o' December 24, an' I spent Chris'mas Eve in the lovin' arms o' m' fam'ly. They proceeded t' beg an' t' try an' convince Tree t' stay inside a white man's house, an' he did, though later he told me it was mighty strange t' look up an' not see the sky through a smoke hole like in a lodge. In some ways, even as sick an' hurt an' tore up as I was, it was the best Chris'mas o' m' life.

The nix day, carried on a litter by Tree an' a uncle o' mine named Jeb Harris, I was able t' give m' sister's hand away in marriage. They was a great many prayer's said, an' a great deal o' cryin' o' sweet, sweet tears, an' the thankin' o' God an' o' Jesus fer m' deliverance. I've hear'd tell that the Lord do work in m'sterious ways, but near as I could cipher it was a humble, red-skinned Injun, not Jesus, what deserved the thanks this time.

EPILOGUE

A note from Doe Harris-Mead: Many years later there was a marker put up by the state road department on US-160 highway a little bit west of Parsons in Labette County in Southeast Kanzas. It says:

On the high prairie a mile northwest, beyond the nearby Mound which bears their name, the Bender family, John, his wife, son and daughter Kate, in 1871 built a small house. Partitioned in two rooms by a canvas cloth it had a table, stove and grocery shelves in front. In back were beds, a sledgehammer and a trap door above a pit-like cellar. Kate, a self-proclaimed healer and spiritualist, and reported to be a beautiful, voluptuous girl with tigerish grace, was the leading spirit of her murderous family.

The house was located on the main road. Travelers stopping for a meal were seated on a bench backed tight against the canvas. In the nix two years several (people) disappeared. When suspicions were finally aroused the Bender's fled. A search of their property disclosed eleven bodies buried in the garden, skulls crushed by hammer blows through the canvas.

The end of the Benders is not known. The earth seemed to swallow them, as it had their victims.

THE END

BOOK ONE

DIAMOND SPRING

BOOK TWO

CHAPTER 1

Between bein' snake bit, robbed, beat up by a ruffian in Chicago, startin' a hellacious fire, bein' attact'ed by a cougar an' dang near kilt, then fallin' in with a fam'ly what came from Hell an' barely escapin' with m' life, then later t' 'ave survived a savage attact by Pawnee Indians fer m' trouble, bein' shot with one arrow in the shoulder bone an' another through the left side, collapsin' a lung, an' then bein' sca'ped, it had not been a real good year fer me! Even back then when I was young I was doubtful if I could survive 'nother like it.

I had promised m' sister, Lizzy, that I would be home in time fer her weddin' on Chris'mas Day, an' with the he'p o' a lot o' people, but mos'ly m' best friend in the worl' a Kaw Injun feller named Tall Tree, by God I had made it! Granted, I had t' be carried in on a stretcher, but I was thar!

Her an' her husband', a Welchman called Domination Jones, er "Domm'", as he was know'd, they had planned a trip up t' Westport fer they hunnymoon but she was afear'd t' go after seein' the guesome condition what I was in. I could talk, by this time, though weakly, but I convinced them newlyweds that m' little sister, Doe, (who is a' takin' all this story down fer me) an' m' friend Tree was more than capable o' takin' care o' me. An' by cracky, they was, too.

It came a snow that night, the first big one o' the winter, an' the nix mornin' was plumb beautiful from m' winder. They was a big hedge wood fire a snappin' an' poppin' in the fireplace an' a full table was set. Them girls had stuffed an' roasted a wild turkey what Tree had shot the day a' fore, an' a goose, give t' us by a kindly neighbor. Also, they had baked sweet 'taters, bread puddin', fresh bread with strawberry preserves. We had smoked venison an' mint jelly. We had pickled cucumbers an' sliced onions, dried green beans (you bile 'em fer two er three months an' call 'em "leather britches"), poppin' corn, parched corn ("horse corn", m' Papa called it, which is field corn that you try t' "pop" but gen'ally only manage t' scorch), sauerkraut, jellied gooseberries, a crock jug o' sweet cider, some home brew an' more! I et some o' ever'thing. As bad off as I was, I found m' appytite was healthy.

Neighbors stepped by on they sledges t' compliment the newlyweds an' was surprised t' find me at home. I'm shore that they was even more surprised t' see the pitiful condition I was in but mos' was kindly an' said nothin' 'cept fer one little feller, Timmy Williams, who was jest 'bout 5 year old, who took one look at m' haid an' ran screamin' from the house an' nary threats ner promises would git him to come back inside. His folks claimed the youngin' had nightymares fer years after he had laid eyes upon me.

I was a awful sight, I reckon! The cougar attack had left some tarrible scars on m' noggin an' down the side o' m' face includin' chewin off more'n ha'f o' one o' m; ear lobes.

The recent scalpin' had been a dam' sight worst. The hairs from the front t' the tippy top had been yanked up an' cut out with a knife that was none too sharp, an' in places the haidbone was exposed. Tree took a great big needle an' thread an' sewed it up as well as he could an' I told him that the pain had been worst that the scalpin' had been. He laughed over that a' though I will confess I did not.

(M' haid really never did heal up an' is tender an' bright red as a monkey's ass t' this very day, all these years later. Cain't never let the sun t' it, no-sir-ee!)

I had mos' my teeth knocked out on one side an' my jaw was broke in sev'ral places…it never did heal jest right which made eatin' a unsightly an' painful ordeal. My nose had been bashed in too many times to count, rangin' from a severe kickin' or two from Lucifer the mule, to the beatin' at the hands of that Chicago heathen, which had also broke the bones 'round my left eye, which caused it to droop some, to jest getting' knocked aroun' consid'able here an' thar in a gen'ral way. The coug attact had left thick, ropey bands o' whitish scar tissue all over m' face and haid an' down my neck an' shoulders. As time passed them scars draw kinda tight which lifted my bestest eye 'bout a inch higher than it shoulda been which meant it was 'bout 2-inches higher than my droopy eye, I reckon. They warn't no body in no kinda hurry to paint my pitcher, let's say.

The arrow wound t' m' shoulder never did heal right neither an' still pains me consid'able during wet er cold weather. I guess it is somewhat fort'nate that that inj'ry was t' the same arm which had been snakebit. It was kinda withered up anyhows.)

The neighbor women he'ped m' sisters t' clean the house an' do what la'ndry they could do, bilin' the clothes an' all, then hangin' 'em outside t' freeze stiff as boards. Event' ally they will dry that way an' smell wonderful clean!

They tore up some old sheets fer dressin' fer m' wounds an' carried on over me so that I was beginnin' t' like it.

The men took care o' the stock an' went down t' the timber an' brought back enough cut wood t' last the winter. Then they all came in an' drank the home brew an' asked me 'bout eleventy million questions 'bout m' "ad-ventures", as one o' 'em called it. I was tired but tried m' level best t' obligee 'em.

Nobody said nothin' agin' Tree bein' in m' house, as mos' o' 'em know'd by now that he had saved m' sorry life an' that even in m' decrepit condition, I was likely t' stand up an' thrash the dog what said anything insultin' t' him.

~

It was late spring, May er early June, I reckon, a' fore I was up an' 'round agin', though I still warn't what you'd call "spry." I had spent the winter inside bein' coddled by Doe an' looked after by Tree an', 'cept fer the pain, I actually spent a purty nice time thar. When they got back from their hunny-moon, old Domm' had did a powerful lot o' work t' m' house (our house) an' had bilt on two more bedrooms, a big old sittin' room an' a verandy style porch what had net an' wire screen t' keep the bugs out in the summertime. Lizzy an' Doe had planted many trees an' flowerin' bushes so it was a pleasure t' watch the springtime come on from a soft, feather cushion on the porch swing.

Tree was gittin' mighty restless (he had taken t' sleepin' out in the yard) an', t' tell true, so was I. Now, as I have said many times earlier, I ain't much on dates, but t' the best o' m' reckonin' this would have brought us t' the spring o' 1872.

Er '73.

(Mebe it was 1874 by this time?)

I had took t' readin' a newspaper, when I could git one, an' I do 'member that Grant was the Pres'dent—er had jest been— an' that sometime 'round here I recall that they was a great fire in the city o' Boston which caused over eighty million dollars o' damage, an' (after m' experience in Chicago I was right proud t' say that I had been nowhar's in the vicinity o' Boston, Mass. at any time prev'ous t' er immediately follerin' that great conflagration.)

They was still lots o' hard feelin's ever'whar in the country over the Great Civil War, as some was now callin' it, an' the South had become the scapegoat. Some in the North said we should he'p 'em rebuild, while others said, "Hang 'em! They brought it all on theyse'ves." An' they was equal hard feelin's t'ward the Negros on both sides, although I was never shore why it was people was angry with 'em? It seemed t' me that they had less t' do with the country's problems than anybody!

The U.S. Cavalry had jumped from the skillet (the War Between the States) right into the fire, by launchin' a full-scale campaign t' eliminate the "Indian Problem" onc't an' fer all. They was fixin' they own "final" solution.

That's jest what it was, too, make no mistake 'bout that! Some people later called it a "relocation" program, But that's horse crap! The Injun's had already been crowded out o' the East an' now the Midwest was bein' filled with more an' more pioneers, settlers an' sod busters ever' day. We was pushin' an' pushin' an' they was no whar's left t' push 'em people t', so Grant, an' Little Phil Sheridan was usin' military genies like Custer an' his ilk t' eliminate the Injuns onc't an' fer all an' don't you doubt it.

They was almost finished a' slaughterin' the great, migratin' herds o' buffaler, knowin' that the Indians couldn't live without 'em an' wouldn't want t'. The image o' the brave Cav'rymen locked in mortal combat with the attackin' savages was a lie, pure an' simple, an' it is a lie that continues t' this day. The "Indian Wars", as they came t' be know'd, is a shameful chapter in our hist'ry, jest like slavin' an' stealin' land' from Mexico.

(It is almost clear fergot now, but both Grant and Robert E. Lee served the U.S. in the Mexikin War an' both o' them men was quoted at differ'nt times as a' sayin' it was the most shameful thing that either o' 'em had ever got involved with.)

Mos' o' the attacks agin'' Indians was launched by whites, unannounced an' unpr'voked, on defenseless villages. If the men was away on a huntin' party, the soldiers liked it even better 'case it meant they could rape an' kill unarmed women' an' childr'n by the hun'ded with little er no opp'sition, so they did!

Them soldiers committed atrocities on 'em folk that makes me shudder t' this day. It was done on both sides, shore, but the extent that it was did by them soldiers bother'd me more an' here is why: They Indians was tryin' t' preserve a way o' life, they families, an' what land' they had left. It was they intent t' do what ever they could, no matters how awful, t' show settlers that it warn't worth the risk t' move in on Injun land'. Looky at it from thar point, the settlers was *nothin' more than invaders!*

The soldiers? Well, they was in the army fer work er t' escape the law, but when it came t' killin', mos'ly they did it t' break the boredom er jest plain fer fun!

One time L'il Phil Sheridan was asked if he didn't think it was wrong killin' Indian childr'n an' he said somethin' that became purty famous. He said Indian's didn't have childr'n, that they had "nits," an' nits, he said, grows up t' be lice! This was the publicly held 'pinion o' one o' the top leaders o' the Amerikin military force in the land' o' the "free" an' the home o' the "brave"! It still riles me up some t' talk 'bout it!

But a few months later L'il Phil said somethin' even more famouser. This time, when som'body asks him warn't it wrong killin' children and "good" Indians, Phil said that he didn't think o' them as children or adults, or as men or women, or as good or bad. He jest thought o' 'em as Indians. "And the only good Indian," Little Phil said, "is a daid Indian."

Why, if two er three white settler's was killed while squattin', illegal like, on Indian land' it was a "massacre." If a village o' Injun women an' childr'n was slaughtered an' mutilated it was called a "military vict'ry"!

Indians would "tech the pen," that is, put they mark, signin' the treaties givin' over they land' an' they rights, jest hopin' that then they would git left alone t' live as they always had.

Them treaties was signed by the Pres'dent hisself an' rattyfied by two thirds votes o' the U.S. congress. They was legal contracts! They was *law*!

Law, that is, till som'body decided that we whites wanted that land'. Mebe it was good grazin' land', mebe they was gold thar er, later on, like down in Oaklyhoma, oil.

Whatever the reason was, if'n it was decided that we wanted the land' that we had promised t' the Injuns, even if it was only weeks er months since the agreement was made, why them treaties was declared as nothin' but empty words writ on fragile paper an' the promises this here country made was dust in the wind an' ashes in the mouths o' the Red Man.

Now, I ain't gonna say that some o' 'em soldiers warn't brave, some was, I reckon, an' mos'ly a dam' sight braver than me! An' some o' 'em believed that what they did was the right thing, bein' raised t' believe that we was super'or bein's. But what the Gov'ment an' the top military brass did was jest low-downed cowardly an' it is a shameful thing t' our nation, which I guess is why we' still tryin' t' hide it an' sugar coat it t' this here very day, all these many years later!

In our neck o' the woods, which is Eastern Kanzas, things was no better. You know, in later years I've hear'd Negro's talk 'bout how pore they was treated, an' they was, no doubt 'bout that, I ain't arguin'. But person'l, I don't think they bad treatment kin even hold a kindle t' how the Injuns was done.

Well into the 1900's, signs on business door might read, "No Dogs er Indians Allowed." A Injun' could still be shot on sight, like a coyote er a woof, an' any o' his possessions could be taken by the feller what shot him! They wasn't even viewed as Amerikin citizens until well into the 1920's! Now, this ain't no "ancient" hist'ry. They is still folks alive who 'member these times besides me!

Shameful! Thar, now. I said m' piece.

~

By 1872-73 all o' the land' that had belonged t' the Kaw, Tree's people, had been "bought" by the Fed'ral Gov'ment from the Osage Nation, as it was know'd, er from the squatters what jest took it over.

The state o' Kanzas had been named after the Kanza Indians, also know'd as the Kaw, but they warn't no more than a han'ful o' 'em people left in the land what they had know'd as they home fer thousand's an' thousand's o' years.

The last reservation fer the Kaw, near m' home o' Di'mond Spring, was swaller'd up by the state in '73, an' the camp whar Tree had grow'd up an' whar his Pa an' his brother was shot down like dogs a' fore his eyes whilst they tried t' pr'tect they home an' they fam'ly, an' the spot whar they was laid t' rest, that land' was now off limits t' him under "pain o' death" if he was caught even lookin' 'round thar!

One time he was up thar tryin' t' find out what had become o' the remainders o' his family after their daid stands had been knocked down. A U.S. Marshall came up and told him, t' his face, that he was a trespasser! The Marshall said he would be well within his rights t' kill Tree whar he stood and said that he would sure as hell do it, too, if'n he ever caught him skulkin' 'round them parts again. This land now belonged t' the U.S. Gov'ment and the Army Corps o' Engineers.

~

I do not know how it was that Tree could still call me his friend after what m' people did t' his. I believe it shows a deep, spirit'al side that most of us whites jest don't understan'. We called his people "primit've" 'case they was able t' live with the land' druther than t' crush it under 'em. But I will always believe that they was closer t' the Great Spirit an' t' the truth o' what life means than me an' mine will ever be.

~

As soon as I was able, me an' Tree got t' takin' walks in the countryside. Well, let's say he walked while I jest hobbled. Lizzy an' Domm' had come home from they trip an' was busy gittin' ready t' start a fam'ly o' they own. Legally, I owned the house an' the land', but I didn't want t' be in the way, so I made a deal with Domm' that if he was t' build me a two room cabin with a well down near the crik, then I would sign over all m' claims t' the house an' the rest o' the property 'cept fer ten acres right thar 'round the cabin.

He jumped on it, o' course, like a chicken on a June bug, an' with the he'p o' his own fam'ly they had ever' thing right as rain within a month's time an' I signed 'em papers an' never did regret it nary one bit. Tree had convinced me long ago that a man kin no more "own" the land' than he kin own the breeze. He kin live on it fer a while an' he kin use it, but he kin never "own" it. When it's all said an' done an' they throw that first shovel full o' dirt on the coffin, then it's the land' what owns us!

The cabin they b'ilt fer me was right nice an' it was bigger'n what I'd asked fer an' they was plenty o' room fer me an' Tree, if'n he decided t' stay on, an' fer a wife if'n I was t' decide t' take one an' if I could find someone who would be willin' t' marry a feller who looked like me, all scairt up an' ugly as a toad.

Domm' was a good enough feller and, as I say, he made shore I got more than I bargained fer. This warn't no little hillbilly cabin he had made fer me.

They was a smallish room with a settee an' leather chairs an' a small stove an' shelves fer books an' souvyneirs, an' a big room with a cook stove at one end an' a pump an' b'ilt-in sink, an' nice winders all 'round fitted with gen-u-ine glass. They was a big loft which served as m' bedroom, an' a little privy room complete with a copper bathin' tub. They was also a big, screened porch, the type which I'm so fond o', that went the length o' the south and the east side o' the house. Yup, ol' Domm' had kept his end o' his bargain with me, an' more.

On one o' m' walks with Tree he took me down t' a bend in the crik, told me he had a surprise fer me. He shore did, too! Down by the water, hobbled in a meadow, was a beautiful, buckskin mare! She was bigger than a Injun pony but warn't as big as the Cav'ry horses. Since I am a smallish man in stature, she was perfec' fer me an' she reminded me a great deal o' m' old horse, Bess, what had been stoled from me by the Pawnee. Tree said that this horse's name was "Cloud" an' he had caught her down in New Mexico territ'ry an' broke her hisself!

(It seems t' me that Tree was the mos' generous feller in the worl' an' it made me feel mean an' small that I had nothin' o' any value t' give t' him in return, as was the cust'm o' his people. He said it was o' no importance t' him an' I believe that was true. Still, it seemed t' me that I would need t' give some serious thoughts as t' what I might do someday fer m' bestest friend)

By the middle o' June I felt like I was ready fer a long ride, if'n we didn't try t' cover too much ground ever' day, t' see what they was left, out thar in the worl'. We took off ridin' west one beautiful mornin' jest as the sun was raisin' itself up over the back horizon an' the worl' was colored pink an' gray. Cloud was a fine horse but she loved t' run, full speed, an' I was not physically able t' stand the constant jarrin' that ridin' a horse over rough ground causes.

I was stove up and sore as hell fer the first few days an' Tree would have t' he'p me on an' off o' the horse as was needed. He never complained. I commented on that an' he 'splained by sayin that it 'peard t' him I was doin' enough complainin' fer the both o' us.

I did make him laugh one day, though, when, after a partic'lar rough ride, I was finally able t' reign Cloud in. Tree rode up an' ask' me if'n I was alright an' I told him, yes, but he could do me a big favor if'n he would ride back up the trail a piece an' see if'n he could pick up any pieces o' m' spleen what he might find scattered 'round.

Evenin's 'round a fire b'ilt o' daidwood er buffaler chips, I would relax, lay back an' listen as he played a flute carved from a piece o' willer wood, an' the music would echo off'n the hills an' it was hauntin' an' sent chivers down m' backbone. Sometimes he would tell me the legends o' his people, 'bout Coyote the Trixter an' Crow the M'sterious an' Raven the Harbinger o' Death. I do regret that I did not set some o' 'em tales down. Like the people what first told 'em stories, they is mos'ly as gone as the smoke from our fires.

~

One mornin' 'bout a week into our journey, we topped off a ridge an' down in the shallow bowl o' the valley we spied a curious sight! They was a feller down thar, a white man with a gold hat an' a blue Cav'ry shirt an' buckskins, an' he was surrounded by woofs. Without a word we flanked 'em horses an' we took off t'ward this pore soul, hopin' we could reach him a' fore the woofs tore him apart.

As we draw'd in closer we see'd that 'em warn't woofs a'tall, that they was some kind o' dogs ("stag hounds," I l'arned later). They was ten er fifteen o' 'em a circlin' this feller. The dogs was jest actin' crazy an' he was laughin' an' playin' with 'em! When we rode closer still, we see'd that it warn't no gold hat he was wearin', but his hair! I'll be dam' if it warn't old "Iron Butt" hisse'f, old Yallar Hair Custer! (An' I should note fer the record that, whilst his hair was still long on the sides an' in the back, it shore had grow'd mighty sparse up top!)

Thar he was, smack dab in the middle o' nowhar's, as far deep into hostile Injun country as you kin be, a gambolin' with 'em dogs, an' his horse layin' daid as a hammer 'bout 30 yards away! When he hear'd the hoof beats he turned, quick as a snake, with a huge, dog-laig pist'l in his hand, octagon barrel like one o' 'em buffaler rifles, an' he had it p'inted at me an' Tree. We pulled up an' he looked back an' forth at us an' we looked down at him.

I was right impressed an', though he would never admit it, so was Tree, I betcha. Tree was a educated man now, read newspapers an' sech, an' he shore as hell know'd who we was a lookin' at this time.

(As I believe I have said, after the first time I'd met 'im, Custer's hair weren't really yallar, at all! It was strawberry colored but quite golden whar the sun had bleached out the curls. It was purty, er would have been on a woman. 'Cept, as I say, he was goin' real bald on top an' didn't like t' be see'd without his hat. He cast 'round fer it till he saw it layin' on the ground, a big ol' soft hat with a extry wide, floppy brim with a brace o' pheasant plumes stickin' out the ban', an' he picked it up an' smashed it down on his haid.)

He was wearin' a dusty, major general's undress uniform from the War, shirt wise, with high topped buckskin gloves t' match his coat, buckskin moc'sin boots an' a fancy, red satin scarf tied loose 'round his neck!

He had piercin' blue-green eyes an' pale, freckled skin that was flushed as pink as a baby's butt! He had a long, hawk-nose an' a curly mustache an' a goatee on his lower lip (like mine). He had thin, red patches o' whiskers stickin' out on his face like he hadn't shaved in a day er two, at least. Up close he was not a big man, fact is he was thin an' rather small, actually, but he appeared big. (Does that make any sense?).

(Tree said later that Custer looked big an' tall 'case that's how we wanted t' see 'im and how *he* wanted t' be seen! It was clear that this was a man o' big, pow'rful "medicine" an' he could *make* other's see him as he wanted t' be see'd. It sounds sort o' crazy t' me, but I reckon Tree was right.)

While we was a sizin' him up, he was doin' the same t' us an' Lord knows what he thought, lookin' at a han'some, civilized Injun with sacrificial notches took out o' his face, an' a scarred up, crimpled up white feller like me.

He had a medal on his breast an' he seemed t' jut that out t'ward us as he tetched the brim o' his oversized, floppy hat an' said, "Greetings, Gentlemen! How fortuitous for me that you have arrived. I am General George Armstrong Custer, commanding officer of the 7th Kanzas Cavalry, at your service." (I know'd he was only a *brevet* General, during the War, an' that act'ally only a Colonel at this time, but I warn't 'bout t' argue the point none with him. He was still holdin' that hog pist'l in his hand, 'though now it was danglin' at his side.)

Tree said, "Good morning to you, General! Pray tell, what are you doing in the heart of the land owned by the Noble Red Savages, alone, with a dead mount and with only a single revolver as protection? Are these wonderful hounds a part of your troop?"

Well, you could have knocked ol' Custer down with a feather t' see his face upon hearin' a red man talk so! His eyes narrow'd an' he looked at me, "Your red friend has a marvelous command of the English language! You sir, are you as well versed as he?"

I laughed an' said "nope," an' introduced m'self an' Tree. I asked him what he was doin' out here, all by his lonesome, an' he motioned fer us both t' dismount, which we did, an' t' sit a spell with him on the ridge o' a buffaler waller. He took his fancy, kid glove off'n his right hand an' sat, twirlin' the end o' his red mustache, still studyin' us both closely. I noticed his hands was pink and soft an' oddly woman-like.

Satisfied that he was safe, fer the minute, he said, "My men and I are headed west to quell a problem with the Indians, forgive me sir, (nodding t' Tree) out in Colorado. Among us rides my younger brother, Boston Custer, and we, he and I, have a wager going as to which of us will be the first to fell a buffalo by any means other than a rifle.

"Earlier this morning my hounds spied a small herd of antelope and took chase, I, of course, in hot pursuit. After riding some distance I spied a lone buffalo cow standing by her dead calf. At our approach she bolted and ran, with myself and my dogs giving chase, forgetting the antelope for the time being.

"I rode up beside the cow and pulled this sidearm and was prepared to deliver the coup'd'gras.

"I was in no hurry as I was savoring the moment, don't you know? Jest as I squeezed off my shot, impeccably aimed, I'm sure, suddenly the beast stopped, short, and turned to confront me! In the twinkling of an eye, the horse foolishly, shied and raised it's head at exactly the same instant that I fired! The missile exploded in the poor thing's skull, dropping it instantly, stone dead, which threw me over, headlong into the prairie, injuring only my pride, only my pride!" He laughed, gen-u-inely, at his misfortune.

"I was quite helpless on the ground but the old cow jest looked at me and snorted, as if to say "serves you right, noble adversary," and she trotted away, leaving me in the somewhat embarrassing situation that you have found me in. I certainly do regret the loss of a good mount, though!

"It is a case of 'Custer's luck', though, as my men call it. This 'luck' has again come to my rescue as, indeed, found I am! I will of course, solicit your help in returning me to my outfit, but, embarrassment upon embarrassments, unfortunately I confess that I have absolutely no idea in which direction we should seek them!"

Tree kind o' giggled which brought a sharp look from the "General." Tree mounted up on his pinto, whistled fer Custer's dogs, which all foller'd him like they was off t' Sunday school, an' rode up t' the nix crest t' git the lay o' the land'.

Custer looked at me, "Interesting chap, that one, 'Tree', did you call him? And just what is his lineage?"

"'Scuse me, sir?"

"Of what tribe is he, your gallant Indian friend? I should guess he is Comanche, with his coloration the facial scarring and his noble brow."

"He's Kaw," I said.

"I doubt it," Custer replied, more to hisself than to me. "How is it that you two are traveling together?"

I 'splained a little 'bout m' life an' 'bout how I had see'd him a' fore, years ago, leadin' his men off t' the West. I told him I had hear'd 'bout the Washita River incident an' some others, an' that I did not approve o' the Army's treatment o' the Indian women an' childr'n.

In reply he simply called 'em the "Innocent yet unavoidable victims of a war which they themselves have engaged, yet cannot win," an' that he was jest a soldier, doing what he was bid t' do by his commander-in-chief, the Pres'dent o' the United States o' America.

I told him that I had hear'd that the voters back East was gittin' weary o' the taxes required t' support the Army an' o' the stories o' the atrocities committed ag'in innocent Indians. It was plain that he was becomin' peeved that I know'd 'bout what was a' goin' on in the worl' an' had the audacity t' question him, an' at m' last statement, he blow'd up.

"'*Innocent Indians*'? Sir, you are but a babe in the woods if, for one single moment, you believe in the concept of 'innocent Indians'! You, sir, are deluded! They are noble adversaries and I admire them greatly as such, as well as a race and as warriors, but never, *never*, believe for one moment that they are either human beings, in the true sense of the word, or that they are the hapless victims of military 'aggression'!

"The Good Lord Himself has destined that the white men shall rule this great country from sea to shining sea, and something as insignificant as a few hungry, vagabond heathens will deter us not from this glorious *Manifest Destiny*".

"It is not merely our *right* to seize this land, my misshapen friend, it is our *duty*, as Christians and as Americans. Onward, Christian soldiers!"

It was clear that Long Hair had beat o' me when it came t' words an' I did not resist him. He was one o' 'em fellers who could see his self as part o' a bigger plan an', right er wrong, a feller like me warn't gonna change him one whit!

I jest sat an' stared at him till he grew uncomf'rtable an' he stood up, pacing, an' finally he asked, "Where has that damned Indian gone off with my hounds, do you suppose?"

Jest then Tree came back over the rise an' rode up t' us, dogs millin' 'round him like flies. He smiled an' said t' Custer, "Sir, your men are about six miles to the north of us. Climb up and we'll take you to them." Tree held his hand out t' the Colonel.

Custer looked at Tree's hand, then over t' me like he expected me t' say somethin', so I did. I said, "*Colonel*, as you kin see, I'm a bit chewed up an' I have t' spread m'self all over m' horse t' be a'tall comfortable. You kin either ride behind m' friend on his horse, er, sir, you kin walk. Makes no never-mind t' him er t' me."

He glared at me fer an second then swung his self up behind Tree. The three o' us rode off t' the north amid a sea o' happy dogs!

When we was in clear sight o' the dust cloud the 7th was makin', I reckon 'bout a ha'f a mile er so from 'em, Custer yelled fer us t' stop. We pulled the horses up an' he slid t' the ground. He took off his hat an' dabbed at his forehaid with the end o' his fancy scarf.

"Gentlemen, I thank you deeply and sincerely for your assistance, if not for your conversation," he said, lookin' straight at me.

"I'm certain that it has been quite an honor for you, regardless of your politics. My men, as you can plainly see, are just ahead and it wouldn't do at all for them to see their Commanding Officer come riding up with two, um, two such singular *gentlemen* as yourselves, no offense meant, of course. And so it is that I shall take my leave of you now. I shall send the hounds ahead and they will fetch someone back here.

"I am sure, of course, that this incident today will provide years of fodder for the generation of tales that you are certain to share amongst your friends and family and your grandchildren, should you be fortunate enough to know them," (here he cast an odd glance at Tree).

"Making the acquaintance of the patriarch of the 7th Cavalry surly has made it a great day for you both and you have been of great assistance to your country. Tell your tales to all who will listen and believe them. In the unlikely event that they should come back to me, of course I will be forced to deny them in their entirety."

An' with that that arrogant sono'abitch turned an' walked away, follerin' his dogs which was already runnin' ahaid t'ward the column o' men, barkin' they haids off an' gallivantin' 'round like they had good sense!

Now, if'n anybody who might happen t' read this here paper o' mine should doubt me, go down t' yer town lib'ary, if you got one. Ask 'em fer a copy o' "My Life On The Plains" by General George Armstrong Custer hisself, they'll have it, an' if'n you'll read it through you will find the story I have jest told, exac'ly right in ever' detail but two! He don't mention neither me m'self er Tree, the *real* heroes what saved his smartass, pasticatin' rind!

~

Over these many years I have hear'd a lot o' stories 'bout George Custer, some folks loved him, some folks cussed the ground he walked on. I cain't say that I felt that strong 'bout him, as a soldier, either way. But I doubt that thar ever breathed a man on God's green earth who was more convinced in his own heart that he was the greatest warrior what had ever lived!

He dreamed o' bein' the Pres'dent, someday, an' mos' o' the hist'rian folk believe they is no doubt he would have been nominated in '76 as the Democratic Party's kindidate fer the Pres'dency er as Vice

Pres'dency, at the very least. But mebe the good Lord, seein' what he had unleashed on the worl', decided t' change his plans as far as Custer's future was concerned. Er mebe neither the Lord er George Armstrong Custer took Sittin' Bull, Crazy Horse an' the whole Sioux Nation into consideration. Then again, mebe both o' 'em believe a little too strong in Custer Luck.

"Custer Luck", indeed!

CHAPTER 2

Tree an' I talked 'bout our meetin' with Custer off 'n on fer a few days an' he was a puzzle t' us both. I believe that Tree was a sight more impressed with 'im than I had been. Tree see'd 'im as a great warrior, I see'd 'im as a glory monger who would put his troops in jeopardy at the drop o' a hat if it meant that Custer might grab some more glory for hisself. (He proved that when he abandoned a feller o'ficer named Elliot at the Washita River fiasco. Custer led a group o' men off in another direction when they should have backed up Elliot an' his squad what was suddenly swarmed, overran, and wiped out t' the man. Elliott paid the price fer Custer's foolish pride! When yer down thar at yer lib'ary, look up the battle o' the Washita. That will might jest show you a side o' George Custer that yer hist'ry book fergot t' mention.)

~

M' sca'ped haid was painin' me consid'able an' as we rode we kept a eye out fer yarrow which is a yarb that I would twist up an' mash into a mat an' I would put it on m' haid, under m' hat, an' it soothed me some.

We lived the Injun life, sleepin' when we felt like it, ridin' when we wanted t' an' eatin' when we could. They was still so much wildlife on the pra'ries that any man who could shoot straight could eat good. Tree was a right fine cook 'case he know'd the yarbs t' add t' meat t' make it taste right, but I never had no interest in that sort o' thing* an' I guess I warn't much he'p 'cept fer bein' able t' shoot straight.

I had become a better than average shot with both a rifle an' a pist'l. I also carried a 10 gauge shotgun in a case fasten'd t' m' saddlebag but, hell, anybody kin hit a targit with a shotgun like that one!

(*Now, don't git me wrong! It ain't that I *cain't* cook, 'case I kin, an' the only folks what ever got sick from m' cookin' is 'em what et too much an' I would say so even in a court o' law!)

Tree tried sev'ral times t' teach me t' shoot a bow an' t' throw knives an' the sech, but I never did take t' it, much. Not like him, anyways.

We was basically loners. It jest warn't safe fer us t' ride up t' a farm er a ranch, what with his bein' an Injun, 'case as I've said, people jest nat'rally reacted bad. As fer me, I was no pict're o' perfec'shin, neither. I had not shaved since we'd took out an' had grow'd a purty nice beard which he'ped cover the scars on m' face some. I *always* wore a hat, not jest t' hide 'em scars, which it did, but beca'se even the blowin' o' the wind over the raw skin and exposed bone o' m' haid caused me pain.

Tree was adaptin' his looks, though, an' was startin' t' look less an' less like an Injun an' more an' more like a dark skinned Mex. He had got away from that Crow style hair he'd been wearin,' an' now had whacked it short, nearly like a white man, an' he'd took t' wearin' a wide brimmed hat that some folks was now callin' a "cowboy" hat, like cowboys had invented it er somethin', but it was jest a Mex hat t' me. Not one o' 'em big, silly-lookin' sombrero things, that look like a dam' table on yer haid, but a regular gaucho style hat. I don't think the av'rage person would assume he was a Indian, no more.

As I have said, Tree was uncommon dark fer a Injun, an' I think that some folks might have even thought he was a high-toned Negra, but mos' would jest think him a Mex. I'll grant you, Mex's ain't the mos' popular folks in these parts, neither, but they is a dam' sight more welcome in town than is a Injun!

~

I waked up one mornin' t' find a old, sow bear rummagin' through our supplies. I had always been partial t' roasted bear an' Tree was plumb wild fer it, but bears, like a lot o' things, was growin' scarce. That mornin' they became one scarser 'case I popped this one in the haid with a rifle ball an' dropped her whar she stood without me even have t' git up out o' m' bedroll.

We cut her throat clean 'cross t' bleed her, then strung her up from a cott'nwood tree an' dressed her out. You ever dress a bear? It's easy! Jest do it the same way as you would a hog. They is almos' the same thing an' parts o' the bear, like his hams, ribs an' the shoulder, tastes a good deal like pig when they's roasted!

We spent mos' o' the day stakin' out the hide an' rubbin' the bear's brains all over the inside o' it, which he'ps it cure nice, an' tans the inside. I was in charge o' cuttin' the meat up. We roasted a big hindquarter that night in a pit we dug an' lined with cattails an' the sech. By the nix mornin' it was purty much done an' we feasted like kings!

We rendered down some fat an' Tree packed into a pouch he had made from the bear's belly. Injuns value bear fat as emerg'ncy grub, salve, an' hair dressin'. Could be the reason I 'member that day so well is 'case that was the last bear meat I ever et. I wished I had me some now, by dam'!

~

I never was one fer cities, 'specially after the fiasco back in Chicago, but Tree got t' talkin' that he would like t' see a white man's town 'case he had never been near one, 'cept fer Council Grove, an' that ain't no city, not by a long shot! I reckoned we was a way's west o' Wichita, so we swung back t' the east an' a little bit north an' I figur'd we'd run into it sooner er later. I hadn't never been thar, neither, but I hear'd it was a comin' thing so, what the hell? We was jest out fer a ride, anyways.

CHAPTER 3

M' sister, Doe, who is a' takin' this all down as I tell it, jest ask me t' say a word er two 'bout the cattle drive days which is jest whar I was haidin' with the story, as a feller cain't tell 'bout Wichita without tellin 'bout cattle drives.

When the Great Spirit made this worl', he must have decided that he needed the perfec' place t' graze his grass eaters, like the buffaler an', later, the cattle herds. That's why he made Kanzas, I reckon, 'case they is no finer land' t' fatten 'em beasts upon than this! Nowhar's on the planet! T' this very day cattle is shipped from ever' where in the U.S.A. t' graze fer a summer a' fore goin' on t' slaughter.

A feller named Zeb Pike, who came through Kanzas in the early 1800's, had writ: "The inhabitants would find it most to their advantage to pay attention to the multiplication of cattle, horses, sheep and goats, all of which they can raise in abundance, the earth producing spontaneously sufficient for their support, both summer and winter, by which their herds may be immensely numerous." From what I kin make o' that, he hit that nail right smack on the haid!

Now, first off, they is lots o' *trails* in Kanzas, some trails made by beasts, others by Indians. Right now I am gonna talk 'bout the Chisholm Trail which took it's name from Jesse Chisholm* who was, his se'f, a ha'f breed Cherokee. This feller could speak 15 different Indian lingo's an' sev'ral white man languages inludin' English an' Frenchy an' what is called Rooshian, whatever in Hades that is! He came in mighty handy as a guide an' a in-terpreter among whites an' Injuns, as well as from one tribe o' Injuns t' another.

At the end o' the War he took off fer Southern Oaklyhoma t' buy up furs fer a trader at the Wichita Indian village. The feller asked him t' drive some cattle up on his way back, up t' the railhaids in Kanzas. On his way down t' Texas he had picked up on a route whar he know'd they was gen'ally plenty o' water an' passable terrain. It only made sense fer him t' take the same trail back, so he did. The trail went from clear down in north-central Texas up t' north-central Kanzas, an' later came t' be know'd as the Chisholm Trail.

Other feller's started t' drive they cattle up that same trail so's they could fatten 'em up in Kanzas an' t' find a railhaid t' ship 'em out o', too.

Well, that was Abilene, Kanzas which was one hell o' a town fer a while, the Texan's even named one o' they own towns after the one here in Kanzas. It was wild an' woolly an' a lot o' things happened in Abilene, but that thar is a whole 'nother story.

(*Now, jest so's not t' confuse ye, some folks claim the trail is named after a feller named John Chisholm, who Doe (who is a takin' all this down} says really spelled his name "Chisum", an' who raised cattle down in West Texas an' as far south as the Concho. But the trail had it's name a' fore that feller ever set foot on it, jest so's you know the truth o' the matter.)

In '71 Abilene lost the claim o' bein' the only railhaid as the Atchison, T'peka an' the Santy Fe had b'ilt a new one down jest a few mile t' the south in a town called Newt'n, so Abilene lost a lot o' the trade.

Now, Newt'n was one hell o' a town too, more so, I reckon, than Abilene had been, as far as bein' mean an' ornery an' hell raisin'. In '73 a even bigger railroad depot an' cattle pens was b'ilt in Wichita jest as soon as the Army killed off the Wichita Indians an' drove the remainder o' the tribe off t' the west. That year the Texans drove between a quarter an' a ha'f a million cattle t' Wichita!

Later on, Dodge City was a big shippin' point, too, but by then they was plenty o' business t' go 'round an' the city o' Wichita had b'ilt other attractions as well, an' soon became the biggest town in the state. Still is, t' this day.

The whole time o' the cowboys didn't last no more than 'bout twen'y year at the very most! In that time they say that more than a million horses an' 10 t' 15 million cattle an' countless pigs (yes, *pigs*!) was drove from Texas an' Mexico up t' Kanzas shipping points!

(I drove cattle fer near a year m'self an' I'll tell ye 'bout that later if'n you want t' hear 'bout it an' you reminds me!)

(That thing 'bout pigs is true, too, but it don't sound near so romantical t' sing, "I'm a lonesome pigboy," so most folks jest 'member the "cowboy" part. Would you want t' be seen wearin' a "pigboy" hat, er a new pair o' "pigboy" boots? I didn't think so! Years later, when movin' pitchers came t' be, would ol' Gene Autry, who I know'd, would Gene wanted t' have been know'd as "The Singin' Pigboy"? If I know'd Gene, an' as I said, I did, I don't think so.)

~

Tree an' I rode into Wichita 'round the first o' July. He had wanted t' see a white man's town, an' by gawd, he got his se'f a eyeful! 'Cept fer Chicago, I ain't never see'd so many people in one place. They was ever' kind o' people, too, jest like in Chicago, but these here was mos'ly jest drunks an' cowboys an' "Soiled Doves" an' pimps an' the like.

They was a few real houses, but mos'ly it was a ramshackle mess, with sheds an' tents servin' fer stores an' shelter. Mos' o' the real stores was saloons. They had divided the town into what they called "blocks" an' ever' block had at least 5 er 10 saloons sellin' tepid beer an' rotgut whiskey t' anybody with a five cent piece. The Soiled Doves hung 'round the bars an' on the corners an' tried t' talk the drunks into spendin' time an' money with 'em an' some would an' some wouldn't. Fer the most part these was sad old gals, drunk and diseased and many a' year past they prime. T' tell you true, they was a purty pathetical lot.

A cattle drive could take anywhar's from 30 t' 60 days, dependin' on the weather, the Injuns, and whar they was comin' out o', an' a feller works up a powerful thirst, an' hunger, in that length o' time.

A cowboy's job was dam' dangerous. Big herds o' cattle is hard t' stop er turn once they git movin'. (I never hear'd o' anybody gittin' kilt in a pig stampede, though). They was snakes an' scorpions, lightenin', pra'rie fires, hostile Injuns an' robber bands o' Mex's, accidents an' murders, mean horses an' meaner companions. It was a hard life as I know'd first han'.

Well, when 'em fellers finally gots t' whar they was goin', t' Newt'n er Wichita er Dodge City, why they was wild, man, jest wild! Some o' 'em fellers was only youngins, first time away from home, first time drunk, first time with a woman.

They had money in they pockets, sometimes more than they'd ever see'd in they lives, an' in ever' cowtown at the end o' the line they was som'body, a thief, a gambler, a shyster er a whore who was jest itchin' t' git they hands on some o' that "jack"!

The first thing we see'd was a drunken feller a staggerin' down the street, which was ankle deep mud an' horse scat, an' he stops, standin' thar in broad daylight, an' starts takin' a leak! A feller standin' up on the second story balcony o' a brothel heaved a empty whiskey bottle down at this feller an' it caught him smack in the back o' his haid, knockin' him face down into the mud! Ever'body on the street laughed till I thought they'd die!

Finally, this drunken feller stirred a bit an' then he set up an' we see'd that the blow from that bottle on the back o' his haid had popped one o' his eyeballs out an' it dangled down the side o' his cheek! He twisted his good eye 'round an' see'd what had happened an' then passed out backwards, from fright, I reckon. How they howled at that! We was wonderin' what t' do when two fellers came out o' a barbershop an' carried the drunk inside. Mos' barbers in 'em days doubled as doct'rs. I figur'd they'd pop his eye back in an' clean him up an' relieve him o' ever' cent that he had fer the trouble.

I turned an' looked at m' friend Tree an' saw somethin' in his face an' eyes I had never see'd a'fore in all the years I had know'd him. It was fear.

CHAPTER 4

Well, it occurred t' both o' us that this here was a bad, bad mistake, our even bein' here, an' that we'd be lucky t' git out o' this filthy mess alive! They was mud an' piss an' horse manure ever'whar! A few o' the stores had sidewalks made o' wooden planks but mos' didn't. An' it was o' little matter, anyhows, what difference did it make t' walk ten feet on a nice wooden walkway an' then have t' walk the nix forty in mud?

The scale o' sinnin' appeared t' be Biblical in pr'portion! Ever'whar they was drunkenness an' human filth. Women would sling open a winder an' dump out the night's leavin's from a chamber pot right onto' the street below, an' too bad if'n you happen t' be standin' underneath that winder! The smell made yer eyes water an' yer nose runny!

We kept a ridin' t'ward the center o' the town an', I must admit, the craziness o' it all started t' die down a bit, er else I was already gittin' used t' it. In this part o' Wichita they was actually a active police force, sech as they was, an' they also was a bunch o' soldiers in town who was not on leave an' tharfore was required t' behave theyse'ves, an' t' he'p the police out as much as they could, which I guess warn't all that much, judgin' from the way things looked.

It was clear, though, somehows, that this here was a town with a future. It weren't some little flash-in-the-pan, as they say. They was layin out proper grids as buildin' zones fer *big* buildings. They had already started on a new hotel, The Eaton, they done had the groun' floor an' a second storey finished an' 'peard to be a workin' on a third an' they was some who claimed when it was all said and did that it was goin' t' be *ten stories tall!* 'Course I didn't believe that one. I might be from the country but I ain't no hick!

We was lookin' 'round fer a place t' eat some grub, as Tree had never been inside a resta'rant in his life. We found us a little place called the Rooster's Roost, an' it looked almost clean an' was at least quiet. They had posted they bill o' fare on a chalkboard outside the swingin', saloon style doors. Beefsteak an' all the fixin's was 10 cents, pork steak was a quarter. They also featured catfish, quail, pra'rie chicken, an' mutton.

They also sold a fried chicken dinner with taters, gravy, bread, coffee, corn on the cob, green beans an' biled cabbage fer 15 cents!

Tree had never et a fried "barn yard" chicken, I had an' I liked it plenty fine, when I could git it, so that's what we ordered from a sour-faced, baldhaided feller in a long apron who writ ever'thing I said down on a little pad o' paper like he was a savin' it t' read over later, in his spare time.

He looked at Tree an' said t' me, "Yer friend, here, now he ain't some kind o' negger er a Injun, is he, 'case if'n he is, he cain't eat in here." I looked at him, shocked, an' said, "Him? Old Jeremiah? A negger, you say? A Injun? Why I should say he ain't! Why, whar's yer brains, old feller? Jerry here is a Frenchyman, ain't that so, Jeremiah?"

Tree looked up an' said, "Wee-wee. That, my good fellow, is French for 'yes'. Now, would you be so kind as to not delay us any longer, as my friend and I are famished and have heard glowing reports about the prowess of your chefs and their culinary expertise."

"Yessir, right away, sir, I will person'l git this here order turned in t' our cooker. Oh, by the way, sir," he said t' me, "I will have t' ask you t' remove yer hat while in this here café as it is the rules o' the house. You see, we's owned by a certain Mrs. Callahan an' she is somewhat of a, hmmm, how do you say it? a *bitch* when it comes t' table manners". (Tree had already took his hat off when we'd walked through the door). I re'ched up an' slid mine off an' when the waiter feller saw m' noggin he actually gagged!

After a minute er two he regained his composure and said, "Well, would sir kin'ly keep his hat on his haid an' jest this once't we will ignore that thar partic'lar rule?"

Well, this food he brought out t' us was laripin'! It was as fine a store bought meal as I've ever tickled m' teeth with. I thought Tree was goin' t' eat till he busted! Between us we et a whole chicken, an' a plump one at that, plus all 'em other things I told you 'bout, an' two loaves o' fresh baked bread which was light as a feather, white as snow inside, an' didn't have a single rock er piece o' grit anywhar's in it, at least not so's that we noticed!

We was jest diggin' into huge slabs o' hot, apple pie with fresh cream pour'd over it, when a mighty fancy lookin' lady came a walkin' in through the front doors. I know'd right away that this here was either that Miss Callahan er a whore, an' it was!

Miss Callahan, I mean t' say.

Well, she caught sight o' me an' came a b'ilin' right on over. "Sir," she said, with a heavy Irishter or Scotch accent, "I see that m' worthless man, Hank, haint told you none 'bout how I am intendin' t' bring sivil'ization t' the god forsaken shite-hole o' a town. Now! Might I cordially invite ye t' be off with that goddam' hat, sir!"

Well, m' Mama always taught us kids t' be mindful o' the requests o' a lady so, agin', I retched up an' whipped off m' hat! Considerin' that Miss Callahan had apparently jest finished her breakfast, toast an' aigs I'm guessin', from the looks o' what ended up on the floor, it was entir'ly the wrong thing t' do!

I throw' a dollar on the table an' wished her an' Hank a pleasant mornin' an' hoped that they would hurry an' git that mess that she had made on the floor cleaned up a' fore feller's started comin' in fer they midday meal. Old Tree laughed so hard he got choked like he'd swallered a chicken's laig bone er somethin', an' I was afear'd he might lose his lunch as well.

~

We walked down t' a tavern a few doors down from the "café," as that feller, Hank, had called it. This place was called the "Bucket o' Blood."

M' gosh, what a thing t' see! Here it was not yet noon an' they was fellers actin' like you would think it was midnight. They was playin poker an' faro, drinkin' whiskey an' beer, they was a banjer player an' a pianer player who had put tin pie pans jest above the strings inside it so's when he hit the key's it made a rattly, tinny sound that went right nice with the janglin' banjer.

They was sawdust on the floor an' if a man had t' spit er t' puke, he jest did so whar he stood an' nobody seemed t' care er t' pay no mind t' it, jest piled some fresh sawdust over it an' let her go! I never did see nothin' like it a' fore an' I was tol'able ashamed o' m' race in front o' m' Indian friend.

If he was shocked, he didn't show it none! He jest had a funny kind o' look on his face but show'd no real emotion a'tall.

The bartender ask him was he a negger er a Injun an' we said no. Agin'. Tree ordered a sarsaparilla an' I had a warm mug o' bitter beer. A whore came over our way but I waived her on a' fore she had a chance t' give us her spiel. A argument broke out over a card game an' one feller busted a empty whiskey bottle over another feller's haid, an' laid it open so's the blood gooshed ever'whar. (It seemed like the name o' this 'ere saloon was not made as a boast but as a fact.)

A drunken cowboy staggered by an' tripped over his own feet an' turned an' told me t' watch whar the hell I was goin' an' I told him I hadn't been goin' nowhar's, jest leanin' up agin' this here bar, an' he said don't sass-mouth him 'case he weren't the type o' feller t' take it an' I said "oh yeah?" right off the top o' m' haid, witty like, an' he said, "yeah," an' away we went!

He took a swing at me an' missed me by six inches! I brought m' knee up into his groin, a' mashin' his tenders, an', as he was goin' down, I punched his haid so hard that they was a knot risin' a' fore he hit the floor! He kind o' paused, in mid fall, so I punched him agin', this time in the mouth, an' I had t' pull one o' his front teeth out o' the skin on m' middle knuckle whar it stuck.

A drunken buddy o' his see'd what was happenin' an' he stands up from whar he had been sittin' at a table with a Dove, an' I see'd him slip his hand down into his boot top an' draw out a fearsome long knife an' t' start fer me. I yelled out, "Stop right thar, mister, er I'll kill you a' fore you've had a chance t' eat yer dinner," an' he said, "Like hell you will," an' he raised the knife up an' lunged fer me, so I did!

Kill him, I mean!

They was somethin' in me that I did not know was thar. I reckon I had know'd it first when I shot down that pair o' John Bender's last winter. It was though I didn't even have t' think 'bout what I was a' doin,' er didn't even try t' aim, er nothin'. Like m' hand jest found the gun by itse'f, pulled it from the holster an' placed a dreadfully acc'rate shot, all jest nat'ral like.

One second this feller was chargin' at me like he thought he was a bull er some dam' thing, an' the nix he was standin' thar makin' goo-goo sounds, lookin' pitiful stupid, with blood gooshin' out o' his mouth an' ears an' a smallish blue hole, jest 'bout big enough t' stick the end o' yer pointin' finger in, thar in the center o' his forehaid, with smoke jest a bilin' out o' it!

It was unfort'nate that the contents o' his brainpan made a mess on ever'body an' ever'thing behind him. 'Parently the bullet took a upwards turn, as one o' the lamps what hung from the ceilin' busted an' dripped coal oil ever'whar, but at least the bullet didn't harm nobody 'cept fer the feller it was intended fer.

M' big Smith an' Wesson had a powerful roar an' it seemed t' echo agin' the walls fer quite a time an' then it was real quiet. The barkeep said, "Watch 'im, boys, while I git a constable," an' he left out. No body paid much attention t' me, though, an' they went back t' the card games, an' the whiskey drinkin', an' the cussin', spittin', an' pukin', what have you.

Ever'body jest stepped over the body thar on the floor and purty much went 'bout they business.

I looked over t' Tree who still had not changed his expression an' I suggested that they is always a back door in these places an' that we should mos' likely find it. We was almos' thar when a voice called out, "Halt, damn you, or I'll drop you where you stand!"

I turned 'round an' found m'self starin' down a uncommon long pist'l barrel. M' eyes foller'd down that thar barrel till I met 'em eyes what was lookin' down it from t'other way, from the "boss" end, an' I found m'self lookin' into a killer's eyes! The face on the other end o' that Buntline Special pist'l was non other than them o' Wyatt Earp!

CHAPTER 5

We stood, lookin' at each other, him 'n me, fer some time, an' he didn't so much as blink, he jest looked through me, so t' speak, an' his eyes looked t' me like a rattler's! I ain't no coward, an' I'll whup knots on any man what says I is, but I was shakin' in m' boots, I'll say!

"Howdy, Mr. Earp, do you 'member me?" I asked, kinda feeble like.

"No," he said, "I most certainly do not remember you! Sir, you are, without a doubt, the ugliest sono'abitch I've ever seen in my born days, and had we met before, why I guess there is no doubt that I *would* remember you! Hell, had we met before I'd have *nightmares* about you!" (Which made ever'body laugh!) "Where, pray tell, do you think know me from?"

"A couple o' year' back, you an' one o' yer brothers, Virgil, I believe was his name, why I met youin's at the Hays House in Council Grove, it was snowin' mighty fearsome an' I advised youin's t' git yerselfs a room instaid o' tryin' t' travel on. I am mighty glad t' see you fared the storm, sir," I said.

He puzzled over that fer a minute an' then he said, "Claimed you was an agent for the Army, as I recall, I do remember you! Looks like you 'arrested' that Indian you were looking for," he said, nodding at Tree.

"Oh, him? Why, I don't believe he's no Injun, sir"

"Hell yes he's an Indian," Earp roared, "Do I appear to be blind, to you, son? I *know* Indians, and I know that it's against several city ordinances to bring one into a tavern or to serve one whiskey! Now, I can see he's drinking sarsaparilla, so you have me there, but he damn sure isn't supposed to be in here!

"By the by, son," he said thoughtfully, studyin' m' face, "what in the hell *happened* to you? You were a fair looking young man, as I recall! Did you tangle with a bear?"

"A cougar, sir. An' some Pawnee," I said, liftin' up m' hat.

He screwed up his face an' said, "Sweet Mother of God, son, put your hat back on! Do you want me to lose my breakfast? Don't ever do that in a public place! I swear, your head looks like the nekkid ass of a baboon!" an' ever'body busts out laughin' agin', me too, in a nervous kind o' way.

"Yessir, I have thought the very same thing m'self, Mr. Earp," which was a true fact.

Wyatt looked over t' the body a layin' in the sawdust and said, "Why'd you kill this man, son?"

"Had t', sir, he was tryin' t' knife me." Earp looked down at the daid man an' clearly see'd that big, old Bowie knife still clutched in his clenched up hand. I went ahaid an' 'splained t' him m' side o' the story an' mos' ever'one in the saloon backed me up, least wise them what was payin' attention did.

Earp let the hammer down gently on his Buntline an' he slipped it into the holster, an' I would be a liar if'n I was t' say that I warn't a sight relieved by that!

He told me t' take m' Injun an' t' git out o' the saloon. He thought a minute an' then said, hell, git out o' Wichita, whilst we was at it, an' t' not come back no more.

Now, I ain't no fool an' I weren't goin' t' argue with the likes o' Wyatt Earp. Shore, I had hear'd the stories 'bout how mean he was, how he could draw an' shoot with daidly ac'uracy! But, even if I hadn't hear'd none o' that, I had see'd them eyes! They was somethin' awful to see!

As we was leavin' his two brothers, Morgan an' Virgil came in with a friend o' they's, they boss, Bat Masterson was his name, an' I see'd Morgan had 'em same kind o' woofish, killer's eyes. Folks sez he was the hothaid o' the Earp clan, an' had it been him what had come t' the scene 'stead o' Wyatt that I'd a' been pushin' up daisy's by sundown.

Now Virgil, who I had see'd a' fore, he had grow'd some, he was a big, plump, good natured feller. An' Masterson was right frien'ly, too, an' a "Dandy," I guess, what with his tailor made suits an' a gold haided walkin' stick with a eagle's-haid handle. But I'm shore that they was both thoroughly dangerous men, ('fact is that they is some what claim that it was Virg who was the nastiest o' 'em all,) but they had a "reg'lar" look 'bout 'em, not dog-mean, like Wyatt an' Morg.

All these boys, along with another friend o' 'em, Doctor John Holliday, who was a drunk an' was dyin' o' the tuberc'losis, had met up thar in Wichita. Wyatt had been warned sev'ral times by the city council t' make shore that 'em fines he collected ended up in the city treasury an' not in his pockets, but I don't reckon that they did. Who was gonna call him on it?

They made enough money in Wichita policin' an' gamblin' an' dealin' cards, t' move on over t' Dodge whar they was t' git in on the ground floor, so t' speak, an' more er less ran the town fer a year er two. They had another brother name o' James Earp, who had been purty shot up in the War an', as I recall, didn't have no use o' his gun hand. All in all, I'd say 'em Earps' was fellers t' avoid. They made a few friends in Kanzas but a dam' sight more enemies! I cain't say that I was either one er t'other, m'self, jest glad t' say that I met 'em an' lived t' tell.

~

We hadn't been in the big city more'n two hours an' already we was bein' run out o' town by Wyatt Earp an' his posse! We had et a good meal, see'd the sights, an' I had shot a man t' death an' been threaten'd by Wyatt Earp so it seemed like a purty full day an' a good enough time t' move along. Tree was disapp'inted that he didn't git t' stay in no fancy hotel, but like I told him, hell, they was plenty o' time t' do that later, let's ride west

CHAPTER 6

As we meandered westerly, in no partic'lar hurry, we decided t' spend three er four days in an Injun camp with some friends o' Tree's. He know'd 'bout whar they would be camped out on a crik off'n the Smoky. We entered into the vicin'ty an' we didn't have t' look none too hard fer 'em as we both know'd they'd find us first, anyways. They did.

As we rode along I ketched sight of a horseman a couple a hundred yards off…then another, an' another, an' so on. Gradual like, they fell in, closer and closer till they was ridin' with us, like a flank o' guards, an' up over the lip o' the nix hill we see'd the campsite.

This was a big Cheyenne camp; mebe upwards o' three, four hun'ded tipi's spread out over the valley. It was a sight t' see as we rode in, escorted by a dozen er so warriors what had "found" us. The haid man was a fearsome ha'f-breed named Quanah Parker, who had his own band o' warriors what called theyse'ves the *Kwahadi*.

They was famous all over Texas an' the Territ'ry, but they was bein' hunted by both the U. S. Army an' the Texas Rangers, so they old tribal huntin' grounds up here in Kanzas was a welcome restin' place fer 'em t' be so's that they could hunt, stockpile some grub an' spend time with they families. The fact that they was wanted by the Ranger's an' the Cavalry was the main reason why Fort Sill was sech a busy place, down thar in the Territ'ry.

It was the belief o' the Kwahadi that, since the whites would not listen t' reason an' refused t' honor the treaties what they theyse'ves had writ, that each an' ever' one o' 'em must be killed on sight. See a wagon er a wagon train? Attack it an' leave no survivors! A cabin, stagecoach, trapper camp, miners, whatever, attack, burn an' kill!

Quanah was a chief, I guess, though as I've said a' fore, that didn't hold much water. (Chief's warn't elected like a mayor, they jest came t' be. If people trusted a man an' was willing t' foller him an' t' listen t' his advice, gen'ally at least, an' t' his opinions, then that feller jest became a chief, nat'ral, like. Now, as I said, this gave him abs'lutely no real power, t' speak o'. He couldn't tell a tribe member t' do a certain thing an' expect that it would be done, that is unless that person he told wanted t' do it.)

Quanah became a chief beca'se he fought plumb berserk! 'Em that see'd him, whites as well as Injuns, agreed that he was jest crazy an' had no fear a'tall! He would ride int' battle against riffles and sabers with a pist'l, which was his weapon o' choice, with his face an' chest painted black, on the back o' a black pony, an' folks l'arned t' fear him in short order!

Some soldiers act'ally thought he was a fer-real demon, like in the Bible, an' they did not believe he could be killed er even wounded.

The Cheyenne was a Northern tribe what had moved down into this area voluntary, a generation er two a' fore white settlement had begun. They gots a hold o' some wild horses, decedents o' 'em the Spanish had left behind, an' when they did they became kings o' the pra'rie! They could ride better'n' faster than any other Injuns, bred a better line o' horses, could shoot straighter from the back o' a horse at full gallop than the average man kin standin' still, on his own two laigs.

The Comanche was also a big tribe, with relatives scattered from Kinada t' Mexico, 5 different bands, in all, an' the two things they all had in common was that they was Comanche an' they loved to fight!

They plagued the Mex's fer years, runnin' off they cattle an' a' stealin' horses by the thousand's an' then jest disappearin' into the land. The Apache l'arned a lot from the Comanche warriors. Once't the Texans started comin' in an' settlin' the land', the Comanche didn't mind a whit, it gave 'em somethin' t' do an' somebody else to torment.

Quanah's ma was named Cynthia Ann Parker, an' she was white. She had been stole away from a stockade in Groesbeck, in east-central Texas, when she was jest a little girl. Her Pa had been murdered in a mos' guesome way while she looked on. Her ma was stripped nekkid an' pinned t' the ground with lances through her hands, but was allowed t' live. The Injun's took Cynthia an' four er five other childr'n with 'em when they left out. She grow'd up in the Injun camp as a Injun an' later married a feller named Peta Nocona who was, his self, a chief o' a band o' Cheyenne.

They had three childr'n, one o' whom she named "Quanah" which means "Smells Good."

The Cheyenne had taditional'y had small fam'lies an' so three kids was a passel! I guess they was all happy, as some years later when some whites tracked down Cynthia an' planned t' take her back t' the white worl', she had declined, sayin' she had childr'n t' care fer an' a husband' who she loved.

Quanah, like other childr'n in the camp, l'arned t' ride a' fore he could walk by his self, an' I mean that as a true fact! They studied war as soon as they could ride. They is a sayin' amongst 'em " A brave man dies young," an' Quanah was out t' show he was a brave man, fer certain. He fought his first battles, an' kilt his first men, a' fore he turned 15 year old.

In '45 the Republic o' Texas joined the U.S. an' immediately sought out Fed'ral troops t' do somethin' 'bout the Comanche. Prospect'rs on the way t' Californy stopped t' he'p the settlers an' the army t' shoot a few Injuns fer sport, an' they did, but the worst thing was that they left behind a particular mean kind o' cholera, which managed t' kill off great numbers o' Comanche an' Kiowa, sometimes killin' off more than ha'f o' a village in a matter o' jest a few days.

(You youngins who is a goin' to school, 'member this: The U.S. Cavalry claims vict'ry in the Indian Wars. But it warn't jest the soldiers what killed off the Injuns! No, 'em soldiers had disease an' the white man's ways on they side, an' t'gither that's what did it. Cholera, the pox, dip'theria an' the bottle kilt far more Redskins than bullets ever did!)

In '60 Quanah's band was hidin' out from the Texas Rangers along the Pease River. Mos' o' the men was off on a hunt an' women an' childr'n was dryin' hides an' smokin' an' curin' meat. 'bout twen'y cavalry troops an' forty 'er' fifty Texas Rangers swept into the camp like a cyclone an' killed more than ha'f o' 'em. They also took sev'ral captives, among 'em was a woman with blue eyes! They took Quanah's Ma an' his sister, Pra'rie Flower, t' east Texas an' they was gone!

Quanah had loved his sister an' his ma an' so this only made him hate the whites even worst than a' fore. It warn't long a' fore both his pa an' his brother died from disease an' Quanah went off t' live with the Kwahadies.

They was among the few tribes who did not go t' the big Medicine Lodge parlay in '67, but he hear'd 'bout the fate o' his ma an' sis from another Injun what had attended the council. His ma had tried t' escape back t' the tribe so many times that they kept her purty much as a pris'ner.

Later, when little Pra'rie Flower died from disease, Cynthia Ann decided she'd had enough, so she starved herself t' death!

Long 'bout the time that we came t' be in they camp, Quanah's Comanche was bein' hounded by a feller named o' Colonel Ronald S. Mackenzie, who was much admir'd by the Injuns beca'se he was a fearsome fighter an' did not give up, ever! He had been on they tails fer the past two years, with no luck so far.

~

When we rode into the camp it is needles t' say that I was the center o' attention. Even though I was travelin' with a Injun, it was beyond the Cheyenne's power o' belief. They wondered whether it was that I was brave enough er stupid enough er crazy enough t' jest sashay into that camp like I owned the place. I didn't show it none, I reckon, but I was scairt spitless!

We rode up t' the lodge o' a medicine man name o' Isa-tai, who came out an' took one look at me an' gave me m' Cheyenne name, somethin' like Tse Osa Het, which means "Brave Man With Ugly Haid", er jest Ugly Haid, fer short. He invited me into his tipi an' inside is whar I met Quanah Parker.

Although he was ha'f white, he shore looked all Injun t' me! He was very tall, lots o' Comanche was, men an' women both, an' he was partic'larly well built, real musc'lar. His hairs was long, parted in the middle with two plaited braids hangin' down either side. He was real dark skinned, though not quite as dark as m' friend, Tree. He had the classic Indian nose, long, hawkish, an' a unus'ally large mouth which I have hear'd described as "cruel," an' I kinnot disagree with that.

He stayed sit-down when we walked in until he see'd Tree, who was a old friend o' his, an' he stood an' shook hands with the younger man, ignorin' me completely. He offered Tree t' sit an' t' smoke an' they did, neither one sayin' a word. I do not speak much o' the Cheyenne, so when he finally did start talkin' I had very little idear as t' what they was talkin' 'bout. I did understan' the word "Ugly Haid" an', t' tell the truth, I was purty shore that was one nicky-name I was not goin' t' be fond of.

Tree talked fer a long time an' I found, if I listen'd real close, I could understan' a little o' his talk, as from time t' time he throw'd in a word er two o' English er Kaw and some Sioux now an' then.

It seemed that he was tellin' his old friend that a' fightin' with the whites was like fightin' with the wind an' that Quanah Parker should think 'bout his love o' his people more an' his hatred fer the whites less. The Chief jest looked at Tree, smoked, nodded an' occasionally gave out with a grunt that could be read as a "yes" er a "no" t' whatever point Tree was tryin' t' make with him.

After 'bout a hour, an' much t' m' surprise, the Chief looked up at me an' said, in passable good English, though with a purty heavy accent, "My young friend, Tall Tree, tells me that you are a good and a brave man. He is a man of wisdom beyond his years. Although I have not known of these traits before in the whites, you are welcome in my lodge on the strength of his words. Perhaps you are different from the others, and can show me another way to deal with the people who are killing my buffalo, stealing my ponies, shooting or stealing away my loved ones and pilfering away my land?

"The soldiers come to us and told us that they represent our Grandfather in Washington, and they ask us to tetch the pen to their treaties which are written in ashes that blow away when the white man wants something, anything, that the Indians have.

" Your people have brought much grief to this land and we want them to go away and to leave us alone, but they will not. Tall Tree says that they will never leave and that we must learn to live with them or that we must die, that their numbers are as many as those of the stars in the sky.

"I have not yet decided which of these two things that I will choose to do, to fight or to make peace. Is it in your power to help me? Sit down an' smoke with me and let me hear your thoughts."

Chapter 7

I do not believe, 'ceptin' fer m' sisters, nobody had ever ask m' opinion 'bout nothin' important a' fore, an' I felt right tetched that sech a great Chief as Quanah would care a whit 'bout what I thought! I wish I know'd what it was Tree had told him 'bout me, as it must have been a fine speech.

I sat down beside Quanah Parker an' he passed a long pipe t' me that had been beautiful' carved an' painted t' look like a mallard duck, an' was dec'rated with inlaid stones an' eagle an' hawk feathers. I never was one t' smoke much an' I draw'd in on that pipe an' proceeded t' choke. They was tears runnin' down m' cheeks an' I know I turned bright red 'case m' face felt like it was inside a oven!

When I would finally ketch m' breath an' start t' say somethin', well, I would choke agin', an' start a new fit o' coughin'! Even though I felt like a danged fool, The Chief did not laugh at me, er act perturberated. He jest sat pat'ently until I finally gots m' wind back. By then the pipe was cold so he took it from me an' laid it down beside whar he was sittin'. (Injun's usually smoked a mix o' t'baccy, dried willer leaf, with mebe wild grape leaves er sage mixed in. They believed that the smoke was the breath o' the Great Spirit an' that they prayers rose up t' His nostrils in the smoke.)

The Chief said, "Tell me, Ugly Head, have you been t' the great cities o' the white man?"

I told him 'bout Wichita an' Chicago.

"Are these cities as large as m' village?"

I almos' laughed, but thought better o' it (an' I'm glad that I didn't, it would've been hurtful.) I told him they was much, much bigger. He asked me how many white men lived in 'em cities an' how many white men did I think that they was in the East? I could have lied, it would have been easier, but I felt that I owed him the truth, as best as I could tell it.

"Chief, they is more white men than they is buffaler left on the plains, more than the leaves on a cott'nwood tree, than on a *forest* o' cott'nwood trees! I believe that they is uncountable. I am told that they is more on the way from 'cross the ocean, the big water, in what they call the Old Worl'.

"It ain't none o' m' business but I'm gonna tell you anyway; ever' battle you fight with the whites you kill a few, an' they kill a few o' you. They is more white men a'comin' into your land' ever' day, *ever' day!* Whar' is the new Cheyenne warriors a'comin' from? Is they ship loads an' train loads an' wagon loads o' brave, young fighters a' comin' from some whar's I don't know 'bout? Is each o' your women' havin' ten er fifteen babies *ever' year,* 'case even if they was, it still wouldn't be enough t' stave off the tide!

"M' bestest friend in this here worl' is a Injun, not o' your tribe, but still he is one o' your brethren. His folks treated me as if I was one o' they own. He found m' dear Mama's body after she had been drownded in the floodwaters an' he brought her t' me. He'ped me t' bury m' own Pa when he passed away from this here life. I have no more feelin' fer white's than I have fer red men. I have nothin' t' gain by tellin' you the things you don't want t' hear, things that might turn yer heart ag'in me.

"I rode into this here village at yer mercy, but by God, I'm a tellin' you the truth! You kinnot win a war with the whites! It jest cain't be done. They will trample you down into the dirt an' they will kill yer women an' your childr'n, too! They will hang yer scalps from they stand'rd poles, right 'neith the Amerikin flag. They will fashion the skulls o' yer children into cups t' drink they whiskey from. They is plannin' t' kill *all* the buffaler so's they kin kill *all* o' you!

"The big herds is already gone. Onc't you could ride and in a day, er two, you could find more buffaler than you could kill. Now you must ride for a week er more jest t' find a pitiful handful. The buffaler is like the Cheyenne. The days has been counted and the buffaler is dyin' out and they ain't no more comin' in from somewhar's else t' replenish they number.

"Whatever it takes; that is what the whites plans t' do! They intend t' poison yer ponies, t' foul yer water and t' sew pestilence into yer blankets. They will stop at nothin' t' wipe you off'n the face o' this worl'. If you give them the 'scuse they will rub you out t' the man, fer you is the livin' witnesses t' the evil that they do."

With that I stopped an' looked into his face. He was lookin' back at me an' his jaw was set like stone an' his eyes was like chards o' flint. I didn't know if'n he was angry with the brashness o' m' speech er if his heart had been moved by it. Without a word, he stood up an' walked out o' his lodge an' left me sittin' in the near darkness inside.

Sev'ral women came in an' one o' 'em handed me a bowl o' antelope stew an' an' some Injun flatbread, another fetched me a bowl o' water an' a han'ful o' sweet, blackberries. They left, too, an' I spent the rest o' that day inside the tipi alone, till they brought me supper which was more o' the same. Finally, I fell asleep on a heap o' robes an' skins.

Sometime in the middle o' the night I got up t' go outside so's I could relieve m' bladder. They was a full moon an' it seemed near bright as day. They was a dog er two snifflin' 'round on me, Injuns always had too dam' many ugly dogs, an' off in the distance I could hear a night hawk creakin' his way through the sky with that lon'some call which, t' me, sounds like the wind in a ship's riggin'.

Away off in the distance I could hear a dreadful, frightful sad sound, it was a whine er a chant. I took a few steps an' listened so's I could pinpoint whar the sound was a' comin' from, an' finally I see'd a lone figure a hun'ded yards er so away, standin' on a outcrop o' rocks. His arms was spread wide an' his face was tilted t'ward the moon an' it was him that was makin' that baleful sound! I could not he'p but t' think o' a old, lone woof, pourin' his heart out t' the moon an' stars. It must've been Quanah Parker, asking his heathen god fer guidance, an' I do believe it was the sorriest, lon'somest sound I ever did hear.

~

The religion o' the Cheyenne was purty simple. They believed that all things have a spirit, an' that if they could git as many o' 'em spirits as they could t' hear the plea's o' the people, that the Great Spirit hisself would intercede on the Injun's behalf.

T' do this they might chant er sing fer hours er days, they might starve an' thirst theyse'ves, stare into the sun until they was blind. They might cut little hunks o' skin an' flesh from they own arms er they faces as offering's, sech as Tree had did as a expres'ion o' grief when his fam'ly was rubbed out.

In perfound cases they would have they own version o' what the Sioux called a "Sun Dance", whar a special hut was b'ilt an' only men could enter it.

Inside a hot, smoky fire was b'ilt an' the men folk would sit 'round poundin' a continuous rhythm out on drums, blowin' on eagle bone whistles, while 'em that was participatin' in the dance would take sharp objects, like a bear's claw er big eagle's talons, an' shove 'em through they skin an' in behind' a tendon er a muscle, usually in they arms er breast. Then the point was attached t' a long, thick thong o' hide what was draped up over the wooden cross pieces o' the lodge's roof'.

The dancer's friends would then hoist him up in the air, suspended an' danglin' from the hooks piercin' his flesh. He would spin thar fer hours, the "dance" part o' the rit'al, all the while a' singin' an' a' prayin' an' implorin' the Great Spirit fer guidance er t' send a vision, until the flesh tore through an' he fell down t' the floor.

These was devout, spirt'al people!

~

I listened fer a while t' the moanin', sing-song chant, but it kind o' felt t' me like I was eavesdroppin' so I turned back 'round an' went inside the empty tent. I laid down an' went t' sleep an' had another one o' them dam' dreams like I have, and this was one o' the worstest dream o' m' life!

Once't I see'd a pict're in a book o' a drawin' o' Death, it was like a man with a skelyton's face an' hands, all covered up in a dark, hooded cowl, holdin' a hourglass, with the time run out in one hand an' a scythe t' cut men down in t'other. In this here dream o' mine, that was me! I was death hisself!

I was in the camp o' Chief Quanah Parker an' I was handin' out bundled rations like the Injun agents do on the reservations? People would take the bundles an' when they opened 'em up they was full o' human bones, skulls, ribs, an' the like. The people would look into the bundle an' scream in fright as the skulls grow'd skin an' turned into the faces o' they loved ones what had been killed in the fightin' with the whites over all the many years.

I would walk up t' the people, men, women an' childr'n, an' I would poke 'em in the middle o' they chests with m' finger an' when I did all they breath would "ooof" out o' they mouths, like the seed does from one o' 'em puffball toady-stools, an' they would jest fall down, daid, on the ground. They could not run away from me an' if they tried alls I had t' do was t' p'int m' bone finger at 'em, an' crook it, an' they was drug t' me like I had a rope 'round 'em.

I walked an' walked, an' p'inted an' p'inted. I took no pleasure in this a'tall, but it was as if it were a job which I had t' do! I was sickened by it, an' I would try t' tell some o' these folks I was killin' that I was powerful sorry. Either they couldn't hear me er I wasn't makin' no sound. In this here dream they was a full moon an' it began t' turn red, an' turned even redder with each one I "fetched."

Final'y, I walked up t' the Chief his self an' he saw me an' weren't a'feared o' me. He told me he was a'goin' t' save his people an' he raised up a fearsome war ax with a stone haid. He held it high, in both hands, an' was ready t' smash it down onto' m' ol' ugly haid when I reached out an' tetched his breast with m' finger an', poof', he dis'ppeared into a cloud o' smoke, an' out o' the smoke they flew a black raven, an' it flew t' the West over a pra'rie that seemed t' be alive an' movin', but it warn't earth an' grass, it was a pra'rie o' Buffaler skelytons, hide's all mangy an' rotted an' draggin' on the ground as they ran an' they ran an' they ran, all o' 'em movin' westerly, with that raven flyin' overhaid until they disappeared from m' sight behind that blood red moon.

I waked up an' spent the rest o' the night shiverin', although I was covered with thick hides an' furs.

~

It was late the nix afternoon when Quanah Parker finished his vision quest an' returned t' his lodge. He found me whar he had left me, an' without nary a word, he sits down beside me an' took up his pipe. He filled the bowl an' lit it with a twig off'n the coals that was all that was left o' his fire. He took a deep draw an' passed the pipe t' me. I took a little puff an' I did not choke up, this time.

After nearly an hour he turned an' said, "Tell me of the terrible dream that you have suffered my friend, and perhaps I can divine a meaning from it that will help me to decide the path for me and my people to walk upon"

I didn't much want t', but I told him 'bout that dream an' when I finished I had tears runnin' down m' face. I don't s'pose I ever felt this low in m' life. When I had told him all that they was t' tell, he stood up an' I did the same.

He reached out an' embraced me then called fer a woman an' told her t' fetch Tree. He told her t' have some other women t' pack us up some pouches o' food an' skins o' water, 'case we was leavin'. He then called in a young man named Horse o' Three Colors an' said fer him t' gather up some warriors an' t' make shore that we was escorted safely out o' this valley, westward.

(It was some days later a' fore it even occurred t' me, but how did he *know* 'bout that dream? We had not said so much as a word t' each other, in fact I had spoke t' nobody 'bout nothin', let alone 'bout that dam' dream! I thought 'bout it over an' over, an' I 'member clear as a bell his sayin,' "Tell me of the terrible dream that you have suffered…"

(Thinkin' 'bout his jest sayin' it, out o' the blue, gave me the creepy-crawlies then, an' still does t' this day!)

CHAPTER 8

Tree, bein' the man he was, asked me no questions 'bout what had gone on between me an' the Chief. He show'd no sign o' jealousy that I had spent the night in the comf'rt his friend's tipi while he had slept out on the ground, an' when I tried t' bring up the subject o' m' horrible dream he raised his hand t' silence me. Either he didn't want t' hear it, er one he already know'd the way it was.

Nix day we came upon a column o' soldiers a waterin' they stock at a pool in the crik an' the o'ficer in charge, after eyein' Tree real close, ask' me had I see'd any sign o' hostiles. I told him that we had, 'bout 20 mile' t' the north, which was the total, oppersite direction o' Quanah's camp. That was the direction that they turned an' haided as we rode on.

Grad' ally the dark mood lifted from me, an' Tree told me that we should rejoice in the endless pra'rie 'round us an' that, as this very well might be our last trip t'gither, we should relish as much o' it as we could.

We came 'cross a herd o' migratin' buffaler which was shor'ly one o' the last o' they kind, prob'ly down from the Black Hills country er Kinada. It was posat'lutely huge! We sat on our horses up on a high ridge an' jest watched 'em, movin' south, grazin' along the way. After the better parts o' a hour we dismounted an' lay down on the ground an' watched 'em until the sun went down.

~

Nix mornin' we decided t' foller the herd fer a spell an' so we turned back 'round t' the south east. 'bout midday, Tree spied smoke on the horizon an' so we rode over t'ward it. It turned out t' be a stage depot o' some kind. It had been burnt t' the ground an' we found the co'pses o' three men an' a old woman, staked out an' flayed. They is no need t' go into the ugly details, but it was a rough thing t' see. They had all been sca'ped an' was full o' Kwahadie arrows. Onc't agin', they was left as a sign!

We had no way t' bury 'em folks but we did drag they bodies over t' whar the fire was still burnin' an' we stacked 'em up thar, an' covered 'em with some daid branches off'n a old locust tree in the hopes that they would ketch fire an' burn.

They was a ol' saddlebag with it's contents strew'd over the ground an' I found a yallar'd page from a Denver newspaper with a story 'bout a new military campaign agin' the buffaler (an' tharfore the Injuns) whar the Army planned t' use the new Sharp's high powered rifles that could; "fell a bison at 600 yards! General Philip Sheridan of the U.S. Army said he was proud of the program which will enlist the help of civilian hunters who will, he said, 'Be instrumental in destroying the Indian's commissary. For the sake of lasting peace, lets kill, skin, and sell them all until we have exterminated the buffalo. Then your prairies will be covered with speckled cattle and the festive cowboy'."

("Festive cowboy?" What in the hell was he a' talkin' 'bout? If by "festive" he meant drunk, ugly, dirty an' mean, why I reckon he was right.)

I took the paper over t' the coals an' tucked it in thar amongst 'em an' watched it curl an' smolder, an' then bust into flames. We mounted up an' rode off in leisur'ly pursuit o' the herd.

~

It s'pose it must have been the middle er the end o' summer, by now. We had rode fer days an' had see'd nobody, which suited us both jest fine. They was entire days on the trail when neither o' us spoke nary single word aloud. It was like we was goin' t' someplace whar we didn't know, but we was bein' draw'd t' it. We didn't know how t' git thar er when we would, jest that we was part o' somethin' bigger than we could think 'bout. They was no hurry an' yet I felt a certain yearnin' t' git on t' whar'ever it was that I was s'posed t' be.

Event' ally we rode t' North Texas, then down into the middle o' it, an' finally on down 'round a bay near whar the Missionaries called the Body o' Christ. It had took us some consid'able time, a couple o' weeks, mebe more, I reckon.

South o' the Mission we both see'd the ocean fer the first time an' the sight o' it an' the smell o' it scairt our horses an' made tears run down Tree's face.

We spent another week er more, ridin' on the sand an' through the surf. We ran into a batter'd, ruined band o' Cherokee an' they was starvin' an' pitiful. They had no horses but had somehow still managed t' outrun the Cav'ry. They told the stories o' how they had been force marched over hun'deds an' hun'deds o' miles, place t' place fer near a generation er more, an' told us how they was *still* tryin' t' find they way back, but that the Great Spirit had abandoned 'em t' woofs an' the white man, t' starvation, disease an' the soldier's guns.

We had nothin' t' give 'em people an' we left 'em. They kept on walkin' east, wailin', cuttin' at theyse'ves with stone knifes, an' lashin' at theyse'ves with branches an' old pieces o' ropes, tryin' t' punish they own bodies fer displeasing the Great Spirit so!

They would roll in filth an' cover theyse'ves with ashes. It was the mos' plumb pathetical thing I ever did see an', I'm 'shamed t' say, but it made me cuss they heathen god, an' m' own as well.

~

That night I told Tree I wanted t' go back t' Kanzas as I felt I had see'd enough.

Injuns believe that they is an order t' ever'thing an' that ever' creachture has it's place in the worl'. Tree said that the Great Spirit had a plan fer 'em pitiful peoples we had see'd, but that, fer the life o' him, he could not figure what it must be! Neither could I. I jest wanted t' go on home t' m' little cabin on the crik an' hide, I reckon.

I had no belly fer travelin' no more, I was sick o' worryin' over Injuns an' they problems. I could hardly face up t' the long ride ahaid o' me an' I only felt worse when Tree told me that he was not comin' along!

I could not *believe* what he was sayin' an' I got right angry with him an' called him a "dam' fool." I said he could ride back an' stay on the crik with me, but he said "no", that they was a voice callin' t' him in the wind, an' that he had t' answer it.

I told him he had spent too much time with Quanah Parker an' his like an' that, if'n he only wanted t', he could go whar he wanted t' go, passin' his self off as a Mex er some other feriner, but, no, he wouldn't have none o' it. He was too dam' stubborn, I said.

"Brother Oscar, a prairie flower might believe itself to be a giant oak tree, but when the cold, north winds of winter blow the great oak will survive and stand tall and see another springtime, but the fragile blossom will wither and die away. Such is the way of the life of a prairie flower."

I was plumb disgusted an' disheartened. When I see'd that m' anger would not turn him I tried actin' hurt an' when that didn't work neither, I tried reason.

Hell, they *ain't* no reasonin' with a red Injun! They is all stubborn as mules an' pig haided, t' boot! I told him that I was washin' m' hands o' him an' that I was glad o' it. I told him t' ride off an' t' join up with Quanah Parker, er Cochise, er Crazy Horse er any other o' 'em that he chose t', t' git his self killed by Yallar Hair er Little Phil Sheridan, an' t' see if I cared!

He looked at me fer a minute an' said, "You are my friend and my brother. You are all the family left to me in this world. Your words are not as sharp as you would have me to believe and I know that it is your heart that is hurt. It will heal, and we will meet again. If not in this lifetime, then in another."

Sayin' that, he turned an' rode off, along the shoreline o' the sea, t'ward the east an' that sorry ban' o' Cherokee.

Me? I turned Cloud t' the north an' rode off feelin' as low as a snake's belly in a wagon rut! I was headin' home, by God, an' fergit they was any worl' a'tall beyond Di'mond Spring.

CHAPTER 9—A NOTE

(Dear Reader:

(Hello. My name is Doedie Harris-Mead. I am Oscar's sister, "Doe," who has been taking down his life's story on paper. Firstly, I will apologize for popping in so late in the narrative. Other than the note inserted concerning the Bender family I have tried purposefully to stay out of his story other than in my role as a character. Please understand that it is only by way of explanation that I am inserting this short addendum to his story at this implausible spot.

(As has been mentioned several times, he is very poor with dates and tends to ramble on some and I am doing my level best to put things in some semblance of order when I know to do so. Unfortunately, I often do not. When I was a young woman I worked for a time as a stenographer and was fairly adept at a system of writing widely known as "shorthand." I can keep up with what he is saying, for the most part, but I simply cannot vouch for the time frame.

(Because my experience in stenography is somewhat rigid I am trying to adapt to his cadence and vernacular as I am writing this. I am trying to use the colloquial spellings to convey the written words to the reader as he *pronounces* them. Unfortunately, it isn't working out very well for me, or at least not as well as I had hoped! I have sadly noticed, while going over our notes, that there may be certain slight inconsistencies in both spelling and with Oscar's impossible grammar.

(This is not necessarily because I've changed a particular spelling so much as that Oscar changes his *pronunciations* of the very same words from one day to the next, sometimes from sentence to sentence! For instance, he will use the words "Indian" and "Injun," or "buffalo" and "buffaler" interchangeably, sometimes seemingly in the same breath which is, as our dear reader may hopefully imagine, very frustrating for me!

(For some reason I recall an incident many years ago when he said to me, "Doe, I'm a' goin' off south on a *buffaler* hunt an' with any luck at all I'm gonna bring you back a white *buffalo* robe!"

(I have also noticed another peculiar trait in Oscar's speech patterns that no one else in our family ever developed, though I have heard it used by the rather less educated Southern classes. He will drop a "g" from one word while retaining it in a following word even within the same sentence.

(For example, he might say that he went "huntin' an' fishing," or, "roping an' ridin'." For the life o' me I do not know where or how he picked that up, though I cannot remember a time when he didn't talk that way. Both of our parents, although they came from far away, had a good command of the spoken word.

(Oscar was always flighty minded and he might be telling one story and suddenly go off into another totally different tale before the first one is finished! This is both confusing and exasperating to me and, several times, I have nearly given up on our ever finishing this project! I have threatened and cajoled him to no avail. Although at times it seems hopeless, it is so very important to him, and to m'self and to his family that all this be recorded, we can but muddle on.

(In an effort to hopefully clarify at least *some* of the possible confusion for you, dear reader, the time of which he is presently speaking would have been shortly before and/or jest after September 3rd, 1874. I know this for a fact as, unbeknownst to him at that time, our dear sister, Lizabeth, passed away during childbirth on that date. There was, of course, no way for us to let Oscar know about his dear sister, as we had no idea concerning his whereabouts at that time, other than that he was on a hunt with his life-long friend, Tall Tree.

(Anyway, it is due to my clear recollection of the sad event of our beloved sister's death that I was able to make this connection and to coincide dates.

(Again, please accept my apology for this improbable interruption at such an unlikely time but I felt, that regardless of what has passed before, it was necessary to finally establish this particular date as accurately as possible. Bear with us. In the end it is the story that matters more than how it is told.

Sincerely,

Doe.)

(*PostScript: The baby survived to become our beloved nephew, Simon Harris-Jones. Simon's pa, Domm', stayed on at our home place as did I. He was a good Papa to his son and I became the boy's surrogate Mama. In later years Oscar and Simon were inseparable and the boy never made an important decision without first consulting his "Uncle Oss."*)

~

Well, I was as worthless as the teats on a boar hog fer some months after the departure o' Tree. I meandered north, back into the Oaklyhoma Territ'ry, whar I worked as a full time drunk fer a while. It's good work, easy enough an' thar ain't much pressure on a feller, but it don't pay none to speak of. Event'ally I found gainful employment with a skinner. Ever'body was all het up t' finish the buffaler off, once an' fer all. What with the new style o' rifles an' a bigger market fer buffaler products, the only thing that slowed down the slaughter was they warn't enough experienced skinner's 'round.

A buffaler is a dam' big creachture, an' it ain't like skinnin' a rabbit! It took a couple two er three hours o' hard work t' do it right, gnats an' flies in yer face in the summer, freezing blood from yer haid t' yer toes in wintertime. But the pay was real good.

I started savin' up m' money, which I never had did a' fore in m' life, until I had enough t' buy a smallish wagon an' another horse t' pull it. I still had Cloud, o' course, but she was fer ridin', not fer pullin'. I then started m' own business as both hunter *an'* skinner.

I know'd the Injun way t' hunt the big critters, an' I would hide m'self up on a ridge with a older style Sharp's er a Henry rifle an' pick 'em off one at a time. The secret, you see, was if they was, say, twen'y buffaler millin' 'round, grazin' below? Well, a feller'd shoot's the back one first. The others will skitty 'round when the one what's been shot falls, but they settle right back down an' go back t' eatin' the grass. They ain't uncommon smart.

It was also important t' shoot the cows a' fore the bulls, 'case fer some reason killin' off the bulls first would likely scare the cows an' calves into runnin'.

I have killed up t' eleven in one day, but it was too dam' much work gittin' 'em all skinned out an' butchered. As it ended up, coyotes an' woofs got into the co'pses at night an' I ended up wastin' as much hide an' meat as I took. After that I slowed the pace an' would limit m'self t' no more than five a day, which was still a hell o' a job, I'll say!

I cain't say that I took no partic'lar pleasure in killin' the pore ig'orant beasts, but it was easy fer me t' convince m'self that if I did not do it then som'body else would! Ever'one was guilty, even the Injuns, who would kill an' sell as many as they could drop, jest like the white folk did.

It was a mighty bad time fer me in gen'ral, from what I recall, an' I don't much like thinkin' er talkin' 'bout it too much. It depresses me an' I'm shore it would depress anybody who happens t' read 'bout it, so I'm jest gonna kind o' skim on through it.

Event' ally I found m' way up t' Fort Sill whar I hung 'round as a part time scout an' tracker. I was also a wrangler thar, which means I took care o' the horses an' mules, in particular, an' all other livestock in general. I thought it would be nice t' spend Chris'mas at home with the fam'ly an' I was homesick fer Kanzas, an' so one mornin' I loaded up m' wagon an' tied Cloud t' the back o' it an' we started out. I'd also hear'd that there was somethin' a' doin' up in Powder River country an' around the Black Hills. There had been some mighty big rendezvous betwixt the Cheyenne and the Sioux up in that country and they was consid'able trouble with white settlers movin' through the land. I thought event' ally I might git on up there and snoop around fer a spell.

I reckon it was the middle o' December by now, although it was uncommon warm. I made good time an' within a few days I was back in Kanzas, jest north o' a little burg called Sedan, when it started t' rain. Oh, Lordy, did it rain!

Now, I've always believed that they ain't nothin' finer than a rain shower out on the plains. You kin see it comin' at you from miles away, the air takes on a fresh smell t' it, an' the rain washes the dust out o' the air an' leaves it as clean as a whistle!

Now, this here rain started out as nothin' much, really, it looked t' be a small storm an' I could see sunlight on the horizon in ever' direction 'round me. I'm a fair hand at jedging the weather an' I figur'd this little squall would blow itself out in less than half a' hour.

But it jest kept up, rainin' all that day an' into the night, sometimes so hard that I let the old draught horse lead us 'case I couldn't see a dam' thing in front o' us! That night I slept underneath the wagon, which had a consid'able number o' leaks. They was no fire, o' course, as even if I could have found some dry wood, rain was comin' down hard enough t' drownded out anything a feller might git started. I was lucky t' have some trail biscuit an' buffaler jerky fer supper.

The nix day was jest some more o' the same. Sometimes the rain would let up fer a spell, like it was goin' t' blow off, then it would start up agin', blindin', so hard 'em drops would sting m' hands an' face! I ain't lyin' t' tell you that most o' the time it was as dark as night an' right down eerie.

M' horses was well-seasoned but the lightenin' was so thick an' close it scairt him purty bad. The thunder was deafenin' an' it never seemed t' stop. As soon as one clap would start t' fade away here comes another, seemingly closer and louder than the last! I reckon it sounded like cannon fire in a big war and it shore got on my nervous chord and on the horses, too.

By the third day, things was jest in a total mess! The biscuit an' jerky had caught the dampness an' had turned moldy an' warn't fit t' eat. The wagon was gittin' stuck ever' few feet an' finally I had t' 'bandoned it, leavin' behind m' whole load o' hides an' supplies, includin' at least two nice rifles.

I unhooked the old hoss an' slapped her rump an' sent her off. I mounted up on Cloud, with what few things I could carry in saddlebags an' a few pouches of this er that, an' haided off in what I hoped t' be a northerly direction. If I'd had a lick o' sense I would have made me some kind o' a travois so's t' be able t' pack them rifles an' some extry supplies druther than t' jest leave it out on the pra'rie t' rust an' rot.

As I say, I was hopin t' head off t'ward the north, but it was rainin' so hard that it was impossible t' say fer certain jest whar we was haided.

~

I was soaked through t' the skin. I had been wearin' a leather jerkin an' it was as cold as death nix t' m' body. Even little ol' slews an' criks had become roarin' rivers, an' I found m'self goin' sev'ral mile' out o' m' way t' git 'cross.

As night approached on that third day, they came a fresh round o' thunder an' lightenin' an' then, o' a sudden, it turned so cold that m' whiskers froze an' they was icicles hangin' off o' me an' the pore horse! The rain turned t' sleet an' then into stingin' pellets that warn't quite sleet, snow, er hail, but was more like a combination o' all o' 'em all. I know'd that this was turnin' into a per'lous situation, an' that a man an' his horse could both freeze t' death in short order. We could not stop, as it was necessary t' find some kind o' shelter an' some way t' build up a fire t' warm us.

Then, o' a sudden, it switched back t' rain an' I got plumb scairt. I don't know if'n you've ever see'd weather like this, but even if'n yer inside it shore ain't funny. The rain froze instantly and the ice clung t' ever'thing. The weed's and grass turn into sharp blades or bust into little, needle-sharp shards like busted glass.

The wind started a' risin' up out o' the north an' seemed t' blow stronger an' colder by the hour! It was t' the point that the ends o' m' fingers could not feel t' hold the reins an' pore, old Cloud had ice so thick on her face that her eyes froze shet! It was real scary! I 'membered that time I had crawled into a buffaler carcass t' hide from Injuns, an' I know'd that if we didn't find a place t' stop soon I would have t' shoot m' horse, gut her, an' crawl inside t' hide from this here weather!

Somethin' that scairt me more, mebe, was when I dismounted t' walk fer a spell an' warm up m' feet, which was becomin' too numb t' feel, an' I stumbled over somethin' in the trail. The lightenin', which hadn't let up a'tall, show'd it t' be a daid coyote. Beca'se it weren't tore up none it didn't appear that he'd been kilt by some other varmit. I figur'd that he had jest plain froze t' death.

Now, that might not mean a great deal t' you, but a feller raised up like I me, out on the plains, knows that when the weather is bad 'nuff that the ol' Trickster hisself cain't take it no more, woe be onto' some pore, frail creachture like a human bein'!

We kept on goin', Cloud an'' me, not knowin' our direction. The rain turned t' snow, with flakes as big as silver dollars an' comin' down so fast as t' make a feller dizzy. I must've slipped into some kind o' a dream, er what they calls a "haloosination" an' I saw m' Ma, Pearline, a waivin' at me from a distance. She was standin' in a single ray o' sunshine.

I called out, "He'p me, Mama," but she couldn't hear. All o' a sudden, though, her face was right nix t' mine an' she leaned over an' whispered in m' ear, "Oscar, son, did you clean the stovepipe like your Mama ask ye?" an' then she disappeared! I swear, I could feel the warmth o' her breath agin' m' freezin' skin!

I had not taken ten more steps when I tripped over what I thought was a tree stump, an' I fell down, face first, on t' the frozen mud, a' bustin' m' nose an' m' mouth. The pain cleared m' haid up a bit, an' I ran m' hand down m' britches laig an' felt a tear in the cloth an' the warmth o' m' blood a' runnin' from a deep gash jest below m' knee. I stood up an' tried t' hobble on, but the pain was jest too strong!

I sat back down on the cold, wet pra'rie an' I started t' weep like a child. Cloud came over an' put her icy muzzle down on m' shoulder an' her breath was hot on me an' it felt good. I figured the run was up. I shor'ly never thought I'd die like this.

Clear as a bell, I hear'd Mama's voice agin', sayin', "Oscar! The stove pipe!"

I raised up m' face an' looked off into the rain an' the snow, an' by the light o' a bolt o' lightenin' I see'd that stump I had tripped over an' it caught m' eye! I crawled over t'ward it, the storm lightin' m' way, till I was close enough t' tetch it. It warn't no tree stump, it was a piece o' steel pipe a stickin' out o' the ground! "Oscar! The stove pipe!" Ma's voice said agin'.

I waited fer another round o' lightenin' an', shore enough, I could see a drop off, jest a few feet away from me. I slid over t' it, looked over the edge o' the ridge. Shore 'nuff, I was standin' on the roof' o' a dugout cabin! I crawled 'round an' slid down the side o' the ridge an' into somebody's "front yard."

Som'body had dug that cabin right into the side o' the hill that me an' Cloud had been a' walkin' on! Crimpled as I was (agin!)I hobbled over t' the front an' they was a strong, wood door. I pounded on it fer a spell, an' when nobody came, I put m' shoulder t' it an' it popped wide open, as two o' the four leather hinges had rotted through.

When the door opened 'bout a million bats swarmed out, t' they deaths, I reckon, in that weather! I had never been partic'larly afeard o' 'em, but I cain't say that I enjoyed a' standin' in the middle o' sech a swarm as they made! I limped inside an' it stunk purty bad from the bat guano, but warn't it warm? The bats had made a mess o' it, for shore but I don't reckon they had been usin' it as a roost fer too long, considerin' that the droppin's was all purty much jest up 'round the fireplace.

I leaned back outside an' whistled through m' fingers fer Cloud. She came a' slippin' an' a' slidin' down the far side o' the embankment an' came right up t' me.

Now, I don't know that she had ever was inside o' a barn er any kind o' buildin' a' fore, but when I stood aside she waltzed right inside that cabin without me havin' t' ask her twice! She snorted some, at the smell o' the bat scat, I reckon, but that horse was smart enough t' git inside out o' that weather which is a site more 'n' I kin say about some folks I've know'd. I pulled off the saddle an' m' bags an' pouches which was froze solid now, as they had been soaked through by days o' rain.

~

They was no way t' build up a fire fer warmth an' light, as ever'thing I had was soaked an' it was too dark inside t' see if'n anyone had left behind a striker rock on the h'arth. I dug around fer a spell fer a little tin box in which I always kept some extry Lucifer matches, but I didn't know which pack they was in an', like I said, it was dark.

But we was thankful, me an' Cloud, an' it was a dam' sight warmer in this cabin what had been carved into the side o' the livin' hill. An' it was dry, hally-loo!

I felt m' way 'round in the pitch darkness, but couldn't tell much 'bout the room. Finally I felt m' way into a corner an' settled down onto' the floor, which surprisin'ly enough, was wood. Usually a house sech as this would have a dirt floor an' a hide hangin' in the front fer a door. The feller that b'ilt this one had intended t' stay, I reckon, havin' gone t' the trouble o' findin' enough trees out here whar they's scarce, an' t' cut 'em down an' t' hew out planks fer a floor an' walls. It made me wonder what had become o' him an' his.

I took the time t' say a prayer o' thanks t' the Great Spirit, a habit which I had only recently acquired, fer our good fortune in this, a time o' need. I asked him t' bless the soul o' the feller what had made this shelter in the wilderness an', also, I said a prayer fer m' Mama, who had led me here.

(When I told this part o' m' story t' m' sister Doe, who is, as I might have mentioned, takin' this all down fer me, she cried! She said that it was Mama's spirit a'talkin' through me an' that this is what is called a "psychotic episode"! She said that she was proud t' have a brother who was psychotic, like me, an' she p'inted out that all o' 'em dreams what I have related here, have true an' deep meanin's. Who'd a' guessed it?)

I slept deep, from exhaustion, I reckon, an' when I waked up nix day Cloud had got out through the doorway somehow, mebe she was smart enough t' pull the hasp with her teeth, an' as I had busted some o' the hinges it warn't shet tight anywise. She was a standin', nibblin' on dry grass, outside o' the dugout by a little shed an' a fallin' down outhouse.

It must have snowed like hell durin' the night as, even though the front yard was clear whar the wind had swept it, the snow had drifted high on the sides o' the ridge. It was tarrible bright an' tarrible cold.

The first thing was t' build up a fire, somehow. I dug around in m' pack agin' with no luck, so I prowled 'round in the one room o' the dugout, lookin' fer the striker.

I found two straight-backed chairs, one broke up an' t'other still serviceable, an' a extry fine rockin' chair with a cushion, a rusty bed spring with a straw tick mattress that needed airin' an' a night stand with a good pitcher an' wash basin on it. They was some dry bark an' branches stacked up neat on one side o' the fireplace, an' a heapin' stack o' buffaler chips on t'other. Some o' the bats had flew back in through the stovepipe durin' the night, an' I shew'd 'em out with a old broom which was still in good shape, too.

I reckon the rest o' the swarm had either froze they little bat asses off er had kept a'flyin' t' some whar's else.

At one point er another a 'coon had b'ilt a big nest in the far corner out o' sticks an' dried grass an' whatever junk it could gather up, although I ain't shore how it got in the place, as the front door had been closed an' they was only one winder an' it had good wood shutters which had been closed, too. I never know'd one t' climb down a stovepipe a' fore, but I reckon it had.

They was a table, in tolerable good shape, which still had a blue chiney vase with the dried stems o' a han'ful o' flowers pokin' out. They was two high stools at the table, an' they was a steel bucket an' a short milkin' stool in the corner, by the door. Hangin' above the fireplace was a old, flint lock rifle, but it weren't o' no use t' me. On top o' the stone mantel they was two books, one called "SLAVERY: THE EVIL WITHIN", an' t'other, "TALES O' THE BROTHER'S GRIMM," an' a wood box full o' Lucifer matches which had caught the damp an' was o' no use.

They was also mos' o' a full bottle o' store-bought whiskey, a lantern with a little oil in it an' a dozen er more homemade kindles. They was a brocade rug on the floor which I took up so's t' shake it clean an' found a trapdoor underneath it which was another lux'ry an' a surprise.

I opened it up, but it was too dark t' see an' I didn't want t' be crawlin' down into some hole without a light. Tellin' the truth, the first thought what popped into m' haid was o' that tunnel back at Bender's Mound. I decided I would shet the door fer the time bein's, till I could find away t' light 'em kindles, an' I continued t' prowl 'round.

Among the other things I found was a rusty razor, sev'ral cakes o' good, lye soap, some near new hand towels, a framed picher o' Jesus as a babe in the arms o' the Virgin Mary, another pict're o' old Abe Lincoln, a wood dipper, a good steel pot an' a skillet, rusty, but in good shape otherwise.

They was a set o' four matchin' dishes, cups an' saucers, some good, silver spoons, var'ous knifes an' kitchen things. It appeared that they had been foodstuffs, but that 'coon had hisself a party an' invited a few rats over an' they had purty much ruined ever'thing.

They was two glass jars o' pickled beets which was prob'ly still good t' eat, an' two jars o' green beans which prob'ly warn't. The jars had zinc lids an' they warn't too tarnished, but I was leery o' 'em beans, as I had et 'em a' fore, one time, which had either gone bad, er had not been put-by right, an' they made me sick as a frog. Who ever had lived here hadn't been gone fer mebe a year, a year an' a' ha'f at the mos', I reckoned. I noted, as I would sev'ral more times in the comin' days, that they had shore left in a hurry.

They was also two jars o' kinned t'maters, three jars o' kinned taters an' sev'ral small containers o' greens which someone had writ on, in a fair hand, "collards".

I walked out t' the outhouse an' opened the door. It was leanin' t' one side purty bad, but it seemed safe enough t' use, so I did. I even had the lux'ry o' a bucket o' dried corncobs an' the remainders o' some brittle, yallar newspapers, which was no longer serviceable fer they, uh, "intended usage."

When I finished thar, I walked over t' the little shed an' pried a rusted nail back, which had held the door closed, an' I looked inside.

This here was a good find as they was a steel jug full o' coal oil, a strikin' device which is made o' stiff wire with two pieces o' flint rock what you hold in yer hand an' "twitch" t'gither an' it makes a good spark. They was also a moldy leather harness, a hoe, a rake, a old hat, a long, hide duster coat, (which I immediately put on an' which fit me perfec' 'cept that the sleeves was too long an' the back o' it dragged the ground.)

They was three er four rusty steel traps hangin' by chains from a nail in the wall, a sack o' shelled seed corn, which was goin' t' mold. I gave a big han'ful t' Cloud an' she seemed t' like it jest fine.

I found another bucket o' dried cobs, a han'saw an' a wood toolbox which had sev'ral useful items inside it, some hemp rope an' some twine. They was also a bolt o' burlap fabric which would make me a good blanket, with plenty left over t' make a shawl fer Cloud.

They warn't much else in thar 'cept fer rusty wire an' the like. Behind the shed they was some old pens made o' chicken wire, like you might use t' keep rabbits er hens in, an' a single harness plow an' a hand tiller with a big, steel-spoked wheel.

I made sev'ral trips, haulin' what stuff I could use back t' the house and then haulin worthless junk from the house to the yard.

The wind was blowin' hard, an' the snow was comin' off that ridge an' the roof' o' the cabin an' blowin' high over m' haid. The hill was a nat'ral windbreak an' I could a' lit a sulfur match down here in the yard, if'n I'd had one.

This shore was a fine place fer a home an' I felt kindly sorry fer the folks who had b'ilt it an' then had t' leave it behind, which, as I have said, they must've did in a hurry, considerin' all the fine things what they left behind.

Fer instance, 'em hand tools. They was rare an' valuable in 'em times, an' a feller in his right mind wouldn't have left 'em 'less he had t'. Same fer the silverware.

After I had gathered ever'thing t'gither in the cabin, I b'ilt a fire, which weren't nothin' hard now, what with the twigs an' scraps from the 'coon's nest an' the coal oil an' the striker.

Cloud stuck her haid inside the door but did not want t' come in. She seemed content, an' she stood thar an' watched me as I worked, a' cleanin' an' a sweepin'. I sang a little song fer her 'bout the "L'il Red Hen an' Her Rooster Bo", an' even with my sore laig I managed a little daince, between you an' me, an' that horse stood thar an' watched me, an' I swear t' you, she was a laughin'! I think we was both thankful jest t' be alive. Lots o' fellers don't make it through what we had.

It didn't take more than a hour er two an' ever'thing was purty much right. I fixed the hinges on the door by cuttin' some new leather from the harness riggin' I had found. I was mighty hongry, so I took the time t' git a small rifle out o' the bag, which I hung from the saddle. I rubbed it down good with a rag soaked in coal oil, then took the time t' rub ever'thing I had that was made o' metal, that had been exposed t' the wet. I even went so far as t' clean each o' the bullets fer both m' rifle an' the pist'l. I warn't worried none 'bout food. I was always shore o' m'self when it came t' huntin'.

Cloud didn't seem t' be in no big hurry t' leave, so I left her at the cabin an' took off a' foot. I had not limped more than a hun'ded yards when I kilt a cottontail. I left it t' lay in the snow, after pullin' off it's haid so's it could bleed. Jest atop the ridge I shot another rabbit an' that was plenty. I had killed enough meat fer a laripin' meal usin' up only two shots, without havin' too far t' walk, neither.

From the ridge they was a good view o' the land', which stretched out empty an' wide an' lonesome an' lovely. I felt mighty fine, truth be know'd. It was like that storm had been some kinder test fer me, an' I had come through it, an' had see'd m' sweet Mama, besides!

All o' that bitterness an' the business o' hard feelin's fer Tree, an' the sickness I felt fer what was happenin' t' the Injuns an' t' the land' itself, seemed t' be a lighter weight on me, now. The weight was still thar, I could feel it, it's jest that it didn't seem so heavy.

From whar I was a' standin' I could see Cloud a' walkin' t'ward a small knot o' bare trees 'bout two hun'ded yards beyond the out house, an' I guessed that they would be fresh water thar, as nobody b'ilt they cabins too far from water, an' I could not see a crik er a river near 'bouts, an' they warn't no well. (It turned out that the horse was right, they kin smell water, if'n you didn't know it, as they was a small spring thar in a rocky outcrop, with a flow 'bout the size o' m' arm.)

It was dam' cold up on the ridge so I took a last look 'round an' breathed a few deep breaths o' the fresh air. I walked over an' picked up the second rabbit an', a' fore walkin' down fer the first which was on m' way t' the house. I stopped an' said another little Injun prayer o' thanks fer the bounty what had been gave t' me an' I humbled m'self an' 'pologized t' the spirits o' 'em two rabbits fer takin' they lives.

CHAPTER 10

I fried one rabbit an' et it, then I fetched up water from the spring an' started the other one on t' bile, in the hopes that I could scrounge up a few winter yarbs an' make a stew. They was a crock o' rock salt under the table an' some dried peppers an bulbs o' ga'lic hangin' from a nail on the wall. I went back down t' the spring an' poked 'round some, but didn't find nothin' thar t' use, but I did find some dry sage that had been growin' b'side o' the shed.

I got t' thinkin' that they may be eatables down in that cellar, so I went back into the cabin t' have a look.

I open'd up the trap door an' stared into the dark fer a bit, then decided that now was as good a' time as any, so I fetched the lantern an' stuck a spare kindle into m' pocket an' went down the ladder, thinking' of the face of that ol' goblin, John Bender all the way down.

It was a fair sized room, not quite ha'f as big as the cabin itse'f, an' the feller had worked *hard* on it. Two walls was smooth dirt, one was lined with stacked limestone, an' the fourth seemed t' be a solid piece o' limestone that had been thar, nat'ral. I expected it t' be musty, but was surprised t' find it right dry an' pleasant.

I found ha'f a barrel o' rotted apples an' sev'ral baskets o' 'taters, mos' o' which had gone t' vine, but they was sev'ral dozen which was eatable, though they had gone mighty soft. I found a basket o' turnips, which was a might shriveled, but was still good, an' a whole pacel o' onions an' some more ga'lics hangin' in bunches from the ceilin'. They was a crock o' lard, which was rancid, some kraut an' sev'ral stone jars o' cider what had turned t' vinegar.

The cellar was warm an' comfor'ble, an' not at all like the last cellar I was in, on Bender's Mound. It had been dug at the same time as the dugout, an' it must've been a hell o' a backbreakin' undertakin'.

I don't think it could have all been did by one fam'ly an' I reckon that they might o' had consid'able he'p. Folks used these cellars t' store food in, o' course, an' also as pertection from cyclones an' Injuns. A feller would hide his fam'ly down thar if a huntin' party show'd itself.

The folks what lived here had big dreams, I reckon. Sometimes when the dugout cabin sech as this one was finished, folks would start buildin' a wood frame house an' barn at a more leisur'ly pace, since they already had a roof' over they haids.

Once the "real" house was done, then they would use the cabin as a chicken coop er a house fer farm hands. Sometimes a dugout will still be 'round generations after the main house is gone. They was good, practical shelters, 'specially ones like this one, which was dug into the side o' a hill. Hills ain't know'd t' collapse, er burn down er blow away like houses is, don't you see?

I brought a armload o' useables up with me an' put some o' 'em things into the stew. My, it shor'ly did smell fine! The smell o' hot, cookin' food did consid'able t' bring new life t' the old place! I ended up havin' t' go back t' the spring agin', fer more water, as the stew pot held consid'able, an' a feller cain't really overcook a stew none. It was m' intention t' jest keep a addin' t' that pot so's that I could live on it fer a week er more, easy.

I took m' rifle with me, in case I see'd game, an' went t' fetch the water. On m' way back, I swung over t' the east, some, t' whar they was a small orchard o' bare fruit trees, nix t' a small corral made o' split rails, whar it looked like they had been pilin' up rocks fer a foundation fer either a big house er a barn.

The rocks had been dressed an' stacked three er four foot high in places, an' a few weeks more work would have finished the foundation wall. Inside the wall was the solvin' o' the m'stery concernin' what had happened t' the folks what had homesteaded this land'!

Up agin' the north wall, the highest part, a' sittin' thar in the snow, they was two skeleyt'ns. They was entwined as if they had been holdin' tight t' each other when the end had come fer 'em, each with one arm 'round t'other, an' they free hands was clasp'd t'gither.

The bigger o' the two, the feller, jedgin' by his size an' the rotten overalls still hangin' on the bones, had what appeared t' be two bullet holes in the forehaid.

The smaller skelet'n, still wearin' what was left o' a checkered gingham dress an' a apron, had the right side o' the skully bone smashed in, splintered an' cracked from the center, clear down t' the lower jaw, jest shattered! It was a pitiful sight an', I admit, it made me choke up, some. It would have been easy t' blame this on Injuns, but, somehow, I jest didn't believe it was so.

First off, a lot o' Injuns in these parts an' in those times still used bows an' arrows. Also, even if they kilt settlers with a gun, they would still shoot 'em full o' arrows t' leave as a sign fer others t' see. Plus, I don't think Injuns would have kilt the woman. They would have took her off as a breeder, if'n they could. As I have said, Injun's gen'ally stripped the clothes off the daid, an' would mutilate 'em, so's t' crimpled 'em in the nix worl', an' t' make 'em weak.

Although I see'd a laig bone an' some ribs scattered 'round, it would be m' guess that this had been done by varmi'ts after the body's had been thar fer a while. I imagin' that 'em bodies bein' inside the stone walls had been pertected some from critters, as mos' animals gen'ally do not like t' enter into boxy places, whar they might git trapped.

'Course the birds had done did tarrible damage t' the haids an' faces, an' they was really nothin' left t' speak o'. The feller had a patch o' dark, leathery skin left with the heavy stubble o' a nappy, black beard, an' the woman had sev'ral loose hanks o' hair attached t' her skully bone an' they was some more hairs scatter'd here 'n' there, in clumps. Same sorta hairs, like the feller's beard. Curly, like a buffaler's.

As I said, they clothes was still recognizable, an' they bones was still held t'gither with gristle an' sinew an' had not yet fell apart.

I reckon that they was a young couple, as both had mos' er all o' they teeth an' they was shiny white an' in good shape. He was a wearin' some old, clodhopper work boots, an' she must've been barefoot, 'else som'body took her shoes. As I say, it was plumb pitiful, an' I decided then an' thar, that whether er not I wintered out in this 'ere young couples home, er whether I moved on in a week er two, that I would come back here, nix spring, an' see t' it that they gots a good, Christ'an burial. In a way, these pore, daid folks had saved m' life, an' I was beholdin'.

Tellin' true, I shore felt strange. I went back t' the cabin an' et, an' fidgited 'round, hummin' blue tunes, an' feelin' sad 'bout the worl' but glad 'bout me. It was growin' dark, but I warn't sleepy, yet.

I cleaned the place up some more, always thinkin' 'bout 'em two, an' how I thought that they would be glad t' see me takin' care o' they place, an' all, an' 'bout how the smell o' the stew a bilin' in the pot made it seem like a home agin'.

I cut me some covers from the bolt o' burlap, stoked up the coals, an' laid me down t' sleep, but I could not. My mind would not shet itse'f off.

I got up an' opened the door an' stared out into the night. It was cold but very still, an' they was a huge, silvery blue moon straight overhaid. Cloud looked up at me from whar she was standin' aside the shed, an' she murmured some at me in horse talk, which I don't know too good, but I reckon mebe she was a tellin' me to get back inside and shet the door and keep warm.

I know that they is folks who would think what I did nix t' be strange. I went back in an' pulled on m' boots, an' put on that young feller's duster coat, an' I grabbed up a big piece o' the burlap. I walked out t' that foundation, the snow an' frozen grass cracklin' neith m' feet, an' I found the bones o' 'em two people. I stood thar, fer a while, jest lookin' at 'em. I could see m' breath risin' skyward like a prayer.

I bent down an' I wrapped 'em up snug an' tight in that rough cloth, then I ask' the Great Spirit t' bless they souls an' t' tell 'em thanks fer me, an' that I would do right by 'em when the ground thaw'd.

I know'd that they was people who'd a' said I was crazy t' do sech a thing. But I did it anyways an' I reckon I felt better fer it.

I walked back t' the cabin, undressed an' laid down in m' bedroll by the fire, an' I cried m'self t' sleep.

CHAPTER 11

I warn't in no real hurry t' leave. I had been mighty homesick down in the Territ'ry, but bein' back in Kanzas had took the edge off'n that, some. I liked the cabin fine, an' it occurred t' me t' haid into Sedan, one o' these days soon, an' t' see who held the deed. That way I could find out the couple's names so's I could carve it in they grave marker an', if they was no other claim t' the land', per'aps I could call the claim an' buy it m'self.

They was plenty o' game t' shoot, they was fresh water an' a good, solid roof' over m' haid. I had never been no hand at farmin', though I shore know'd how, an' I began t' consider it, fer the first time in m' life. They was shore as hell worst places in this worl' whar a feller might end up than this little dugout in the hills o' Southeast Kanzas.

They was nothin' unusual 'bout the weather. It would snow an' blow an' be cold as hell, till you would think it would never end, then I'd wake up nix mornin' an' find the snow meltin' an' the breeze from the south, like it was springtime. Then, that night er the nix, er the night after that, it would snow an' blow an' be cold as hell, agin'. Jest what a feller'd expect from Kanzas.

They had been a covey o' quails a scratchin' in the dirt on the west side o' the soddy, whar I throw'd out table scraps. I had been hankerin' fer some fresh game birds but I did not have me no shotgun, an' they was too small t' waste a rifle bullet on, besides which it would have blow'd 'em t' bits.

One snowy afternoon I went out an' fetched one o' 'em old, wire pens I had found behind the shed, an' I brought it 'round t' the cabin. I propped one end o' it up with a stick, an' I took a piece o' that hemp twine an' tied it 'round the stick, an' ran it along the ground up t' the little winder by the cook-stove.

I took me a han'ful o' the shelled corn an' pounded it some, with a hammer, an' I mixed in some o' the trail biscuit from m' bags which had got soaked, so's I had stacked it up on the mantel t' dry. It was some months old, by this time, an' it was hard as rock, but I did manage t' pound some o' it up into a kind o' meal without breakin' the hammer, an' I mixed it up with the corn an' spread it all 'round under that cage.

I went inside an' opened up the shutters on the winder an' grabbed a'holt o' the end o' that twine, pulled up one o' the tall stools an' waited. Shore enough, in 'bout fifteen minutes, along came 'em quails. First one, then another, then another still.

If you ain't never seen 'em I am sorry for you. They is han'some, fat little birds and they'd druther walk than fly 'case they gots short little wings. When they walk, well, actually they run, and they do so in a straight line. Fer all the worl' they look like tiny, round soldiers a' headin' out on maneuvers.

They all gather up into a covey and would peck 'round in that meal, until ever' dam' one o' 'em birds was underneath that cage. Snap! I jerked on that twine, an' yanked that stick from under the edge o' the cage, an' down she came, trappin' ever' blessed one o' 'em birds inside!

They fluttered an' flapped, but they was caught! I took some pliers from the toolbox an' went out an' snipped a small hole big enough t' put m' arm through, an' one at a time, I pulled 'em birds out an' twisted off they haids. I killed 12 birds, enough fer two meals fer me. It might have made three meals fer some folks but I am fond o' quails and had been hankerin' fer 'em.

They was two cocks an' four hens still left inside the cage an' I let 'em go. I patched the hole in the screen by crimpin' scrap wire into place with he ragged ends that I had cut.

I plucked 'em little birds, an' fried ha'f o' 'em that night, an' roasted the other ha'f the nix day in a iron skillet, with a heavy lid, which I shoved into the coals in the hearth.

You ain't et fowl 'less you've et quails! I did sorely miss haven' some flour, though, an' some milk fer gravy. But I did count m' blessin's an' open'd up a jar o' taters an' brought 'em t' a bile an' then smashed up with salt an' ga'lics an' all, all that was missin' was butter, gravy an' some fresh biscuits.

~

The days an' weeks went by, uneventful, as you might say, an' I got t' thinkin'; I had more money put back from m' job on the fort than I'd ever had at one time in m' life, an' they was nothin' special t' keep it fer, so I decided that I would saddle up Cloud an' ride back into Sedan t' buy me up some supplies, an' t' mebe check on the deed t' the cabin.

We had wandered 'round in that storm fer three days after havin' rode through Sedan, so I was a might put out t' find it was only 'bout a 2 hour ride from our cabin! I ain't ashamed t' admit that, though, "case the best dam' scout in the worl' couldn't have found his ass with both hands in that storm. I figure that we must have doubled back once, er mebe twice, a' fore we accidental found the cabin. (Doe says that was jest part o' Providence's plan, an' I reckon she's right).

Sedan was not much o' a town back then. (I reckon it never was, an' I doubt if it is, now). They was two main streets what formed a cross, as they gen'ally do. I will admit that these streets was special nice, in that they was extry wide an' paved with red bricks.

The town was a tradin' post on the Chautauqua river, as I recall, an' mos' o' it's trade was with the Injuns an' the pikers an' outlaws which holed up in the Territ'ry, as the boarder line was less than five er six mile away.

As it turns out, it was a Friday, 'bout noon, when I rode into town, an' som'body said it was the first day o' the month o' March. Ever'thing was real quiet, though the local folks said that Satan hisse'f came t' town from the Territ'ry mos' ever' Saturday night.

It was a bright day, an' a warm one, an' though I cain't say fer shore how I 'member, er why, they was a funeral goin' on at the Baptist church. (Mebe that's stuck with me 'case it goes t' show that it had been warmin' up enough fer the ground t' thaw so's they could be a buryin'.)

They was a train depot, which doubled as a telygraph o'fice, whar a feller could send er git messages from almos' anywhar's, in nearly no time at all, that is, when the Injuns hadn't cut the wires er pushed the poles down, which was among they favorite pastimes!

Also, they was a blacksmith shed, a dry goods store, a hardware, a barber, a druggist an' a dentist (who also worked on watches), a feed an' grain, four er five saloons, at least two o' which had "Doves", an' 'bout six churches. They was prob'ly a schoolhouse out in the country, a ways. Sech was a average small town in Kanzas in 'em times.

Som'body said they was a feller goin' t' start up a newspaper a' fore summer an' that he planned t' install telyphones, although at that time they was nobody who could tell me what a telyphone was. Lookin' back, if they had know'd an' would a' told me, the chances are good I wouldn't have believed 'em, anyways.

I rode Cloud t' the smithy, a nice feller named Stuckey, an' ask'd him t' trim her hoof's an' t' shaw her fer me. He was finishin' up a plowshare an' he said he would have her ready t' ride in a hour er two.

I strolled over t' one o' the Saloon's, The Spur, an' drank the first beer I'd had since m' drunk days. It was chilly-cold an' tasted so good that I had me another! I ate a pickled aig, which made me hongry. The barkeep said that they was a free "lunch", a fancy new word fer dinner, which would be served up 'round one of th' clock if'n' I could wait, so I said "ducks".

I walked back over t' the smithy an' asked him if'n he know'd whar a man might buy a small cart t' pull behind a rider an' a single horse, an' he said "shore," an' we struck a bargain fer a little two wheeler with a light harness. He was askin' ten dollars an' I said, "five." He said, "eight, includin' the shoes an' the hoof trimmin'", an' I said, "deal"!

I walked up t' the dry goods store, which was act'ally a gen'ral store, which was run by a nice lady name o' Mabel Call. She he'ped me pick out supplies an' I got flour, salt pork, cured bacon, sugar, coffee, a gallon tin o' fresh milk (I wanted more, but it don't keep), a laripin' chunk o' sweet butter in a stone crock (that *will* keep, fer quite a spell, down in the cellar) an' three loaves o' store bread, which is gen'ally better than nothin'. I also bought some fresh trail biscuit an' some dried meats an' veggytables an' froots (sic).

I bought some more roots, sech as onions an' turnips, white 'taters an' sweet yams, a ha'f dozen aigs (I will always 'member Ma Samuel an' her "hen apples") a rooster n' two layin' hens. It cost me dam' near six dollars an' I was afear'd it wouldn't all fit into that cart, but Miss Call he'ped me t' fetch it all over t' the smithy, an' she was a good hand t' pack it, an' made it all fit, 'cept fer the chickens, fer which I had t' buy two wooden crates that the smithy had fer two bits, an' we hung 'em, one on each side, 'round the saddle horn, the hens in one, rooster in t'other.

M' bridle reins was worn mos' through, down whar they attach t' the bit, so Mr. Stuckey braided 'em, no charge.

I went back over t' the saloon whar they was layin' out the free lunch, an' I had a ha'f gallon o' wheat beer an' woofed down some biled ham, sausages, black bread, biled aigs, pickled aigs, biled 'taters, onion pickles, pickled pigs feet an' knucks', an' some laripin', salty sardines what had been packed in mustard an' oil.

After I had et, I waddled back over t' Miss Call's store an' bought me up some tins o' sardines an' a small crock o' 'em pig's knucks, as I did not git m' fill o' 'em. (I was 'mos' full o' ever'thing else a' fore the bar keep's wife had brought 'em out. Had I know'd she was gonna serve 'em, I'd have waited t' eat, as I am wild fer knuckles!)

By then it was nearly two thirty an' it would be dark by five of th' clock. It had took me better than a hour and a half, nearly two, t' ride in, but now I was toting' the cart an' that would add at least another hour as I would have t' foller what trails as I could. I settled m' accounts with ever'one an' I bid 'em good day. I planned t' git the supplies home an' then t' ride back into town, either t'morrow er the nix day, an' check on the deed.

The cost o' the supplies reminded me o' how exp'nsive things was in boarder towns an' concerned me some as t' the price o' the property I was a' wantin'.

Luckily, they was a big full moon on the horizon a' fore the sun even went down. Cloud 'membered the way home, though I had t' remind her 'bout the cart, from time t' time, an' I sang her "Jimmy' Crack Corn", "Down In The Valley", an' the one 'bout the l'il red hen an' her rooster bo, which is Cloud's favorite. I told her she could daince if'n she was feelin' like it, but she didn't.

It was still purty warm although I could still feel the chill o' the season in the air. I could hear a redwing blackbird, down in the willows by a slew, an' that's 'bout the shorest sign they is that spring is comin', right fast! The countryside was real purty, an' it was startin' t' look more like Kanzas ever' day.

We scairt up a big flock o' pra'rie chickens, a hun'ded er more, an' I had a chance t' shoot a deer but did not, as we was already haulin' a full load. They would be more deer t' shoot, some other time.

I enjoyed the ride. In fact, it had been a real good day, all 'round, I reckon. But I 'member thinkin' t' m'self, "I'm tired, an' I want t' git home."

Home.

CHAPTER 12

I turns out that it was five days a' fore I got back t' the town. I got busy on some things. I pulled out the harness plow from behind the shed an' replaced what leather I could. Fortunat'ly, the metal was all still in good shape. I made a list o' things I was gonna need in Sedan, includin' some leather strops, buckles, nails, brass brads an' the sech. I had also b'ilt a crude, little ladder t' lead up into one o' the wire cages, so's the chickens had a place t' nest. It was a waste o' time, as they made they nests in the tall grass behind the outhouse.

I was kind o' lookin' forward t' goin' back t' Sedan, mebe spendin' a night in a hotel er a boardin' house, if they was one. I had looked into a small mirror that I had found with the lady's brushes an' things, an' I see'd that I didn't look so bad as I had feared. I used the man's razor an' had trimmed up m' beard, an' had whacked off the longest parts o' m' hairs with some shears, as best I could. The scars on m' neck an' face had healed up consid'able, 'though I still would have t' keep m' hat on, as the top o' m' haid was still purty guesome t' look at, I reckon. I added a note, "by a nu hatt" t' m' shoppin' list.

So, the nix Wednesday, ol' Oss Harris went t' town ("ridin' a billygoat an' leadin' a hound, ever' time the hound would jump, a spider would bite him on the rump, e-i-e-i-o." I'm sorry, Doe!).

Stuckey told me that they was a town assay o'fice inside the post o'fice, so I walked over t' ask 'bout the deed. The feller what worked thar was a snotty little sono'abitch 'bout five feet tall (smaller than me, even). He had a mutton chop mustache an' burnsides, shiny hairs,

262

slicked back an' parted in the middle an' a shiny, gold tooth right smack in the middle o' his mouth.

I told him m' name an' I give him the directions t' the place an' a description o' the property, an' he opened up a great big ledger book an' poked an' sniffed 'round, an' he hummed an' he haw'd t' his self. He found the names o' John Henry Bohannon an' his wife, Hazel Rae, an' he said they had filed the claim in '72 fer one an' one ha'f sections o' land'.

I asked him whar I would go t' buy up the claim an' he looked at me, suspicious like, an' asked me how'd I know the place was even fer sale? I said, well, I jest know'd, an' he said well, we had better go over an' talk t' the sheriff, an' I said, fine, let's go. So we did.

The jail house was a little stockade type buildin' in the alley back o' Miss Call's gen'ral store. The o'fice was no more than 8 by 10 feet with two er three little boxy rooms attached behind it, with the winder's covered with laced strops o' flatiron, an' which was used as cell houses.

The sheriff was a giant man with a huge belly an' his name was Tom Pope. Sheriff Pope wore a big, black, Mex style sombrero hat, a yallar leather vest, a pinkish colored shirt with a big silver badge pinned t' the left breast, an' a pair o' pearly handled, Colt .45 Peacemaker pist'ls facin' backwards on either hip. His job must've paid better than mos', as 'em guns cost near $40 each. (Some o' these lawmen got t' keep a big share o' the fines they collected as well as the monies they took in from sellin' var'ous items confiscated from thieves, pickpockets an' footpads, which was prob'ly a consid'able amount here on the boarder o' the Territ'ry, an' is prob'ly how he came into possession o' sech a fine brace o' pist'ls).

He was a gruff man with a gravely voice, but he was frien'ly enough, I reckon, considerin' the natures o' his job. He seemed like the kind o' a feller who would listen t' a body's story a' fore lockin' him up er hangin' 'em.

Well, Pope wanted t' know the reason fer m' visit, an' that little twerp assay man, who's name, I l'arned, was Earl Paske, he jumps right in, tellin' the Sheriff who I was an' that I was askin' questions concernin' the Bohannon place. I asked was they a law agin' buyin' land', here 'bouts, an' the Sheriff kinda laughed an' said, no, they warn't, but how was it I came t' know that place was available? Did I know the folks what owned the land', an' I said, well, no, I did not.

He said, "We ain't see'd much o' the Bohannon's fer a while. I'd say, what, Mr. Paske, 'bout eight, ten months er so, don't ye reckon?"

Paske didn't answer, he jest grinned an' took on a extry sly look.

The Sheriff went on, "Would you happen t' know the wharabouts o' 'em folks, Mr. Harris?"

I said, "Well, sir, I reckon I do. I believes that they is daid."

"Daid?" the Sheriff asked, "Now how would you know if'n' they was daid, Mr. Harris?"

"Well, sir, I jest came on t' the place, accidental like, durin' that big rain an' snow storm, a while back, the first big blow o' the winter, a' fore Chris'mas? Well, I see'd the place appear'd t' be abandoned. A few days later I came upon two skeleyt'ns hunkered down whar a new foundation was bein' laid, fer a barn, it looks like. Looked t' me like they's had met with foul play."

"'*Skeleyt'ns*'? 'Foul Play?' Now, Mr. Harris, that has been sometime back, three, goin' on *four months*, an' yer jes' *now* gittin' word t' the Sheriff's o'fice? Why, that seems t' me t' be the *first* thing that a feller would do! An' you say you didn't know these folks?" (I shook m' haid, "no"). "Well, that does seem a might strange t' me. Don't that seem strange t' you, Earl?"

Paske shook his haid "yes," real eager, t' side with he Sheriff. Well, I tried t' tell 'em 'bout m' findin' the place whilst I was gen'ally lost, an' ha'f daid, an' all, an' how I warn't even shore how far it was from the homestead t' town, an' all that. But it seemed the more I talked, the less sense any o' it made, an' finally the Sheriff stood up an' said, "Mr. Harris, I'm afear'd I am goin' t' have t' lock you up on the charge o' suspicions o' murder."

"*Murder?*" I cried, "I didn't *murder* nobody! Fer Christ sake, fellers, I shore wouldn't *kill* a man, a man *an'* his wife, not fer a little bit o' land' an' a cabin! Hell, I own m' own place, over in Di'mond Spring, up by Council Grove? Dam', you jest ask up thar an' mos' anybody will tell you I ain't no *killer* er no claim jumper. Jest ask, that's all!"

"Well," the Sheriff said, "I guess I will have t' do that very thing, Mr. Harris. I will send a wire this afternoon. But till I hear back, Mr. Harris, you is goin' t' be a guest o' the county. The room is small, but you will be by yerse'f, at least until the weekend, an' believe me, that is preferable t' some o' the comp'ny you might yet be a' keepin' when the rowdy's come t' town. You git two meals a day an', as the weather warms, a bath ever' second week. Assumin' o' course, yer with us that long. Now, do I need t' shackle yer hands, er will you come along, peaceable?"

"What 'bout m' horse?"

"I will see t' it that yer horse is took care o'. They will be a circuit jedge in town end o' nix week, weather permitin'. That's 'bout nine er ten days from now. If he let's you out, yer responsible t' Mr. Stuckey fer boardin' the horse. If the jedge decides t' let you stay with us a spell, the proceeds from the sale o' yer mount will he'p t' defray the cost o' yer livin' expenses here in the lap o' lux'ry pr'vided by Chautauqua county.

"C'mon, now, Mr. Harris, an' I will show you t' yer room. By the by, is they anybody in partic'lar I should contact, up in Council?"

"Yes, sir. Miss, I mean missus, Lizzy Harris-Jones. She's m' sis, an' she will git the sheriff up thar t' wire you back an' clear this whole dam' mess up."

They was nothin' t' do then but t' go with him. I did not blame the Sheriff none fer doin' his job, though I shore as hell would have liked t' git a good poke in at that Earl Paske. He was grinnin' like a 'postum as the Sheriff lead me into the back.

CHAPTER 13

So, thar I was, in *jail!* Oh, but it was a pitiful thing! I hadn't never been locked up a' fore an' it made me wonder if'n' I would go crazy! Finally I figur'd out that even if I did go crazy it didn't matter none. The mos' I could do was t' injure m'self a' slammin' agin'' 'em bars, an' what not, so I struggled t' keep ca'm, but they was panic not far from the surface all the time.

This here cell was nothin' but a little, square box. It smelt like piss an' was cold as the tomb, even thou I could see the sunlight filterin' in from outside. I could see m' own breath when I blow'd it out. It was 'bout six-foot by six foot small. They was a iron bed frame hangin' from the wall, a piss pot an' nothin else! I had no sooner laid down upon the cot when I could feel bugs a' crawlin' all over me. I stared up at the ceiling' fer a hour er two, an' then the Sheriff hisself brought me some food.

It was a big meal, I'll say that, an' it were hot an' purty good, too, I reckon. They was coffee, two pieces o' butter'd bread, a heap o' fried 'taters an' a big, greasy pork steak an' some kind o' greens, collards, I reckon, er poke. I had not et no pork, other than a bit o' sausage an' bacon, in a long spell, an' it tasted fine. The problem was that they was no salt t' anything. But havin' lived as long as I had on the trail, I was used t' doin' without salt.

The Sheriff, bein' alone with me now, seemed a might more friendlier than he had a' fore, when that knothaid, Paske, had been moonin' 'round. He commenced t' stir up a little bit o' a fire in a tiny little coal stove jest outside m' cell, an' he talked a might while he worked on some papers an' while I finished eatin'.

He told me he had sent the wire but had not hear'd back yet. I told him I had never been in a jail a' fore, an' he said, well, if that was true, I should know it t'weren't no big shakes an' that I should try t' relax an' enjoy the time t' m'self. Then he said somethin' that struck me odd, like.

He said, "Don't worry 'bout it, too much, son. They ain't a'gonna hang you even if'n' you did kill 'em two. I know'd this district jedge an' he fought fer the Confed'racy. Besides, here on the edge o' the Territ'ry an' all, well, ever' one's sympathies will be on yer side, I reckon. Now, that shore don't mean that I approve, I don't, but what happens t' you ain't exac'ly up t' me, so I reckon that's how it will go fer you."

He ask' me did I have a lawyer in mind.

"A *lawyer?*" I ask him, surprised, "Does it look t' you like I am gonna need *a lawyer?*"

"Well," he said, "I cain't say fer shore that you'll need one, with Jedge Morrison on the bench, but I'll ask 'round fer ye, anyways. We got two right here in town, if'n they's not off somewhar's throwin' a big drunk, as they usually is."

I finished m' food an' he took away the spoon an' the tin plate an' was kind enough t' ask me did I want some more coffee, which I did.

~

Long t'ward the middle o' the afternoon a man in a dirty suit came by an' ask me if'n' I was Oscar Harris. I asked him jest who the hell else he might have been expectin' t' find at this here address, an' he jest laughed. He said he was a lawyer an' his name was George K. Armstrong. I told him that I warn't gonna pay fer no lawyer, as I had did nothin' wrong, 'cept t' try an' buy a little piece o' land' with a dugout on it, legal like, an' that I wanted t' hell out o' this outhouse what they called a jail.

He waited till I ca'med down, some, an' he said, "You ain't t' be charged no fee fer this, son. The Order will pay fer m' services."

"What you mean, 'The Order'", I asked him.

"The Order o' the Knights. The *Knights*, son, git me? The *Knights* o' the Ku Klux Klan," he said, but it must have been clear from m' face that I didn't git his gist. *"The Klan*, boy! The K.K.K.! Don't tell me you ain't never hear'd o' the Klan?"

I told him that not only hadn't I hear'd o' the "Clan," I said I didn't even know what a goddam' "Clan" was, less it was somethin' like a "clam" er some other kind o' creachture!

He jest laughed an' said, "Well, son, a "clan" is a type o' a fam'ly. I am talkin' 'bout *the* clan, only we spell it with a "K." We's a type o' fam'ly, too, you might say. A 'fraternal organization,' might be a better choice o' words, though.

"You see, the Klan is a purty new organization, Mr. Harris, at least 'round here. We are made up mainly o' soldiers an' citizen's an expatriates o' the Confederate States o' America, an' it is our goal t' wipe out the injestice bein' done t' us in the name o' the Union Army, Ulysses S. Grant, the Jewish an' Catholic communities, an' the United States Gov'ment.

"Now they is tryin' t' tell us that the slaves, that is the Negro race, is gonna be a part o' our society, jest like ever'one else! They have set 'em free, an' now is givin' 'em money an' land' an' homesteads that rightfully belongs t' whites! They even says that the day is comin' when a, uh, Negro, will have the right t' vote!

"*T' vote*, Mr. Harris. Kin you *imagine* that? Jest like a *real* citizen o' the United States! Why, if we don't react t' this now, the nix thing they'll be tellin' us that *Injuns* kin vote, too!

"Now, any thinkin' man knows this fer the hogwash that it is. The Negro is not even a real person, Mr. Harris, they are not what is called "human bein's." The Klan has decided that we want t' see the Negroes shipped back t' the Afrikin continent, whar they came from an' whar they belong, in the jungles with the apes an' the monkeys an' the other animals. If they do not want t' go, then they must be convinced that it is in they best interest, that they is nothin' fer 'em here, in spite o' what they is bein' told.

"In this we even have some half-assed support from the Federals. As you may or may not know, the United States has already made the purchase o' a large area o' land in the northern half o' Africa called, Liberia, purchased fer the express purpose o' relocating the Negro. It was one o' the few good plans made by Abe Lincoln, that sono'abitch.

"Anywise, as you might already know, sir, 'Bleeding Kanzas' is bearin' the brunt o' this bad situation! Our statehood was one o', if not *the* main issue, what brought our nation into a divisive war in the first place, the results o' which is well know'd t' ever' breathin' Amerikin. It is as though we is now bein' punished, as it were, by havin' the bulk o' the Negro population thrust upon us agin' our will!

"Now, as a form o' payment t' the Negro fer formin' military units t' he'p fight the war fer the North, the state o' Kanzas has been open fer virtually *free* Negro settlement! M' God, they is already entire towns bein' formed by these 'Exoduster's', as they call theyse'ves, towns sech as Nicodemus and Dunlap, as you might have hear'd, Mr. Harris.

"But the Klan feels that it is wrong t' take this land' from the hands o' the white settlers who has worked hard t' clear it an' t' take it away from the savages. And fer what, Mr. Harris? Jest t' turn it over t' savages o' a different color? I don't believe anyone kin honestly see sech a thing happenin', Mr. Harris, kin you?

"This country no longer has a use fer the Negro race an' we do not want 'em stayin' here, rapin' our women, livin' in our towns an' cities nix door t' good white families, takin' farmlan' from 'em what is deservin' o' it. Simply put, Mr. Harris, we want the *neggers* t' go home!

"Convincing 'em t' go home is hard, though, when they hear talk 'bout homesteads an' other handouts that Pres'dent Grant an' the Congress an' the Jew's that control the nation's purse strings seem more than willin' t' give t' 'em.

"The Klan feels that we have give 'em enough, already! We have taught 'em the ways o' civilization, t' grow crops an' t' raise livestock, t' form families an', Mr. Harris, we have gave 'em the greatest gift o' all, the gift o' the knowledge an' rekinition o' our Lord, Jesus Christ, an' o' the Church that he has founded.

"As you might know, sir, this country is on the verge o' financial ruin! We cain't pay fer the reconstruction o' the South, a noble 'case, certainly, *an'*, at the same time, *buy* homesteads an' houses with the taxpayers money, then turn 'round an' *give* it all, lock, stock an' barrel, t' a bunch o' *neggers!*

"Why, what's nix? Will they ask us t' allow the Injuns into our towns, our schools, our churches? I think that we cain't allow any sech thing t' *ever* happen, an' that this whole way o' thinking must be nipped, Mr. Harris, *nipped in the bud!*

"So, when a negger couple sech as the Bohannon's come t' a bad end, it is not somethin' that we applaud, necessarily, but we cain't say we're sorry, either. In a way, they has brought this all down upon theyse'ves, pretendin' t' be white, er as good as. The Lincolnites an' the liberal Gov'ment o' the United States has put good, honest, God fearin' folks, sech as the members o' the Order o' the Knights o' the Ku Klux Klan, into, what is know'd in the legal community, as a 'wholly untenantable position'.

"The Honorable Jedge Morrison, hisself a Grand' Wizard o' the Order, is shore t' see his way clear o' findin' you 'not guilty', er at least greatly reducin' the charges agin'' you. Do you understan' all this, Mr. Harris?"

I looked at him blankly fer a spell an' then I said, "Hell, I don't think I understan' *none o'it!* You mean t' say that the couple who owned the place whar I been stayin' was black?"

"Precisely, Mr. Harris. Negro's. Lazy, good fer nothin' *neggers!* Shor'ly, now, you do not want t' hang fer *they* 'murders'? 'Murder' is a term we use, legally, t' describe the violent an' wrongful death o' a *human bein'.* That is how I will argue your case, need be; that this couple was not 'human bein's', they was *neggers!*"

~

A young feller came over an' told the lawyer that he had t' git back t' his o'fice, right now, as they was fellers there t' pay a bill what they owed him, so he took off like a mule with a burr under its tail, shoutin' back over his shoulder that he would be back later t' finish our strategy fer the trial.

I spent the rest o' the day a noddin' an' a nappin', in an' out o' m' mind with a pecul'ar combination o' dread an' boredom. Fer no reason I would wake up freezin' cold, then I'd drift off agin', then wake up a' bilin' hot!

I was still a' doin' this when, 'bout dark, I hear'd a fearsome ruckus outside o' the jail. I couldn't see nothin' much, less I stood up on m' cot an' pulled m'se'f up by the bars so's t' peak out through a little triangle o' winder, but I could hear drums a beatin' an' shouts, an' I could see they was a passel o' men carryin' kerosene torches.

Finally, some feller crawled up 'top a buckboard wagon an' I could jest see him from 'bout his knees up. He looked jest like a goblin o' some sort! I thought I was still sufferin' from some kind o' delirium, when he reached up an' took off a tall, white, p'inted hood what had covered his haid an' face an' I could see that he was a real man. He started talkin':

"Now, brothers, we's gots us a real job here a' fore us, t'night! Our Sheriff has locked up a innocent man in that thar yonder cell! A man what ain't done nothin' wrong 'cept fer mebe killin' a pair o' breedin'-aged neggers! Why, this here is one o' 'em "miscarriages o' jestice", as they say, an' I think it is our Christian duty t' git that pore feller out o' that 'ere jail, even if'n' we gots t' bus' down the jailhouse wall t' do it!

"What has he did, brothers? Nothin', that's all! (The whole gatherin' cheered wildly) He ain't done nothin' more than a man does when he shoots a buffaler er feeds his hongry fam'ly, by puttin' his foot on a chicken's haid an', by a grabbin' the chickens feet, pullin' that haid off so's he kin pluck that chicken, so's his wife kin cook it!

"He was a doin' what a man gots t' do! He is takin' what a man has a right t' take! (More cheers) He is reclaimin' this here land' from the wilderness, by a fightin' off the savages an' by killin' off the dangerous creachtures, which in this here case is nothin' more than killin' neggers!

"A negger *ain't* a man, an' killin' one ain't no more than killin' off a wild cat er a bear er a dam' *Injun*! If this man is punished fer doin' what he *should* be a' doin', fer stakin' his right t' the land' that *God*

Almighty has give t' white folk, then what is nix? Will we start puttin' fellers in the poky if'n they's t' kill a bear, er a wildcat, er a Injun?"

("No," the crowd roared!)

"Then I sez we *bust* him out o' that jailhouse an' that we does it *now*! An' if'n the Sheriff gits in our way, er anybody else, I sez *'hang 'em'*!"

The whole crowd roared an' seemed t' surge forward an' then I hear'd a dam' big boom from up above. Som'body told me later that it was the sound o' the Sheriff's shotgun. Him an' a han'ful o' deputies had climbed up on top o' the jailhouse. I listened an' I could hear his voice jest a boomin' down from above me, like the trumpet o' Joshua, an' he said:

"Jest one o' you sonsabitches takes another step t'ward this jail an' I'll cut you in two, startin' with you, Mr. Bigmouth," I could tell he was a talkin' t' the feller who'd been makin' that speech.

"I have fought in wars, an' I have lost a good many o' m' friends an' fam'ly a' fightin' in wars, from Mexico t' Shilo, t' defend the Constitution o' the United States. If you think I'm gonna be backed down by a bunch o' mealy-mouthed cowards dressed up in the night sheets off'n they wives beds, you'd better dam' well think 'bout it agin'!

"Each one o' us up here is armed with a scatter-gun an' each has eight brass shot cat'ridges filled with steel, an' by God, we will cut you'ins t' ribbons, as shore as I stand here. These men o' mine has been ordered t' aim fer yer guts, an' we should be able take out a consid'able number o' you a' fore we fall. Now, come ahaid, goddam' you, come right on ahaid if'n yer men enough!"

Well, you could have hear'd a pin drop, an' fer a minute they was real tension in the air. Then I hear'd the sound o' feets a shufflin' off, but I never did hear nary a peep o' talkin' an' finally I laid back down on m' cot an' drifted off into sleep. It was a good an' restful sleep, too.

~

Nix mornin' that lawyer feller, Mr. Armstrong, came back an' he was a might more subdued than he had been yeste'day. He took in like he was tryin' t' comfort me, sayin's how they had been a show o' strength among "his peoples" last night, an' that he was shore that neither the Sheriff ner Jedge Morrison was goin' t' be willin' t' hang me fer m' "alleged crime", an' that he know'd that if'n they did hang me that they would be trouble, trouble, trouble, an' that I should know, if'n I was hung, that that they was folks who was willin' t' sacrifice all t' avenge me. As I recall he said I would be forever know'd as a "Marty t' the Cause," whatever the hell that meant.

I was jest gittin' ready t' tell him that I didn't want t' be no Marty nor t' hang fer nothin' 'case I had not done nothin', when the Sheriff came in. He walked right up too me an' said, "I got word back from Council Grove, Oscar. They *was* a Lizzy Jones, but son, she is daid! I'm sorry, young feller, but she died last fall, givin' birth."

I felt sick.

"I did find out from the deputy down thar that purty much ever'thing else you told me is the truth, though. Now I'm goin' t' decide whether er not you have t' stay in jail, here, till Jedge arrives, er if'n' I kin let you go.

"You would have t' promise me that you would come back t' yer trial, though. The wire said you was kind o' a shiftless feller, an' not much good fer nothin', but that, as near as anybody could 'member, you was honest an' that you shore ain't no killer.

"Now, fer no reason other than so's you'll know, I ain't too dam' shore that I am in agreement with Mr. Armstrong, here, nor Jedge Morrison, fer that matter. It seems t' me that we jest finished up a ugly little meetin' last night, an' a ugly war which, er so I was told, was goin' t' determine, once't an' fer all, whether er not *all* men was created equal."

Armstrong raised his hand but the Sheriff cut him off.

"Now shet up, Armstrong, jest save it, don't git up on yer high horse with me, I know yer feelin's on this matter completely, an' if I didn't know it a' fore, I hear'd all that trash that was said by yer cohorts last night. But person'lly, I *do* believe that the Negro's in this country is humans an' I don't think it is right fer one human t' buy er sell er enslave another an' I don't think it's right t' go out huntin' fer two legged prey regardless o' whether they is white, black, brown er Injun. That is m' opinion, sir, an' goddam' you, I am entitled t' it!

"Yer always braggin' t' folks that you represent *the law*, Mr. Armstrong, but god dam' it, I *am* the law! I will caution you that you have little t' gain by causin' me grief, on this matter, an' that you have consid'able t' lose. It would be mos' unfortunate fer Mr. Harris here t' find out that, on the very day o' his own trial, that his defense att'rney was, hisself, locked up on charges o' disturbin' the peace. On t'other hand, come t' think o' it, that might not be sech a travesty fer Oscar, after all.

"In a nutshell, Mr. Armstrong, I will give t' you the same advise m' pappy used t' give t' me when I was gittin' a might t' big fer m' britches. He'd jest say, 'Shet up', an' it was always right wise o' me t' do so. Immediately.

"So I say t' you, Mr. Armstrong, 'shet up'."

The Sheriff turned an' looked at me, "Oscar, if I thought fer one minute that you killed that couple, you would stay in this cell fer a long, long time. If the Jedge said you was innocent I would have t' let you go. But you'd have t' jest keep goin', otherwise I would have yer ass back in here, the nix day, fer stealin' chickens, er bein' drunk er fer jest pissin' in the wind! Whatever the reason, any one that I could find! I would see t' it that you paid fer what you did.

"Havin' said that, I must also say I ain't got no doubts that you is innocent. An', havin' said *that*, I reckon I have jest convinced m'self that I should let you out o' here an' t' send you on yer way.

"Know this, though, Mr. Oscar Harris, if you ain't standin' in m' o'fice nix Friday mornin', at 11 of th' clock, I will hunt you down, an' I will find you, an' I will assume your failure t' present yourself is a admission o' both yer guilt, an' m' failure t' see it in you! I am a man mos' capable o' dispensin' jestice, Mr. Harris, *total* jestice! Is this all clear t' you?"

(He rested both his big paws on the pearly handles o' his backward facin' pist'ls jest t' make shore I ketch'd his drift, which I did, clear as a bell.)

I told Sheriff Pope that I did understan', an' that I 'preciated his trustin' in me.

I turned t' Mr. Armstrong an' I told him that I did not want him t' represent me, as I was innocent an' was shore the jedge would find me so.

A' fore I left out the Sheriff handed me the telygraph so's that I could read what it said 'bout Lizzy fer m'self. He was a purty straight feller, I reckon.

CHAPTER 14

Miss Call rented me a room over her store t' stay in fer the days remainin' till m' hearin' at the cost o' 25 cents a day. Shor'ly I need not say that it beat the devil out o' that closet they called a cell.

Stuckey, the smithy, told me he was glad t' see me free, an' he only charged me two bits fer takin' care o' m' horse. That was a powerful nice thing fer him t' do, I reckon.

A lot o' people in the town, who I didn't know from Adam, would stop me, an' tell me that they had hear'd 'bout me an' m' troubles, an' that they was glad t' see me out o' jail.

The problem that I had with all o' this was that I never know'd was they glad t' see me free 'case they believed I was innocent, er was they glad t' see me go free 'case they thought I was guilty o' killin' a couple o' Negro's?

It riled me some an' I found I did not sleep well fer the entire time a' fore the hearin'. I was also in a state over the sudden news 'bout Lizzy. I was t'rmentin' m' self as how much o' the news was true, an', if it was the truth, an' that if I had haided fer Di'mond Spring back when I'd first intended t', could I have been able t' do somethin' t' prevent her death, though I know'd hardly none o' the details?

~

The hearin', which is all it was, not even a real trial a'tall, lasted 'bout five minutes. The Sheriff read the charges agin' me, then added that he did not person'l believe that I was guilty. Armstrong said he was representin' me an' that we pleaded "not guilty."

The jedge asked me t' speak an' I said that Armstrong *did not* represent me, that I was innocent o' any crime, but that I hoped the Sheriff would find the true killer er killers an' that they would hang till they rotted.

The jedge looked at me over the rim o' his specs, as if t' study if I were sayin' was m' true feelin's, er if I was jest puttin' on a show fer the benefit o' the small crowd in attendance.

After a minute o' thought he pounded his gavel on the Sheriff's desk an' said, "Case dismissed. Insufficient evidence. The State o' Kanzas relieves Oscar Harris o' all implication in this here case. Court is adjourned. We will resume with further hearin's after we've et lunch at the Spur. I am hankerin' fer some pickled hen-apples an' knucks'."

The jedge was a Missouri man.

~

I did not join 'em fer they meal. Instaid, I went back t' m' room an' gathered up m' things. I saddled Cloud, an' tied a jug o' coal oil t' the saddle horn, an' stuffed a pasteboard box full o' Lucifer matches into one o' m' bags. I put a new spade I had bought from Miss Call into m' rifle sling. I thanked her kindly an' got directions t' the Methodist church south o' town.

~

I made it back t' the cabin 'bout three, four of th' clock, I reckon. I worked till almos' dark, diggin' one extry large grave. I dug it as deep as I could an' lined it with fresh, green grass an' some o' the first wild flowers o' spring which I had cut with the scythe.

I unwrapped the skeleyt'ns and sep'rated 'em as best I could and then wrapped each in a fresh layer o' burlap an' fetched 'em, one at a time, first him, then her, an' I laid 'em down on the grass an' the flowers in the grave. They was so light that it was like carryin' a sheaf o' dried corn husks!

I gathered up any spare bones that I could find an' put 'em in a kinvas bag at the feet o' the skeleyt'ns. I laid what was left o' her hand on top o' his, an' then I laid the joined hands down on top o' a bran' new, white leather Bible I had got from the Methodist Preacher in Sedan. I covered both o' 'em up with a patch quilt from the cabin. The western sky was bright pink an' lovely.

I don't reckon I had ever prayed right out loud a' fore then, other than jest mumblin' t' m'self. But now I turned an' faced the dyin' sun an' I said:

"Great Spirit, thankee fer the gift o' this here day. It was a beaut'. I stand a' fore you in good relations with the Earth an' her creachtures. I stand here t' give praise, t' say m' thanks, an' t' ask fer blessin's.

"Bless me an' m' horse, Cloud. Bless m' pore, dear sister Lizzy an' her little baby an' the rest o' m' fam'ly, an' if'n Lizzy *is* fer shore daid, well I guess you already know it, so please giver a kiss from me.

"Bless m' friend Tall Tree, an' keep him safe, whar ever he is. Bless his people, too, if'n' it ain't too late. Bless the Earth Mother herself, fer without her we would all perish. Bless this here couple fer which I have did m' best t' lay t' rest here. Thankee fer puttin' 'em on this earth fer a while, 'case without 'em I would not be standin' here, m'self, I reckon.

"I ask a blessin' fer the beasts o' the fields an' the forest an' the waters, fer the birds in the sky an' fer 'em creachtures what live beneath the water an' the soil itself. Bless them that is hunted er injured an' scairt. An' when I hunt fix it so's that m' bullets kill clean er miss clean so's that nothin' suffers what don't have t'.

"I ask fer yer pertection from evil, both that which I kin, an' that which I kin'ot see. I ask that you bless the pure o' heart an' the innocent an' t' grant 'em more power in the human worl', an' I ask fer punishment o' 'em that does evil.

"I don't always know whar I am, er whar I am goin' t', but Great Spirit, I ask that you guide m' feet along whatever the path is that you've chose fer me t' take. Ho'kah Hey! Hecel lena oyate kin nipi kte, Ho'kah hey!

"Amen."

~

They was a little sliver o' moon left, unus'al bright, an' between it an' the dyin' light from the sun I could see plenty well t' cover the grave up an' t' strew a few flowers over the top. I walked t' the shed an' got a wood cross I had made, a week er two earlier, an' I got me a hammer an' two small nails.

Cloud was standin' by the shed, still saddled, an' I fetched a small, copper plate that Stuckey had made fer me, from one o' m' saddle bags. He had engraved it nicely, with block letters, what said "Bohannon." I nailed it t' the cross. I went over an' hammered the marker into the ground at the haid o' the grave.

~

By now it was purty dark, mos'ly. I walked back t' m' horse an' got the bottle o' coal oil hangin' from the saddle horn an' took it into the house whar I sprinkled it ever'whar. I opened up the trap door an' pour'd some down thar, as well. I walked outside an' pour'd some o' the oil in the outhouse an' some in the shed. What little bit was left I poured on a pile o' rags inside the walls o' the foundation, as I had a bit more work t' do thar, an' I was goin' t' need some extry light t' see by.

I walked Cloud down t' the spring an' I left her thar, tied loosely t' some o' the willers which was now in bud. I grabbed out the box o' Lucifer matches an' walked t'ward the house, strikin' an' pitchin' the matches into the dry grass along the way.

I throw'd a lighted match into the outhouse an' I reckon it caught the coal oil first an' then some o' the gas from the sewage, an' it made quite a 'splosion, which near t' knock'd me down, but didn't hurt me none, other than t' singe the hair on m' arms an' face a might. The 'splosion caught the shed a'fire as well.

I was a little more careful when I pitched the first few matches down in the cellar. One finally caught, with a "whoosh," an' flames spread quick t' the upper room. I stood fer a minute an' watched things ketch fire, the straw tick mattress went first, then the floorboards an' the chairs. Abe Lincoln looked back at me from his pitcher frame as the flames went higher an' higher.

I pitched a match into the coal oil I had spread inside the walls o' the foundation an' on the pile o' rags there. By the light o' the fire I pulled some o' the stones down from the wall, an' I used 'em t' cover over the mound o' the grave.

It was very still, that evening, an' the smoke rose straight up, thick an' gray. The stars was bright enough t' see through the smoke, even though the fire made consid'able light.

I walked down t' the stream an' took Cloud's reins an' mounted up. We both looked back at the blaze, what had grow'd quite fearsome by now. It had reached it's peak an' was jest startin' t' die down, some, when I turned m' horse t' the northwest an' gave her a gen'le nudge in the flanks. We was haided home t' Di'mond Spring.

EPILOGUE

Well, m' sister Doe tells me that she is plumb tired out, an' I shore as hell am, m'self. They is shore a lot more t' tell 'bout the things I did an' the peoples I know'd, but it's time fer a rest.

M'be me an' Doe will git t'gither agin' an' kin start in with me a'talkin' an' her a' writing' an' I kin tell you 'bout that time I met Sittin' Bull an' Crazy Horse. An' 'bout whar I was an' what I did on the 26th day o' June in '76 up on the Greasy Grass, an' 'bout a couple o' Pres'dents who I met an' he'ped out, some.

I won't like it but I reckon I will tell ye, too, 'bout the day I see'd the worl' come t' a end fer a whole race o' people on a frigid December day in a place called Wounded Knee.

They was m' trip t' the Carolinas an' two brothers thar name o' Wright what I he'ped out an' a feller named Edison, an' another named Ford, both o' who became rich an' famous in part beca'se o' m' advice! An' they was some battles I fought, an' a hell o' a feller I met down Cuba way named Teddy Roosevelt.

I'll tell you 'bout m' first aut'mobile ride, an' how I flew in a areoplane! An' I went t' Europe an met me a Queen thar in Englan' who shore talked funny an' how I laid up in one o' them castles fer a spell!

Oh, yes, an' I kin ketch you up on m' old friend Tree! You ain't gonna believe what became o' him! Oh, an' they's more, a heap more!

But fer now, m' nephew Simon, who spent his childhood on m' knee, but is t' big fer it these a days, he's a sittin' on the floor beside me, with his haid a' layin' on his arm which is curled up 'cross the same knee what he use t' set on. He's sound asleep an' he looks fer all the worl' jest like he did when he was a little feller.

We's all sittin' in front o' a fine fire in m' little cabin back home in Di'mond Spring an' m' cat, Button, is a' sleepin, wrapped around m' neck like a scarf. They's a snow a' fallin' an' Chris'mas is in the air. An' m' sweet, dear, little Doe says that's all that they is.

Fer right now, anyways.

THE END

S. C. DIXON
P O BOX 1309
724 Commercial Street
Emporia, Kanzas 66801-1309
scdixon@osprey.net

Lightning Source UK Ltd.
Milton Keynes UK
UKOW042006300812

198299UK00001B/106/P